Sky Tribe

Sabrina Chase

Cover art by Les Petersen

ISBN: 978-0-940006-27-7

CONTENTS

ACKNOWLEDGMENTS

Many thanks to everyone who has enjoyed the Guardian's Compact adventures and wanted more. I hope the latest installment meets with your approval—I had fun writing it! Thanks also to my editor Michael J. Totten, beta readers Darla Raitt and D. Jason Fleming, and supreme proofreader Roger Ivie.

- S. Chase

CHAPTER 1

Twilight was best for rooftop travel. People weren't around, generally, and couldn't see Triss hanging from a window ledge or shimmying up a drainpipe very well. She, on the other hand, had just enough light to see a loose roof tile or dirt that might make her grip slip. Not that she needed to see much for this. She'd gone this same route many times now. So why was it suddenly so difficult?

It was late winter and cold, but she was used to cold. Heights had never bothered her.

Cousin Nicu would say she had become wood, a dangerous thing for acrobats. Triss shook her arms and rotated her shoulders, reaching for the remembered feeling of fluid strength and pushing away her worries. Look ahead just far enough and no farther, Nicu had said. Not at the rope under your feet, but at the platform the rope was tied to. *Never* at the ground below. Looking at the ground would pull you down.

Triss swung smoothly from one hand and reached with the other, grabbing the stone decoration that protruded from the window frame to pull herself up to the sill. No, she was not imagining it. There wasn't as much room as before. All this soft living, indoors all the time—it was making her too plump! She would be as round as Tia Drina soon if she didn't watch out. Triss shook her head. She would fix the extra roundness later. Right now she had to break in quickly and silently.

She reached back to the thin leather sheath that lay flat along her back and pulled out the slender knife Toa Mihai had given her. Scowling in deep concentration, Triss edged the blade between the window casements and pushed steadily upward. The oil she'd applied previously made sure that the latch opened smoothly without a sound and that the window hinges didn't creak. Triss quickly dropped inside and closed the window, unable to stop the broad smile on her face as she looked around at the riches inside.

Books. Books everywhere, on all the walls and on smaller shelves in the middle of the room. It would take her years to read them all, especially since she had to clamber over the roof from her tiny garret room to get to them. Baron Heufritz, her employer, was a young noble who never bothered with his library, keeping it locked since he inherited the title. The housekeeper only dusted and cleaned the library once a month. Once a month, and she'd just told the maids that cleaning would be next week. Triss could not risk anyone noticing missing volumes then. Everything she had borrowed had to be returned.

That wasn't the real hardship. Once she read a book, Triss remembered it vividly, every page. No, the hard part was that she wasn't able to take any new books back with her this time, not even a small volume from a lower shelf. The housekeeper was a stickler for cleanliness and would have the maids dust *everything* before inspecting the library herself.

Triss glanced out the window. Darkness was falling fast, and she had to return to her room without detection. She took the books she had carried in a small cloth bag tied to her back and hastily reshelved them before perching back on the windowsill. With a little more deft knifework, the latch dropped in place from the inside and then she launched herself at the sturdy metal gutter of the adjoining roof. Going back was much easier than getting in.

She paused at the ridge of the roof, looking at the bare trees lining the carriageway and distant rooflines of the city of Baerlen. Pale clouds obscured the moon, drifting low. As she watched, a dark shape emerged briefly from the clouds above, drifted, then floated out of view again.

Triss rubbed her eyes, astonished. The thing had looked almost like a *boat*. But boats didn't float in the air, did they?

Then she heard a distant voice, so faint she barely heard what was said.

"Dunderhead!"

"Well I'm sorry, but they moved the control levers to add the viewscope," Dieter Theusen said, running a hasty hand through his already messy hair. "And switched them around in the process …"

Jens-Peter gritted his teeth and waved the hand that didn't have a death grip on the safety cable. "Did anybody on the ground see us?"

"It's rather dark, and we're in the clouds." That was Jochim, peering happily through the new and experimental viewscope. He was the only one who could see anything useful at the moment since the levitation ship was once again enveloped in mist. "Also, this location is not very busy at night. I saw no one on the ground. I believe we avoided notice."

"Some good news for a change," Jens-Peter grumbled under his breath. This levitation ship was just the original experimental prototype, but everything about the levitation ships was still an Imperial state secret. If he revealed anything about them, his chances of ever piloting one of the *real* ships would be nil.

Maybe it already was. He had been promised the first real ship completed, but then the Kriegsa had commandeered it for "trials" a month ago, and it hadn't been seen since. Nobody would answer his questions either. It was true that the Kriegsa was the organization responsible for magical defense and that the levitation ships *used* magic, but non-magicians, like him, could operate them. The Kriegsa magicians didn't like that fact, or his skill.

Stefan Arendt peered up at the large bag filled with the levitation dust, then climbed up the creaking rope ladder to poke at one of the bronze fittings.

"Anything wrong?" Jens-Peter had to repeat himself to be heard over the wind and the gentle whir of the propeller.

Stefan shook his head. "Modifications appear to have worked as intended. The controls are much more powerful and stable. Maybe why the altitude adjustment was larger than we thought it would be."

Jens-Peter felt a brief wave of optimism. While it was true that the new ship was bigger and better looking, he knew *this* one inside and out and had made many of his own improvements without detection while making various repairs. Perhaps that would count in his favor later on.

"Are we done here?" Stefan continued from above. "I have a *Praktikum* review tomorrow morning."

Jens-Peter wanted to stay out longer, but his friends were already doing him a favor by coming at all. "Very well, I'll take us back."

"Drop us off at the beech grove," Dieter said. "Unless you need help docking?"

"No, I can manage." If it was just the distance between the university grounds and the experimental facility outside Baerlen, Jens-Peter was confident now. The repairs were solid. "And now I have an excuse to do a fast vertical!"

A fast vertical was intended to be an emergency move, going from one altitude to another with no lateral motion. Once the levitation ship reached the university grounds, Jens-Peter used an override lever to allow the altitude control to move freely and moved it sharply down. The ship dropped immediately, forcing Dieter to stifle a yelp. In the dark, no one would see the ship and with the motor off, it was silent. Levitation ships were practically *designed* for students to evade curfew.

As soon as the last of his friends had dropped from the ladder, Jens-Peter reached for the altitude lever and pushed up until it hit the limiter bar. He'd adjusted it to account for the lighter weight from the missing passengers but it was more of an art than a science at the moment. He watched the altimeter and winced as the ship's levitator bag contracted for lift. Off by ten feet. If Dieter didn't eat like a starved wolf, it would be easier to make weight estimates.

Jens-Peter started the motor again. Now alone on the ship, his thoughts became gloomy. He was still a student, at least for now. But all his time was taken up with the levitation ships, and recently he'd had to take part in an emergency rescue all the way around the globe in Ynde at the request of the King. Someone official had made the right noises, so Jens-Peter wasn't in trouble for *that* unexcused absence. It was just all the others that were the problem.

He supposed he should go to classes tomorrow. The wear and damage done during the rescue had been repaired and checked so he really had no excuse to hang around the Kriegsa facility at the moment. Especially since von Koller, the head of the Kriegsa, barely tolerated his presence. If he and his university friends hadn't been involved in the discovery of the secret levitation design none of them would be allowed anywhere near the ships now.

Thinking back on it, that was probably why von Koller glared at him so much. Even though the late Professor Siebert, Dieter's advisor, had started the research on flying craft, the person who had truly invented the levitation ships was Dominic Kermarec. That wasn't the problem, nor was Kermarec's profession of author. The problem was Kermarec's wife, Ardhuin. Who was, more precisely, the powerful Mage Guardian of Bretagne and the one person who enraged von Koller simply by existing.

And every time Jens-Peter showed up with the levitation ship, von Koller was reminded of the whole unpleasant history. Even though it wasn't his fault!

He checked his heading, using the compass with the dial of mother-of-pearl that showed up well in the darkness. Since they did so much of their flying here at night, for secrecy, he'd gotten fairly skilled at it. Rivers gleamed if there was any light in the sky at all; a light dusting of snow picked out roads and fields but not forests. When he saw the dark spike of the Tegel church tower, Jens-Peter locked the wheel and went forward to the beacon. He carefully wound the bronze shutter spring mechanism and tripped the catch. The shutter clicked open and shut, allowing a bright blue light to escape. It was all magic. Somehow the little bead inside the cryselectrum-lined beacon case glowed in the open air, and the shutter flicked open and shut until the spring wound down. They had found that a flickering light did not need to be as bright as a steady one to be seen.

Having to use bronze was annoying. It was brittle and prone to breaking, but nothing else worked as well in close proximity to magical fields. The whole ship used wood and bronze as much as possible.

Peering into the dark, he finally saw the answering flashing blue light of the secret facility, deep in the Tegel Forest. Slowly drifting down to float a few feet above the ground, he edged forward until he saw the tall white poles, one on either side of the open grassy area before the large structure that looked like a barn but wasn't. A figure ran out, and shortly afterward he heard the clank of a connecting hook and felt the tug of the tow rope bringing the levitation ship in.

Someday they would let him just *fly* in … but maybe not in the dark.

Triss trudged up the steep, narrow stairs to her garret room, clutching a precious candle stub in the hand that wasn't holding the railing. Even though she was exhausted, the candle was unlit. Why waste precious reading light on something as simple as stairs? The housekeeper was strict but fair. Triss had heard that other households didn't allow their servants to have personal candles and that everyone had to go upstairs to sleep at the same time so they could share one. Triss didn't need a candle for these stairs, even at night. She'd memorized them after the first week.

She was tired but happy. The cleaning of the library was complete, and her unsanctioned visits had not been detected—although she had a bad moment when she saw a dead leaf on the floor that must have come through the open window. She picked it up without detection and continued her cleaning, resolving to be more careful next time.

In her tiny room, barely large enough for an iron cot and a rough washstand, she lit the remains of the current candle and took out the cheap paper envelope from her pocket. There was no return address, but she knew who it was from without opening it. Only one person wrote to her: Toa Mihai. The crucial question was whether he had written it himself. Toa Mihai was barely literate, and sometimes his words reversed direction, changed from one to the other midway, or emerged as new creatures altogether. If so, the letter would have to wait for daylight to decipher.

This time she was in luck. The carnival troupe was wintering in Eisenach like it usually did, and Father Ogeli had kindly transcribed Toa Mihai's message in clear, delicate script. The bulk of the letter was family news, mostly concerning the continuing struggle of the troupe to stay financially solvent. Cities expected flashier shows and a great many trained animals. Small towns were often not welcoming to a zigane troupe. The remaining options were few, and the fashion was changing to musical shows rather than carnivals. It was why Triss had been placed out as a maid over a year ago. Her acrobatic skills were good, but not as good as the best in the troupe. There was also the problem with her hair …

She hadn't *meant* to overhear, but it had been raining, and how many dry places were there in the caravan, anyway? She'd hid under one of the *vardo* carts, hoping Mata Sheri wouldn't find her and make her do chores. The chief of the troupe—Faad Tobar—and Toa Mihai were arguing, and that was not unusual. Arguing about Triss was.

"How can you say this about family?"

"Mihai-*che*, yes, she is your family. But in truth, she is not zigane blood. And it shows! You know what the *gadje* with evil thoughts will say. Yellow hair, we must have stolen her."

"She has been with us since she was born!"

Faad Tobar sighed. "They do not know this. Or they think we lie. You love her like your own bones, but she is not and I must think of all of us who are. It invites *zumala*."

"Triss is *not* bad luck. You should not say that!"

"Aiye, invites only. Think, you. Even if she dyes her hair or covers it, she is pretty enough to draw eyes and those eyes will wonder." The two men were silent for a moment. "You are still her *toa*. That does not change, wherever she is," Faad Tobar added gently.

Not long after that, when they passed through Eisenach, she had been brought to Father Ogeli who had found a place for her to work through his church network. Toa Mihai and the others had not liked her going all the way to Baerlen, but the promise of high pay and a household where the only young man, the master, was never in residence won them over. Triss trusted Father Ogeli, who had taught her to read, but she was also reluctant to leave the troupe and the only family she'd ever known—until he used the magic word *library*.

She had heard of libraries. Father Ogeli had nearly a hundred books of his own, in the church study. But a whole *room* full of books? Was that even possible?

Triss knew the troupe needed money. She was not the only young person sent out to earn an income, just the only one sent so far away. She knew it was because she did not look zigane, so it was safe for her to do so. The others had to work as day laborers or hire on to barges. Being a maid, even in Baerlen, was not so bad. It was just lonely.

She sent half her earnings to the troupe even though it wasn't much. Toa Mihai sent her letters and sometimes charms, if the letter wasn't going through the church, but it wasn't like being in the cozy family atmosphere of the troupe. The servants in the house were very, very *gadje*, and the maids near her age focused on local gossip and hair ribbons and the like. Not books.

Triss changed into her only threadbare nightgown, and while the last fraction of the candle stub sputtered and smoked, she did a few back walkovers and handstands to work out the kinks in her back before crawling under the covers. At least the library had been cleaned and locked up again. Now she could safely go back and get some new books!

The gazebo by the lake was not far from the main house, but given that all three of them were either injured or missing limbs, it was to be expected that the walk would take much longer than Gutrune cared for, given the cold. Heinrich had adapted well to his artificial leg, but not to the extent of being casual about ice and snow. He insisted on helping her up the few steps, ignoring Markus's outstretched hand, and pulling out a chair for her to sit on. Ostensibly so she would have the best view of the icy lake but more likely to place her away from Markus.

Markus himself exhibited his usual air of urbane courtesy, but having known him for some time, she noted the small signs of mischievous amusement and sighed internally.

"If you would be so kind, Herr Asgaya?"

Markus nodded and gestured. It was a subtle effect, but suddenly the sound of the wind vanished, and the chill breeze was no longer present. "We are secure. I can detect no magic present."

While Gutrune had almost completely recovered from her extensive injuries, Heinrich insisted it was still too much for her to endure riding in a carriage. This meant that meeting at the warehouse that functioned as the secret office of the Dragonhunters was not possible. Markus had also been badly injured, but his wounds were primarily burns. Still, they had important matters of great secrecy to discuss that could not be delayed, so Markus had come to them at the von Kitren family home. A decision Heinrich was clearly regretting.

"We do not have much information, but the little we have obtained recently is concerning." Heinrich removed a slim sheaf of papers from his case. "One of the *geas*-bound we captured after your return had been observed at the usual haunt of a band of street thugs. This one, unfortunately, led by a fairly intelligent man. All we know is they were hired for an important task in a few days and were paid well. If it weren't connected to Denais and Korda ... but it is. If they are moving the extract now ..."

Yes, that would be bad. The magical extract that *anyone* could use to wield powerful magic. Even she had done it, accidentally. The mage Denais had found a way to extract it, and even though he was now dead, his former subordinate was still alive—and had been stealing the extract from under Denais's nose for several months. They were reasonably sure, from captured records, that at least nine hundred pounds of the material had been created. Only one hundred pounds had been intercepted, and none of them believed the remainder had been destroyed in the fight in Bhuta. And since Korda had managed to hide his theft of the extract from Denais, they had little hope of tracing it now.

"You think it is related to transporting the extract?"

Markus nodded. "Smuggling is a specialty of that gang. I have not been able to learn anything further."

Heinrich shifted. "Do we not have more people to investigate? Must we do things personally?"

"For something as secret as this?" Markus threw up his hands. "It's a miracle we were able to hire as many Dragonhunters as we have. It isn't easy finding intelligent, capable people who can hide, strangely enough, and that's completely setting aside the ability to handle dodgy magical investigations and not reveal secrets to the wrong people. What about the Kriegsa—have they responded to your inquiries?"

"No." Heinrich glowered in silence for a moment. "In fact, more than once they have done exactly the opposite of what I requested. Or they state that the Kriegsa is the Imperial *War* Magic Department and that smuggling, even of magic, is not important enough for them to pay attention to. I have mentioned it repeatedly to His Majesty but without success."

"If they would bother to read our reports, this all dates back to the *Mage* War, and we are trying to prevent another one! How is this outside the scope of their duties?"

Time for her to give some insight, if not excuses. "His Majesty is in a very difficult situation at the moment," Gutrune said, tucking her hands more securely around the small handwarmer in her fur muff. "He must rely on the support of the Kriegsa during the selection of our Mage Guardian." It was unfortunate, but replacing the assassinated Professor Siebert was also critically important for defending against Korda and any other magical threats—not just the extract. To keep the Kriegsa soothed and more likely to agree to a suitable replacement, the King was keeping a low profile in such matters. They would have to rely on their own efforts.

The extract was dangerous, but it was also important for Preusa to have its own Mage Guardian again. If for no other reason than to deal with all the magically enslaved people created by Denais using the horrific *geas* spell and then later further enslaved by an additional layer of magic by his unwilling assistant, Korda. Who had escaped in Bhuta, was probably insane, and was convinced everyone wanted to kill him and was defending against that fear with all the magic he could steal.

"We can use the regular police if we don't reveal what we are actually looking for," Markus said, leaning back in the flimsy chair. "For example, the smuggling routes I found. Getting them shut down makes it more difficult for Korda. I've also made a list of suspicious materials for the secret police. Since we know the extract reacts to iron, they will have to use special shipping methods."

Heinrich frowned. "Will it make that much of a difference? Didn't you bring back some of this extract by steamer and train?"

"One jar." Gutrune suppressed a shudder, remembering. "And we had a Mage Guardian assisting every moment of the trip. To ship in bulk as they did … now I understand." She saw the confusion on the men's faces and hastened to explain. "When I found the crates of extract in Anatoli, they were being shipped both by small boat and by cart. I had thought it was merely for stealth, but it might also be because those methods do not have much iron present."

"Ah." Heinrich rubbed his bearded chin thoughtfully. "So that explains something that had puzzled me." He handed Gutrune a page from a report. It contained information on an intercepted message found on one of the captured *geas* servants. Whether bound to Denais or co-opted by Korda, they all would go to specific locations to report and get further instructions. Someone from the Dragonhunters was tasked to watch these locations and arrest them. It was unfortunate they were not able to interrogate the men; the *geas* prevented it, and removing the *geas* had proven difficult. First, only the Mage Guardians were permitted to know *geas* magic and second, many of the *geas*-bound went mad from the damage done while the spell was in effect.

The actual wording of the message was cryptic. *The mages have created a secret mechanism of travel that cannot be intercepted and the master orders us to capture it from them. Go to the house at Arconaplatz and follow the instructions given there.*

Gutrune looked up. "And at Arconaplatz, what did you find?"

"Nothing. They had departed a long time ago." Markus got up and paced in the gazebo. "However, one of the smugglers was seen in that area at the same time. We've set the secret police to try and trace their movements, but we should be cautious. It's near several secret Kriegsa facilities and we all know how much von Koller would love to make trouble for us."

"Then we must move quickly." Heinrich gestured sharply with one hand. "They must not obtain this method of transportation. And if we catch them in the attempt, we can hopefully find the rest of the extract." He stood carefully with the aid of his cane. "You must not stay out in the cold too long, Tru. Asgaya, shall we return?"

She glanced at Markus. His polite calm did not change one iota. He merely offered an arm to assist her, preempting her brother, which naturally meant Heinrich was left to open the door and follow. Even though she could not walk very fast, they somehow managed to outpace Heinrich. She suspected Markus of doing something magical to effect this.

"Your brother is becoming more obvious," Markus said, allowing a slight curve at the corner of his mouth. "He hopes to have this matter dealt with before you can take any active part."

"He also wishes to keep you occupied anywhere but here." Even through her gloves and the thick wool of his overcoat, she felt the muscles in his arm tense.

"Ah. So he has been aware of my true purpose all this time?"

Gutrune tilted her head briefly. "Suspected. But now, I think, he is certain."

A flash of his usual smile. "I suppose I cannot expect him to be unconcerned in matters regarding his only sister." They had already reached the path to the carriage drive and the low stone wall and gate that separated it from the grounds. It was both open and out of sight of the gazebo and the main house. Markus turned and raised her hand to his lips. "And what concerns does his sister have?"

"That you derive too much enjoyment from baiting him. Do not forget our greater purpose."

All amusement on his face vanished. "Seeing you like this, and because of that extract … How could I possibly forget?" His grip tightened on her hand. "Your safety is also my concern. He is not the only one who worries for you. And these are dangerous times."

CHAPTER 2

The lectern was tall, and the professor even taller. Jens-Peter didn't even try to look the man in the eye. For one thing, with his short height he'd get a painful crick in his neck. For another, Professor Schenk combined a gaunt, hollowed out face with a cloud of thin muttonchops attempting, and failing, to disguise that gauntness. Exactly the sort of thing to give a student nightmares, especially when giving that student a painful ultimatum.

"Yes sir, but I had leave to absent myself from classes," Jens-Peter interjected, trying to appear respectful.

"*Retroactive* leave," huffed Schenk, "and not for the first time. How dare you treat my lectures as a trifle to attend or not, as you please! Furthermore, this behavior has been a constant theme of your attendance here. If you refuse to learn, remove yourself at once!"

"But I have been learning! Didn't I get top marks on the spring exam?"

Professor Schenk leaned down from the lectern like a vulture. "There was a subsequent exam, young Oberacker. Which you *missed*. Since your powerful friends have exerted their influence, I am not able to expel you from the university for this glaring omission like any other student. However, I *can* determine the means to evaluate your knowledge in place of the exam." He smacked the top of Jens-Peter's head with a sheaf of paper. Fortunately his student cap cushioned the blow. "There. A research paper, the outline of which I have given you, to be completed in two months. If you fail to complete this task on time or to my satisfaction, you will no longer be a student at the University of Baerlen. Have I made myself clear, student?"

Jens-Peter couldn't help protesting. "That's impossible!" Which was a mistake, as he realized once he saw Schenk give a tight, wintery smile.

"Oh, I do hope so."

Meeting for lunch, his friends expressed only perfunctory sympathy. "I did warn you," Wolfgang Mauer said between bites of schnitzel. "Huber never notices students skipping his classes since he's blind as a bat, but *alte* Schenk is rumored to see in the dark. *And* he holds grudges."

"But two months! For a project like this?" Jens-Peter waved the sheets of paper wildly. "Structural failure modes of architectural masonry, with personal analysis of a recent case? It will take me two months just to find something like that, never mind analyze it. When am I to sleep? Or eat? Or have a little fun?"

"You can sleep in class, like the rest of us do." Stefan Arendt grinned and took a swig of beer from his mug. "Why are you so distraught? I thought you didn't care about graduating."

Jens-Peter scowled. "That's my decision, not theirs!" He felt a very slight pang of guilt. He barely remembered his deceased mother, but his father had constantly told him how much she had dreamed of her son becoming the first university graduate in the family.

"Pending your elevation to president of the University Baerlen, you're delusional," Mauer said rudely. "You're lucky it's just a matter of a paper."

Just a paper! Jens-Peter fumed. All right, he *had* skipped a lot of classes. But to assign so much work just because of a missed exam, and right before the Little Holiday too! Everybody else would be out beer-drinking and relaxing before the next quarter began. Classes were mostly suspended. What if he were seen at the library? He'd be mocked as a kettle, the term for a diligent student he loathed above all others.

It was all because Schenk hated him. He hadn't even given Jens-Peter the option of retaking the exam—which would have been unpleasant, true, but then it would be *over* and he could go have fun with a clear conscience.

His gloomy mood continued on his walk to the ornate stone building housing the university library. There was no help for it: he'd just have to get it over with as soon as possible. If he did a decent job, even if *alte* Schenk wanted to expel him, Jens-Peter could protest to the Burschenschaft or even the dean. That's right, he'd prove Schenk was an ignorant old fossil!

This mood of righteous purpose lasted until the library closed that afternoon and the assistant came to toss him out. "Why so early?" Jens-Peter asked, puzzled.

"Reduced hours during the Little Holiday," the assistant droned. "Will you be checking those out?" He looked without enthusiasm at the pile of books Jens-Peter had stacked on his table.

Now he really was in a bad mood. He couldn't park himself at the library to work until midnight as he'd planned, and some of the books he needed could not be removed from the premises. Well, he'd just have to find another way. Bundling the books he was allowed to take with a strap, he left the library and headed to his quarters, a room in a run-down boarding house convenient to several beer halls. This had been a prime consideration when choosing accommodations but now was an annoyance. He heard the cheers and laughter as he tried to work.

Finally he couldn't take it any more. "Gaaah, *burschen!* A herd of wild pigs is quieter!" he shouted out the window.

"Have some gruel, grandfather!" replied a slurred, laughing voice from the crowd, which became even more boisterous than before.

It was impossible. Not only was it impossible to think, it was a constant reminder of the fun he couldn't have at the moment. "There's no place I can go … No, there is one place that is guaranteed to be quiet!"

The old *rittershalle* at the military barracks in Tegel had been repurposed as the levitation ship dock. The current king had reduced the military ranks, and that particular barracks was no longer in use—and the buildings other than the *rittershalle* had been torn down. Jens-Peter even had a pass allowing him to use the Baerlen Ringbahn train for free, getting him to Dalldorf which was a short walk from the dock building. Of course, he was technically only supposed to use the pass when he was working on the ships, so he packed up his books in the worn leather bag he usually carried tools in, not forgetting ink, paper, and the notes he'd already started.

He read a bit on the train, but the light was fading. By the time he reached the dock building, after passing the guard post and signing in, it was dark.

"Who's there?" The gruff voice changed to a more genial tone when Jens-Peter turned around. "Ah, Oberacker. You've not come for more work, have you?"

Otto Reber was the night watchman at the dock building. He was an old soldier, strict with his routine but also extremely proud of the secret Preusan levitation ships. As one of the main engineers behind them, Jens-Peter was therefore included in his stern approval.

"Evening, Otto. Afraid so. They're always coming up with more tests, you know." Carefully leaving out who was doing the tests, and why. "I'll likely be here all night."

He climbed the dock scaffold stairs to where *Einzl*, the very first levitation ship, was tied up. In the dim light, he could barely make out the large, loaf-shaped bag containing the pulverized levitator dust, but the wooden deck it supported was illuminated by moonlight from the clerestory windows all along the upper wall. Ahead and on the other side of the *halle* was a deeper shadow of the new ship. Jens-Peter blinked. It was back already? A pity it was too dark for him to take a look at it.

It was cold enough that he grabbed a canister of fuel from the supply cabinet for the little stove onboard. That way he could heat water for coffee, which kept his hands warm enough to write. He stumbled on a long, low wooden crate on the deck, hiding in the shadows, and stifled a curse as pain radiated from his bruised shin. He recognized the crate. He'd tried to get it tossed off previously, and here it was back again, taking up precious space and doing nothing useful. "Why would a secret project need safety flares?" he muttered and kicked the crate out of the way. "Stupid regulations."

He really should have come here to work on his paper sooner, he realized. The levitation ship dock was completely still at night. He spread all his books out on the deck, lay on his stomach, and worked to his heart's content. Years of experience as a poor student made a single lamp more than adequate for his purposes and easier to hide from anyone that might come through to make sure the levitation ships were secure. Jens-Peter firmly believed in the principle that it was easier to seek forgiveness than permission, and nobody had forbidden him from studying in the ship he worked on at odd hours, had they?

Somebody else had been working on it recently, though. Several of the guy-wires from the control post were loose and disconnected, and one of the steering motors was disassembled on the other side of the deck. They must have started working on the suggestions he made after the test run a few weeks ago. When he got this annoying task completed he would have to take *Einzl* out for a flight to evaluate the changes.

Pen scratching on paper, Jens-Peter started to feel his research idea coming together. He'd need some information to support it, and he still had to find an actual masonry collapse to examine ....

Clink.

Jens-Peter lowered his pen, frowning. The sound had come from the direction of the berth of the large new ship. No one should be there; even Otto would just walk by and give it a once-over from the ground. But something had just fallen from the ship to the concrete floor of the barn.

He didn't want to give himself away if it was one of the Kriegsa or, God forbid, von Koller himself, but he was definitely curious. Jens-Peter turned down his lamp, pushed it against the bulwark, and crawled carefully to the side.

Faint flickers of light were visible in the dark, and moving human shadows. More than one. Jens-Peter blinked, rubbed his eyes, then pulled out his cheap pocket watch. Three in the morning? Nobody in the Kriegsa would be about at such an early hour, and even if it were some secret mission, they wouldn't need to creep about here. No, someone was up to no good. But what could he do about it?

Einzl was tied firmly to allow for all the repair work. It wouldn't shift much if he moved. Jens-Peter thought for a moment, blew out the lamp, and carefully climbed down the ladder.

The new ship was officially named something pretentious, but he and most of the others connected to *Einzl* referred to it as *Zwo* or Two, emphasizing that *their* ship came first. It was larger and had actual cabin space and a fixed dock. Moving carefully, Jens-Peter went up to *Zwo* in the shadows. He heard more stealthy movement, creaking of ropes and wood hitting wood. No voices. He took another step, trying to get a better look at the figures on the deck of *Zwo*, and stumbled on something heavy.

Heavy, and soft. A person, who hadn't made a sound or moved since Jens-Peter had landed on him. Then he realized that his hand had landed in a sticky pool on the floor beside the man, and that his skin was cool to the touch. Jens-Peter scuttled back, heart pounding. Dead. Not just dead, *killed*.

This had gone beyond illicit study locations. Why would someone …

Somebody was stealing *Zwo*. He couldn't see the dead man's face, but the only person who should be inside at this hour was Otto. There were also guards, perhaps ten or so, outside. Since the strangers were being careful to not make noise, they probably hadn't killed all of them.

Jens-Peter tried to stop his teeth from chattering while his thoughts went around in frantic circles. What should he do? He wasn't big and strong like some people, so attacking on his own was out. He had to get the attention of the guards in a way that didn't reveal his location to the thieves. But how?

There were only three exits: the big main doors for the ships and smaller doors front and back for people. The invaders were between him and the big doors and one of the smaller doors. If he got outside, he'd need to be certain none of the enemy were present before raising the alarm, and the dock was big enough that it would take time to run until finding the guards. He needed something loud and long-range, like a gun. No weapons were stored in the dock. Maybe he could find something outside?

Then he remembered the crate he'd smacked his shin on. Flares would be perfect for this situation! He'd just skip outside, light the flare, and the soldiers would be alerted and the thieves would never know he'd been there.

He stumbled a bit in the darkness, still shaky with fear, but managed to get back to the scaffolding and climb up without trouble. Rummaging in the crate, he found the long sticks and pulled out two. Patting his vest pocket to make sure the box of matches was still there, he threw one leg over the side to head back down.

A low rumble made him lose his balance and drop one of the flares over the side. That sound—it was coming from the main doors. They were opening the doors! There was no time to run outside if he was going to stop the theft. He would have to aim the flare at the open door instead.

Jens-Peter squinted at the big doors, fumbled for the matchbox, and tried to balance the long stick with the flare at the end while striking a match at the same time. The fuse—he could barely see the fuse in the dark, and lighting it with one hand and keeping the flare aimed was not going well. He'd tried three matches in a row without success.

Until the fourth attempt succeeded. Too well.

The fuse spurted to life with a shower of sparks, and he dropped the stick in shock. The fuse rolled against the bulwark of *Einzl*, tilting as it went, and a second later the flare launched. Toward the roof.

Horrified, Jens-Peter watched the flare riccochet off a beam and head directly for the deck of *Zwo*. Startled shouts erupted from the thieves, then a scream. Was the light from the flare supposed to be that … large?

No. The flare had set *Zwo* on fire.

I was only trying to help …

More yelling and scrambling figures, at first trying to put out the fire and then giving up and escaping. Jens-Peter felt a surge of hope, thinking that meant the guards had finally arrived, but then one end of *Zwo* sagged down and the levitator bag snapped up and smashed into the roof beams. The connector cables had broken.

The good news was that *Zwo* was not going anywhere now. The bad news was that the thieves, realizing this, remembered there was another, smaller ship that could also be stolen and were now headed for him and *Einzl*.

Von Koller was already going to be enraged if he ever found out that Jens-Peter was involved with damaging *Zwo*. If *Einzl* was stolen as well he'd demand his head. And probably his immediate expulsion from the university as well.

There was no time to think. Jens-Peter ran for the controls, started up the navigation engines, and ramped the levitator bag until the ship was straining at the ropes.

In the light from the fire, he saw that the shadowy figures were streaming toward him, one even grabbing the ladder. Jens-Peter pushed it away from the ship and grabbed a small hatchet stowed nearby. He ran to the front and cut the bow rope.

Einzl shifted nose up, dislodging more invaders. Jens-Peter fell to the deck and slid to the stern, catching a connecting rope that went by just in time for him to swing and cut the remaining rope holding the ship to the dock. *Einzl* shifted free, and he quickly adjusted the altitude and moved forward.

The ship moved sideways. Jens-Peter cursed. Of course, one of the rear navigation engines was missing! And the main door wasn't open wide enough for *Einzl* to go through sideways.

He still had both bow trim engines, right? They were tiny but still had an effect. Slowly he got the ship in trim just before colliding with the edge of the door. *Einzl* scraped, hung for a terrifying moment while the dark-clad thieves ran after and grabbed at the trailing rope, but then the ship broke free and drifted up.

Jens-Peter fought to get control of the ship, which was spinning in a slow spiral in the wind outside. The fire inside the barn was bright enough that he could see the guards running up. He even recognized one of them, Sergeant Becker. Becker was staring at him with a stunned and horrified expression.

"They tried to steal the ships!" Jens-Peter yelled, pointing at the barn. "They killed Otto!" He swore, grabbing at the controls as *Einzl* lurched and smoke came from one of the bow trim engines. "No, don't die … Help me get this thing under control!"

Sergeant Becker stared, motionless. Then brought his rifle up and aimed.

"No! It's me, Oberacker! Don't shoot!"

Becker fired, and Jens-Peter heard the bullet hit the side of the ship a few feet from him. Time to run. He could explain later.

CHAPTER 3

The evening sky seemed ominous to Triss, glancing out the tall kitchen windows while sweeping. Dark, and threatening snow. Not only had she finished the books she had, it would take days for the new snowfall to clear away from her roof route. It would never do to leave footprints, after all. Yes, even though it was cold she should go to the library tonight to return the books and get new ones.

She would need to wear her stockinette tights, usually worn for acrobatics, under her dress for warmth. Also tie a shawl, because the one dress she had left that was comfortable to move in no longer covered everything it should. It was somewhat of a relief to learn that she was not getting fat so much as growing ... out. It still was very inconvenient for her evening activities and Triss had not reconciled herself to the change. But she had started using a safety rope for the tricky section near the library itself, just in case the window ledges really were too narrow for her to balance on now. If the troupe ever found out, she would *never* live it down.

When she went out, she found that it was windy as well as cold. As she carefully shifted over the roof, Triss made her plans. Maybe she'd take one more book than usual this time, to tide her over. Surely the snow would clear before the next cleaning day? It would be a pain taking them all back at once, but ...

A dark shadow loomed out of the clouds. Triss blinked, wondering why it looked so familiar. Except this time, the boat in the sky looked closer. She could almost imagine seeing the trailing ropes and the wooden barrel that rolled off the slanted deck, or the person frantically pulling on lines and gear handles, or ...

It was really close. So close that it was going to hit one of the chimneys. The edge of the boat scraped and ground, making the whole thing pivot.

"Oh nooo ..." The man cursed and pulled harder. The boat seemed to float up, strangely, but then bobbed and tilted. "*Gottsverdammt* ... Stuck! Axe ... where's the axe?" He looked around and caught sight of Triss, crouched on the roof and still trying to understand what she was seeing. "AAAAH!" he screamed. "What ... why are you on a roof? Why? I hate my life ..."

His face was smeared with something dark, and his hair was tousled. Whoever he was, he was in need of help, and it was bad luck to leave rope trapped. Triss shrugged and shuffled her feet on the ridge, crouching for balance, until she reached the rope. It had gotten firmly wedged, and she had to exert all her strength to pull it free.

And just at that moment, the wind surged. The rope jerked her off her balance, and she clung to it, wrapping her legs about it instinctively. The man was cursing under his breath above. Triss looked down to find her footing and nearly cursed herself. The roof was far below her and moving rapidly away.

"Aaaaah!" She couldn't help it. A strange sky boat was taking her away from the house, and the *library*!

"What?" A tousled head peered over the edge of the boat. "You! Get off!"

"*How?*" Triss shrieked. "Put me back on the roof this instant, you ... you kidnapper! I was *helping* you!"

"I didn't do it on purpose, it's the damn wind! If I could steer, I wouldn't have gotten stuck in the first place!"

Triss gritted her teeth and started climbing. Her hands were getting too cold to hang on to the rope much longer, and she couldn't see the ground any more. The boat would be safer, for now.

She swung herself over the edge and looked around. It looked very much like a real boat, only it had no sail and a row of cables from the edges to a looming, rounded bulge as long as the boat and covered with metal latticework. The deck was covered with a mess of ropes, wooden crates, strange devices, and ... Triss blinked. A pile of books?

Everything loose slid as the boat tipped hard, including Triss. The man was darting back and forth between a large dark metal housing in the back and a brass armature with a large handle—or he was trying to. Every time he let go of the brass handle, however, the ship began to dip and turn, and he had to run back again.

"Look, you, whoever you are, I've got to get this engine going or we'll crash! Hold on to this!"

Everything on the deck slid to the side again, but Triss was ready this time and didn't fall. She grabbed the brass handle and braced herself against a metal tube bolted to the deck. The top was open and a metal gear was sticking out.

With the boat somewhat steady, Triss turned her head to see what the man was doing. He was completely focused on the machinery—the

19

engine?—grabbing tools from a large leather satchel and muttering what sounded like bad words in a desperate tone. Something dark was smeared all over his face and clothes, and there was a lingering smell of smoke.

"Please work, please work …" The engine made a loud bang followed by a grinding noise. He gave something a whack with a large metal tool and tried again. This time a low rumbling noise caught and continued, gradually growing softer. The man sagged to the deck, dropping his face in his hands and looking completely exhausted.

The flying boat felt different now, not wallowing but moving with creaking sounds. Triss caught glimpses of darker clumps of trees on the ground moving past.

"Is this going to crash now?"

The man looked up, startled. "You're still here?"

Triss stared. "Where would I go? I don't even know where we are. Or how to get down to the ground. And if I'm not back before dawn, Frau Heusler will dock my pay!" Not to mention she still had to return the books without anyone noticing. "What is this thing?" She gestured at the flying boat.

His shoulders drooped. "I can't tell you," he muttered. "You aren't supposed to know about it."

"I'm *in* it."

"Don't remind me! What a horrible night. If I'd just missed that chimney—hold on, what were you doing on the roof, then? And what's that sack on your back? Are you a thief?"

He seemed more interested than angry, but Triss felt her temper boil. "I'm a housemaid! And I wasn't stealing anything, I was putting things back!"

"Housemaids clean roofs? At midnight?" He seemed skeptical, and Triss couldn't blame him. "Putting what back?"

She pulled the bag over her shoulder and opened it. "See? Books. *Catapultam Habeo*, *Travels in Alba*, and *A Journey Underground*."

"Oh?" He picked up one of the books. "Graeco-Roman siege engines? Not to pry into your personal affairs, but do housemaids need to know about that sort of thing?"

"I like reading. The place I work has a really big library but they keep it locked all the time so I go over the roof and through a window." Now that she was explaining it for the first time to someone, she could see how it might be considered unusual. "Look, can you make this go back to where it was now? I'll be in trouble if I'm late."

"I'm afraid you're already in trouble," he said slowly. "Not as much as I am, but … this is a secret. A government secret. I can't just let you go, not after you've seen this."

Triss felt a chill beyond what the wind created. "You … you're going to make me stay here?"

"I don't know!" He threw up his hands. "Someone tried to steal this tonight and killed some people to do it and I've been shot at and set on fire and I didn't mean to bring you along so I'm sorry." He took a deep breath. "I don't know where I can go for help. I thought I was safe at the … the place I was. There were even guards!"

He didn't seem like a criminal. He hadn't tried to hurt her, even when she suddenly appeared on his flying boat, and he seemed really worried. Triss pondered. What would she do in his place?

"Can you go to your family?" Zigane trusted family first above all, sometimes *only* family.

He shook his head. "Too far away. I can't let this be seen, so I have to get it out of sight before dawn."

"Friends you can trust?" Triss said doubtfully.

"Well, there are my fellow students." He rubbed his chin, thinking. "If I can get to them in the town. Wait, I keep forgetting it's Little Vacation. Not Dieter, not Stefan … wait! Wolfgang Mauer is staying with his cousin in Kladau. It's not that far, and even better it's in the countryside. Oh, I suppose I should introduce myself. I'm Jens-Peter Oberacker." A quick smile flashed on his grimy face.

Triss regarded him in silence, then started picking up the fallen books. Until they got closer to the ground, there was nothing else she could do.

He'd been too focused on survival to notice previously, but the girl—Triss—was amazingly calm and matter-of-fact dealing with the levitation ship and being so high in the air. It didn't seem to trouble her at all to climb the rigging to repair one of the control wires, and she'd even climbed up the rope to get on board in the first place. On the trip to Kladau, now that he'd mostly regained control of the ship, he had time to think about exactly how odd she was.

Since there wasn't much to do, Triss started leafing through his engineering books.

"That's a pretty dry topic for most people. You'd probably be better off reading the books you brought."

"I already read them," Triss said without looking up.

Usually what happened when young ladies attempted to read his engineering texts, which wasn't often, was a polite effort that quickly ended with the book being closed and firmly ignored after a few pages. Triss, on the other hand, looked at each and every page with a serious expression. She even fished out and relit the lantern to read better. Jens-Peter had her string a tarp to cover the light, just in case. Not that there would be many people out at this hour, but he didn't want to get in even *more* trouble.

If he remembered correctly, the place Mauer was staying was on Lake Havel, on the other side of the lake from a small forest park. Jens-Peter had gotten skilled at navigating from landmarks at night with all the secret runs he'd been doing. He peered over the side. Was that it there? He'd only been there once before. During the day. There was a walled garden with an orchard, definitely. And he thought the house itself was white, with red roses. Which wouldn't be blooming in winter, and hard to see from the air even if they were blooming.

"I think that's it," Jens-Peter said softly, squinting in the distance. Voices carried more than you thought.

"The place your friend is staying?" Triss put the book down and looked over the railing, intrigued. "Will he be awake?"

"Probably not." It was going to be tricky waking Mauer up without also waking everyone else in the house, exactly what Jens-Peter wanted to avoid. "I guess I need to find a place to hide this thing, then wait for morning."

That got him a glare. "No! I have to get back as soon as possible!" Triss hunkered down and stared at the house in the distance. "What if I can get him to wake up now?" she said with hesitation, as if unsure how Jens-Peter would react.

"Huh?"

She pointed. "Take it over the house. I can go down a rope and knock on his window, if you know which room he's in."

Gnawing his lip, Jens-Peter considered. It was not risk-free but better than his other ideas. Triss could definitely do it. "All right, get ready. There's three guest bedrooms, though, so we may need to check first." As he moved in, he gave her a quick description of Mauer. "Oh, and he wakes up in a vile temper, so I will apologize in advance for any intemperate language he might use."

Triss just nodded, attaching a rope to a cleat fastened to the deck in a practiced manner and tugging it. Perching on the railing and holding the rope, she glanced over at Jens-Peter.

"I can't control the ship height precisely, but I'll do my best to get you close." He was whispering now. "It's those second floor rooms there." He pointed. Damn, there was a faint light on the first floor. Servants? They'd have to be careful.

Triss nodded and swung over the side, sliding down and out of sight. He really needed to ask how she got so comfortable with ropes and the like. He wished he could see what was going on, but he needed to focus on the ship. To help avoid notice he had reduced the engine speed, but he didn't dare shut it off entirely. It might not start up again with his luck.

No sound. He felt the ship sway a bit and guessed Triss was shifting to a different window. Then he heard increasingly loud tapping noises. Had she found the right room? Silence. A metallic scrape, a creaking noise, then a burst of profanity. What had Triss done to him?

"Whose idea is this ass—"

"Mauer! Come to the window, it's an emergency!" Jens-Peter hissed as quietly as possible. Triss scrambled back up the rope, and he waved at her to take the controls.

"You ape, von Koller will gut you! What are you doing?" Mauer still sounded half-asleep.

"Get up here and I'll explain! You think I'd do this for fun?"

"Yes." Mauer snarled, then sighed deeply. "Oh, what's the point, I'm already awake. Let me find some pants. Then I'll kill you."

Triss found a rope ladder and thoughtfully fastened it for Mauer's use. In a few minutes Mauer gasped and struggled his way on board. His hair was wet. Apparently Triss had tossed water on him to wake him up.

"What the hell happened? The ship looks half-wrecked." Mauer gestured helplessly as he glanced around. "You really did it this time. Von Koller is going to kick you out, maybe into a jail cell, and I can't blame him."

"And I'm telling you I didn't have a choice!"

"Can you take me back now?" Triss interjected. Mauer whipped around to face her, staring.

"And who is she? Oh, you idiot. You can't have …"

"I don't know what you are thinking, but you're wrong. I found her on a rooftop and she helped untangle the ship and things just sort of happened." Jens-Peter rubbed his head. "It's been a long night. Someone attacked the ship dock. Otto is dead, and Sergeant Becker thinks I'm involved." He couldn't give all the details with Triss in earshot, but that should give Mauer some idea of what was going on. "The … other one was damaged by fire. They were trying to steal it."

"Who?"

"I don't know. A bunch of people."

Mauer frowned, leaning forward. Then he turned, crouched under the tarp and picked up the lamp, holding it up to Jens-Peter's face. In the light Jens-Peter could see Mauer's face go pale and the angry expression in his eyes turn to fear.

"Jens-Peter … why are you covered in blood?"

CHAPTER 4

The grim stone facade of the Kriegsa held no happy memories for Wolfgang Mauer, and there was little hope of improvement. He fought a sudden overwhelming urge to yawn, staggering and brushing up against the wall before lurching upright again.

"Will you stop?" Stefan Arendt whispered, glancing about the hallway. "You look half-drunk. Go back."

"Oh, Gods, if only I were drunk! I didn't get any sleep last night thanks to that disaster-prone midget. And now that my bed is all wet, I won't get much if I go back, so you're stuck with me for now."

Arendt suddenly stopped, making Mauer crash into him. "What happened?"

Damn, I really am tired. Mauer rubbed his sore nose, fear jolting him alert. He'd agreed to keep the girl's presence a secret, after all. "Dumped the entire washbasin on me. What happened to knocking on doors? And calling at reasonable hours? That water was freezing."

"Seems to have worked."

Mauer realized that no one had expressed any sympathy for his plight, and his gloom increased.

The inhabitants of the Kriegsa were likewise lacking in cheer, and they had, presumably, woken in a less violent manner. It made him wonder if Arendt was right and something major was happening.

Of course, ordinary citizens like them could not enter the inner sanctum of the Kriegsa, but they could send a message asking for Stefan's brother, Ermut.

"Will he come?" Mauer muttered, feeling his headache grow.

"He cautioned me about coming here for trivial matters, and I've never done it before. He'll come." Stefan appeared quietly confident. "Wait, Jens-Peter dumped a washbasin on you?"

Mauer winced internally. If he weren't so damn tired—and still slightly damp—he would have refrained from mentioning the incident entirely. He and Jens-Peter had agreed that he was in enough trouble and mentioning Triss's presence would only make it worse. She was not going to be mentioned unless absolutely necessary, and they had taken steps to ensure her secrecy. Fortunately at that very moment, a worried Ermut came in view, and Mauer gave silent but sincere thanks to whatever guardian spirit had saved him from having to either lie to Stefan or end up repeating Jens-Peter's completely implausible "I found her on a rooftop" story. He had the sinking feeling he was going to get blamed eventually, but exactly when and for what was yet to be determined.

Stefan whispered in Ermut's ear. He hadn't said more than a few words before Ermut went completely white and gestured to him to be silent. Ermut left in a hurry and then returned with some very serious men in uniform, who escorted Mauer and Stefan to a room and asked a large number of agitated questions.

"Has the levitation ship been left unattended?" This was from a man with lean features and light-brown hair, who did not sit back fully on his chair.

"No sir, Oberacker is with the experimental craft. It's hidden. The other ship was badly damaged."

"Yes, we know. Do you have any information on who did this? And where is Oberacker?"

"He said he would hide the ship somewhere in the Halensee Forest before dawn." And after dropping off the girl, presumably to the same rooftop he had found her on. Mauer felt his headache increase. "He didn't say exactly where. And he didn't get a good look at the thieves, but there were a lot of them. At least twenty, and they were armed."

One of the men made a noncommittal noise that could be taken as agreement or merely an encouragement to continue speaking. "The ship is damaged but can still navigate." In a slow, wounded-bird fashion he did not want to experience again.

The lean-faced man frowned. "So you don't know where he is. Is he going to be reporting in after hiding the ship, or meeting with you somewhere?"

Even through his pounding headache, Mauer was aware of something odd in the man's tone. Nobody had asked anything about Jens-Peter being injured or about the extent of damage to the ship. "He didn't say. He was pretty busy just keeping it in the air and worried about keeping it concealed."

"And letting the Kriegsa know," Stefan added helpfully.

"Absolutely. He kept mentioning it." Mauer desperately wanted to leave before someone decided to make this officially his fault. "So, what should we tell him if we see him?"

The officials glanced at each other, then at Mauer and Stefan. "He should report in immediately."

"We shall do so." Mauer stood up and kept moving, hoping against hope they would be allowed to leave.

No one stopped them. Letting out a pent-up breath as soon as they left the Kriegsa grounds, Mauer continued walking at a casual pace.

"Er, the university is in the other direction," Stefan mumbled.

Mauer nodded, but didn't say anything until they reached Schutzenstrasse, with a number of cafes and bakeries. The smell was tempting, but even though he was starving, food was not his goal.

He glanced at the plate-glass windows lining the street and with a sinking feeling realized his suspicions were well-founded. They were being followed.

His first mistake—that day—was thinking the engines had been fixed. They'd worked well enough to drop off Triss and then Mauer, but shortly after Jens-Peter noticed an uneven vibration in the deck, followed by visible smoke wisping out from the housing. Jens-Peter quickly throttled down and glanced about, hoping for inspiration. He could see the Halensee Forest ahead faintly in the predawn light. The trouble was that he wasn't sure he could reach it before the sun came up.

They had to keep the levitation ships secret. That had been made extremely clear to everyone involved. If he couldn't reach the forest in time, what else could he do? Land in a field and cover the ship with branches or something? He didn't see any houses nearby, fortunately. But there was a road, and the numerous ruts told him it was well-used. Gritting his teeth, Jens-Peter pushed the throttle again.

A thicket ahead … but it wasn't large or dense enough for concealment with the leaves gone. He could see right through it. At the edges of the forest were a few isolated clumps of trees. Would one of those work? They weren't very large, from what he could see in the gloom.

The troublesome engine popped twice, then burst into flame. Jens-Peter hastily shut it down and grabbed the one sand bucket that had survived the previous adventures and tossed it. The flames vanished, but dark smoke continued. That would also be visible soon, and he looked frantically for something to cover the engine with. The canvas tarp Triss had used when reading … it would have to do.

He couldn't take the time to tie it down. With one engine missing, the ship was handling poorly, and Jens-Peter had to constantly adjust the controls to get anywhere.

The second engine died. The levitation ship coasted silently but slowly, too slow to reach a good hiding place. Muttering curses, Jens-Peter managed to get the engine started again, but he could tell it wouldn't last long. For one thing, the fuel was nearly gone. They'd done a lot more flying than usual with no resupply. He had no choice; he'd have to make for the closest clump of trees and pray.

The engine died for the last time just as he reached the trees. The ship glided over the top of the branches. *This isn't good. I can see the ground from here. Anyone who walks by and looks up will see me.*

The first rays of sunlight appeared over the horizon. Jens-Peter scowled at the lovely scenery and gathered up the line with the grappling hook. If he pulled the ship down between the trees, it might help conceal it a little more. He swung the line, snagged it on a branch, and pulled. The levitation ship eased over, and he gathered up the line. Was there a better location, or should he tie up here?

A neighboring clump of trees caught his eye. One tree still had most of its leaves, although they were all a withered brown, and it was quite large. Large enough that *Einzl* would be concealed. If he could get to it … but he no longer had any means of navigation. The engines were gone.

He looked at the line in his hand, then at the trees near to him. Maybe there was a way.

It took well over an hour of exhausting work, pulling the ship by hand into place and then compacting the levitation bag for a little more altitude. It also made the ship's profile smaller, and Jens-Peter decided it was worth the effort.

After so much work, he was ravenous but there was no food on the ship. The tree he'd anchored the ship to turned out to be an oak, and a few bunches of acorns still lurked under the leaves but he couldn't remember if they were edible. He'd have to go find something to eat and maybe send another message.

He looked over the rail and stifled a yelp. It was one thing to be so high up when he had a working levitation ship. Now he was *much* too high above ground, and the only way to reach it was by climbing. Why did it seem more terrifying when solidly anchored? And he didn't have a lot of anything to climb with either. Jens-Peter got everything he could find on the boat together and started working out a strategy.

The upper branches were sufficiently close that he could drop from one to another, but soon it got more complicated. He was lying on a limb and wondering if he could use a simple length of rope or the only rope ladder for the next section when he heard voices calling in the distance.

Should he yell? He couldn't be sure they were Kriegsa people coming to rescue him until he saw them, and if they weren't, he ought to be well away from the tree with the levitation ship to keep it safe. He needed to get to the ground, then yell.

He tied the rope and tugged it to make sure it was secure before taking a deep breath and dropping slowly from the branch. It had seemed so easy when Triss did it.

It was not easy. His feet flailed, trying to pinch the rope between them, and his arms burned from supporting his weight on their own. And why was the rope suddenly made of bristles?

And it's too short. Jens-Peter plummeted down, purely unable to climb back up and try another option. He landed with an impact that drove all the air from his lungs, and all he could do was gasp soundlessly. When he could move again he stumbled away from the oak tree, after first tucking the end of the rope in the crook of a branch. If he was found, the ship needed to stay secure.

Everything hurt, and he was still hungry and cold. Then he saw some figures coming out of the forest, and fear displaced his discomfort. They were wearing dark clothes and one had a slung rifle. Hunters? He hunkered down behind a deadfall and watched. Even if they weren't here to rescue him, maybe they had food.

They kept walking, circling the edge of the trees. They were close enough now that Jens-Peter could hear the occasional word.

"… find it."

"Alone? We need …"

It certainly looked like they were wearing Kriegsa uniforms. Jens-Peter sagged with relief. Just a little closer to be sure …

"… sure?"

"Yes. A clearing in the forest. That's what they said."

It was definitely a Kriegsa uniform! He opened his mouth to call out.

"But don't kill him until you've got that ship."

Jens-Peter froze. Kill? Who? Him? But he hadn't *done* anything!

The two walked away, still talking. He didn't dare move, especially when he saw other dark figures in groups of two and three at the edges of the forest. He lay there for hours, even as the light faded and his stomach growled. At last he realized he had to do something or he would freeze to death. Besides, he hadn't seen any movement for a while now.

He got up and had to stifle a groan. Staying still for so long, he had stiffened with the cold and his aches and bruises had only gotten more painful. Where was the nearest town? The area he could see now was farmland, but surely he'd seen buildings on the way here, or had he been too busy with the engines?

A sudden sharp crack split the air, and something hit the snow next to him. Jens-Peter froze, his mind a blank. He knew that sound.

Instinct made him run. Another sharp crack, and this time a searing pain in his left arm that made him stumble, and another shot went over his head. He dived behind a stone fence along the field, shaking and terrified. His arm was bleeding, but it was hard to tell how much without removing his coat.

No, it didn't matter right now. He had to get away before they found him and did *more* things that would make him bleed. As best he could with his various injuries, he crawled alongside the stone fence.

Something was very wrong. He'd been shot at when he took the ship out from the dock too. Why would the Kriegsa think he was one of the thieves? Unless someone knew about the ships, enough to know where the facility was and who would be guarding it. They hadn't known he'd be on *Einzl*, though. And now Kriegsa people were looking for him after he'd passed a message—that had apparently gotten through from Mauer—but they were not here to help him. They were here to take the ship and kill him. Which meant someone inside the Kriegsa was involved with the thieves.

Now he really needed help. And he had no idea where to go to get it.

Triss hauled the last heavy basket of wet washing to the large room of the cellar that did duty when weather made using the clothesline impossible, put her hands to her aching back, and sighed. She'd gotten no sleep at all the previous day and very little since. And today was laundry day in addition. How could she sleep? *They had her books.*

Grimacing, she started hanging the washing, using a little more force on the clothespins than necessary. It was all that Mauer fellow's idea. She'd gotten what she wanted then—back to the house before dawn. Dropped off on the roof with just enough time to change into her day clothes and start down the stairs, only a little late. But to make sure she kept quiet, they kept the bag of books.

They were going to send her a message when she could get them back, but it had been two days already without any word. Triss didn't want trouble with the law either, so she understood why they were worried. But what if she didn't get her books back in time before the monthly cleaning? Who would she tell about the flying boat who would believe her?

Whose blood had been all over Herr Oberacker? She didn't want to be involved in that kind of trouble. Toa Mihai would be angry.

Triss was the youngest of the maids, so in bad weather she was the one who had to take the sweepings to the trash heap. It was near the stables and the back gate, and seeing a young boy loitering in the vicinity was not unusual. What was unusual was the urchin hissing and making a jerky motion for her to come closer.

"What'se?" Triss used the zigane dialect to see if he was a messenger from the troupe. But the boy only gave her a puzzled look.

"Gotter message for yer. Toffer said, tell yer 'books.'" He held out a grubby scrap of paper.

Reluctantly, Triss took it. It was a torn section of a bill that only had "past due" and an amount. Then she looked on the other side, which had an address scribbled in pencil and a date—tomorrow's.

The junior upstairs maid, Therese, leaned out the kitchen door, scowling. "What do you think you're doing, girl, dawdling like that? You should be ashamed, meeting men on the sly!" The urchin darted off before Triss could ask him any further questions, so she turned back. "Do you want Frau Heusler to turn you out without a reference?"

"I've never seen him before. He was looking for a different house." *And he has at least five years to go before anyone would call him a man,* Triss thought but didn't say. Therese had always disliked her and found any excuse to cause trouble. Gloomily, Triss realized that if she didn't get those books returned, she'd be turned out anyway, so the threat had even less of an effect.

With a great deal of persuading and promises to take some of the more hated chores from the other maids Triss managed to switch her half-day holiday to the date on the note. Her stomach clenched in worry. What would she do if this failed?

She managed to find out exactly where she needed to go, and how to get there, before the next morning. It took several of her carefully saved pfennig to ride the town coach to the river park, but that was the only way she could get there in time and still return before dark.

Since the weather was cold the park was not crowded. Triss looked about for Jens-Peter as she walked, but no one she could see had sandy hair like his—or if they did, they were not short. Her irritation grew. Why make her come all this way for nothing? Was he late? Or had he come and then gone off again? *Stupid gadje.* She should have known better than to trust a stranger who showed up on a rooftop.

Motion caught her attention, and it took her a moment to realize a dark arm was waving to her from behind a wooden building at the edge of the river. A face peeked out—that Mauer person, the one she'd had to wake up. Toa Mihai must never know she had gone into a man's bedroom at night. Triss shuddered. She'd even gone through the window. What had she been thinking?

"About time you showed up. There's a nasty wind off the river, and I'm nearly frozen solid." Mauer glanced about, then opened a side door. The interior was dark, but enough light came through high windows to show several small boats on racks along the sides and a channel of dark water leading to two barn-sized doors.

"If you'd just let me take the books we wouldn't have to do this at all," Triss pointed out. "And why are you acting so strangely? Where is Jens-Peter?" She made sure to stay near the door, just in case she needed to run.

"That's what I'd like to know," Mauer said bitterly. "He's usually nothing but trouble, but he's reached new heights even for him this time. We can't find him or the ship. And the Kr—the people who are in charge are mad at all of us."

"Even me? But I didn't do anything." Triss slowly reached for the door handle, hiding the motion from Mauer.

"You saw the ship." His face got a grim expression. "We didn't tell them about you, and now I'm glad we didn't. Something odd is going on, and even though he's a pain, I don't want Jens-Peter dead. I need to get help I can trust, but they're following us because they think we know where Jens-Peter is. I need you to take a message to someone." He held out a familiar canvas bag. Her books! "Promise me you'll do it, and I'll give this back right now."

She forgot entirely about escape. "Where do I need to take this message?" Triss asked, first eager and then suspicious. "Is it far? I'm already using my half-day for the month, so unless…"

"It's in Baerlen. The warehouse district, off Gastimerstrasse." Mauer gave her the rest of the directions. "When you ring the bell, show them this." He pulled out the copy of *Underground Journey* from the bag. "Tell them you've brought the fish the author needs for his pet. That should get you inside. Don't mention me or Jens-Peter or the ship out on the street, understand? Even if you can't see anyone. There … there are magicians involved." It wasn't her imagination. Mauer looked pale and desperate.

"So what do I tell them? What's the message?"

Mauer rubbed his forehead. "Tell them everything you saw that night. And that I need to make *secure* contact as soon as possible and that the Big Idiot is furious and suspicious. They'll know what to do. I hope."

Something thumped outside the boathouse, and Mauer jumped. Holding up a finger for silence, he clambered up the racks of boats to the row of windows at the top of the wall. Mauer stared outside for several minutes, saying nothing, until he finally glanced down at Triss and waved toward the door.

Triss didn't hesitate. She picked up the sack with the books from the floor where he'd dropped them and darted outside.

She didn't look back.

CHAPTER 5

The buildings got increasingly shabby the closer Triss got to her destination, and there weren't many people. She felt uncomfortable and more than once thought about turning back. Toa Mihai wouldn't like her being here—but he wouldn't like her "borrowing" books either. She hugged the bag of books tighter and pressed her mouth into a thin line. She had promised, and that Mauer person had given the books back in return for that promise. Taking something without fulfilling the obligation, well, that was just asking for *zumala* and she needed more good luck, not less. Besides, Mauer and Oberacker knew where she worked. If she didn't do it, they might come looking for her, and she'd lose her job. Toa Mihai would be *really* angry then.

The address given was an intersection, and after eliminating the other three corners, Triss stood before the one remaining building. It was possibly even shabbier than the rest, and all the doors were closed and windows opaque with grime. Seeing so much dirt made her hands itch. Taking a deep breath, Triss went up to the smaller entrance beside the carriage door and pounded with her fist since there was no bell rope in sight.

Nothing happened. She pounded on the door again, wondering if she was mistaken. What would she do if no one was there? If she knocked on the other buildings, would they know the right location? Then again, Mauer had been quite insistent on secrecy, so perhaps that would not be a good idea.

Still, she could look around. Triss had stepped down from the stoop when she heard a rasping noise behind her. A panel in the door had opened just enough to reveal a pale blue eye, staring at her.

Fumbling in the bag, Triss held up the correct book and repeated what Mauer had told her to say. The shutter slammed shut and she heard muffled

32

voices for a minute or so. Then the door creaked open, only enough for her to enter, and was immediately closed and locked.

Standing beside the door was a lanky young man who said nothing but kept glancing between Triss and a dark archway off the courtyard. Inside was an open courtyard of a three-story building. The windows were cleaner here, and the cobblestone court was remarkably free of the trash and weeds visible outside. In an open bay Triss saw something like a cart or a carriage in the shadows.

When the young man remained silent Triss sighed. "How long is this going to take?" The gangly boy went red and shook his head so hard his dark hair flew. "I just need to leave a message. Maybe I can write it down or something? The last carriage omnibus leaves in an hour or so, and I—"

The sound of a door creaking open made the gangly boy snap his head around. Out of the archway came a man in a dark uniform with no obvious insignia. Triss blinked. The man himself was dark, with bronze skin and short black hair with a shocking slash of white.

"*Kakot?*" Triss blurted before she could stop herself. But even as she greeted him as a zigane she realized he wasn't one. The bones of his face were different, and he walked with the assurance of the gentry.

"Pardon?" He spoke like the high-class visitors to Baron Heufritz's house, too, with a polite, calm expression on his face. He didn't look at all like a Preusan, but he also didn't have an accent. Triss shook herself, trying to ignore all the oddness he represented.

"Um. I'm supposed to deliver a message. He didn't say to who, but …"

The corner of the non-zigane man's mouth twitched. "Please excuse the interruption, Miss, but precisely who sends this message?"

"Herr Mauer, although I guess it's from Herr Oberacker, too, really."

The tolerant amusement on the man's face vanished, replaced with intent coldness as he held up a hand for her to stop. Gesturing for the lanky boy to leave, the man waited until they were alone to indicate Triss could continue. She told him the entire story, even, with a gulp, her reason for being on the rooftop that night. As she spoke his calm, aloof manner became more rigid, and the expression in his eyes glazed over.

"You … *happened* to be on the roof. Just in time to see the one time Oberacker went by." He raised an elegant eyebrow.

"Well, it might have been the second time," Triss admitted. "I saw something that looked like a boat coming out of the clouds a few days before."

The man winced, rubbing his face like he wanted to wake up from a bad dream. "I can't imagine how this would all be a cunning plot, but if I don't make sure I'll undoubtedly regret it." He pulled something from an inside pocket. It was on a fine chain and had a lens like a monocle, but instead of being round, it was a narrow rectangle about the length of her little finger and set in a bronze frame. He stared at Triss through the lens for a long time, finally sighing in relief. "Well. You're not under a *geas*, at any rate."

"Huh?"

"A forbidden magical compulsion." His eyes went cold.

This man was a magician? Now she remembered that Mauer had mentioned magicians, but she hadn't taken him seriously. She didn't want to have any dealings with a *gadje bruje*. "If there is nothing else, sir, I should go now." It helped to be extra polite when dealing with the gentry. "I must catch the carriage omnibus from Königshoferstrasse."

"That's a long walk. I can send you back if you prefer, as recompense for your trouble." Triss opened her mouth to turn down the offer, but then he called, "Willem! Take the cart and return this young lady to her home."

Willem was the inarticulate door guard. Triss considered him for a moment, then nodded. Willem was probably safe, and it was a long walk to the bus. She could have him stop well away from the Heufritz mansion so no one would see them.

The magician came up to Triss when she was seated in the cart. "I must ask you to not repeat anything we have discussed," he said softly. "A dangerous secret is involved. Your life might be in danger if anyone discovers your connection to it."

Triss hunched her shoulders. "I won't say anything." She wanted to forget the whole incident, especially getting kidnapped off a roof. Then she realized if she was in danger simply for knowing, what about others? "Will Herr Oberacker be all right?"

"I intend to find out." The magician nodded to Willem and reached for a small lever on the wall of the courtyard. When he pulled it the two large carriage doors swung inward silently and smoothly. The horse didn't even twitch an ear, but Triss was startled.

"What sort of place is this, anyway?"

Willem mumbled something incoherent, speeding up once they were on the street.

It didn't matter. She'd done what she'd promised, and she'd gotten the books back. It had nothing to do with her any more. She'd never see any of them again.

The trouble began, as might have been anticipated, with a meeting. To be precise, a *demand* that Markus Asgaya present himself at the head of the Kriegsa's office on Tuesday, at nine o'clock precisely.

"Are you going to go?" Heinrich von Kitren asked in an off-hand manner. "It makes it sound like you are an erring schoolboy."

Markus raised an eyebrow. "That was exactly von Koller's intent. Which is why I replied that my many duties did not give me leisure to attend to him, and proposed the following day instead. And mentioned His Majesty might well call me to consult on the *other*, more important case so I could not be confident in my attendance but would be sure to send a trusted subordinate should I become unavailable for consultation."

That got an appreciative chuckle. "You'll give him an apoplexy yet."

They were sitting in the official offices of the Dragonhunters in a smaller building on the Palace grounds but not in the Palace itself. The practical offices, of course, were in the shabby warehouse in the commercial district. Markus was almost sure von Koller knew about them, but he'd taken his own steps, with discreet assistance from the powerful Frau Kermerec, to make sure he could not spy on them there.

Von Koller did not like the Dragonhunters. First, in his opinion they should not exist at all. The Kriegsa was all that was needed for Preusa's magical defense. Second, if they *did* exist they should be under von Koller's command. Instead they reported to the prime minister, at least on paper. In reality they had a direct conduit to the King himself, through von Kitren, and von Koller was infuriated about that as well.

"I have been officially instructed not to pour oil on open flames." Markus waved a hand. "However, I cannot permit overreach either. The head of the august and mighty Kriegzauberkollegium wishes to meet the head of the Dragonhunters? I will accommodate him—but on my terms. I am afraid von Koller will continue to be aggravating until our Mage Guardian is appointed and can act as a buffer. Which might be why we are having such difficulty finding one," he added. Just by saying it, he had a sudden insight. Who would want to deal with von Koller on a constant basis? He didn't want to either. "And I'm not just being difficult for the fun of it. I really am busy with the salts business."

Von Kitren sat up stiffly, looking surprised. "This is another matter?"

"The levitation ships incident." Markus rubbed his forehead, wincing. "One ship badly damaged, the other missing, and still no information on the perpetrators. Although it may, possibly, be connected to the salts since that message we intercepted was likely referring to the ships. They also do not use much iron and would be very appropriate for stealthy transport. I have mentioned this to von Koller but he does not agree. Or rather, he still does not consider the salts a serious threat."

Von Kitren muttered something profane under his breath. "Have you tried approaching someone else at the Kriegsa?"

Markus shook his head. "As paranoid as von Koller is? Very, very bad idea. He dislikes us enough now; if we went behind his back to his own people it would be even worse."

"Why is he calling you in now, and so urgently?"

"A good question." Markus leaned forward, elbows on the desk in front of him and resting his chin in one hand. "And a puzzling one. It seems, from what that housemaid told us, that Oberacker's friends properly contacted the Kriegsa to inform them of what happened and that he needed help. Yet *after* that message was passed on Wolfgang Mauer was followed by Kriegsa people and we still have not heard anything about Oberacker or the ship. It's been nearly a week. If they have not found him yet, why not?"

Markus continued to ponder that question even as he entered the grey, intimidating Kriegsa building the next day. Perhaps von Koller was withholding what *he* had learned? Granting the inclination, the head of the Kriegsa was too cunning to make such an obvious move that would bring down the wrath of the King once discovered. It also didn't fit the tone of his letter, which was more like accusing Markus of hiding information.

Something was off.

He was accustomed to stares and chilly expressions, given his visibly non-Aeropan appearance. There seemed to be an added element of unfriendly interest this time, and oddly not uniform but only in a scattered few. He was escorted to the imposing office of the Kriegsa head.

Von Koller was as usual gaunt and unsmiling, only his usual stony demeanor had changed to one of visible annoyance. Markus saw no reason to prolong the agony and decided to charge the ambush.

"Before proceeding to the matter you wish to discuss with me, may I ask if you have heard from Oberacker? Have he or the ship been located?"

It was brief, but Markus caught it: a flicker of hesitation in von Koller's eyes. He had not been expecting that question from him. Interesting.

"Are you telling me you have had no contact with that criminal?"

Markus raised an eyebrow. "Have we already concluded the attack on the ship dock was his responsibility? Really, if one university student can take down the armed might of the Kriegsa, perhaps some changes are in order." He observed with satisfaction von Koller's darkening face.

"If he didn't do it he's in league with those who did. We have witnesses that saw him take the experimental craft out of the dock, and he has not returned."

"I seem to recall reports of gunshots during the incident, and several guards killed. Perhaps Oberacker was wounded?"

Von Koller scowled. "He was alive enough to make contact through his friends!"

"Which is hardly the action of a hardened criminal, would you not agree? But it is proper for a loyal subject and member of the secret levitation ship project. Now, did he mention a rendezvous point, and if so has a team been dispatched to that location?"

His sense of something off was only getting stronger. Asgaya knew he had to disclose that Mauer had contacted him about Oberacker, but if that information was only going to be used to hunt Oberacker down, he would delay as long as possible.

"There was a location. I sent Gehrig to investigate, but he found no sign of him or the ship." Von Koller sat back in his chair, narrowing his eyes at Asgaya. "Which makes me think it was a diversion to allow him to escape. That's why a criminal would make contact. And I find it very curious that you are so eager to defend him—and reluctant to tell me if he spoke to you recently."

Truly, the man's paranoia was beginning to wear on Markus's nerves. "The last time I saw Oberacker was shortly after leaving Bhuta, months ago. Do you have reason to think otherwise?"

Markus spoke in a leisurely tone but he was far from relaxed. Von Koller clearly believed he and Oberacker were acting in concert with one another, but he didn't know what made him think so. He watched von Koller's reaction carefully from under lowered eyelids, and saw a momentary hesitation.

So he doesn't have any proof, just a great deal of suspicion.

"Let me remind you: the secret facility is heavily damaged due to fire. The new levitation ship will take months to repair. Six of my men are dead. Oberacker was present at the time of the attack, late at night when he had no valid reason to be there. He may have been loyal once, but he has complained to everyone about not getting command of the new ship. Why would he not destroy it and steal the only working ship we have?"

Asgaya stared at him, astonished. This level of creativity was new. "Aside from the entire Preusan military hunting him, plus the Kriegsa,"— he remembered in time to *not* mention the Dragonhunters or the Mage Guardians—"what could he accomplish?"

"Revenge. He may not have plans for the ship, but he is in league with those that do. Didn't you find a connection with the smugglers you were tracing?"

Asgaya gritted his teeth and reminded himself that von Koller had little interaction with Oberacker and could come up with these unfounded hypotheticals without embarrassment. Oberacker was easily distracted, barely graduating, relentlessly cheerful, and loved nothing more than working on the levitation ships and making them better. Asgaya couldn't imagine him successfully plotting anything or getting angry enough to plot. And Asgaya would never forget the sight of the little levitation ship coming to rescue them after the explosion in Bhuta that left them trapped on a cliff, badly injured and unable to use magic because of the danger of triggering yet another explosion. Oberacker had rescued them all. And if he had not, Gutrune would have died.

He clenched his hands into fists. No, he would require much more than von Koller's unsupported theories before suspecting Oberacker.

"There are indeed troubling links to smugglers, but none to Oberacker.

As you would know if you read our investigative reports." Asgaya got up to leave. There was no reason to stay, and he had only come to keep the peace with the Kriegsa.

"If you or any of your people find Oberacker, you must notify me immediately."

Was the man deliberately trying to infuriate him, or was he simply oblivious to how rude he was? With an effort, Asgaya reined in his temper.

"Should contact be made, that information will be shared with the proper authorities."

Outside von Koller's office, a Kriegsa magician was waiting, a man Asgaya did not recall meeting before. He had light brown hair, and he glanced at Asgaya sharply.

"Come in, Gehrig," von Koller snapped. "I want you to search south of the city."

"But sir, what if he's still—" The door to the office closed.

Asgaya raised an eyebrow. They hadn't found Oberacker in the Halensee Forest, according to von Koller, but the man in charge of the search wanted to keep looking?

I wonder why.

CHAPTER 6

This was the building. Jens-Peter was certain of it. It had taken much too long, over three days, to find. Mostly because he was trying to stay out of sight but also because he couldn't walk very fast due to his injuries. Besides the bullet hole in his arm that was still painful, he had a fine collection of bruises and scrapes from falling out of the tree, falling over stone fences, and generally falling. Running for his life in the dark had many disadvantages. He certainly didn't have enough money for transportation, and it would be too dangerous to use his railway pass. He'd finally given in to his ravenous hunger and bought a sausage roll from a vendor, but it had been late at night and in a shady area where he hoped the regular customers were also people avoiding official notice.

The house was a large stone mansion with a well-maintained front garden, even in winter. Things looked very different on the ground than they did in the air, and he'd been busy and terrified at the time, but he could hardly forget the copper finials on the roof that had snagged the trailing lines. This is where he'd encountered Triss. Now, how did he go about contacting her?

Jens-Peter's knowledge of housemaid habits was minimal. In his own home, Frau Zinkler ruled domestic matters with an iron rolling pin and did not encourage mere males to intrude in her domain, even if they were her employer or his son. He was vaguely aware that maids did chores in the house but did not know if those chores involved going outside at any point. He *did* know that servants would never use the main entrance, so he watched the back until he saw people begin to stir. Eventually an older woman showed up with a large basket, knocked, and was allowed inside.

It must be a delivery of some kind. Presumably, he could pretend to be delivering something to Triss. Nobody at this house knew him besides her. It should be safe. But delivering what? He patted his pockets. He had a pencil, a small notebook with mathematical formulas and other useful references, and a wad of paper for the initial draft of the paper he had to write to satisfy Professor Schenk.

An idea sprang instantly to mind. A letter! He could say someone asked him to deliver a letter to Triss. And it would be true! Sitting on a low wall, Jens-Peter scribbled a quick note and then carefully constructed a folded envelope from another sheet of paper. It looked a little lopsided, but it would have to do.

Taking a deep breath, he stood up and headed for the servant's entrance. *I'm just a messenger, I'm just a messenger...* Assuming a bored expression that did not match his jumpy nerves, Jens-Peter knocked on the door.

It was opened by a pretty, dark-haired woman with a demure smile, a smile that vanished when she saw him. "Letter for a servant girl that works here," Jens-Peter said while putting a hand to his cap. It looked polite and helped shade his face. A sturdy, grey-haired woman in a flour-dusted apron suddenly appeared and snatched the letter from his hand, and Jens-Peter backed away quickly.

"Hold on. Who is this for?" Her tone was sharp.

"Isn't it written there?" He couldn't remember if Triss had told him her last name or not, so he'd scribbled something illegible. How many maids named Triss could there be in this place?

"Therese, how many times have I warned you about your loose behavior? This is—"

"It isn't me! I've never seen him before!" The dark-haired maid pointed angrily at Jens-Peter. "He's just a tramp trying to stir up trouble."

The apron woman, who he guessed was the cook, and Therese continued to argue until the old woman with the basket, who had been sitting by the fire, rose stiffly to her feet.

"Can't think of any of Therese's young men what know how to write, let alone her reading anything they sent that wasn't money." Ignoring Therese's furious response, she held out a gnarled hand for the letter while fumbling for a set of lenses attached to a much-knotted string. "Written by a drunk chicken, from the looks of it."

Jens-Peter decided that now was an excellent time to depart and started shifting back toward the gate. His injured leg spasmed when he put weight on it and he stumbled, only saving himself from falling by holding on to a fencepost.

"Where do you think you are going? Ach, Josef, grab that troublemaker!"

A large, iron-hard hand had his upper arm in a vise grip. Jens-Peter looked up into the grim face of a man dressed like a coachman.

"I swear I just came to deliver a letter ..." Jens-Peter stammered while being dragged inside the large kitchen. "Ow! Hey, let go!"

There were more people inside the kitchen now, staring at him and Therese. The old lady was still attempting to decipher the name on the letter when a calm blonde maid wearing glasses looked over her shoulder. "That's Triss, not Therese. Although I can understand your confusion. That's really horrible handwriting."

Jens-Peter gritted his teeth. *You try writing gracefully with a broken pencil and frozen fingers with a stone wall for a desk, you old biddy!*

"I've brought Triss," someone in the crowd said.

Triss was wearing a common maid outfit of a long dark skirt, pinafore, and white shirtwaist. Jens-Peter was startled at this normal attire, very different from her roof-climbing outfit. Triss took one look at him and her eyes widened in shock before her expression went blank.

"Of course it's her, she reads *books* any chance she gets!" Therese said. "Who else would get a letter here? And there was that other boy that came by to see her the other day too!"

"Hmm." The old lady with the basket peered at Triss through her glasses. "Now I remember where I saw you. In a cart, three days ago, by the park gate." Her hawklike gaze turned to Jens-Peter. "Wasn't him driving, though."

"See? You all accuse me but it's really *her!*" Therese started to cry.

Triss stared at her. "What?"

"Look at the letter! See what it says!"

Jens-Peter relaxed. The contents of the letter were completely ordinary. Just a request to meet, nothing criminal. As soon as they understood that, everything would be fine.

Triss hugged the bundle of her possessions to her chest, numb with shock. What would she do now? It was already starting to get dark, and the wind was bitingly cold even though she was wearing extra layers of clothing to make her bundle smaller.

She had some savings—that she had intended to send to the troupe—as well as her month's wages. She'd never had to find work on her own before. This position had been found for her by Father Ogeli. Did she simply go around and knock on doors? Then she remembered she'd been turned off without a reference, which would make finding a new position in any decent household impossible.

And this was entirely the fault of that idiot Jens-Peter. "I should never have freed that rope," she muttered, hunching her shoulders. Then she wouldn't have been kidnapped or lost the books and then been forced to meet that strange magician to get them back. She stopped in her tracks, stifling the sudden urge to cry. She would never be able to return to the library, to read the books she hadn't gotten to yet. There were so many!

"Psst!"

Triss snapped her head around. There, hiding behind a hedge—and not very well at that—was that same idiot who had caused all her troubles.

"You!" She glared. "Haven't you done enough?"

Jens-Peter gave her a puzzled frown. "It was just a letter, and how else was I supposed to meet with you?"

"You *weren't* supposed to meet with me! Housemaids aren't supposed to have, um, gentlemen friends!" Triss clenched her teeth, trying very hard not to shout. What made it even more frustrating was the confused innocence in his eyes, like the expression of a large but untrained puppy. She sighed, fighting back tears of frustration. "There's no reason to see you again. I got the books back. And now because of this ..." A tear betrayed her and fell down her cheek. "They've turned me off and the troupe *needs* that money to survive and I don't know what to do to find work here."

Now Jens-Peter looked horrified. "But ... why? You didn't do anything wrong! It was all me! Please don't cry."

"It's not all your fault," Triss said and sniffled. "That Therese, she's got a caller she spends time with regular. And maybe more than him," she added slowly, remembering some things. "I think she may have been frightened that someone saw her and tried to put the blame on me to hide it.'"

"Oh, Therese is the dark-haired girl? She did seem to be expecting someone when she opened the door." Jens-Peter shook his head sharply. "Never mind her. What did you say about needing money to survive? What troupe?"

Triss wiped her eyes and sniffled again. "I don't have time to explain it to you. It's getting dark, and I need to find someplace I won't freeze." She trudged off.

"Can I come with you?" Triss looked back over her shoulder. Jens-Peter was limping behind her, his eyes not meeting hers. "I'm on the run these days. That's why I needed to see you."

"Why? I passed on the message your gloomy friend gave me. Didn't those people help?"

Jens-Peter silently and awkwardly took off his coat. There was a bloody bandage tied around his left arm, and a hole in the matching coat sleeve. "The Kriegsa people who were supposed to help me shot me instead. You're the only person who can help me now without getting in danger."

Triss kept walking, her temper rising. "You're getting shot at and you want *my* help? Sounds dangerous to me."

"It's not just for me," Jens-Peter panted, struggling to put his coat back on. "This is some kind of government plot, I'm sure of it."

"Then I *really* don't want to be involved."

"I'll help you find another position!"

Triss stopped and looked back. Jens-Peter was gasping, his breath visible in the cold air. His face was grey around the edges, his lips pale. He wasn't lying—he really was injured, and in his current state, if he stayed outside tonight he'd freeze too.

"All right, you can come with me." Triss sighed. She'd probably regret it, but she didn't know anyone in the area except for him and being alone was dangerous for her too.

Hope flickered in his eyes. "Where are you going?"

"You can't talk about it, understand?" She glared to make sure he understood she was serious. "Just follow me and don't make any noise."

Triss had been worrying about what to do as soon as she understood she no longer had a place to sleep. A regular inn was out of the question; even if she found one that would allow a girl by herself to stay, it would either be in a dangerous location or cost more than she could afford. Even more so now that she had a visibly injured young man in tow, one with pursuers if he was telling the truth.

The trip back from the river park in Baerlen was curiously useful. On the way she saw a large, busy structure with many large carts going in and out. A sign said Tauscher Carting and Deliveries on the wall next to the large gates. Carters kept their horses on the premises when not in use and even better had people coming in and out at all hours. It was unlikely the barn would be locked until late at night.

They had to stop a few times to allow Jens-Peter to rest. He was not looking well, and despite herself Triss shared half the loaf she'd been given by the nicer of the two upstairs maids. By the time they had reached the carter's building, a large half-timbered structure with a walled yard, it was full dark and the streetlamps lit. Few people were out, with the weather and the location. She would have to move fast.

"You wait here," Triss said, indicating a dark alley with her chin. She handed Jens-Peter her bundle. "I'm going to look things over."

Not only was he barely able to move at this point, he would draw the wrong kind of attention as the kind of person with no legitimate business at the yard. A young girl, however, especially one dressed like a maid, would be ignored if she seemed to be on an errand. Even the lecherous were too busy working, although that would change soon.

The yard had two main gates, arranged so the carts could drive in one and leave from the other. The barn was located in the far corner, away from traffic and inconvenient for sneaking into. At first Triss thought the entry gate would be safest, but that would mean going by the main office, the busiest location. In contrast, the exit gate had the goods warehouse on one side and the staging area for the empty wagons. They would be closing that gate first, though. If she and Jens-Peter were going to do this, they would have to act soon.

Triss watched for a few minutes, memorizing the location of the nearest empty carts and the doors of the warehouse, then went back to retrieve Jens-Peter.

He had fallen asleep in the alley, clutching her bundle. Fortunately, no one had seen him and robbed him. She stifled the urge to kick him and instead shook his shoulder forcefully. Once sure he was awake and paying attention, Triss described what she had seen. "When I tap you, run inside and under the first wagon near the gate. Get inside and don't make a sound. I'll move when I'm sure nobody has seen you."

"We're not staying in the cart, right? That won't be any warmer than here." He waved at the brick alley.

"No, we'll be in the barn. But we can't get to it until the gates have closed and all the horses put away."

They were able to follow the first part of her plan. Jens-Peter stumbled on his bad leg while running but landed without making too much noise and eventually limped to the cart and got in. Triss joined him in a desperate rush when she saw two large men leave the office and head for the exit gate, presumably to close it and put down the bar for the night. They were talking with each other and had come from a brightly lit location, so they did not see her slip inside and merge with the shadows.

She heard the solid thump of the bar dropping, followed later by a more distant but similar thump. Both gates were now closed. Triss peered over the side of the wagon. The barn still had light inside and faint voices.

"How long do we wait?" Jens-Peter whispered.

"An hour, maybe less." That was what it usually took for the last horses to be fed and their tack cleaned and hung up.

"Can you tell me about the troupe now? I'm going to fall asleep again if we just sit here." Jens-Peter sounded drowsy. Too drowsy. Triss felt a sinking sensation in her stomach and reached to place a palm on his forehead. It was hot. One of his injuries, probably the bullet hole, had gotten infected, and he was feverish.

Triss sighed. It was rather complicated to explain, but it would keep him awake. "My family is a traveling acrobatic troupe. Mostly in the Sachsen area. They don't make a lot of money going to lots of middling towns all over, so a lot of the younger people who aren't part of the main act hire out and send their earnings back. Usually it's the boys who go, and they do manual labor, but they had to find a job for me in service to the gentry. Toa Mihai insisted on that." She hadn't minded once Father Ogeli mentioned the gentry usually had libraries in their homes.

"If the towns don't earn enough, why not go to Baerlen? I know there are acrobatic shows all over the place like in the Tiergarten."

Triss huffed. "We don't have the horse acts that they like. And there aren't enough of the middle-sized towns. We can't keep showing up every month. The novelty wears off."

"So go to lots of little towns, maybe?"

"They don't like zigane." Triss blinked. She hadn't been meaning to say that. She must be more tired than she thought.

Jens-Peter was silent for so long that she thought he had fallen asleep. "You don't look zigane."

And that's why I had to leave and work, even though every other zigane girl my age is married already. "I know. My mother took up with the troupe when I was barely old enough to walk. My Toa … he's not really my uncle, not by blood. But they are still my family, even when Mother died. They are all I have." And it hurt to be told she had to work outside, away from everyone she knew. Toa Mihai's explanation made no sense. She knew he loved her like his bones, so why did she have to leave?

"Acrobats. Is that how you learned to go up and down ropes?"

Triss nodded, then remembered he wouldn't be able to see her in the dark. "We all learn, and everyone practices when we aren't performing. Rope climbing is easy." Mentioning rope climbing made her remember their first encounter. "What happened to the flying ship? Shouldn't you be taking care of it or guarding it or something?"

"It's damaged too badly to move." He sounded upset. "I had to hide it. And now that something odd is going on at the Kriegsa, maybe it's a good thing I can't move it now. I don't know who these people are, but it's too dangerous to let something as powerful as the levitation ship get in their hands." He sagged against the wagon side, wincing when he made contact.

"If it's so important, so dangerous, why are you trusting me?"

He gave a soft laugh. "You've never tried to kill me. Even when you're mad at me."

Despite the cold, the pain of his injuries, and the constant worrying Jens-Peter dozed off more than once while hiding in the cart. He was having a hard time thinking. And remembering. And understanding what Triss was saying. Eventually he understood he was supposed to stay there until she waved him over.

He watched, blinking, as she flitted from one shadow to the next on her way to the barn. The door wasn't barred, but she still chose to climb up a barrel to the roof of a nearby shed, and from there to a smaller shuttered window in the barn. Triss opened the shutter slowly, then slipped inside.

Jens-Peter felt his eyes drift closed and jerked awake. That was the other thing she had said, fiercely. He couldn't sleep, not yet. He pinched his earlobe until tears came to his eyes and watched the barn.

No sound, no motion. Then the main door inched open just enough for a familiar arm to appear and wave. Jens-Peter got to his feet, stifling a groan, and limped forward. The yard was completely silent and empty, but he still kept a careful eye for any sign of returning carters. When he reached the door Triss yanked him inside and silently shut the door again.

It was warmer inside and full of the soft sounds of horses shifting their feet and rubbing against the walls of their stalls. It also stank in a way that woke him up even more than Triss's iron grip on his arm.

"Go up the ladder," she said in a quiet voice. "We'll sleep in the hayloft." It was too much effort to argue, so Jens-Peter started up. Slowly, since his injuries had gotten more stiff and sore while he waited in the cold.

The only light in the hayloft was faint moonlight coming through cracks in the wood walls. When his eyes adjusted he saw Triss's bundle next to two roughly person-sized holes dug in the hay. The air was dusty, and he stifled a series of sneezes that made his head throb.

"Don't make so much noise!" Triss came up the ladder, burdened with horse blankets. Even now her angry voice was pitched low. "We can't be found now. Here, wrap yourself up, and I'll do the rest for you."

Puzzled, he took the offered blanket. It smelled strongly of horse, but it was warm. He lay down in one of the holes only to see Triss spread yet another blanket on top, weighting down the edges with old horseshoes, and then, from the sounds of it, tossing more hay on top.

"Burial is premature, don't you think?"

"Shut up. It will keep you warmer."

More rustling noises, followed by silence. She must be constructing her own hay cave before sleeping. It occurred to him that Triss was quite familiar with the process, and he wondered how many times she'd slept in a hayloft before. She was right, though. He was warm again, and his numb hands were burning as they thawed. Not just warm—he felt like he was roasting. He struggled out of the blanket and pushed the blanket roof aside at one end, wiping sweat from his face and wondering why he couldn't sit up straight.

"Don't come out. You have a fever." Triss handed him a small jar and a collection of rag strips. "I don't have anything for the fever, but you can use this liniment for your injuries."

"I thought you were asleep," Jens-Peters mumbled. The liniment had a strong herbal scent that wasn't unpleasant. He took off his jacket, wincing when the dried blood attaching to the cloth pulled at the wounds.

"I had to do some *obeza*, and there won't be time in the morning. We have to leave before dawn."

"What's ... oh-bay-sa?"

Triss took a deep breath. "When you ... um, take hospitality without asking, zigane have a custom. First, leave no trace. No damage, don't leave things behind. This is for others who may come after to the same place, you understand. If no harm is done it is more easily forgiven if discovered. Second, *obeza*. This is a … hmm. Service in thanks? You make the place better somehow, as payment for the shelter and for good luck. There was bucket handle about to break, so I fixed it. Also cleaned a stall that was forgotten." She scrubbed her forehead with the back of a grimy hand. "You should do something as well to thank them. That's their horse liniment you're using."

CHAPTER 7

Accustomed to waking early to clean and work in the kitchen, Triss had no problem rising well before dawn. She shifted the hay back to its original location, then gathered up the horse blankets and brushed them clean. Faint snoring noises were coming from Jens-Peter's location, but after thinking a moment she turned and let him sleep. He was sick and needed the rest, even a few minutes more.

She put the blankets back where she had found them, placed her bundle near the door for a quick exit, then did a quick wash with ice-cold water from the barrel. Only then did she go back up to the hayloft and shake Jens-Peter awake.

"Get up. We need to leave quickly before they come to harness the horses." He made a vague grunting noise, eyes still half closed, but didn't move. "Suit yourself. I'm leaving."

By the time she had one foot on the ladder, Jens-Peter was fully awake and upright. Once on the ground Triss eased open the door and looked outside. No sign of movement or lights, but there was a thin layer of frost on the ground. She grimaced.

"Wait for me!" It was a hissed whisper in a frantic tone. She darted to the ladder to tell him to keep it down, and was nearly buried in a pile of horse blankets dropped from the loft. "Oh, sorry! I can't see very well in here."

Fear of abandonment definitely got Jens-Peter moving. After getting him sorted out, Triss took a careful look at the interior of the barn. She was the best of the troupe at this—remembering *exactly* how a place had looked before. She shifted a bundle of rope that had been knocked askew, removed a wisp of hay from the loft ladder, then glanced at Jens-Peter. All the clothing was the same except for the new bandages she'd given him the previous night. He hadn't been carrying anything, and she had all of her belongings.

Time to go.

"Follow where I step, do you understand? There's frost on the ground and we can't leave footprints."

Jens-Peter nodded, confused but willing, and they left the barn in silence.

Edges of buildings didn't have the frost, and rougher ground was safe too. It just took longer. Eventually they reached the same location they had waited in last night. Triss glanced at Jens-Peter again. From what she could see in the limited light, he was doing better. Either he just needed sleep or the carter's horse liniment was excellent quality. He'd started out moving very stiffly but that had improved as well.

She wasn't sure if she really would have left him behind. It wasn't just the position he'd promised to find her. The zigane said each day traveling with a person tied a string to you, and they were careful to avoid joining the unlucky or the untrustworthy for that reason. But did this really count as traveling with Jens-Peter? She did feel a twinge of responsibility, especially since he clearly couldn't survive on his own. And, she reluctantly admitted, for all his ignorance once she had shown him what to do he never forgot. So he wasn't *stupid*. Just dense.

I'll get him to his friends, and then never see him again. No more strings.

"We should plan what to do once we get out," Triss whispered. "You need to stay out of sight."

"I'm starving." Jens-Peter was shivering so hard his teeth chattered.

"Won't your friends have food?" Triss was not happy at the thought of having to spend her few coins on feeding him.

He snorted. "They're college students, like me. Poor and hungry."

Motion caught her eye. "Looks like they are getting ready to start the day. Don't talk anymore, and follow me when I start to move."

She felt more than saw him nod, and she went back to watching the yard. It was much the same as what they had seen before, only in reverse. Men went to the barn, others went to the warehouse building and started loading carts. Eventually the large doors to the yard were opened, horses were brought out and harnessed, and the first carts left for delivery. The sun had just risen over the horizon.

Triss looked back at Jens-Peter, making sure he was awake and alert. He did look better than before, less feverish. She tapped his arm to get his attention, pointed at the gate, and stood up slowly. The trick was to wait until the cart had left and there were other people on the street.

As she moved she saw him shift his balance to lean forward, and she jerked hard on his sleeve. He winced. "No running!"

She forced herself to move at a usual pace, bundle in her arms and an annoyed expression on her face as if she disliked being sent on an errand.

No voices raised in alarm sounded behind them, and after the carter's yard was out of sight, she allowed herself to relax.

"I was thinking while we were waiting. We need to go see Mauer. If he can't help, he can find other people who can."

Triss frowned, remembering the flight on the floating ship. "It will take days to walk all the way out there. Isn't there anyone close by?" Jens-Peter was still limping, too.

"Nah, he was only in Kladau because of the Little Vacation. Classes start up again today, so we just need to go to the university. Or rather, you. I'll be recognized there. He's even met you before." He grinned.

The university? Maybe she could get this entire problem fixed today. That wasn't far at all. Still, they should be careful. Edging into an empty alleyway, Triss put down her bundle and rummaged around, pulling out a worn black-and-grey scarf with holes in it. She took off the thicker blue scarf she was wearing, handing it to Jens-Peter.

"Wrap this around your face. And don't lose it!"

He held the scarf and looked at it, then at her. "Why are you giving me this one? Shouldn't you—"

"This one was a gift from my mother." The gift just before her mother had died. She tucked in the ends of the black-and-grey scarf and braced herself for questions or objections, but surprisingly Jens-Peter silently wrapped the blue scarf to hide his lower face without saying anything further.

The streets were not empty despite the early hour, but most people looked like Triss and Jens-Peter did—poorer laborers and servants. Jens-Peter's clothes were originally high quality, but adventures had added grime and wear to the point he blended in quite well.

As they made their way toward the center of Baerlen where the university was located, Triss found what she had been looking for. A bakery, just starting they day's baking. A heavyset woman with flour still dusting her forearms was sweeping the front step of the shop, looking tired. Damp hair stuck to her forehead.

"Excuse me. I know the new baking isn't up yet, but might you have some of the old bread left?" Triss held out a copper half-pfennig. That was to show she wasn't begging, and it worked. The woman's initial scowl faded.

"Mmph. Got a few rolls, but they gone hard a bit."

Triss had expected that too. The trick was to find a bakery that hadn't yet brought out the freshly made bread. Any of the old bread was unlikely to sell after.

"That's no problem. Although if you have some hot water to spare, we could dunk the bread in to soften it up a bit."

The woman folded her arms and gave her a considering look. "Ah, that's a clever notion. You can come inside if you don't track dirt in. I'll give you a roll each and hot water." She took the coin and went inside.

Triss demonstrated the fine art of knocking dirt off shoes using the curb edge for Jens-Peter, then followed the woman inside. This part didn't always work, but it was worth it when it did. They were now in the warm shop, eating a crusty roll and had a mug each of hot water to get it down with. Jens-Peter got a little more color in his face, and to her relief he appeared to understand her whispered order not to talk. His accent would have given him away as not truly belonging to the working class.

When they finished, Triss handed the mugs back to the woman and took the broom to sweep the floor. They hadn't dropped any crumbs but it was *obeza*. That earned them a not-unfriendly nod and two small, slightly burnt ginger cookies, still hot.

"Did you look for a bakery because they start work early?" Jens-Peter glanced about the street and quickly pulled down his scarf to eat the cookie.

"Yes, and because it will be warm. You have to time it after they start the first baking but before they take it out. They aren't rushed then and are happy to make a sale that clears space for the new bread." They had been lucky this time. This area of Baerlen was close to Lüneburgerstrasse and more well-off than the areas Triss usually spent time in. "When we get to the university, how do we find your friend?"

Jens-Peter blinked. "I'm still figuring out how to get inside first."

"Why?"

"The university has walls and a gate. They'll be looking for me," he said patiently, "and you aren't a student or employee." He smiled. "But you can climb walls, right?"

Back on familiar ground Jens-Peter fought the urge to relax. If anything it was more dangerous here—more people could recognize him. And Professor Schenk would be first in line to turn him in if he were discovered. He shuddered. In addition to everything else, he still had to finish that paper.

At least they were inside the walls. True to form, Triss had barely even slowed down when faced with the wall. He was still not in very good shape with the bullet wounds and bruises, so if he hadn't known the trick to using the worn bricks on the fence pillar he'd still be outside.

He led the way by narrow paths to his destination. There was a shabby gardener's shed located, appropriately, behind the botany building. The windows were dusty and crusted with cobwebs and, even better, there was a pile of poles and other gardener-type equipment covered with withered vines along one side. It didn't provide much protection against the cold but it did offer concealment, desperately needed now.

"Where did all these people come from?" Jens-Peter fumed, peering around the corner of the shed. "They aren't students; why are they here?"

"Probably cleaners," Triss said, perched on an old wooden crate. "Servants have to clean when the masters aren't using things."

"I suppose that makes sense." Jens-Peter scratched his head. "But does the university *need* cleaning?"

That got him a scornful look. "You'd know pretty fast if it wasn't cleaned. Or maybe *you* wouldn't, but other people would."

He snorted and pulled out one of the folded sheets of paper in his pocket. "Here, I'll make you a map of where you need to go to find Mauer, when he gets here."

"You mean he isn't here now?" Triss glared at him. "Why did we go to all this effort to break in? What if he doesn't show up today? We should go to his lodgings instead." She'd been impatient ever since he'd met up with her but now she looked truly upset.

"Lectures don't start for at least an hour, so he's still asleep. You know how irritable he is when woken up—and more importantly, his lodgings are likely being watched by the same people trying to get me. Plus there are a lot more places to hide here." He did not mention that he was quite willing to wake up Mauer but did not want the enemy, whoever they were, to start noticing Triss.

Triss muttered something under her breath but made no further objections. Instead she crouched and opened her bundle. It didn't have much, mostly a few items of clothing and a comb, a tangle of ribbons, a thin packet of letters, a tan leather pouch the size of a fist, and a string of blue and white beads. Undoing her hair, she used the comb and a ribbon to redo her hair in a tidy braid wrapped around her head, then removed her old, rough coat, put on a long white apron, and rewrapped the bundle. She looked like one of the regular servants on campus now.

"I would have thought you'd have at least one book, the way you go on about them," Jens-Peter commented while adding more detail to the map. It would be bad if Triss got lost, on her own.

She looked up from her bundle. "Why would I keep a book I've already read? I can just remember it."

Confusion kept him silent for a few minutes. Jens-Peter had the distinct feeling he had missed a crucial part of the conversation, but he shrugged and showed her the map he'd drawn.

"So, this is where we are now, the botany building. The chancellor's house, which has a tower, is over here. Beyond that is the library, and next to that is Tellenbach Hall where the classics lectures are—"

"Library? That's where the library is, in that building?"

Jens-Peter paused for a second. "You can see it from here if you look around the corner. That cream stone building with the large windows?

That's the library."

"The whole *building* is the library?" Triss was staring, eyes wide, and her mouth open in shock. "*All* of it?"

"Yes. Is that bad?"

Triss shook her head, eyes shining. "So many books …"

He hoped this wasn't going to be a problem. What if she decided to take a detour and forgot her primary task?

"Largest collection in Preusa, I've been told. You should ask Mauer to let you take a look. I can't get you in right now, because of everything." He gestured at his bandaged arm and stifled a sigh of relief when the rapturous look faded from her eyes. Getting word to Mauer took precedence over everything. "Now, back to the hall. You can get inside without being seen if you use the staff entrance on the lowest level. I marked it on the building floor plan. This arrow points to the corner stair access to the lecture hall entrance. Go up three flights. Mauer likes to sit in the back. There's a doorway on the other side of the stairs you can hide in, wait for everyone to be seated, then open the door and get his attention." He hoped this would work, that Mauer wasn't being followed by whoever was behind this. If they were desperate enough to sit through one of Professor Ludeker's classics lectures, though, death would be a merciful release.

"What excuse should I use if someone catches me?" Triss stood up and dusted off her skirt and pinafore. Seeing his blank gaze, she added, "What would a maid be doing at a lecture hall?"

Good question. Anything academic would involve sending a junior student rather than a maid. Students in town rarely had their own maids, so that was out. No, they had just come off holiday where most students went home. A family emergency of some kind? That couldn't be handled by a letter?

"You've been sent by his family, with another servant, to deliver the luggage he forgot and need the key to his chambers. And you have to get back to the family house before sundown or the master will beat you." That would excuse the urgency. "Here, take the map. You should leave now and find a place inside the lecture hall to hide and wait. It will be warmer inside too."

Triss ignored the paper and turned to go. "I've already seen it once; I won't forget."

He raised one eyebrow. "Really? How many buildings will you pass on the right side on the way to the hall?"

"Four, if that little box next to the word 'Santry' is a building. What's a 'Santry'?"

Jens-Peter stared at the map, scowling. She was right, even about the scribbled label for the sentry box that yes, he hadn't written very well. Fortunately, it was not staffed these days. "How many rooms on the floor plan?"

A brief pause. Triss had her eyes closed. "Eleven." Right again. This was becoming disturbing. She really had memorized the entire map. How was that even possible? "Keep watch on my bundle while I'm gone. It's everything I own in the world."

"Of course." Strangely, the curt reminder made him feel better. Triss would not simply abandon him, not if he had her belongings. He watched her leave while tucking the unneeded map back in his coat pocket. What an odd girl she was ... but he'd been lucky to run into her and even luckier that she'd grudgingly agreed to help him. For a housemaid she was amazingly resourceful.

He sat back down where he could glimpse anyone coming to the gardener's shed, ignoring the pangs of hunger from his stomach. He hoped Mauer would be able to bring him some food.

CHAPTER 8

The university grounds were more like a park to Triss compared to the city streets. Buildings were separated by wide expanses of lawn, now somewhat lifeless in the late winter chill. More people were out, but they were all clearly students and professors and all male. Triss started to avoid any strangers she saw by taking side paths or walking slower until they were out of sight.

When she reached the library building, she stopped for a moment. The building was huge, larger than Baron Heufritz's mansion—was it possible for there to be so many books in the *world?* Impossible. Jens-Peter had to have been teasing her. It had many tall windows with a half-round of smaller panes at the top. She fought off the urge to sneak up and take a peek. That would be dangerous if she got caught. She'd just have to hope Mauer could, as Jens-Peter promised, take her inside somehow.

There was plenty of time. Maybe she could pretend to be lost and ask for directions? Resolutely Triss turned around and marched away. No. She had to do this right. Not only was Jens-Peter injured and in danger, he had to be safe to find her the position he'd promised. If she was lucky, the troupe would never need to know she'd been dismissed. The letters were always forwarded through the church anyway. She didn't like deceiving Toa Mihai, but she also didn't want him to worry. And what could he do to help if he did know, so far away?

The Tellenbach Hall was just as Jens-Peter had described, although he had neglected to mention the hedge that concealed the lower entrance from the path. Triss had to go all the way around the building before finding the door.

The door itself was heavy and battered, and the glass panes at the top opaque with dust and cobwebs. Triss was shocked. Clearly no one cared to clean much in a university! Opening the door, which was, as promised, unlocked, she saw that the inside was not much better. The walls were scuffed and grimy, and the floor was filthy as well. Then she remembered this was considered the cellar of the building. Still, it could be a little cleaner!

The entrance was clearly not much used. She didn't see anyone else, and the doors on either side of the hallway were all closed. She found the corner stairs and started up. After the first flight the bare wood steps were covered with worn carpeting, and the walls and railing were cleaner. Midway through the second flight, she heard a door open and voices behind her, and she sped up as much as she could without making any noise.

The voices followed her up the stairs. Triss darted out of the stairwell on the third floor and looked around frantically. Where was this supposed doorway she could hide in? The lighting here was dim. Was that the doorway? No, it was just a shallow indentation in the wall that wouldn't hide anything. Desperate, Triss slipped through the only door she could find just as the door to the stairway opened again.

She found herself in a large, empty room with steeply sloped seats. The third-floor entrance was at the top of the slope. Where could she hide? It was all seats everywhere…

No. Columns were scattered about the room. There was one just a row down from where she was. If she got on the other side of it, no one in the main area would be able to see her. Only someone standing at the podium at the ground floor, or someone looking back. It was risky, but what other choice did she have?

There was no seat on the other side of the column, fortunately, only an empty space. Triss sat down and scooted back as far as she could against the wall. She could only see the part of the lecture hall directly in front of her.

She waited, nerves stretched tight. It would be hard to explain her presence now if she was found. Voices, then footsteps. She couldn't see anyone, but she heard the voices move about. Too far to hear what they were saying. Hadn't Jens-Peter said she would get there early? Then why were people here?

Then a few more came in, one with a clear, carrying voice, and Triss understood. After being away for so long, a group of friends were meeting up. One owed another money, and all were planning some sort of celebration later, possibly unsanctioned. She shifted her position carefully so her legs would not go numb.

After some time the rest of the students came in. As Jens-Peter had predicted, most sat in the lower rows and none in front of her hiding place. Now, where was Mauer? Her hiding place was actually too good now as it prevented her from seeing anyone else.

Triss carefully shifted to her knees and glanced around the column. It was darker here, but her eyes had adjusted while waiting. Still not much help. The students wore dark clothes and from the back one looked very much like another.

A door creaked open below and shut with a sharp bang. This sound was followed by a rough voice from the podium, and all the students stood and chorused a greeting to the professor, who waved a thin hand and promptly began to lecture in a dry monotone. Triss ignored him, for she had finally located Mauer. He was only three rows away from her. Unfortunately, she was behind him and out of his field of vision.

If she moved, the handful of other students in the upper section would see her. Triss really didn't want to spend the entire lecture waiting, especially if there was a danger that Mauer would leave before she could safely intercept him. If only she'd been able to get to that outside doorway to hide in!

Maybe she could throw something, something small. She wasn't carrying anything, though. That paper with the map would have been perfect, but she'd left it with Jens-Peter. Was there anything around her that would work?

Much to her disgust, there was plenty of odd debris under the seats within her reach. *Do they* never *dust here?* She ended up with a handful of missiles: three buttons, a broken pipestem, a cork, and a chunk of sealing wax. The dessicated apple core was unlikely to produce a favorable response, so she discarded it.

The cork, chosen for being less likely to cause injury, was also too light to be thrown accurately. Two buttons eventually provoked a response. However Mauer just turned around again even after she waved at him. Had he not seen her? Or more likely, not recognized her?

Triss debated whether to throw the pipestem or the sealing wax, then realized Mauer had suddenly stood up and moved seats when the professor had his back turned to the audience. Moved closer to her, close enough that she could crawl behind his seat without being seen.

Now that she could see him better, he looked tired and worried, glancing nervously about.

Triss whispered softly. "It's me. The one who wanted her books back."

"Why are you here?"

Triss tried not to roll her eyes. "To find you. Because he needs help again."

Silence, then Mauer sank his face in his hands. "He's alive?" His voice was shaky, and Triss hurried to reassure him.

"Yes. A little beat up, but alive."

"Thank God." She could barely hear him now. "We can't talk here. Follow me out when I leave."

Mauer didn't say anything more but watched the professor intently.

When the man picked up a thick volume, placed pince-nez on his nose and began to read, Mauer stealthily stood up, crouched, and slowly left the room.

Triss wasted no time scrambling to her feet and following. Mauer unhesitatingly darted down the same narrow stairs she had used and even went all the way down to the basement level. The hallway was, again, empty.

Mauer turned quickly to face her. "What happened to Oberacker? He was fine when I left him, but now there are people outside my chambers at night recently, and I think I'm being followed." As before, his voice was low and intense.

"We didn't really talk that much. He just showed up where I work … *used* to work, got me dismissed, and has been following me about being a nuisance ever since, getting sick and all." Triss frowned, remembering the night in the barn. "Someone shot him," she admitted slowly. "He did say something about Kriegsa people being involved. What's a Kriegsa?"

Mauer's eyes widened, and he looked quickly about the hallway. "Don't say that name!" he hissed. "They are dangerous people, and magicians. Where is Oberacker?"

"I'll take you."

Some people got confused reversing their trail, but Triss never did. She'd seen the path once, hadn't she? And even if it were confusing going the other way, she'd seen the map, and all she had to do was mentally turn it around.

The reappearance of the library, however, did distract her.

"Is it true that building is full of books?" she asked Mauer.

"The library? Of course. Thousands of them."

"Ohhh." Triss stared at the library, suddenly realizing she'd stopped walking. "Do you know if they have maids? If it's anything like that filthy lecture hall, they need a lot!"

The first time he'd seen the girl, all suspicion and headkerchief, Mauer had concluded that Oberacker had suffered a severe head injury that affected his judgment. She looked exactly like half the junior kitchen help in Preusa, thin and weary. He had to admit, though, that she was surviving Oberacker's acquaintance without difficulty, so there might be more to her than met the eye. She had certainly managed to find him without detection.

Then he witnessed her turn into a statue when he confirmed the purpose of the library building, and his earlier doubts reemerged.

He glanced around the pathway, worried that her unusual behavior would attract attention. "Come on, we can't stand around here. I don't know if those people are following me here." That at least got her moving again.

"He said you could get me inside," Triss muttered, glancing back over her shoulder at the library.

"At the moment we need to stay out of sight." Mauer pulled her behind a sad-looking yew tree until a group of students passed by.

Triss scowled, pulling her hand away. She didn't say anything more. Now that he thought about it, how sure was he that she was safe? He'd never actually seen Oberacker since meeting her at the boat house, had he? And now she was leading him to a lonely corner of the grounds where an abandoned, ivy-covered shed stood. Mauer slowed his pace, nervously glancing about.

Triss darted behind the shed and then a familiar tousled head peered around the corner. Mauer sagged in relief.

"What have you been *doing*, you pickle-head? She said you were shot, for God's sake!"

"It's not like I did it for fun," Jens-Peter groused. "It still hurts like hell, even after she put horse liniment on it."

Horse liniment? "Why did she …" Mauer blinked, glancing at the resigned face of Triss, then shook his head. "Watch your language, blockhead. I know you're tired but—"

"I've heard worse." Triss waved a dismissive hand. "If you two are going to argue you should do it behind the shed and out of sight. More people are walking about."

It was an interesting space between the main university wall, the wall of the shed, and a pile of various gardening things all covered in ivy. Jens-Peter crouched on a large, upturned pot, and Mauer found a reasonably sturdy wooden box nearby.

"We spent the night in a barn. Horse liniment was all that was available." Jens-Peter flexed his arm, wincing. Now that Mauer looked more carefully, there was a dark stain on the upper part of the sleeve and a glimpse of a bandage through a hole.

And how was that an explanation? "Before we go any further, why is she here? No offense, Miss." The last thing Jens-Peter needed was more infractions of the rules. It was going to be hard enough as it was to get him back in the good graces of the law without the additional charges of skirt-chasing.

"He asked me to help. Besides, he promised to find me a position to replace the one I lost because of him." Triss scowled. "I'm not leaving until then."

"She already knows most of it anyway," Jens-Peter said with more of his usual grin. "She saw the ship, she's flown on it, and she knows I'm involved. And you. I trust her."

"It's not a matter of trust! This is dangerous, and what if the Kr—those guys find out about her?"

Jens-Peter leaned forward precariously on his pot. "And who was it that sent her to that warehouse to talk to Asgaya, hmm? How is that inconspicuous? What if those guys find out about *that*? You know those two groups don't get along."

Mauer sighed and rubbed his forehead. "All right, you made your point. I didn't have any choice then and we don't have much choice now. But let's keep her out of view as much as possible, yes?"

"She already has a great disguise. Maids can show up anywhere!"

Triss sighed. "So what do we do now? First off, we need a better place to hide out. This is too open and exposed."

"We need food too. I haven't had a real meal in days."

Of course that would be the first thing he thinks about, Mauer sighed internally. "What about the ship? Where is it now? Can you hide there for a while?"

The cheerfulness in Jens-Peter's face dimmed, and he scrubbed his head. "Um. I kinda … can't get to it right now. But it's really well hidden! You can't even see it from the ground." The sudden stricken look in his eyes told Mauer he hadn't meant to say that. "It crashed, all right? I lost both engines, and I was lucky not to smash the whole thing to pieces. It's safe where it is for now. I still don't know who was trying to steal them, but we can't let them succeed. They can't get their hands on *Einzl*."

"Agreed, which is probably why they are trying so hard to get their hands on *you*. As for hideouts …" Mauer hesitated, thinking hard. "My chambers are out. No, not because of her. They've been watched for the last week at least. I don't know anyone else we can trust with this big of a secret either."

Jens-Peter looked up. "Not even Stefan?"

"You know where his brother works. And if they are hunting you, do you want to put him in that kind of dilemma?"

"No, I suppose not." Jens-Peter slumped back down. "Then what about Dieter? We know we can trust him. He's the one that started all this!"

Mauer gave him a look. "You've seen where he lives, haven't you? Not only is his room barely big enough for the bed, it's in one of the rattiest boarding houses in Baerlen and the house mother is a notorious gossip. Besides, he hardly ever stays there. Always working late."

"That's it!" Jens-Peter was cheerfully grinning again. "We could stay here at the university, even!"

"With Dieter?" Dieter probably wouldn't mind or even notice. But how would that help them hide?

"Don't you remember? The first levitation model that blew up? I guess that was an assassination, actually, though." Jens-Peter's voice trailed off, then he looked up again. "That laboratory was destroyed. Then they were going to fix it and start the new prototype there, but the military stepped in.

So it's still empty and unused."

And how could he forget? So much happened that year—and then the year after. Dieter's advisor, Professor Siebert, had been working on an early, not very functional version of the levitation ship when he died in what was assumed at the time to be an accident. As Dieter's friend, Jens-Peter had naturally helped out when a Gaulan visitor by the name of Kermarec discovered evidence that it was not an accident but an assassination and later helped Dieter develop *Einzl*. Because he, and they, knew too much about those events, when Jens-Peter wanted helpers for the levitation ship, he managed to get official permission for Mauer and Stefan to help. Even though he personally had no magic or engineering experience.

"I guess that would work. You'd have to do something about the windows, though. Now we need a way to get you there safely. She's all right, but you look a mess. Even if they don't recognize you, you look suspicious." Mauer thought some more. Dieter's laboratory was on the opposite side of the campus. They could travel some of the distance by means of paths that were not often used or had concealment, but a large open plaza could not be avoided and was often populated by strolling students. Many of whom would recognize Jens-Peter.

Up to this point Triss had been crouched down, arms wrapped around her knees for warmth. She had picked up a coat and scarf left on top of a faded cloth bundle, and put them on as well. "There's a wheelbarrow," she observed, pointing. "He'd fit."

The wheelbarrow was grimy but looked sturdy enough, and she was right, there would be room. "Who will push it, though? It would cause as much comment if either of us did it." He wasn't entirely sure she would be strong enough, but she'd surprised him before. Notably by climbing down a rope to dump water on him.

Triss chewed on her thumb. "If I wore boy's clothes, I could do it."

CHAPTER 9

At one point this had all made sense. Or rather, Triss realized, it was a series of seemingly small decisions that, taken together, resulted in her pushing a very heavy wheelbarrow through the grounds of the University of Baerlen while wearing an oversized coverall and a ratty tweed cap. It had made sense *at the time*. Of course the only one of them who could move freely was Mauer. So she and Jens-Peter had to wait while he found Dieter, got the key to the abandoned laboratory, scrounged up the disguise, and then handed everything off to them before running to his next class.

This hadn't seemed like he was taking the situation seriously until Jens-Peter explained that Mauer's absence would be noticed and questioned. Triss reluctantly agreed that getting found by the attackers would be a bad idea, at least before she had her new job.

The wheelbarrow shifted and nearly tipped over. "Will you stop moving around?" Triss muttered, teeth clenched. "I can barely keep this balanced as it is. Are you made of lead?" It was true that Jens-Peter fit inside the wheelbarrow, even with a covering of burlap and old leaves. For a short person, he was amazingly heavy. Triss paused to lower the wheelbarrow to its stand and wiped her forehead with a rag, careful not to dislodge the cap. Like the coverall it was too big and if it fell it would reveal her pinned-up hair.

"I can't help it! Something is poking me right where I was shot, and it hurts."

Triss sighed. "Move now before I pick it up again, at least." She took a careful look around. So far no one was paying her any attention, but they still had a long way to go. There had been sections where the cover allowed Jens-Peter to get out and walk, but now the route was open and had too many people coming and going to be safe.

More buildings, large and ornate. She wondered if they had books, too, or if all the books were in the library. She trudged on, ignoring the growling emptiness of her stomach. She'd been hungrier for longer, but she hadn't been expected to work as a porter then.

"Will this Dieter person have any food?"

"If he doesn't, he'll know where to find it. Dieter eats a *lot*."

Triss found this information reassuring. If Jens-Peter thought his friend ate a lot, that was impressive and such a person would be very likely to get food for them, too. "Shh, don't talk for a while. There's a group of people ahead."

So they would get to this blown-up laboratory, which supposedly had a roof. Maybe even a stove? She was tired of being cold all the time, although now she was a bit warm pushing the heavy wheelbarrow. It sounded fairly safe—abandoned meant people would have no reason to go there.

Triss thought more. Once the immediate problems were fixed, they still had to figure out how to get Jens-Peter back to the flying ship safely. She was *not* going to push him in a wheelbarrow, that much she was sure of. And why did this university have to be so *large*? There was space for a small village between some of the buildings. It made no sense.

She mentally reviewed the map Mauer had scratched in the dirt back at the shed. If she was right about the buildings, they had already gone more than halfway. Triss trudged on, fatigue burning in her arms and legs. The buildings were less imposing out here, and the people had thinned out too.

"What does this laboratory look like?" Triss had never seen one before. Maybe it looked like everything else here? But if part of it had been blown up, wouldn't that be visible?

"Um, brick."

"Most of the buildings here are brick," Triss grumbled.

"It's not as tall. Long, though, and it has lots of windows. Oh, and several doors. Painted black." Jens-Peter's voice was muffled.

That sounded odd enough to find easily. Triss started to scan desperately. It felt like her arms were going to come loose. She blinked in surprise. "I think I see it. Wait, you said lots of windows? How are we going to hide then?"

They got closer, and she understood why Mauer and Jens-Peter thought it would be a good hideout. The laboratory building was long and low, just like he'd said, and one section of windows had boards across them. If you looked closely, you could see scorch marks on the brick.

The door was still solid and the lock stiff from lack of use. Once it was opened, Triss took a careful look around before helping Jens-Peter out of the wheelbarrow. She then grabbed the now wonderfully light wheelbarrow and ran off to hide it before joining him inside.

The abandoned laboratory was essentially two large rooms joined by a damaged and sooty brick wall. It was rather dark, due to the boarded-up windows, and it smelled musty. It bore signs of cleaning and a few attempts at repair, but lacked much in the way of furniture. There was a stove but no coal. Triss started searching to see what their options were. Maybe there was some wood to burn, even if they had to wait until dusk so the smoke wouldn't show.

As her eyes adapted to the darkness, she could see more of the interior. Someone had collected all the damaged and burned equipment in one corner, including what looked like a broken table and pieces of chairs. She pulled out a nearly intact box that would do for sitting on.

"Be careful making noise. There could be people in the lab next door." Jens-Peter was propped against the wall in the corner, keeping watch out the window.

"Do we have a plan? I know, get food, but beyond that? Don't you need to get back to your flying boat?"

"It's a levitation ship," Jens-Peter huffed. "Yes, I need to get back eventually, but I have to make sure the enemy can't follow me there. It's broken and can't move right now." He was silent for a moment. "I'm hoping Dieter can help find the gear I need to fix it."

Triss brightened. She knew nothing about repairing things, and she'd done what he asked—get him to his friends safely. "You don't need me here anymore then, right?" No one was searching for her either. She could leave. Maybe she could even ask if the library needed a maid since she was already here. She'd need to change out of the coveralls for that, though. And now that she thought about it, since she was not pushing the wheelbarrow anymore, she was getting quite cold. She went and pulled out her coat from the pile of belongings Jens-Peter had brought in.

"Um, actually..." He scuffed his hand over his head, not looking at her. "It's in a tree. I can't get back up."

"How did you get out then?"

"Fell." He gave her his usual quick grin. "That's how I injured my leg. Didn't help when I was running from the people with guns either."

Triss sighed and resumed searching for pieces of wood small enough to fit in the stove. Her brief hope of getting away from the entire situation had vanished, but perhaps she could salvage something from it still. Jens-Peter owed her a position, after all, and she should keep an eye on him to make sure he survived long enough to make good on his promise.

Perhaps she should keep wearing the coverall. She couldn't climb trees very well in a skirt, and it might be useful to pretend to be a gardener's boy a little longer.

"It all depends on fixing the engines," Jens-Peter continued. "I'm counting on Dieter. This laboratory is where the first levitation ship prototype blew up!"

Triss stared at him with concern. He seemed proud of the fact. "I didn't know they could blow up." Maybe she should give up on the promised job, to survive. You had to be alive to work.

"Oh, that was a really bad design. Also it was sabotaged." His eyes went wide. "Ah. Could you pretend you didn't hear that last bit?"

Triss stared some more. She was saved from having to answer by Jens-Peter's frantic gesturing, indicating something was outside. She scooted quietly to the wall under one of the windows. The handle of the door turned, and she held her breath, heart hammering. Then she heard Jens-Peter gasp, followed by "Dieter!"

In a very short time Jens-Peter was happily chewing on a hunk of bread with a sausage in his other hand, amazed at how good it tasted. It was rough food, but he was not complaining. Fortunately, Dieter's ideas of an adequate amount of food were generous since he had not known Triss would be joining them. Dieter himself, however, was distressed. He was displaying an inarticulate chivalry, sure that Triss would dislike the crude meal he'd provided. Jens-Peter suspected, from the experienced way Triss drank from the common jug of beer without touching it with her lips, that this was not the first time she'd eaten like this.

He'd have to pull Dieter aside and reassure him at some point. "Is that actually cheese?" Jens-Peter pointed at a somewhat dark lump, hard to distinguish in the pale light of a single oil lamp.

"It's … pretty hard. It was left over and I thought …" What Dieter thought faded away as his face grew increasingly scarlet.

The color faded when Triss reached behind her head and pulled out a curious, slim knife. Jens-Peter froze. He had not known she had a knife with her all this time, but somehow he was not surprised.

"Looks good to me. No mold." She proceeded to matter-of-factly chop the cheese into three equal portions. Trying to chew his share, Jens-Peter concluded that the knife was quite sharp.

It was the first time in many days he wasn't ravenously hungry. That just meant now he was even more aware of the various bruises, sprains, and wounds that were still aching. Sleep … he'd gotten some sleep in the barn. Not nearly enough.

"Mauer said he'd come as soon as he could tonight," Dieter said with his mouth full. "Don't know exactly when."

"Will he be able to bring some matches?" Triss asked. "I have a few but we should have more."

"I can get some from my … You're not planning to stay *here*, are you?" Triss nodded. Dieter looked horrified. "But there's nothing to sleep on!"

Jens-Peter shrugged. "The first few nights I pretended to be drunk in low bars and slept under the tables. Last night we slept in a barn. My standards for sleeping accommodations have lowered to 'someplace warm where I won't get shot' recently."

Dieter turned his head to look at Triss, who just nodded at him. "I can bring in the leaves I used to cover him in the wheelbarrow—that will help a little." She peered out the window. "I think it's dark enough to light the stove now. If you can move some of the larger things in that pile to make a wall around it, that will help keep the heat in one place."

Dieter ran off to get matches, and Jens-Peter started wrestling with the damaged cabinets that had been pulled down and left in the pile of junk. Triss was crouched down and poking at the stove, having gathered some scraps of paper and slivers of wood for kindling. He was glad. It was definitely getting colder now.

By the time Dieter returned, Triss had a fire going and was stacking more wood scraps nearby, and Jens-Peter had created a rough wall of broken cabinets. It would also help shield any light from the stove from being visible from the window.

"It's not much but better than nothing," Dieter said, dropping an armload of stuff by the stove. "We had some canvas tarps for covering equipment." He'd also found some stoneware mugs, a kettle, a tin of crackers, and some tea.

"Ah, just like home," Jens-Peter said, grinning. It really was starting to feel comfortable, comparatively. Triss gave him a look.

"Where can we get water?" she asked, holding up the kettle.

"It's right here." Dieter scrambled to his feet, then headed for the inner, shared wall which had pipes running along the side. He turned a sooty metal valve and water spurted out. "Should probably let it run for a while. It hasn't been used recently."

The stove hadn't gotten very warm yet, but Triss put a kettle full of water on it anyway. Jens-Peter shrugged and looked at Dieter, who was trying to spread out the canvas tarp in a useful fashion and not succeeding.

"How much of the old engine gear do you still have? I need to fix every single engine on *Einzl* and I think the starboard trim motor is a total loss. Something inside melted, and I can't even get it apart any more."

Dieter winced. "We did, but … almost a month ago, Meisner got tired of having it stored in our space and told us to move it outside. We couldn't keep it here"—he gestured to the empty, burned out room—"because they are going to fix it up."

"What, that again? It will never happen." Jens-Peter knew the university process very well.

"I know, but they still won't let us use the space. And sometime after we moved it, it just disappeared."

Jens-Peter thought hard. "I might still be able to build it with regular parts or at least fix it long enough to get to the facility."

Dieter shook his head. "Mauer said you needed to keep a low profile from the Kriegsa. We've got some of their people working with us now and—"

"Here?" Jens-Peter sat up, a cold chill down his back. "Then I have to leave. It's too dangerous!"

"Relax. These aren't the uniformed magicians but low-level mechanics. Still, they would notice any significant change in our equipment stock and ask questions, and you *know* how expensive some of those parts are, so we don't have a lot on hand."

Taking a deep breath, Jens-Peter calmed back down. It probably was safe if they were just ordinary staff. Maybe. But he'd been counting on Dieter for repair parts, and where else would he be able to get them?

"What parts do you need? Make a list. I might be able to get a few away without notice." Dieter was peering at him, looking concerned.

"As many of the bronze couplers as you can spare, I know that much." Jens-Peter thought hard. "At least a box of #3 locking screws. An entire fuel compression chamber or the parts to build one. And … Do you have something to write on?"

It wasn't just the parts, Jens-Peter realized as he wrote furiously. He didn't have all the tools he needed on the ship. And fuel. The trim engines ran on benzine, but the main ones required a mix of fuels and oil. And when you looked at everything together, how was he even going to move all this gear without a cart?

"I wonder if—"

A soft tap came from the door. Triss froze in the act of pouring hot water in a mug, then set the kettle down and eased over to the wall with the door. He was almost certain the knife was in her hands again, and he could feel his stomach knot.

"Dieter! Are you there?"

Jens-Peter gave a shaky sigh of relief. It was Mauer. And why had he thought it was the Kriegsa? They wouldn't bother to knock.

"I see Oberacker is still alive. Sorry I'm late. I went back to the fencing club for this." Mauer held up a wood case with a handle on top. "Medical box. I understand you're injured. Ah, you have a picnic set up here." He nodded at the improvised seating and eating arrangements. "Very rustic. Do we have any idea what to do next?"

"I need too much equipment to repair the ship," Jens-Peter said, waving the list in despair. "Even if we, by some miracle, find all of it, we'd need a good-sized cart to transport it." His gloom increased. All he'd managed to do was put his friends in danger, damage imperial property, and get chased by rogue elements of the Kriegsa. Not to mention get a perfectly … well, somewhat innocent housemaid turned off. "It's impossible if we have to do it fast before getting found. Maybe I should find someone trustworthy to tell instead."

Mauer raised an eyebrow. "We told Asgaya, didn't we?"

Jens-Peter indicated Triss. "Well, she did. I haven't heard anything from him since then. And I don't know anybody else we can talk to." He remembered some of the other people involved in the Bhuta incident, like the intimidating Fräulein von Kitren, but he didn't know where to find her.

"He knows where to find us," Dieter said with a thoughtful frown. "If he hasn't, maybe that means he can't. I think he would if it were possible. The levitation ships are too important."

"But why can't he?" Jens-Peter slumped where he sat, chin in his hands. It would be so much easier to hand it off to someone in the government. This was too much like work.

"You said someone was following you." Triss sipped from her mug. "Would these people maybe also follow him? Or be able to stop him somehow?"

Everyone thought about it for a moment. Asgaya was a magician and more than likely a very good one. Stefan had told them he was originally one of the *schutzmagi*, the royal defensive magicians. But the Kriegsa were *all* good magicians.

"Maybe. I sure wish I knew what was going on." Jens-Peter sighed, reaching for the mug Triss had put in front of him. He winced as his injured arm twinged. "I also wish we had that old equipment, but I guess it is gone forever now."

"It was metal, right?"

Jens-Peter stared at Triss, unable to see the connection. She had a serious expression, waiting for his response.

"Yes."

"I remember when the old boiler broke down in the kitchen and they replaced it, the old one got hauled away by some men. The cook called them in special, and they even gave her a little money. There are all kinds of people that make things out of old metal." She looked around at everyone's expression of shock. Jens-Peter knew his matched the others. "From what I've seen, nobody does any work here if they don't have to. The rubbish cart may have taken it away from here, but someone probably stole it to sell for salvage. If it hasn't been too long, we might be able to find where it went and get it back."

"I suppose they *might* have been cleaning up, but you are right, it is unlikely. Where does rubbish go, anyway? After the cart leaves, it's a mystery." Dieter scratched his head. "I can ask around tomorrow."

"Meanwhile, we'd better take a look at your war wound." Mauer unlatched the medical box. "Horse liniment can only do so much."

"*Horse liniment?*"

"Baerlen is strange." Triss seemed to have relaxed now that the stove was generating heat and she didn't have to go anywhere. "Everywhere else I've been, people just dig a pit and throw in broken bits and whatever won't burn. Here you have a cart."

Jens-Peter took off his coat and carefully rolled up his sleeve. It still hurt but not as much as before.

"Oh my, what a mess. Looks like the bullet went through, lucky for you." Mauer rummaged in the box, while Triss moved their one lamp on top of a broken cabinet for better light.

"I'd have been even more lucky if they had missed," Jens-Peter muttered under his breath, then hissed as Mauer poured something that burned and stung on his arm. "*Gottsverda* ... uh, *gosh,* that hurts. What the ... Was that turpentine?"

"Tincture of iodine. Good. If it was numb, we'd have to amputate."

Why do I have such unsympathetic friends? Even the only female here seems to think it was all my fault.

"Must have been good horse liniment," Dieter said with a grin. "Say, I just remembered—I think I have the old diagrams of the engines. They moved all the gear, and it got mixed in with our other stuff."

Jens-Peter brightened, sitting up straight until Mauer tightened a bandage and made him wince in pain again. "That would be ... great," he gritted out. "If we end up ... having to build 'em again."

Dieter went out and returned shortly with the rolled-up plans. Triss looked them over as intently as the others. Did she understand the drawings at all? Thinking back on it, Jens-Peter remembered her reading one of his engineering texts when she was on the levitation ship. And not just leafing through at random, but reading each page.

"I think we've done what we can for now," Mauer said, repacking the medical box. "I don't have any classes I have to attend tomorrow, so I can help you then." He paused. "I didn't tell you about meeting with Ermut at the Kriegsa, now that I think about it. It was very strange. Ermut acted as one would expect, but the superiors who came in once he reported only cared about the location of the ship. And it was after that meeting that I started being followed. They didn't give their names, but I'd recognize them again." He scowled. "Something isn't right here. You are a walking disaster but you aren't a traitor or criminal. Why did they automatically assume you were behind it all? You can barely figure out how to slice a pie. How are you going to manage a conspiracy?"

"I could if I really wanted to!" Triss gave a muffled chuckle, and he glared at her, annoyed. He wasn't *that* incompetent. Hadn't he managed to hide the badly damaged *Einzl*? Well, maybe that wasn't the best example.

"Yes, yes, you are a latent criminal mastermind. Very latent. Rest up, I'll come find you in the morning." Mauer peered outside to make sure no one was watching, then he and Dieter left the abandoned laboratory.

The stove's heat was almost comfortable now. The canvas tarp was less so. Jens-Peter shifted and tossed, trying to find a comfortable position that still kept a portion of the tarp as a blanket. When he glanced over at Triss, she was already asleep as if she were in a real bed. Just how rough a life had she lived before? She never complained, and here he was fussing about his sleeping arrangements. Triss simply took care of needed tasks without saying a word. She'd even *carried* him in the wheelbarrow, a young girl like her.

Embarrassment heated his face more than the stove. They both needed to survive this, and he needed to do more to help. He got out of the tarp, relit the lamp, and started looking for more wood to stack near the fire.

CHAPTER 10

The tea that Dieter shared with them was dark and astringent, perfect for waking up on a cold morning. Triss added a generous amount of hot water from the kettle to thin it out a little.

Jens-Peter stirred under the tarp, possibly awakened by the sound of metal on metal. To her surprise he sat up and started putting things away without a word from her. Even more shocking, he made no attempt to add wood to the dying fire. She had been sure he would do so and had sat next to the stove on purpose to prevent it happening. She'd warned him about the danger of smoke showing up where it shouldn't, but she didn't think he'd really understood. He'd surprised her again.

"I'm going to go out in a bit," Triss said. "If I can find whoever does the cleaning around here, I can ask them about rubbish carts."

Jens-Peter nodded and used the last of the hot water to make his own mug of tea. "I guess I can make this place look like nobody has been in it, just in case someone looks in the window." He shivered. "I think the barn was more comfortable." He shifted something, and a metallic clatter sounded. "Oh, it's the tin of crackers. I wondered where that went."

There weren't many left, but he scrupulously split them with Triss. With the tea it was almost as much of a breakfast as she got as a maid. Triss dusted her hands, tidied her hair, and carefully wrapped her shawl about her. She studied Jens-Peter as well as she could in the pale early morning light. His jacket had once been a decent one, but even if she ignored the bloodstain on one arm, it was quite dirty and shabby. Now that she thought about it, he probably had not been able to change clothes in over a week.

"You should ask your friends to get you some different clothes. And something to hide your hair. They probably have a description of you out already, so anything that appears changed from what you are now will be safer. You can't stay here very long if Kriegsa people come."

He just nodded. Was it her imagination, or was the usually chatty Jens-Peter suddenly silent? He didn't look feverish, fortunately. Maybe he was worried about his friends.

Triss let herself out after looking around for any observers and stayed on the less frequented paths until she got to the central area of the university. She was wearing her maid's skirt and apron again, having changed clumsily under the tarp while Jens-Peter snored softly. She wasn't sure she could pull off impersonating a boy if she had to talk to people, so skirts were safer.

They were not, however, very warm. She walked briskly, mentally reviewing the map of the university grounds Mauer had shown her. Any of the buildings with labels were probably of no use. She'd seen how little cleaning got done in the lecture halls. And like at most wealthy places, the location of the trash heap would be out of sight and unobtrusive, far away from anyone of importance.

That left three areas of the map that didn't have labels. The first turned out to be truly empty, a grassy field. The second was much more promising, a low brick building with a cylindrical smokestack and two large doors, like a barn. A smaller door to one side stood open, and an elderly man with a large beard sat smoking a pipe just outside.

"Excuse me, sir." Triss bobbed a curtsy. "I was told I could find the men that do the salvage hauling here?" Which wasn't true, but it would be an excuse to ask more questions.

"Mphm." The old man shifted and blinked at her. "This'n the incinerator, girl. Who's a wantin' hauling then?"

Triss gripped her hands together tightly, glad they were hidden under her shawl. "Um, it was some gentlemen at the laboratories." She gestured in the wrong direction, just in case. "They said they'd had some big metal things taken out before. When we were cleaning they found more of them. So they sent me." She hunched her shoulders and put an expression of weary resignation on her face.

"Ah, who was it then? Some rackety fella, tall and skinny with black hair, was it? They'll cheat you going and coming, that lot."

"I didn't see them, sir …"

It became clear, as the old man ran down the possible haulers, that she was his morning entertainment and he rarely got an audience willing to listen. Triss stayed polite and listened with a serious face, gently nudging now and then toward her goal.

"And there used ta be a great outfit, the boss guy was from Thuringa … or maybe it was Thurienwald? Anyway, one a them places out there. And he …"

She heard a gradually increasing creaking noise, which eventually was revealed as coming from a large four-wheeled cart pushed by two men, followed by a third with a pitchfork. Greatly irritated by the appearance of actual work, the old man rose stiffly from his chair and opened the large doors. Inside were a series of chutes down to a central furnace just getting lit by a helper.

Triss stepped just inside the smaller door, not wanting to be noticed by the cart pushers. They seemed like the rough sort of men who would cause trouble for her or, worse, remember her. She waited, looking around the room which appeared to be a small office, and intending to slip away as soon as they were all inside with the cart.

There was a map of Baerlen on one wall with scribbled notes and other papers pinned near the edges. It was just for a moment, but she caught a glimpse of the words "Rag, Metal, and Bone Collectors" on one of the printed papers.

She darted back outside and away from the building, waiting until it was out of sight to review what she had seen. The old man had told her nothing of use, but the map and papers were a listing of several salvage and refuse businesses. She still wasn't sure which one had gotten the laboratory engines, but the students might be able to narrow down the options.

When she returned to the laboratory, Mauer had shown up with a basket of food. It was only bread and cheese but there was plenty, even with Jens-Peter's appetite. Triss recounted what she had learned at the incinerator.

"The map had five places listed. Mostly in the same area, at the south end of the city near the industrial section."

Mauer shook his head. "That's a large area to search. I'm not sure how much time we have."

"I saw the addresses," Triss blurted.

Mauer gave her a doubtful look. "You can remember them?"

"Kasler & Sons, Bulow and Uhlenstrasse, Roerich Co., Hagelsbergerstrasse …"

"I told you before but you didn't believe me," Jens-Peter mumbled, chewing on a crust. "She really can remember everything from things she's seen. It's uncanny."

"All right, but even if these are the right places we'll have to search them, yes? And you can't do it. You have to stay hidden."

Jens-Peter triumphantly waved the diagrams. "We've got these!"

"One copy." Mauer glanced at Triss. "Oh. I suppose that might work after all. But they look different in real life, especially if you've never seen them before."

Jens-Peter shrugged. "I can sketch the general outlines. We just need to know if they are there after all."

Triss was intrigued. "You can draw?"

"Requirement of the engineering school," he said with a deprecating grin. "It's hardly high art." He tore off a piece of the heavy brown paper that had wrapped the cheese and brought out a pencil. "The most obvious bit is the engine casing." He started to sketch. "They had to make it special to keep the iron as far from the levitators as possible and still operate."

Watching him work, Triss started to see how the diagram worked. It was like a fruit, sliced in half. You could see parts inside that were hidden when it was whole. But the insides determined what the outside looked like.

"What's this?"

Jens-Peter stopped, looking at where her finger was pointing. "Exhaust pipe."

"Is that like a chimney? What's burning then?"

He bent his head again. "Benzine, for that one. Yes, like a chimney."

"But it doesn't go up." It was a small tube, smaller than a water glass in diameter. Triss knew chimneys had to be built right or they would smoke. The *vardo* traveling vans the troupe used had little stoves on them, and they could be quite troublesome.

"Benzine burns hotter than wood or coal. That means the smoke rises faster on its own, so it doesn't need the wind to help draw it out like a house chimney does." He stared at the drawing for a moment, added a few more details, then handed it to her.

There was still half of the paper left. "May I use the pencil for a bit?"

She wasn't sure what she could write that would be useful, but she was already late, and not writing anything would be bad. One of the salvage yards was near the church of St. Erita, where the priest who knew Father Ogeli resided. Triss went there at least once a month to send money and letters, and the housekeeper had even allowed her to go when it wasn't her day off because she approved of pious girls. Well, she could always talk about what she had read and maybe that she had *heard* of the university library being a huge building full of books. She'd also need a plausible excuse for not sending much money this time.

Everything about being out of work and sleeping in a barn alone with a young male *gadje* was simply not going to be mentioned. Ever.

After finishing her carefully edited letter, Triss wrote out the addresses of the salvage yards for Mauer, and while she was doing this Dieter arrived.

"The Kriegsa people aren't coming today," he said, poking his head inside the door. "That's what my advisor said, and I also overheard enough to figure out that they are having them go help fix *Zwo*."

Triss frowned, then remembered. Jens-Peter had mentioned there was another flying ship of that name that had been badly damaged in the original attack.

"Excellent! Then I can go through your lab and look for spare parts and whatnot." Jens-Peter got up, dusting his hands on his trousers. "I'll start immediately."

"I can help," Dieter added, only to be stopped by Triss.

"It's more important to get him a disguise," she said, indicating Jens-Peter. "Working-man's clothes, and something to cover his hair and face. He'll have to go out eventually, and what he has now is too recognizable."

"Oh." Dieter's eyes widened. "Ah, I think I recall a second-hand clothes shop by the river. Would that do?"

Triss nodded, feeling relief that at least one of Jens-Peter's friends seemed to understand the reasoning involved. "We'll be searching for the engines." She really hoped they hadn't been sold already or taken by a company outside Baerlen. An unpleasant thought occurred to her. "What do we do if we find them?" If they were anything like what she had seen before, the engines would be much too heavy for someone like her to carry. She also had no idea how much the salvage people would want for them, and she was extremely reluctant to part with any of her dwindling funds.

"Let's just find them first. They may not even exist anymore." Jens-Peter grimaced and thumped his fist against the sooty brick wall.

"I may be able to borrow a cart," Dieter said. "Not a very *good* one, and the donkey that comes with it is a terror."

"We may have to borrow everything." Mauer shrugged at their inquiring glances. "The cart, money to get the engines… or just borrow the engines."

CHAPTER 11

"That's the wrong way. We have to cross the river before Schmidtstrasse." For all she didn't have a map, except in her head, Triss sounded absolutely certain.

Wolfgang Mauer hunched his shoulders, looking quickly about the road just outside the university gates. Besides the usual groups of students, he didn't see anyone obviously out of place or suspicious, like he had outside his chambers.

"The carriage tram stops up ahead."

"It's cheaper to walk," Triss grumbled, but not very seriously.

"The faster we get there, the faster we can search. I can't spend *all* my time rescuing that idiot. He's just lucky I don't have classes today." Mauer also wanted to move quickly just in case he really was being watched. "I'll pay."

Triss had no further objections. He suspected she also wanted to solve Oberacker's problems as soon as possible. It couldn't be comfortable hiding out in wrecked buildings and barns like she had been recently.

After paying the tram fare for both of them, Mauer voluntarily went up to the open top, which was less crowded, having Triss stay below in the enclosed section. What he really wanted to do, besides minimize the chances of the bad guys connecting the two of them, was watch and see if anyone was following from the outside or would try to get on at the next stop.

After half an hour he was reasonably sure they were safe and relaxed, at least until they started to get closer to the manufacturing area. It was quite seedy, and the people on the streets were rough and uniformly male. The original plan of splitting up to search began to seem more dangerous. Triss was a redoubtable girl, but there was no need to invite trouble.

"The salvage places themselves should be reasonably safe," Triss said when they left the tram. "We can split up inside and search that way."

Never having seen a salvage yard before, Mauer wasn't sure exactly what to expect. The first one was a large, open lot with a slat fence, and the larger pieces sat out in the open with rust at the edges. Smaller items were in bins or on shelves under a ratty roof. The two of them got many dubious looks before the watchman allowed them to take a look, and Mauer saw him following at a distance the entire time they were there.

"I can't really blame him for being suspicious." Triss sighed. "We don't look like the sort of people who need salvage metal."

"I suppose not."

She pointed in the direction of the next target. "We need a story. I know—you're the young master of a notable family and I'm a servant in the house."

"I'm not a servant?"

She gave him a lowering look. "Nobody would believe it. You don't sound like one, and your clothes are quality. Anyway, we are looking for something to fix an expensive bronze thing that got broken and there'd be trouble if it's discovered. That will give us a reason to ask for bronze."

"An expensive bronze thing? Such as?" Mauer frowned, feeling dubious. Bronze wasn't that expensive; it was functional. "Oh, we can just claim it was a family heirloom. But then how did it get broken? It's not very fragile." He was starting to get in the spirit of the thing.

"You were horsing around with your friends. Possibly drunk. I discovered the damage, and you are bribing me to help you cover it up." Triss was very matter-of-fact. Mauer began to suspect she had experienced something very similar in real life. When he mentioned this, she shook her head. "It really did happen, but not at the house I worked at. One of those servants told others, and it got around."

He sidestepped a pile of horse dung lying on the rough cobblestone. The road was not well maintained or even cleaned regularly, and the same could be said of the buildings. Even the paint was faded and peeling.

"I hope we can find the place," he said doubtfully. "They seem to be saving money by not using signboards."

"According to the map, it's there." Triss pointed without hesitation. "The white building with a gate."

She was right, of course. The yard owner was a thin old man with ragged white hair and a suspicious glint in his eye. Mauer gave him a deliberately implausible excuse for looking for bronze items, in a supercilious manner. Triss was standing primly to the side and saying "Yes sir," and "No sir," with an expression of weary resignation.

The suspicious yard master reluctantly admitted he might have bronze scrap, somewhere. He stuck to Mauer like glue but ignored Triss, who soon wandered away into the weed-infested yard.

Mauer kept up a flow of inane small talk to distract the old man. All the bronze he was shown tended to be small and heavily damaged, clearly never part of an engine, but instead decorative. As he examined yet another ornate candelabra missing two branches he glimpsed Triss walking quickly through the far end of the yard. How was he supposed to help search like this?

Then another visitor appeared, one that the old man appeared to know well. As their talk wore on Mauer slowly edged away until he could duck around the bulk of an old boiler. Triss was still at the far end of the yard when he found her, eyes gleaming with faint excitement.

"I think this is one of them," she said, glancing over at a pile of sheet metal. "Underneath."

It was indeed one of the discarded engines, and with a little shifting of the sheet metal he found another. It showed damage as if it had been dropped and the casing was cracked.

"I don't know if it can be used like that … but Oberacker said the parts would be just as useful. Here, you keep watch for that crabby old man. I'm going to move these somewhere more convenient."

The engines were heavy and had too many sharp metal edges that would dig into his fingers, so Mauer didn't want to move them very far. Fortunately, the wall of the yard was close. He heard wheeled traffic on the other side, too, and the sound of horses' hooves. Making a note of the crumbling brick post nearby that formed part of the wall, he moved both engines next to it and then concealed them behind some of the sheet metal. He hoped it would be as easy to find in the dark.

Feeling slightly guilty at the planned theft, he purchased one of the less ghastly small bronze lamps before they left the yard with the still-chatting old men, paying them no attention.

"We'll have to wait until it gets dark. I assume they close up then? We won't be able to get the cart before then anyway."

In a complicated set of circumstances, the cart in question was available, but for a price. Ziegnitz the beermonger had a mule famous for either having a bad temper or being possessed. Debate raged in the student community. However, it still needed shoeing on a regular basis and after maiming a few farriers the rest refused unless the mule was immobilized. Ziegnitz would loan them the cart and the mule, no questions asked, but they had to get the mule shod successfully first.

"I have an errand to run nearby. You don't need to wait for me. I know how to get back in the university." Triss nodded to him and turned to go.

"Shall I escort you? This really isn't a good area for a girl to be walking alone, even in the daytime."

Triss studied him with a frown. "I suppose. It isn't far from here. I just have to leave a letter with the rector at St. Erita's."

"Why not send it by the post?" They started walking. He noticed Triss had a much more energetic pace now.

"The rector is a friend of the priest in the town where the troupe winters. The priest knows where they are going and when they will return. Sending a letter is hard when they travel, and they don't really have an address even in winter."

"Ah, a traveling troupe. So does this mean you have experience handling animals?" Mauer felt a twinge of almost optimism.

They discussed draft animals in general and mules in particular until they reached the church of St. Erita. It was a decent-sized church with a collection of outbuildings and a small charity school, all in grey stone. Triss skirted the edge of the main church building, heading directly to a smaller, two-story structure with diamond-pane windows and a climbing vine over the doorway, now leafless and unidentifiable.

Knocking at the door, Triss waited a moment and then grasped the latch to open it.

"Father Rito is a trifle deaf," she said to Mauer's shocked face. "Father Rito? Are you here?"

A distant, unintelligible voice came from the upper floor. Hasty footsteps sounded on the stairs, and then a round-faced priest with glasses and a cloud of thin white hair appeared.

"Miss Trisstela. What a pleasure to see you again. And this gentleman is?"

"Wolfgang Mauer, student at the University Baerlen. I happened to have business here and offered to escort Tri ... Miss Trisstela on her errand." Triss shot him a warning look. Mauer felt an urge to apologize, but for what? "I'll, er, wait outside." The priest was a nosy, grandfatherly type, definitely the sort to ask questions and Mauer wasn't sure what information to avoid.

"I just have a letter and money to send to my family," Triss said quickly. She brought out a thin brown paper bundle and handed it to the priest.

"Of course. And that reminds me, there's a letter for you!" He beamed and bustled off, followed shortly by crashing and thumping.

Strangely, Triss did not look happy to be getting a letter. If anything, he would have said worried. Was she expecting bad news? She said nothing, but tucked the letter away without opening it and said goodbye to the priest.

She didn't say anything on the trip back to the university either until they had gotten off the tram carriage.

"Once everything is fixed, will I be able to find work quickly?"

Mauer did his best to sound reassuring. "With all of us assisting, I am sure of it." In reality, he was only hoping they would all get out of this mess alive and without going to jail, but it would be impolite to let her worry.

Father Rito puttered about the office, organizing the stacks of paper disordered in his hasty search earlier in the day. His usual tasks had been rearranged by a christening, replacing the pastor who was ill, and then his visitor—not that he minded the girl. His friend Ogeli had taught her well, and he only wished he could spend more time on her education. While she read voraciously, her book learning often had a curious detachment from reality, as he had discovered when she had asked about moon fairies. If she had read it in a book, she accepted it as real. It was a blessing that in her life as a maid, this did not seem to cause her any difficulties. Yet.

The young man worried him. Trisstela was far from her family, and while she had never caused him concern before and the young man seemed decent, Rito was quite sure Ogeli and her kin would want to know. He would send his own letter with hers then. A pity he knew nothing more than the name he had been given.

A tentative knock sounded on the door. Father Rito went to open it and saw the same zigane who had brought the letter for Trisstela. The light had faded from the sky while he had worked, and a chill wind was blowing.

"Old Father," the man said, clutching his cap and ducking his head nervously. Like many zigane, he was reluctant to use Father Rito's name directly. It was their version of respect, Ogeli had explained, from a time when true names had power.

"Please come in out of the cold. The young lady stopped by this morning to pick up the letter and left one to send. She appears to be in good health, so I hope your worries are relieved."

The man, Barzo, stepped inside but did not sit down when invited. He seemed even more agitated. "Where did she go, old Father? I went to the great house she worked at. They said she no longer was there, and they did not know where to find her."

Father Rito stared at him, greatly worried. Trisstela had not mentioned leaving her position at Baron Heufritz's house, the position he had helped find for her. She had not asked for help finding another either. Feeling weak, he sat on the nearest wooden chair and gripped the arms.

"There … there was a young man with her when she came. Quite handsome, I would say, and well-dressed. He seemed polite."

Barzo's face darkened. "What did this *gadje* look like?"

Rito described him as best he could. "He said his name was Wolfgang Mauer. He said he was a university student." He thought for a moment. "Ah, he was wearing a cap, as many of the students do, so it seems likely."

"If she is well … I still must find her and ask." Barzo jutted his chin stubbornly. "I must go to the barge now. Before five days I return to see if you have news of her."

Rito struggled with his conscience and his worry for Trisstela's safety. "The letter … if it is for her family you surely must be permitted to read it. It might tell you more."

Barzo looked away. "I do not read, old Father." He sighed. "And our Triss, if she did not tell you, would she write it down for us? Send it quickly."

"I could add my own note … Should I mention what we know?"

"We know so little, it can only cause trouble for them. If she were hurt or afraid, that is different, no? I do not like it, but we wait for now."

Father Rito, with distress, saw his guest out then sat and worried more. He did not know what else he could do to help. Finding a particular person in a city the size of Baerlen was nearly impossible. True, he had a name—assuming it was a real one—and possible affiliation. Did he know anyone at the university?

Knowing he would need to calm his troubled mind to sleep that night, he went to the church to pray. As he entered he saw a figure in the shadows and went to greet them, wondering if Barzo had come back.

It was not Barzo but a stranger with a sunken face and clothing that hung loosely on him as if he had lost a great deal of weight due to illness. But he was not poor—the clothing was that of a professional man, such as a doctor, and he had a pearl tiepin.

"Father, please help me. I need to find the dark-haired man who called on you today." This was said almost in a single breath, without pause between the words.

"Pardon?" Rito took a small step back. The man did not seem well, in body or in mind. "Many people come to this church. I am not certain who you seek."

"I must find him. The student. He is one of them. *Please.*"

"There was a student visiting today, but I have never met him before and do not know where he lives." Father Rito felt a strange fear of speaking the name. But was it possible to find out more from this very odd person?

The thin man gave a cry of despair, no less wrenching for being so faint, and stumbled away. Father Rito, alarmed, wanted to call for someone to help him, but no one else was in the church or likely to be in hearing this late at night.

There was a lady chapel to one side, before the main door of the church. As the man passed it, his head turned sharply, staring upward at the face of the statue over the altar. Rito felt a chill pass through him. The man's legs were still shuffling unevenly in the direction of the door, but his torso remained turned to the chapel. The man fumbled at his pocket, pulling out a silver coin and stretching to place it in the small offering box on the wall. Although it was too far away, he did not step closer, instead throwing it with a gasp, a look of agonized desperation on his face.

Frozen in place, Rito watched the man leave before slowly approaching the lady chapel. He picked up the coin where it had fallen on the stone floor. It was not a Preusan coin, but what country it came from, he could not say. He placed it in the offering box, shaken by what he had seen. A soul in torment … and seeking the young man who appeared to be Trisstela's protector.

He knelt in prayer, asking for the thin man's peace and for the safety of Trisstela. He closed his eyes, remembering the terror on the man's face, and prayed again for protection against demonic influence.

CHAPTER 12

"No! Don't let him drink, we've still got a long way to go!" Jens-Peter sounded alarmed.

Triss pulled the bucket of beer out of the reach of the mule's mouth, just in time to avoid a lunging attack. "It's still half full."

"We have to make it last all the way there and back," Jens-Peter said, hunched over in the driver's seat. He was wearing his "new" clothes and a knit wool cap. As a disguise it wasn't much, but better than the almost rags he had previously. "He can't get drunk or we'll never get anywhere. Where is this junkyard, anyway? How much farther?"

Triss was too tired to answer. She was beginning to think it would have been easier to just carry the engines, heavy as they were, instead of this insanely complex process of procuring a cart.

It had taken all of them, plus two of the farrier's assistants and the first half of a bucket of cheap beer, to get the mule fitted with new shoes. Without the beer it would have been completely impossible, and the farrier's stable would be in ruins. This accomplished, they now could go to the salvage yard.

Drunkenly.

Urfus, the mule, was owned by a brewery delivery man. Urfus had spent his entire life delivering beer and had developed a fondness for it. He did not need motivation to go to the brewery or to carry full barrels. It was only when the barrels were empty or the direction away from the source of the beer that problems arose. His owner, strangely, had not discovered the cause of his mule's mental issues, but the students had, giving them a secret advantage.

Unfortunately Urfus was much more interested in the location of the bucket of beer than any directions from the reins. Triss had to walk ahead of the cart, which improved their speed, but she had to keep a sharp watch to make sure the mule hadn't gotten too close. More than once he managed to get a good grip on her coat with his teeth.

By the time they reached the salvage yard, it was fully dark and Triss was completely exhausted. She could not rest, however. They needed to scale the wall, and that meant she had to go first with the ropes.

They'd better find me a really good job. With … with two days off a month. And my own oil lamp instead of candles. And permission to go in the library through the door rather than the window. And twice the pay of the last one, with less cleaning! And no laundry work!

The wall along the street was brick, and she could climb it freehand if necessary, but it would be just as exhausting as the journey over. Fortunately, there had been another building next to the yard, now demolished, and the wall there was just wood and much easier to grip and climb. Triss wound some rope over one shoulder and stuck her fingers in the gap between a pair of warped boards, tugging to test the grip. She had changed into her performing tights earlier in anticipation, so it was just a matter of tying up her skirts to be ready to climb.

The boards creaked a little, and Triss shifted her position. Not a good idea to make any more noise than necessary. She *really* couldn't get caught now. If the troupe ever found out she was … well, stealing … she didn't want to think about what would happen then. It was only a small sop to her conscience that she was helping steal something *back*. The police would not consider it an excuse.

She pulled hard, swinging her legs up to the top of the fence. She felt the crinkle of the letter she'd tucked in her vest for safekeeping. She hadn't read it yet but she had a pretty good idea what the contents were. Which was why she was reluctant to read it.

Of course the troupe had noticed the delay since her last letter. During the winter especially they depended heavily on the outside earners. And now she had sent even less than expected, late, with only a brief mention of costs related to "breakage" to explain it. It wasn't a complete lie—the flying ship *had* broken and everything regarding her current situation was directly connected to it.

Her fingers slipped on the dusty top rail. *Focus.* No audience, no troubles, only the rig and the feat to be performed on it. Distraction caused failure.

Balanced once again, she brought her legs underneath and stood up, head tall, and walked precisely and with grace along the rail to reach the brick section of the wall. That was practically a road to Triss, broad and level. They hadn't even put broken glass on the top. A distant part of her mind heard gasps down below and a bray, quickly stifled, from the mule.

Where were the engines again? She paused to orient herself, nodding. Yes. Not far from here. Glancing over the wall into the yard, she saw the sheet metal leaning against the bricks. She waved the others over.

"Move the cart here," she said as softly as she could. "There's nothing to attach the rope to up here. I'll go down and tie it to the engine."

"You'll need help." Jens-Peter handed the reins to Dieter, who took them limply.

Triss shook her head. "You can't climb with that arm."

"I can get to the top of the wall from the back of the cart if you hold the rope, and even I can fall down. I've done it before." His grin flashed in the darkness.

"But can you fall quietly?"

The sooner they got the engines the sooner she could leave. Triss sighed and unwound the rope before dropping to the yard. She found an easy place to wrap the rope and tied a simple but strong knot, then snapped the rope a few times as a signal.

Shortly after that Jens-Peter heaved into view with a stifled groan. He draped over the wall for a moment, breathing hard, before sliding down the rope by tucking it under his arm. He crouched down to see how Triss had attached the rope, nodded, then stood up again.

"Psst! Mauer! The other rope!"

The end of another rope flew over the wall. Jens-Peter quickly wrapped it around another part of the engine and fastened it.

With four of them they managed to get the engine out, first with Dieter and Mauer pulling, then with Jens-Peter and Triss lowering once it was on the other side. While Jens-Peter attached the ropes to the second engine, Triss checked the ropes for fraying. The ropes were not in great shape to begin with and being pulled across brick edges under a heavy load wasn't helping.

With the second engine away, Triss took the two ropes and wound them together before handing them to Jens-Peter. "You go up first."

"But—"

"Go!" Triss smacked him on the back. "I see lights moving in the building."

It wasn't a lie. To her relief Jens-Peter stopped arguing and started climbing. Triss glanced back at the building. No one had come outside yet. Mauer scrambled up to help pull Jens-Peter, who was not having an easy time climbing up the full height of the wall, especially after heaving two heavy engines.

Eventually Jens-Peter sat straddling the wall. Triss gathered the ropes in her hand and started to climb. Behind her she heard a door bang open and a dog barking. She climbed faster … and the rope broke.

Her hand reaching for the top of the wall was grasped firmly, and a hard jerk launched her up in the air. Jens-Peter tugged again, lowering her down to Dieter and Mauer in the cart before half jumping, half falling in himself

85

with a crash.

Triss pulled the ropes free and stowed them in the cart as it moved forward. She didn't have to tell them to go at a regular pace. They'd already gone over that before. Besides, nothing could make Urfus go faster than a walk. She glanced back over her shoulder. The barking had stopped, and nobody was looking over the wall. The people in the yard would have to go find a ladder anyway, and by that time the cart would be out of view.

"Thanks for pulling me up," Triss muttered. Jens-Peter, surprisingly, could move fast when he wanted to. He was stronger than he looked as well.

"You're the only reason we got them out." He tried to grin but it was a tired one.

Shortly it was clear that Urfus had figured out they were not headed back to the brewery and was refusing to move. Triss had no intention of walking the rest of the night, so she rummaged in her bundle and found a sock. It had been darned so many times that the original material was sparse, so the loss was not painful. She still intended for them to pay her for it, however.

Dipping the sock in the beer, she got down from the cart and tied it just above Urfus's nose. "He mostly likes the smell," she said to Dieter. "If he stops again just soak it with beer."

The mule had worked hard, though. *Obeza* said she owed him some beer or maybe a carrot or two. Back in the cart Triss shifted her bundle and wrapped a blanket over herself before trying to fall asleep. This proved impossible. The cart was uncomfortable, and the road full of bumps and rocks. Not to mention there was little space with the two engines in the back.

She spent too much time trying to convince herself that she did not owe *obeza* to the yard owner. Even if they had knowingly taken stolen goods, it didn't change the fact that she had stolen herself. And why had she not refused to help? Just because Jens-Peter was so desperate and so happy when she agreed? *Too many strings. I should have left him in the carter's barn.*

Blearily, she watched the half-full moon move across the sky. With only occasional stops to refresh the sock with beer, it took hours to reach the secret rural location Jens-Peter was directing them to.

Feeling her feet turn into icy lumps, Triss had paid no attention to the fact that the cart had stopped yet again until she realized that nobody had come back for the bucket of beer and that Jens-Peter had gotten out and was trudging into the woods. A short while later, he came back.

"This is as close as the cart can get," he said. "We'll have to carry everything the rest of the way."

Dieter had provided a very clever short stretcher to carry the engines, one by one. He and Mauer did most of the heavy lifting, with Jens-Peter assisting up banks or awkward spots with his one good arm. He and Triss were carrying the other, smaller gear like tools and a canister of fuel. They also had other things from the lab, like blankets, more rope, and a small amount of food.

Jens-Peter led them to the base of a huge oak. "It's up there," he said proudly, patting the trunk. "The leaves help hide it."

"Why does it have leaves in the middle of winter?" Dieter said, puzzled. "Don't they usually fall off?"

"Some oaks keep them until spring." Triss had figured out previously that Dieter had spent his entire life in Baerlen and knew very little about plants of any kind. "I know you are planning on having me climb the tree but how will that help get the engines up to the ship?"

"Oh, we have winches aboard!"

From his tone that solved the entire problem. Having never seen a winch, Triss was more doubtful.

Mauer dropped a wooden box that clanked. "Right, that's everything we brought. We should be able to get Urfus back before daylight. Are you sure you don't want one of us to stay?"

"You're being watched. Dieter will be missed. And until we get it mobile again, everything has to go up and down a rope, including you. There isn't much room aboard either. We'll be fine."

"Really? I just don't like leaving a girl out here in the cold, that's all."

"I don't have anywhere else to go." That sounded a bit abrupt. Triss sighed. "It's not so bad. You forget, I am zigane. It's not the first time."

CHAPTER 13

Jens-Peter leaned against the oak trunk, blowing on his fingers to warm them. He could see the first pale bands of light on the horizon, and he glanced at the heap of blankets that contained Triss. She had refused to climb the tree in the dark, saying it was too dangerous. Even though he was impatient and worried about being discovered, he had agreed to wait. He certainly couldn't risk injuring Triss now. So he had found some branches to help conceal the gear and made plans to stay awake.

First thing was getting working engines again. Either replacing the originals and then raiding them for parts, or vice versa. Next was moving the ship, and that could only happen at night. Where should they go? The people hunting him had come here before, so leaving the forest was a priority. Then again, the fuel they'd brought would not take them far, and they still needed to be in range of Baerlen for more supplies. Where could he possibly hide a levitation ship the size of a cottage?

The bundle of blankets stirred. After a moment Triss emerged, blinking and rubbing her eyes with one hand as she sat up.

"Is there water nearby?"

Jens-Peter pointed. "I remember falling into a stream just over that ridge. It's not very deep, though."

Triss took the kettle Dieter had thoughtfully included and left, reappearing a few minutes later. They made a light breakfast of cheese and crackers. Jens-Peter sketched a quick diagram of the winch and described how to operate it manually while Triss ate.

"It's tedious cranking it by hand but there are enough gears that you should be able to lift pretty heavy loads by yourself. Even me. There's strong cable already attached, so you don't need extra rope. Make sure the ratchet is set like this, with the lever in the lowest position. Move the crank handle clockwise and the cable will come off the spool. When you want to bring it back up, flip the ratchet lever up and move the crank handle the other way."

Triss raised an eyebrow. She dusted cracker crumbs off her fingers and turned around to study the trunk of the oak tree. The trunk was immense and remarkably smooth. How she was going to climb it was not obvious. Triss picked up the kettle, poured some water into her mouth, and shifted the branches hiding the gear. She pulled out one of the longer ropes and tied a wrench to one end.

"I thought you were going to heat water," Jens-Peter said.

"I'd like to, but we'd have to hide the firepit later, and it's too much trouble."

He brightened. At last, an opportunity to give her some good news. "There's a little stove on the ship. The fuel it uses is different than the engines, so there's still some there." Triss stood a little straighter, and her face lost some of its grim weariness.

She moved away from the trunk, circling it while looking up at the branches. She appeared to find what she was looking for and swung the wrench-end of the rope in a vertical circle. When she let go, the wrench sailed up and hit a sturdy branch. She grimaced, retrieved the rope, and tried again.

This time the wrench sailed up and over the branch. Tugging on both ends, Triss looked over at him. "Come hold this steady."

She took off her coat, removed her shoes, and tied a knot in her skirts until they nearly reached her knees. Triss crouched a few times before jumping and grabbing hold of both ropes, wrapping her legs and feet around them.

It looked like crawling, if you could crawl on a rope. She would bring her feet up while hanging by her arms, clamp the rope between them again, then reach up one hand at a time to get a new grip. Triss clearly had done this many times before, and he found himself wondering what her life had been like in the troupe.

Jens-Peter clutched the rope in his good hand, watching her speedy progress until it occurred to him that perhaps he should *not* watch her from underneath, even if he was concerned about her safety. She was wearing some sort of long, thick stockings so her legs were properly covered, but she would definitely be angry if she caught him gawking.

The rope stopped moving, and despite his good intentions Jens-Peter looked up to see if Triss needed help. She was standing on the branch and looking about, confidently.

"I should be able to make the rest of the way up just by climbing," she said, bending down to grab the rope, "but I'll take this with me just in case."

It really was a long way up. Jens-Peter felt his stomach twist. "Be careful.

I didn't see any horse liniment in the supplies."

Triss gave a quick, flashing smile. It was the first time he could recall her smiling at anything, and it was because of his very small joke.

She started climbing and soon disappeared from view, blocked by the dry brown leaves. Unable to see how close she was to the ship, Jens-Peter paced under the branches and worried. She would be fine—better than he would be in the circumstances. She liked to climb around on icy rooftops, for heaven's sake. What was a tree to her?

But what if she got stuck somehow? Or the ship came free? He had tied it securely before leaving, but what if it had come loose in the wind as the tree shifted?

He imagined any number of disastrous scenarios, and he got more and more frantic until he saw a drift of leaves falling down. And then another, and another. He stared at it, puzzled. Her climbing shouldn't have disturbed them. Sticking to the interior branches, there were no leaves to knock free.

Then he sighed and rested his back against the oak, shaky with relief. Triss was on the ship. And what was the first thing she would do when she got aboard? Sweep all the fallen leaves from the deck. He could almost picture it.

Then he heard the clacking noise of the winch. She had found a rope net and attached it to the end of the cable. Inside the net was a wooden box, which confused him until he realized it was probably to prevent the cable from getting caught on branches because it had no weight on the end.

He gathered up her shoes, coat, and the blankets and added them to the net as the first test load, shaking the cable to let her know. After a pause, the net rose up again.

It took them until noon to move all the gear they had brought, even the two engines. After one near-disaster Jens-Peter attached a light rope to help guide the net and contents past potential snags from below. For the last load, Jens-Peter carefully checked to make sure there was no sign of their presence remaining under the tree and cautiously stood in the net.

"Pull me up!" he shouted.

It was very slow and terrifying, and the net bag twisted making him dizzy, so he closed his eyes. If he fell the most he could do is to grab a branch on the way down, but there weren't many in reach. Triss was also clearly becoming tired, even with the winch gears helping her.

"You can get out now," Triss panted. "I don't think I can pull you out."

Her voice was very close. Jens-Peter opened his eyes. Sure enough, the cable had reached the edge of the winch. Very carefully not looking down, he swung the net bag until he could grab the side of the ship. With more awkward struggle, partly fueled by terror, he eventually managed to fall over the sides and into the ship itself.

He spent a glorious moment just looking up at the blue sky and breathing, letting his heartbeat slow. Then he scrambled to his feet. He wanted to get at least one engine working while there was still daylight so they could leave if they had to. He was feeling better now that he knew the ship wasn't visible at ground level, but he still didn't want to be caught out here.

First he unbolted the burned engine from its stanchion and with a pulley moved it as far away as he could on the deck.

"Here. Take this apart as much as you can. Don't worry, it's broken past saving so you can't do any more damage." Jens-Peter found an extra set of tools for her.

"If it can't be fixed why take it apart?" Triss gave him a skeptical look.

"The engine is broken, but the parts inside may still be useful to fix the others. This design was always odd." He demonstrated how to use the tools to loosen bolts and screws. Triss frowned, staring in focused concentration, then got to work.

Jens-Peter immersed himself in repairs. The remaining original engine, the one that had not caught fire, was quickly opened up. As he had feared, a component had broken and in doing so had fouled the combustion chamber. The good news was with the component replaced and the chamber cleaned, the engine should be good as new. The bad news was that the component was not a good design and broke frequently, so the burned engine might not have a replacement either.

He turned to look where Triss was sitting, cross-legged, sooty engine parts surrounding her. She had most of the engine disassembled already.

"Perfect! Let's see if this will pay off." He went over with the damaged component in his hand. Triss glanced at him, then at the component … and reached out to her pile of parts.

The piece she handed him was the exact match.

"How did you know?" That particular component was part of a sub-assembly in the engine, and not obvious to casual inspection. Why had she taken it apart, and correctly?

"Isn't that the right one? It looks the same." She tilted her head. "It was in the diagram too."

Right. She remembered how things looked, and didn't forget. Jens-Peter held it up to inspect. It certainly *looked* intact. "No, you have the right part. I'll clean it and make sure there aren't any hairline cracks."

If there were, he couldn't see them. Sighing, he started putting the engine back together again. The true test was firing the engine up. If it broke, he still had another salvaged engine for parts.

"I've finished." Triss came over, frowning at her grimy hands. "What else can I do?"

"In the cubby on the left side, near the front." Jens-Peter grunted, using all his strength to tighten a bolt. "There should be some field glasses. Take a look outside and see if anybody is out there. When I start up the engine it might make some noise."

There followed shortly a period of clatter and banging, then Triss gave a victorious "Ha!"

"Found it?"

"Yes." Silence for a few minutes. "How does it work? I can't see anything."

He glanced up. She was attempting to look through the larger end of the optics. "Other way." He gestured.

"Oh."

Jens-Peter finished cleaning and reassembling the engine. He found the canister with the precious fuel and started to pour it in the reservoir, then stopped. Before he filled it, he should make sure it wouldn't catch fire first. He didn't have any fuel to spare on accidents.

"See anyone out there?"

"No." Triss walked to the other side of the ship and observed for a while. "I checked all around, even the road."

He took a deep breath. It wasn't going to get any better. He closed the switch and yanked hard on the starter lever.

A loud bang was followed by a choking cloud of thick black smoke, and Jens-Peter staggered back, coughing. At least it wasn't on fire. "I think I know what the problem is," he wheezed. Triss gave him a skeptical look and went back to searching the countryside with the field glasses.

After tinkering, remembering that new parts needed an oil coating, and restarting twice, he got the engine started and kept it running. It was even quieter than before. After a few minutes Jens-Peter shut it down again and started working on the second engine.

"Why didn't you wait for night to test the engines, when nobody is able to see?"

He grunted with effort, getting the engine cover off. "For one thing, if it is on fire, everyone can see it. For another, we can move with one engine if we have to, so getting one working is the most important. I don't want to be trapped here if those Kriegsa people with guns come back."

The second engine, he suspected, would be easier to fix. It would just take longer. Firstly multiple parts were needed, so he started assembling them.

"Where do you plan to go?" Triss crouched down to get out of the wind.

Jens-Peter cursed under his breath. "Someplace nearby, with people I can trust with something as secret as this, that can completely hide the entire ship. I don't suppose you know of any large abandoned barns in the area?" He was being sarcastic, but then he remembered that she had displayed amazing competence in finding a barn to sleep in previously.

Maybe she would know.

"I've been in Baerlen a little over a year," Triss said, wrinkling her forehead. "And I didn't get out much. That time I passed the message to get the books back was the most I've ever … oh!" She stopped and turned her head to look at him. "That person … What a pity, I didn't get his name. The *bruje*. I mean, magician."

"You mean the time Mauer sent you to tell the Dragonhunters about me?" Triss was looking completely confused now. Jens-Peter put down the wrench and wiped his forehead with his sleeve. "Was there a tall man with bronze skin and black hair at that place? White streak in his hair?"

"Yes! I thought he was zigane at first."

"Why do you bring him up?"

"The place I went was a large building, three stories tall. And it had a large courtyard that can't be seen from outside. I don't know if he counts as someone you can trust with the secret of the flying ship, though."

Jens-Peter started to chuckle, then laughed outright. "He knows all about it." He still remembered vividly rescuing the badly wounded Asgaya and the others in the mountains of Bhuta. With this very ship. "This courtyard … is it big enough?"

Triss looked at the levitation ship, from bow to stern, and nodded slowly. "It will be a tight fit, but it should work. The building is in the manufacturing district, south of the river. On Gastimerstrasse."

It was perfect. Jens-Peter didn't even bother asking Triss if she knew how to find it again. With her memory, even locating it from the air would be possible.

"You should get some sleep then. We're going to be very busy tonight."

CHAPTER 14

"I don't like it. We should be arresting every single one we find and lifting that cursed magic. All we need is one survivor to find him." Heinrich von Kitren scowled with narrowed eyes, the clenching of his jaw making the scattered scars more prominent.

Markus sighed. While he was increasingly coming to value his prospective brother-in-law, Heinrich greatly preferred leaping into action given the slightest opportunity. When he was still in the military, it was of no consequence, but now that his injuries and his new job restricted action of any type, the tendency was increasingly pronounced. And annoying.

"We would have to wait for a Mage Guardian to be available to remove the *geas*, remember? We still don't have one of our own, the Bretagne Guardian is, ah, *unavailable* and a source of contention, and the Guardian of the Low Countries is still learning his role. I don't know if he even can do it yet." Removing—and creating—*geasi* was highly restricted magic, and for good reason. "From what I recall, we'd have to capture over twenty to get one that might be sane." He frowned. "Possibly more. Korda is placing a second compulsion spell over the first, and I'm not sure what the effects are. At any rate, we need to capture this fake mage *and* the source of his power. He's paranoid and well-hidden, and the only means we have to find him is tracing his servants. This is too important to make mistakes over, and we may only have one chance."

Von Kitren sat back in the wooden chair, still visibly unhappy. They were in the official Dragonhunter offices in the palace grounds, trying to make progress. They had just returned from a late-night meeting with the King, who was becoming impatient, and they had suffered many barbed comments from von Koller, the head of the Kriegsa. If they didn't have something to show soon, there would be trouble.

"We know he's looking for something, something he considers

94

important. And—"

A knock sounded on the office door, followed by one of the Dragonhunters holding a slip of paper. He had a very confused expression on his face.

"Message from the warehouse, sirs." He handed it to Markus.

SEND HELP IMMEDIATELY STOP GIANT MELON IN COURTYARD STOP PLEASE ADVISE

Von Kitren was shamelessly reading over his shoulder. Markus rubbed his forehead, trying to make sense of the garbled message. Had they decoded it correctly? How could there be a melon in the middle of winter? Was it some kind of magical attack? Illusion?

"Who is on duty there? Is he drunk?"

"Willem. And even if he was drunk, he wouldn't have this much imagination." Or be this frantic. Well. The message said nothing about being on fire or under attack, but Willem was quite upset about something. Enough to use the secure telegraph line. "I suppose I will have to go and take a look." In the spare time he didn't have.

It was late at night and the warehouse district streets were empty. Asgaya had the carriage stop nearby, not wanting to bring any attention to the hideout. The area appeared the same as before, grimy and worn, with no sign of unusual, ambush-like activity.

Using stealth magic he did a quick, low-level scrying of the building. There was *something* magical there, but it seemed diffuse. He knocked on the side door. The shutter was immediately slid open, followed by Willem saying "Thank God you are here, sir! One of them says they know you, and the other is insisting on cleaning up."

No, definitely not drunk. Markus looked about the courtyard, wondering why it was so dark when the moon was out. As his eyes adjusted, he realized a certain familiar boat-shaped structure was taking up most of the available space, and a bulbous floating canopy was barely clearing the walls on either side.

A matter-of-fact young woman with blonde hair was sweeping up scattered broken tiles and shards of glass. She looked familiar, but before he could recall, a cheerful, boisterous voice greeted him.

"Oy! Asgaya! What a relief to see you." Jens-Peter Oberacker jumped out of the ship. "Can I keep this here for a few days? It's still not completely fixed, and people keep shooting at me for some reason."

Willem was making incoherent noises while waving at the levitation ship. "But ... the carriages, we can't ... nothing can get *out!*"

This was true. They might be able to open the large gates but none of the vehicles they had would be able to reach them. Still, it was a tremendous relief to have recovered the missing levitation ship.

"I'm delighted to see you are still alive and the ship intact. But why bring

95

it *here?* The Kriegsa is the proper authority to handle this."

Willem had given up on anything making sense tonight and had lit one of the lamps ringing the courtyard. In its light Markus could see the manic grin on Oberacker's exhausted face stiffen and fade.

"It was people in Kriegsa uniforms who shot me." He gestured to his arm. "I don't know if they really are Kriegsa people, but I overheard them talking about killing me when they found the ship. After that I didn't dare contact them."

Willem gaped. "The Kriegsa ... *shot* you? Why? I thought they were working with us!"

Markus was aware of a gradually increasing, throbbing pain at his temples. He'd suspected something was off before. Now they had proof. If the Kriegsa was compromised, his job was going to become nearly impossible. He also needed to throw von Koller off the scent or, better yet, provide him a distraction, and that had to be done immediately.

"All right, I understand. There's not much I can do now since the hour is late and I still have work tonight. Do you need any medical attention?"

Oberacker shook his head. "The horse liniment is working. We haven't gotten much sleep, though. Or food."

Horse liniment? Markus glanced at Willem.

"There's a cot in the back room," Willem said slowly. "And bread and butter."

"Excellent!" Oberacker turned to the girl. "Did you hear that, Triss? A sort-of-real bed and food! They've probably got something better than the tiny stove for heating water too."

She nodded and put the broom back in the corner. Triss looked extremely tired, too, and her clothes had streaks of dirt. How many days since she had brought that message, and how had she been surviving since then? How had she met up with Oberacker again? It would have to wait until morning, but he was looking forward to getting the full story.

"Then you should rest. I'll be back later." He turned to Willem. "Before I go I'll cast aspersion over the top of the courtyard to help with concealment, but be especially careful even with that protection. There are dangerous people looking for this ship." He really wished he knew who they were.

Triss woke and stared at the ceiling in confusion. Where had a ceiling come from? It didn't have any holes or water stains—although she did notice a spiderweb in a corner. In addition, she wasn't cold.

She sat up. She was on a cot and covered by a rough but warm wool blanket that smelled faintly of pipe tobacco. Now she remembered. They had taken the flying ship into Baerlen, flying so high that both she and Jens-

Peter had to wrap every blanket they had around them to keep warm. Only when she pinpointed the location did Jens-Peter lower the ship, almost straight down, to avoid being seen. Even when it was dark, the streetlights gave off enough light to reflect off the body of the ship.

It had been a little more difficult to land the ship with precision in the courtyard due to wind and only two working engines. Triss had to hang over the edge of the deck, hanging on to a convenient rope, to guide Jens-Peter down the last few crucial feet. In addition, she had not known the balloon took up more space when descending, so her estimate was off. They hadn't broken *that* much of the building, and it was in sad shape to begin with, so Triss hoped it would not get them in trouble.

The room she was in was not a proper bedroom. It was just a small room with a window, now covered by dusty blinds, the cot she was lying on, a worn upholstered armchair, and an oil lamp on a stand next to it. Pale light seeped past the edges of the blinds, so it must be morning.

Triss got up. She had only taken off her shoes to sleep, so she didn't have to get dressed. Seeing her bundle on the armchair she thought briefly about changing but decided against it. Until she knew what would happen today there was no point.

The room was at the end of a long hallway. Across the hall was a washroom and midway the stairs they had taken from the courtyard level. There was one level above this, but the stairs didn't go that far. Once she reached the stairs, she heard the faint sound of snoring. Following the sound to the other end of the hall, she found one door ajar and inside a collection of wooden desks and glass-front bookcases.

Jens-Peter was sprawled on top of one of the desks, cocooned in a blanket. On another desk was a folded-over blue-check napkin covering a half loaf of bread. Next to it was a crock of butter. Triss helped herself to bread and butter and then sat on the edge of the desk and thoughtfully poked Jens-Peter.

"Nooooo," he moaned faintly. "Go away …"

Triss poked him again. "I *want* to go away. You promised to find me a job if I helped you, and I did."

"What can I do? Until we uncover whoever wants me dead, I can't even go outside!" Jens-Peter got up and scrubbed his head, blinking sleepily. "I haven't forgotten. Don't be in such a hurry. If I had any money, I'd hire you myself. You were really clever taking apart that engine." He grinned.

While it had been interesting, engines were much too oily and dirty for Triss to find enjoyment contemplating working with them on a daily basis. She sighed. "I suppose we wait until someone comes. That *bruje* gentleman said he would come back, right?"

"His name is Markus Asgaya, and he's, well, kind of the boss of this department. Don't let his foppish mannerisms fool you. He's very capable."

Jens-Peter looked like he was going to say more, then firmly shut his mouth.

There was nothing for her to do, and there was no telling when this Asgaya would show up. "I don't suppose there are any books here?"

Jens-Peter yawned. "You and your books." He looked around. "You'd think with all these bookcases, but no, they are full of papers. Well, if you don't mind a dry topic my engineering books should still be somewhere on the ship. I think. I don't remember them falling out anyway."

Even if the books weren't there, she *could* tidy up the ship. Triss went down the stairs. To her surprise there were now two men clearly guarding the two large inside gates. They said nothing as she approached the ship, so presumably they had already been told about her. She didn't see Willem. Hopefully he was sleeping somewhere, and calmer.

In the daylight the utter mess of the ship deck was glaringly apparent. Triss gathered all the loose engine repair parts in a wood box, coiled up rope, and generally imposed order until she found one of the books Jens-Peter had mentioned. As she was flipping through it Jens-Peter came out and joined her.

"I probably should be reading too," he said, not meeting her eyes. "I was writing a paper when this whole mess started."

"Students write papers?" Triss was mildly interested. Anything to do with the university with the colossal library was interesting.

Jens-Peter sighed, rolling his eyes. "This student does, unfortunately. I, ah, may have missed some classes. And some exams. But I had a really good excuse! So my professor made me write this paper to make up for the exams or he'll have me expelled. I don't care that much but my father would get angry and cut off my allowance. Evil Schenk!" He stiffened, eyes wide in fright. "And classes started again already, and I've missed them! He's going to *murder* me!"

"Who?" Triss assumed this was a different person than the one shooting at Jens-Peter previously, but she could never tell for sure.

"My professor, who loathes the sight of me, and—"

The smaller door near the gate creaked and opened. Two people entered—the *bruje* Asgaya, and an elegant and beautiful woman with honey-gold hair, who was leaning heavily on Asgaya's arm. Triss knew at a glance the woman was of the upper class, if not nobility, simply by the way she carried herself. Up until now, dealing only with men, Triss had taken in stride her grimy clothing but now she felt very awkward.

They were followed by two men, one carrying a trunk and another a large covered wicker basket.

"My apologies for the delay," said Asgaya, "but I thought it best to bring an important associate. I believe Mr. Oberacker is already known to you, Fräulein von Kitren. This is Miss Trisstela."

Triss covered up her shock by immediately executing a curtsy. How had this person learned her full first name? Was this something a *bruje* could do?

Fräulein von Kitren inclined her head. "Shall we go inside? There is much to discuss."

Following them inside, Triss was surprised to see them pass the stairs and instead go to a metal structure much like a very small greenhouse.

"Have you never seen an elevator before?" Seeing her hesitation, Jens-Peter waved her in. "It's basically just like the winch on the ship, except there's this instead of the net bag." He thumped the metal frame of the structure.

Asgaya pulled a small lever on the side, and the inner cage began to rise. Triss noticed several things about the so-called elevator. It was clearly new, unlike the building. The square area on the side of the cage had several of the small levers with a small ceramic disk in the center of the lever post. The disks had numbers, from one to three, with the topmost one blank.

The cage stopped moving and the accordion-fold doors opened to the second floor Triss was familiar with. Asgaya walked down the hall to one of the closed doors and went in with Fräulein von Kitren.

At first Triss thought it was a dining room. There was a large rectangular wooden table and several chairs pulled up to it. The walls behind the chair were covered with maps of Baerlen and the various Aeropan countries, and at the far wall something she'd seen at Father Rito's school rooms: a chalkboard.

Fräulein von Kitren sank into a chair, briefly closing her eyes. Asgaya said something in a soft voice, watching her face with concern. She shook her head very slightly.

"Please be seated. I understand you have been caught up in these matters through no fault of your own. You worked as a maid in the Heufritz house, correct?"

Triss nodded, sitting ramrod straight in her chair. This was the kind of lady maids feared and respected, the kind who noticed everything and did not tolerate laziness or sloppy work. Allowing Triss to sit in her presence was quite unexpected.

"Oberacker explained that the levitation ship is a secret. A state secret. Fräulein von Kitren and I are members of an organization that, shall we say, protects this and other, similar secrets under the direct command of the King."

Jens-Peter nudged Triss. "It's true! And we've even gone outside of Preusa to do it. I went to Bhuta in that very ship!"

Fräulein von Kitren gave Jens-Peter a level, intense look and he froze, suddenly silent. Triss was very impressed. Getting Jens-Peter to stop talking when he was excited was nearly impossible. She wondered where Bhuta was—somewhere in the south? While she liked to read, her formal schooling was not extensive and her knowledge had significant gaps.

"Yes, Herr Oberacker has been assisting us for some time now with the levitation ships. This building is one of our bases. Unfortunately, while the ship is hidden here it can't remain for very long. For one thing, the enemy behind the research facility attack is still looking for that ship. For another, we believe that enemy has infiltrated the Kriegsa and that the Kriegsa knows about this location and has been watching us. All of which means while we will help you, we still need to think of another place to hide the ship." Asgaya sighed. "Also, this is not the only problem we are facing at the moment. Unfortunately, Fräulein von Kitren and I must focus on a much more dangerous situation, and that means we must ask for your help meanwhile."

Triss kept her face blank. She had noticed that no details of this other danger were being provided, which was suspicious. She had also noticed that Fräulein von Kitren was not well, yet she had come here despite the pain. There probably was something important, something so secret an outsider like her could not know. But they let her know about the flying … levitation ships, which were *also* a big and important secret that someone was willing to kill for. So this other thing was probably even more dangerous.

Too dangerous for her. All of it.

"Begging your pardon, ma'am. I'm just a housemaid. How can I possibly be of assistance? I must look for work to support my family, and the need is urgent." She stood and curtsied again.

"Because of me she lost her position at Baron Heufritz's house, and I promised to help her find another one," Jens-Peter said. "But I can't really do it now, can I?"

"The situation is a temporary one." Fräulein von Kitren rested her elbows on the table and supported her chin in her hands. Her pale face remained calm and remote. "Until it is resolved it is best for you to stay under our protection. This is not only for your safety"—she stopped Triss's objection with a raised finger— "but also ours. You know a great deal the enemy would like to learn, and they are completely unscrupulous in their methods. Even using magic to compel obedience."

Triss felt a chill run down her back. Magic? "I could go far away from Baerlen …" But that would take money, money she didn't have. And she still would need to find a job.

Asgaya shook his head. "They could follow you anywhere."

"May I ask how much money you were sending to your family?"

Triss looked at Fräulein von Kitren, unsure. "Usually three talers a month. Only last month I couldn't even send that."

"Then let me propose this solution. We will provide you with room and board until it is safe for you to go about on your own, and also an equivalent sum to three months of your prior wages. If necessary, further funds will be provided."

"What work will I be doing?" Triss tried to keep her voice calm. Working was acceptable. Exchanging favors, like she had done with Jens-Peter, was also acceptable. Accepting charity was not.

"Any cleaning you are able to accomplish here would be an improvement." The tone in Fräulein von Kitren's voice was rather chilly, but to her relief Triss saw that it was not directed at her.

Asgaya looked up at the ceiling, the corners of his mouth twitching. "As we discussed before, cleaning is very low on the list of Dragonhunter priorities."

"Well, now it is not. I expect to be able to determine the color of the floor in the future." She looked at Triss. "You mentioned that your need to send money is urgent. How have you done this in the past? Do you request a bank draft?"

Triss stared at her, puzzled. She didn't understand the words. "We … banks don't like zigane. I take it to Father Rito at St. Erita's church, and he sends it on. The troupe trusts him …" She wondered if they would understand. Would they let her go to the church to send the money? If strangers appeared, claiming to speak for her, Father Rito would definitely tell the troupe, and Triss would be in deep trouble. "I should … I need to tell him where to send it. The troupe moves a lot." This was not exactly a lie. The troupe *did* move a lot, but not in the winter. And Father Rito often knew sooner than Triss did where they traveled to.

"That should not present a difficulty." Fräulein von Kitren nodded. "We can arrange for a suitable escort with the full sum. Not you, Herr Oberacker. You must remain out of sight."

Jens-Peter sighed. "Oh, very well. If I can get my hands on more parts, I can work on the other engines. And I'll need more fuel in order to leave."

"Inform Willem if there is anything else you need. You as well." Fräulein von Kitren nodded at Triss while drawing on her gloves. "It is unlikely you will find much in the way of cleaning equipment here."

"Yes ma'am." Triss bobbed another curtsy.

Asgaya once again let Fräulein von Kitren lean on his arm as they left the room, but she turned her head before going through the doorway. "Oh, one minor detail. Do not clean anything visible from the street. The dusty and abandoned exterior is part of the disguise." With a faint smile on her face, Fräulein von Kitren departed.

CHAPTER 15

The wind off the river was bitterly cold, and Barzo was working fast to finish so the barge workers could return to the warehouse—which was not warm but at least out of the wind. It was an easy load this time. New barrels for beer, empty and light. The rough wood was still fragrant and made him suddenly recall the sawdust used to cushion the ground when he practiced rope-walking as a child.

Now all his skills were used to balance on the shifting barge and the flexing gangplank up to the brewery dock, carrying barrels on his shoulders. It was not bad work, but it was lonely away from the family, surrounded by *gadje*. The hours were long. Even without daylight they would still work. They had loaded the barrels in the early morning, and the sun was only now beginning to rise.

"Oi, you there. Take the last barrels all the way inside." The brewery man, a stocky individual with a thick walrus mustache, pointed with the stem of his pipe to the large building up a slope from the dock. Barzo glanced at the barge master, who jerked his chin indicating he should go. It wasn't something the bargemen were supposed to do, but often it was a favor done to earn more work or keep what they had.

Barzo walked as fast as he safely could. There were puddles of ice in the mud and uneven, frozen ruts in the ground from carts. There was a cart coming in just as he went inside the large, barnlike main doors of the brewery. He put down the barrel, was told to move it further, picked it up again, and finally put it in the right place.

The cart was stopped in front as Barzo went out. The driver was being harangued by a wiry, thin old man who was not happy about something. Barzo didn't care; he had more barrels to move.

"—use it for a few hours, not all night! And look at Urfus—he's so tired he can barely stand up!"

"He's tired from fighting all of us for more than an hour during the shoeing."A second man jumped down from the cart. "You didn't say anything about how long, just that it needed to be back before morning. We got him shod and fed and everything, just like we promised. Not our fault we got lost."

By the time Barzo came back with two smaller barrels, one on each shoulder, the argument was still going on.

"And what's this over his nose?"

"A … scarf? To keep it warm in the cold night air. Come on, Mauer, we'd better get back if you're going to get to class on time." The pale-haired man slapped the dark-haired driver on the back while snatching a long, narrow cloth from the mule's head. The old man grumbled but led the cart away. As Barzo passed the two men from the cart, he overheard one say in a quiet voice, "That's a girl's stocking, you dunderhead! If *alte* Ziegnitz thought we were out carousing in his cart, we'd never be able to borrow it again!"

"Who would be carousing in this weather?" the dark-haired one grumbled. "Do you think Triss wants it back?"

Barzo slipped on a patch of ice so badly that his usual balance was barely enough to keep him from falling. He ran back to the barge, grabbed the last barrel, and called to the bargemaster.

"Meet you at warehouse! Too damn cold on water!"

The man sighed and waved permission, reluctantly. Barzo knew it was in recognition of doing the extra work. He clenched his jaw. He wasn't cold any more—fury burned through his veins. This must be the one that the priest had mentioned, the man that had been with Trisstela. Both of the men in the cart had round caps, too, and he remembered hearing that they were something students wore. And for them to have her stocking … this was bad. Was she safe?

He didn't have much time. It was faster to go by land to the warehouse, so he could still follow and get back without being late. Still, he had to do *something* to help Trisstela.

The two men walked at a good pace but Barzo was able to follow without much difficulty. He wished he could get close enough to hear more of their conversation, but even when the wind brought it to his ear, he couldn't understand every word. Barzo had learned Preusan from the barge men, and their dialect was rougher and had a heavier accent than the one these two used.

He peered around a corner. They had stopped, and the dark-haired one called Mauer waved and took a different street while the other continued ahead. Barzo thought for a moment and decided to follow Mauer. Both students seemed to have met Trisstela but Mauer was the one the priest had seen with her. He could find out more from him.

Eventually he found himself in an area with shabby but decent houses consisting of several stories. Mauer opened the door to one of them and went inside. There was writing on a board on the wall of the house, but since Barzo couldn't read, it was useless to him. He was wary of speaking to the people on the street to ask since many here did not welcome zigane. But then he saw an errand boy with a basket, and kissing the wind for luck, waved to him.

"You know what this place is?"

The boy gave him a doubtful look but answered. "Says 'Frau Schimmerle, rooms for rent', so a boarding house, I guess?" He shrugged.

"My thanks, and fortune to you." Barzo didn't have much, but the boy had helped him, so wishing luck for him was only right. The boy shrugged again and ran off.

So, a place to stay. It must be where this Mauer lived. But would Trisstela be there too? It was unlikely she could be hidden if there were other boarders, and Mauer did not look wealthy enough to provide a room for her if he was so poor that he was staying here. But perhaps he was only visiting someone?

Barzo worried and looked at the pale winter sun. He would have to leave soon to reach the warehouse in time for the next load, and he still had not learned where Trisstela was.

Then the door opened again, and Mauer came out. He had changed his clothes and now carried several books by the leather strap that bound them together. He was looking at a pocket watch, and grimacing.

He had to risk it. Barzo followed Mauer again, waiting until he turned down a narrow alley that seemed deserted.

"Hey, you *gadje*! You tell, where my cousin now? What you do to her?" In his anger and fear, his zigane accent was strong.

Mauer spun around and stared at him. "What? Who are you, and who is—"

A flash of barely visible light flared in the alley, and a thousand tiny needles stabbed into his body. Barzo tried to scream, but he couldn't move no matter how hard he struggled. And in front of him, Mauer was also frozen in place, eyes wide and mouth about to speak.

Something was moving behind him. He heard footsteps and muffled voices, but he could not shift his gaze to see more. Then dark cloth covered him and he could vaguely sense that he was being lifted and moved.

Bruje. It had to be magic, or how else was he frozen in place? Had Mauer done this? Barzo wanted to think so, but if so why freeze himself too?

He saw nothing, felt nothing. For what felt like hours in the dark, he could only curse fate. Failed Trisstela, failed his family. And the bargemaster. He had kept none of his promises.

When he could finally move again, the first thing Mauer did was rip off the cloth hood over his head. Initially the darkness didn't change, but as his eyes adapted, he saw a patch of pale light, high above his head, that seemed to be a window. He hadn't been tied up, but as he explored the room he was in, he realized why. The walls were thick stone and only interrupted by one very sturdy wood door with iron reinforcements. A lot more iron than seemed strictly necessary for strength, actually.

"Hey. *Gadje.*"

Mauer spun around, stumbling. Whatever had frozen him had worn off, but not completely. In addition the stone room was rather cold, and he was stiff all over. "Who's there?"

One of the deeper shadows shifted, and in the pale light he saw vaguely familiar features. Ragged dark hair, a knit cap, an oversized sweater and a leather vest. The *zigane* man from the alley who had accused him of something involving a cousin? The man's face looked haggard and sad.

"All I wanna know, my cousin safe?"

"Who *is* your cousin?" Mauer snapped. "You keep nattering on about a cousin, but you don't say their name! As if I'm in the habit of kidnapping people for fun!" His irritation faded. "Unlike the people who took us. I'm guessing it's the people who have been following me the last few days, but what did they want with you?"

The grief in the man's eyes changed to confusion. "You said her name. Before, at the brewery. Triss."

Mauer blinked. "Triss? She's your cousin? But … er, you don't look much alike. No offense." Not only was Triss a good deal paler, she had a head of gold hair never seen on a zigane.

"You think that makes for nothing? Trisstela still family! No matter what she look like!" The man snarled fiercely. "Anybody hurt her, I hurt them worse!"

Hearing sounds like determined if clumsy movement his direction, Mauer held up his hands in defense. "Look, the last time I saw her, she was in perfect health and about to climb a large tree to help a friend of mine retrieve some, ah, lost property. I have no idea what you are thinking, but it doesn't reflect very well on your cousin. I've never lifted a finger to her, even after she dumped a pitcher of rather cold water over my head."

"Why she do that?"

"I was asleep." Mauer suddenly realized this topic of conversation was heading in a dangerous direction, considering he was talking to someone who appeared to be a *highly* protective and suspicious male relative. Who would have a very dim view of "she climbed in my bedroom window late at night to wake me up" as an explanation, even if that was exactly what had happened and nothing more. "Look, we need to get out of here. These people don't mean well. Even if you just got caught up with me by mistake, I doubt they'll let you go just for asking. Let's find a way to escape."

"Why I help you? I still not understand, why Trisstela have anything to do with you. Or why you have her stocking." The last few words were growled. "I went to place she worked, they say she no longer working there. Tell me, *gadje,* what you do with her?"

Mauer was in the process of searching the room they were locked in, mostly by feel, but he froze at the mention of the stocking. So he'd heard that conversation at the brewery? Mauer racked his memory for the exact words he'd used. And what had the stocking been used for, and how had it gotten there? More importantly, what was the least inflammatory story he could concoct that would cover all the known facts and still keep the important things, such as the levitation ship, secret?

He tripped over something that slid over the rough stone floor. When he reached out, searching, with his fingers he found that it was the books he had brought, still tied by their leather strap. Mauer sighed. Suddenly being late for class seemed a very minor problem. He picked up the books and walked over to the high wall with the window and sat down. If he put the books here he wouldn't lose them in the darkness again.

"Triss has been helping a friend of mine. This friend had something very valuable nearly stolen from him, and Triss helped him keep it safe." So far so good. All truthful, and no important secrets disclosed. "He encountered Triss at that house she worked at while protecting the valuable thing. But because this happened at night and my friend was not supposed to be there, Triss got in trouble and was sent away." A highly condensed summary, completely ignoring the fact that all of this took place on the *roof* of the building, but still mostly truthful. "What could we do? My friend and I are university students and not well-off. He felt responsible for her loss and wanted to help her. We've been doing everything we can to keep her safe and to find her new work."

Silence fell. Mauer knew saying too much was as dangerous as not saying enough, so he waited until Triss's kinsman spoke.

"The priest said you were with her when she came."

He hadn't expected that response, and it took a moment for Mauer to understand what he was referring to.

"Oh, you mean Father Rito? If you've spoken to him, you already know Triss is fine then. She even sent a letter with money to her family."

"Then why were you there?"

Mauer sighed. "As I said, I am helping my friend help Triss. What, should I have allowed her to go there alone?" He assumed an air of wounded innocence and hoped there was enough light to make it visible.

"You do not say the name of this friend." It might have been his imagination, but the zigane didn't sound as hostile as before. Just wary.

"You haven't mentioned yours either. Not that I blame you; just because we've been kidnapped together doesn't make us acquaintances."

A pause, then "I am called Barzo."

"A pity we met under such circumstances, but I'm glad to have your company. I'm Wolfgang Mauer." He hesitated, then decided to be a little more forthcoming. "I won't mention my friend's name because if our kidnapper is listening it might endanger Triss."

"*Zumala,* no, that not good." Barzo shuffled cautiously to the wall, and Mauer could hear him sit nearby. "We talk quiet, yes? So they not hear."

Mauer sighed, feeling completely exhausted. He hadn't slept for over a day, not counting a few hours napping on the way back in the cart. He definitely hadn't eaten in far too long, and there were no signs that their captors had any intention of feeding them. Plus it was cold and the air musty.

"Did you notice anything coming in? Do you know where we are now?"

"They put bag on head same for me. But, it only been few hours. Pretty sure not far from Baerlen." Some rustling noises and a muttered phrase Mauer didn't understand but sounded like a curse. "*Chor* take my knife. And my pipe bag."

"Nothing to help you escape. You usually carry a knife? I remember Triss does too. Is that a … er, zigane custom?"

Barzo gave a soft laugh. "Trisstela is a girl by herself. Toa worries, he gives her this that can be hidden well. If she show you, she trust you. Me, I work on river. Barges. Big rats sometimes, and sometimes men like rats too. Have a knife no one sees, you live longer, heh?"

Now Mauer remembered. There had been a barge at the dock at the brewery, and people carrying new barrels and a pile of new barrels outside. Barzo had been part of that.

Barzo cursed again, and a meaty sound like a fist hitting stone came. "Thousand curses, me the unworthy! I should be lucky to find work on river again. I was to return to warehouse. They not wait for me. Now family in hard times during cold months, with Trisstela and I not sending money back. Hard to find work in winter." His voice sounded bleak.

"Well we're already finding Triss a job, so helping you won't be that much more effort," Mauer said, trying to cheer him up. "But first, we need to get out of here. Maybe we can overpower them when they come in."

"I fight," agreed Barzo. "But when they come? We here a long time, hear nothing."

It was a fair point. Mauer couldn't tell where the sun was from the one window, but it was still daylight. The fact that nobody had come for them, when they had made the effort to kidnap them, could mean that whoever ordered the kidnapping was not at this location. Possibly could not show themselves openly. Which meant they might not have a chance until nightfall, and even then, what if extra guards were brought?

"I think we may want to leave before anyone comes," Mauer said slowly, thinking it out. "We know they have at least one magician working for them, and if that magician shows up again we'll just be frozen like last time. And I don't know about you, but I'm not going to be fighting my way through much of anything. Whatever they did to us hasn't completely worn off yet. And I'm starving."

"Maybe there is drain? Lot of things drain to river."

They both searched the entire room, mostly by touch. The only drains found were tiny ones, no larger than a fist would fit through. They found a few broken slats of wood, many spiderwebs, and a short length of rusty iron chain. There were no other openings besides the door and the window.

Barzo stood and looked up at it thoughtfully. "This maybe only way."

"How? There's no way to reach it. Even if you did, it's too small to get through."

"Ha. *Gadje* Mauer maybe not, but this Barzo can get through. You see? No bars. Wood broken around the glass. Is maybe only for circus people, but can get through."

Mauer looked at the window and grimaced. If Barzo did fit through that opening, even if the frame were removed, it would be a very tight fit. "Then there is the matter of, well, *reaching* it."

The window was at least fifteen feet off the ground. It was impossible. Then he saw Barzo run, jump, and *keep* running up the wall a few steps. Even with this, his outstretched hands were more than a foot from the sill of the window. A second attempt was closer to the goal, but Barzo scraped his hand badly enough that it bled.

"*Zumala!* I have been too long away, and lazy. Before, I could reach it."

"Are you serious? You could jump that high?" Mauer was seriously reconsidering circus skills.

Barzo patted his stomach. "When younger. Hungrier. Me, I have been eating well and moving cargo. Get big, strong."

"Well you can still jump a lot higher than I ever could. And you weren't that far away from the window. We just need to get you slightly higher."

"Is more than that." Barzo panted, hands on his knees, until he caught his breath. "Gotta get window out, yah? Not gonna hang there and break."

"So we break the window first, from the ground. Where's that piece of chain?"

Barzo instantly understood and suggested his own addition. "Chain maybe go all the way through, not come back. We gotta hold on to it." He pulled a large splinter of wood from one of the broken slats and poked at the edge of his sweater until he had brought out a loop and cut it, eventually unraveling a long length of yarn. "Wool, yah. Strong."

While this was going on, Mauer had been thinking. The only way he was getting out was through the door, which meant Barzo had to bring help somehow. In addition, their captors would know rescuers would be on the way when Barzo escaped, and it was likely he would be moved to a different location. He needed some way to let them track him.

He also needed to keep secret information from Barzo. Even if he could be trusted, he shouldn't be put in danger. *More* danger.

The books he had brought with him were for one of his classics courses. A regular textbook, a Graeco-Roman dictionary, and a personal volume of rare classic text translations. The volume of translations had a bookplate from his family library, complete with the engraved crest. That would serve as proof of his identity. His signature could possibly be forged, but the bookplate would be more difficult, and his friends would know the book was his.

He took out his pen, fervently hoping he'd remembered to fill it recently, and started writing on the back endpaper, all the while furiously thinking about how to provide a way for his rescuers to track him. Rescuers, but not enemies. Tracking … Why was that thought reminding him of something? It was even somehow connected to Markus Asgaya and a very long night, the night he met, without realizing it, the Mage Guardian of Bretagne.

Blood. Mages can track blood.

The crack of breaking glass made him glance up. Barzo had broken the panes with his improvised tool, the length of chain attached to a long, knotted string. He whirled it over his head and let go. The weighted end flew up and reaching the limit of the string, wrapped loosely around the central wooden divider. Barzo tugged lightly, at an angle, to set the grip of the chain before giving it a slow, steady pull.

The rotted wood snapped, and a shower of broken glass fell to the stone floor. Mauer picked up one of the shards and tested it with his fingertip. Sharp enough. He pressed down harder, wincing. He hoped this would be enough. He let the trickle of blood run along the inside seam of the endpaper, where it would be less obvious. But to give a clue, he wrote a well-known classic tag, that translated as "common iron binding softly" and a reference to blood along the edge as well.

"*Hala!* Good, good!" Barzo nodded, a triumphant light in his eyes as he looked up at the now empty window opening. That dimmed, and he turned to Mauer. "But how to get up? Even if I use all the yarn, not strong enough to climb if long enough. And what to tie to?"

"I've got an idea." The trouble with hanging about with engineering students is that their habits rub off on you. Mauer took the sturdiest two slats from the pile, then tied the chain about the middle to fasten it in a lopsided cross. "I watched the way you jumped up the wall. I think if you got just a little more height at the beginning, you could reach the sill and then toss this outside. It will catch on the stone, and the string will let you pull up even if you slip a bit. And the extra height"— Mauer sighed—"will be me. I'll crouch near the wall for you to jump from."

"You think so?" Barzo raised an eyebrow. "I gonna land hard to do this. You no bargeman, *gadje*."

"I know, but I want to live and I think you do too. I'm counting on you to bring help, understand? These people are putting Triss in danger too."

That made the familiar fiery glare return, and Barzo grabbed the improvised window attachment with every indication of immediate use.

"Yeah, I go. No worry, *gadje*. Debts are paid, yeh?"

"Hold on. You'll need to know where to go and who to speak with. I've written three addresses to try. Show them this book so they know it's really me, and—"

Barzo was shifting his feet and rubbing the back of his neck. "You tell me these places, I remember."

Shock held Mauer in place for a moment. How could he simply assume a bargeman knew how to read? Except he *had* assumed because his cousin read enough for five people. "Er. Yes. You'll need to be careful to avoid notice." Mauer gave directions and visual descriptions of the destinations, as well as the names to ask for. He took back the book and added a few more lines. If Barzo couldn't read, it would be safe to add a few more details. "All right, here you go. This had better work," he muttered, and dropped to his hands and knees.

Barzo had him move slightly, glancing up at the window and then down. Then he backed up, gripped the chained boards in one hand and ran, full speed.

The blow of Barzo's first step on his back was like a sledgehammer, the pain sudden and explosive. Mauer thought his back had snapped at first, unable to move. He'd been braced, expecting it to hurt but not that much. He writhed on the cold stone floor in agony, tears blurring his vision. Where was Barzo? Had it worked? As much as he wanted to stay alive, Mauer didn't think he could go through that a second time.

Mauer managed to turn his head enough to look. Barzo had made it up to the window. His head and one shoulder were outside, and he was struggling to get free. Was there a problem? Mauer winced. They'd just assumed the window was within reach of the ground outside. What if it was too high? What could they do now?

But then Barzo vanished from sight. No screams, so with luck he hadn't fallen. Then Mauer saw his dark face peering back inside.

"*Gadje*. I go now. Stay with luck, yah?"

Mauer was in too much pain to talk, so he waved and tried to smile. He'd done what he could. Now he had to trust Barzo.

CHAPTER 16

After two days Triss was bored again. She was only allowed to clean the first and second floors, and while the building had been unbelievably grimy at the start, it was now in passable order. It was a relief to be able to work indoors where it was warm, sleep in a dry bed, and have regular meals she didn't need to pay for. In addition, Jens-Peter was very busy working on the levitation ship, so she had peace and quiet as well.

She hoped Fräulein von Kitren had not forgotten her promise. If she had, how would Triss find her to remind her? The few people who showed up at the building seemed worried and rushed, and since she didn't know her official status here, she was reluctant to intercept them to ask.

Sitting in the larger room with the desks, she helped herself to a meat pastry from the food hamper for lunch and sat on a desk, swinging her feet and wondering what else she could do. Her eye snagged on the glass-fronted bookcases, now gleaming and dust-free. Previously they had been so opaque that she hadn't been able to identify the contents correctly, but now she could see the bindings clearly. She hadn't been told *not* to touch the books, but she'd resisted temptation. This was the only job she had right now and she didn't want to lose it—at least not before she sent the money.

Triss got up and peered through the glass at one shelf. The glass door wasn't even locked. The titles on the spines were things like *Rail Lines of Lower Sachsen* and *Commercial Telegraph Code 36th Edition* and other reference-like volumes. But on the shelf below, she found *A History of the Mage War*, *Gaulan Combat Magic*, and *Final Battles of Guedoc* which seemed more interesting. She decided to dust that shelf first.

Properly dusting a book, of course, meant opening the covers. Generally even the housekeeper at Baron Heufritz's house found clapping the books together a few times and then shaking the book while holding the covers by the edges to be sufficient, but Triss decided a page-by-page dusting was called for here. Besides, if she just shook the dust she'd have to clean the room again. So armed with a clean rag, she started reading about the Mage War.

She wasn't sure if this was something that had actually happened or not. Sometimes books were not about real things, and people would look at her funny when she asked about it. Apparently the Lands of Fayre weren't real. They had seemed real when she read about them, though. And this Mage War seemed very unpleasant with a great deal of magical destruction and some sort of enslavement spell that was never clearly described but always referred to with horror.

I think this is probably one of the not-real books, Triss decided once she finished. Wouldn't something that horrible still be talked about?

She rummaged on the shelf for another book to clean and discovered a small booklet that had fallen behind the other volumes. It had no lettering on the spine, but a pasted paper label read *Symbols de Gloire*. Triss opened it, curious.

The contents were all hand-written and not very easy to read. Each page had two or three small designs with a paragraph of text next to each. Triss squinted, frowning, then relaxed. It wasn't so much the bad handwriting but that the text was in a different language. That was why she couldn't read it. She paged through, wondering what it was all about, before dutifully wiping the pages and putting it back.

She cleaned most of the shelf before hearing voices in the courtyard below. Triss went to a window to take a look. Jens-Peter was standing in the levitation ship, speaking to someone on the ground and gesturing at the main building. When he saw her in the window, he waved for her to come down.

Their visitor was Willem. Willem did not look happy to be there and kept glancing up at the looming bulk of the levitation ship balloon in a worried fashion.

"He's brought your pay and will take you to that church you want to go to." Jens-Peter frowned, appearing doubtful of the wisdom of letting Triss go without him.

She had already donned her coat, anticipating this. "Let's go! I want to send the money as soon as possible." Willem appeared resigned and willing to get it over with quickly, so he made no objections. He even provided funds for a hire carriage, further convincing Triss this was an errand he wanted completed soon.

It was a pleasant, sunny day, despite the cold, and she felt her mood improve with it. The troupe would be able to make it through the winter once they got the money. Maybe it would be enough to avoid questions? No, that was expecting too much. But she had fulfilled her obligations, and

Fraulein von Kitren appeared to be the type of noble who kept promises. She would get another position and not have to worry about any of …whatever this was … again.

Triss was not surprised to hear Willem ask the driver to wait for them once they reached the church. She got out of the cab and headed for the rectory, glancing back to make sure Willem was following. He had the money, after all.

Father Rito greeted her with more than his usual warmth, looking her over and clasping her hands in his. Then he caught sight of Willem. "Now who is this? What happened to the other one?" He seemed agitated.

"This is Herr Willem, and he was sent to escort me from my new job." Not a lie, any of it. "I was given an advance on my wages, and I wanted to send it immediately."

"Of course, but …" Father Rito dithered and stammered. "My dear, your kinsman Barzo came by shortly after your last visit, and he was quite worried about you. And your, er, gentleman friend. He said he would come back, but I have not seen him since that day. Perhaps he found you elsewhere?"

Triss felt her stomach knot. Barzo was already looking for her? "No, I haven't seen him. Please tell him I have work if you see him again."

Willem handed over the money. Triss claimed she did not have time to write a note, but in reality she was only trying to put off the inevitable scolding. If she didn't say anything they couldn't blame her for it, could they? And it was harder and harder to conceal the truth. She would rather wait until she was at a boring household to reassure them.

"Apologies, but I feel that I must ask who this gentleman is and how he is connected to you." The old priest was unusually firm.

Willem silently reached into his overcoat and brought out a slim leather folder. Opened, it showed a metal plate with an enamel crest at the top and writing below it.

"Imperial Police? There is no trouble, is there?"

Is that what the badge said? Triss frowned. That wasn't a term she'd heard before, but something different. Something about hunters.

"The miss is working for one of our offices. Cleaning." Willem had a faintly pained expression on his face.

Father Rito seemed much relieved at this proof of legality and showed them out the rectory door with his calm restored. Triss felt calmer too. She was quite certain a message would be sent even though she hadn't written one, and this would be very helpful. She couldn't be in trouble if she was hired by the Imperial Police, right?

"Thank you," she said to Willem. He may have been unwilling, but one paid debts. "We can return now."

The cab was waiting outside the church yard, where the sun made it slightly warmer for the grey dappled horse. To reach it they had to walk past a narrow alleyway.

A loud voice suddenly shouted from the alley. "Go, think shame on yourself, you filthy drunk vagrant! Go sleep it off somewhere else. You're in sight of a church where children learn, and they don't need to learn about you and your evil ways!"

"No drunk …"

Triss turned her head, frowning. She had been ignoring the noise, but the faint voice responding to the rant seemed familiar.

"We should return, Miss. This is not a suitable neighborhood to spend time in." Willem was watching their surroundings in a nervous but subtle way that worried Triss more than an obvious one would have. She nodded and kept walking.

"Trisstela!"

Triss froze, spun around, and ran. No one here called her by that name. The only people who used it were her family. But who was here?

Halfway down the alley, she saw a man lying in the gutter and a large frowzy woman with a broom raised up to strike him. At first she didn't recognize him with his face bruised and swollen. "Barzo!" Triss yelled.

"I no drunk. Trisstela, you believe?" He mumbled through cracked lips.

The angry woman had stepped back when Triss appeared, but she looked even angrier now. "You know this bum? Get him away. We don't need him here."

"Barzo, what happened to you?" He had no smell of alcohol, but he was clearly in bad shape.

He gave a smile that was more of a wince. "Bargemaster beat me. I miss work, crazy person lock me up with that *gadje* you were with. He tell me get help for him when I escape. But I no find the people he said, I go to bargemaster thinking he help me. I get away but hurt bad, try to get to old Father here."

She could tell he was injured, so badly he was unable to stand for long. "Locked up? Who did this? Why?" The person she was with couldn't mean Jens-Peter, since he was still at the warehouse. The only other person could be Wolfgang Mauer.

"No see. They make us like stone, with magic, cover our eyes. Put us in stone room. The *gadje* helped me escape, but he no could follow, I promise to bring help." With a shaking hand, Barzo reached under his tattered sweater and brought out a slim leather-bound book.

Triss had seen it before, and in Mauer's possession. Even the scrapes and wear on the corners were the same. "I recognize this book. But why …"

"He put words in, himself."

Triss opened the front cover. There was a name, Wolfgang G. Mauer.

She flipped through the pages, seeing nothing unusual, until she reached the back. The entire endpaper was covered with shaky writing, and a dark brownish stain along the inside edge had seeped over obscuring a few of the words.

"I should report back, Miss." Willem was looking quite agitated. "This is … very disturbing and the chief needs to know about it. But I don't have permission to bring outsiders there."

Triss scowled. She didn't like it, but it was true that they didn't know Barzo. "He's my cousin. I can't just leave him! I'll stay with him for now. Help me get him to the church!"

Father Rito was horrified at the sight of the injured Barzo and instantly agreed to allow him to rest in the rectory until a decision was reached. "What a terrible thing to have happen … Who could have done such a thing? I will find bandages …" He shuffled away, followed by the sound of drawers and cabinets being opened and contents tossed willy-nilly.

For all his efforts, Father Rito did not find much in the way of medical supplies. Triss had to make do with a torn-up sheet and hot water. As she cleaned up the blood, her anger grew. Who had done this to her cousin, and why? He was not the sort who started fights for no reason, and he didn't seek trouble.

She did not have a lot of experience, but she had seen enough injuries in the troupe to at least be sure he had no broken bones. His face was sunken and weary. She did not like to think what he had been through the last few days, but he was safe now.

As she was cleaning the blood from his face, Barzo's eyes slowly opened—hazy at first, but then clear. "Trisstela," he whispered. "I worried I would not find you."

"Why? I am not lost." She scrubbed harder, revealing a range of bruises, and he groaned. "You are so beautiful, with the colors of the peacock," she said in the zigane tongue. "Surely now you will find a wife."

He smiled and winced. "Such sweet words my little cousin speaks, like the shy dove at twilight. Surely she will ease and comfort her husband … whenever she catches him and ties him up." He spoke slowly, and his voice was rough with fatigue.

"Bah, bah, if you weren't already wounded I would beat you and save your wife the trouble." Triss sniffled, trying to smile back. "Why did they do this, *nadu*? Why did they take you away?"

"The evil people did not say why. What are you up to, little rabbit? Why are all these *gadje* men looking at your face? Do you think Toa Mihai would be pleased to learn?"

Triss scowled, irritated. "How many are looking? Do you think I keep them like chickens? These men I know, they keep respect, and so I would tell Toa Mihai himself if he were here. Maybe Mata Sheri would not approve … but does she ever?" She was *not* going to mention the various places she'd slept in close quarters with Jens-Peter and no one else. She'd have to warn him never to mention it, especially if he came in contact with Barzo. No, best would be to keep them apart. Jens-Peter spoke without thinking too often.

"Toa Mihai worries. They all worry about you, little rabbit. Grief has put a stone on their hearts since sending you here. Even Mata Sheri." Barzo gently ruffled her hair with a bandaged hand. "Why do you think I looked for you? And then the old father said you came to the church with a man. How could I be your cousin if I did not see him for myself?"

Triss rolled her eyes but didn't say anything. She continued bandaging her way down Barzo's body.

After thinking for a while, she asked, "Did you do anything other than follow Mauer? Anything that might bring evil eyes on you?"

Barzo shook his head. "Only that. I see him by chance, when I bring barrels to a brewery. He was there with another *gadje* in a cart. I hear him use your name and mention a stocking belonging to you." Triss could hear grinding noises and hurried to distract him.

"Ah, that's where it went! They took me in the cart to my new position. The bundle with my belongings must not have been tied completely. Eh, bad luck to good. The stocking was old and mostly darning. Oh! Are you hungry? I will ask Father Rito to get you something to eat."

Triss dashed out of the room, frantically hoping Willem would return soon.

116

CHAPTER 17

"The lack of progress on this investigation is … concerning." Von Koller gave Markus Asgaya a cold stare. "I do not feel the Kriegsa has been given full cooperation by the Dragonhunters. The report you requested my immediate attention to consider contains remarkably little new information. Is this the best you can do? Or are you withholding what you know for a greater share of the glory?"

Markus spread his hands and assumed his most at-a-loss face. "We cannot share information we do not have. We are in complete agreement that the secret of the levitation ships should never reach enemy hands, and the Dragonhunters will do everything in their power to make sure this never happens."

And if the enemy is in your ranks, well, that just means we won't be telling you much. They did have to be careful about still appearing to be helpful, however. The Kriegsa was powerful and von Koller quick to take offense. Sadly, the distraction of the "immediate report" was not sufficient to divert his attention. Markus would have to find something else.

An aide slipped inside the meeting room with a nervous, apologetic expression on his face. He went to Markus and said softly "Willem wishes to speak to you, sir. Immediately."

Markus suppressed the raised eyebrow, then saw that Willem himself was visible outside the open door and felt a sinking sensation of dread. Willem was visibly agitated. How many times had he told the Dragonhunters not to reveal *anything* to outsiders? And Willem was the worst of the lot. Only Markus and Gutrune had the instinctive skill to handle the dangers of the political world, and despite all their efforts to teach the rank and file, it was proving an uphill battle.

Time to contain the damage, but he feared this was already a failed effort. Von Koller was just the type to notice. Markus kept his expression relaxed and mildly amused even though he was cursing inside.

"It appears I have another meeting to attend, and I believe there is nothing more we can accomplish here today," he said smoothly and continued with further pleasant-sounding verbiage that had no actual meaning beyond courtesy. He managed to escape the room, but he was quite sure von Koller's suspicions were raised.

He gave Willem a glare and walked away.

"Sir, it's—"

Markus glanced quickly around, grabbed Willem by the arm and pulled him into a side corridor before casting a sound-muffling spell.

"You idiot, I know it's important, and now half Baerlen knows it too! More importantly, von Koller is going to be out for blood!"

Willem visibly wilted. "I know, sir. You said make an excuse and I did. It's the cousin of that girl Triss. He's badly hurt, but I didn't dare bring him to the warehouse because you said ..."

Markus forcibly held on to his evaporating sanity. "Why did you need to drag me out for this?"

"He escaped, sir. Er, that Wolfgang Mauer fellow was caught too."

Eventually Markus was in possession of the pertinent facts, if not in the order of importance. Someone, probably the mastermind behind the attack on the levitation ships, had kidnapped both Triss's relative and Mauer, but Mauer had not been able to escape.

"Does this man know where they were being held?"

Willem shrugged. "He only spoke a little before going unconscious. Oh! Mauer made him take a book when he escaped. Maybe it is important somehow?"

A book? Odd. But perhaps Mauer had written something inside that would help. "Possibly. Keep the book safe, understand? Take it and that man to the warehouse, but cover his eyes on the way so he can't learn the location. Quickly. Get him awake, and find out where Mauer is." Every minute counted, and unfortunately he had to stay here. If the Dragonhunters could trace the kidnappers, even by non-magical means, it would give him a head start.

"Aren't you going back?" Willem looked panicked again.

Markus sighed. "No. I'm going to stay here and distract von Koller." And send an emergency message to Gutrune. Von Koller must not discover that they were hiding the levitation ship. It also occurred to him that a certain device sent by the inventor of Peran might be useful, and Gutrune could bring it to the warehouse. "And one more thing. Whoever kidnapped Mauer may be looking for others who know about the ship. Send someone to find Dieter Theusen and bring him in too."

While it was good to have time to really fix *Einzl* after all the damage and crashing and so on, Jens-Peter was not fond of the warehouse courtyard. For one thing, it was dreary and cold. The oak tree was also cold, but it had a beautiful view of the countryside and a number of birds that seemed be offering commentary or helpful flying advice. Also, he was stuck and not allowed to go out, and even Triss was completely focused on cleaning and did not talk to him. He didn't even know where she was right now since she left with Willem hours ago.

It was boring.

Jens-Peter sat on the rail of the ship and contemplated whether moving the mid-trim engine was worth the aggravation when someone knocked rapidly on the street door of the courtyard. The guard peered through the slit, then opened the door. Triss darted through and headed straight for him.

"Come help! Willem can't carry him by himself."

Jens-Peter vaulted over the rail of the ship before she finished speaking. He had no idea who she was talking about, but she seemed panicked. Triss didn't panic. Outside on the street was the usual plain carriage that couldn't come inside because *Einzl* was in the way. In that carriage was Willem and a man with what appeared to be Willem's hat pulled down over his eyes and a muffler wrapping the rest of his face.

"Help me get him inside. He's unconscious."

"Maybe because he can't breathe?" Jens-Peter muttered but reached for the man's legs. Fortunately, as a student he had lots of practice carrying drunken comrades, so he knew the most efficient way to move someone who couldn't stand.

They managed to shift him out of the carriage and through the warehouse door. Triss was waiting impatiently inside with the elevator already open. With four people, one a limp body, the elevator was crowded and moved slowly.

"Not to be nosy or anything, but who is he?"

Triss glanced at him. "My cousin Barzo. He was caught by bad people, and they caught Herr Mauer too! Barzo escaped to get help, and he found me at the church."

Shock hit him like a blow. Mauer caught? If Barzo was injured, was Mauer injured too? "How badly is he hurt?" Jens-Peter could see inexpert bandaging on Barzo's hands, and traces of blood.

Triss sniffled. "I think not too badly. He was very hungry, he hadn't eaten in days, and then his stupid boss beat him. As if he could help being late when he was locked up!"

When the elevator finally creaked to a stop, they dragged Barzo out and into the little room with the only real bed. He had groaned once, and his eyes flickered, but he still wasn't fully awake.

"Mauer's been kidnapped? He did mention that strange people have been watching him—but why is your cousin involved?"

Triss's face slowly went pink. "Barzo overheard Herr Mauer and Herr Theusen talking about me and got mad … um, misunderstood something and followed him to ask. That's when the bad guys grabbed them." She pulled out a battered calf-bound book. "There was a high window in the place they were locked up. Barzo could reach it, but Herr Mauer couldn't. Herr Mauer made Barzo take this when he escaped, so it must be important somehow."

"I'm beginning to think circus training is very useful," Jens-Peter said, feeling cold. "Who caught them? Where were they held? We should go get Mauer!"

"I tried to ask where they were, but Barzo can't read street signs and didn't recognize where he was. Then he fell asleep again. Do we have a map of the city?"

"I'll go find one," Willem volunteered and ran out.

Triss went out, too, returning with a cloth and a jug of cold water. She started wiping Barzo's face again and calling to him softly, and his eyes fluttered open. Jens-Peter watched her, frustration and guilt flooding his mind. It must be the same people who attacked the levitation ship facility, the people Mauer had mentioned were following him. Mauer was in danger now and it was his fault for involving him.

"What can we do?" His voice sounded strange to his own ears, tight and flat.

"He made Barzo take this book for a reason. It can't be to prove it was him; I know Barzo and I would believe what he says. We could check to see if Herr Mauer has been at his classes."

"Maybe it was so we'd be sure it was him faster."

Triss raised an eyebrow. "Or maybe he knew he'd be moved. Wouldn't you think so, once they knew Barzo escaped? Of course he'd get help and bring it back to the same place."

The door to the room opened, but it wasn't Willem. Dieter came in. He was pale and wide-eyed and not nearly as calm as he usually was. "So it *is* you. These men just pulled me out of the lab and brought me here! Something about I could be in danger because of that damn ship and pretty much dragged me by force. Is this a joke? What's going on? I'm too busy for this."

"Somebody got Mauer," Jens-Peter said dully. "It's not a joke."

"What…Is he dead?" Dieter went even more pale.

"Not dead, not when I go." Barzo shifted, tried to sit up, and winced. "Alive, not hurt."

Dieter stared at the zigane, puzzled, until Jens-Peter explained. "This is Barzo. He's Triss's cousin and was caught at the same time as Mauer and the only reason we know any of this."

Triss was still examining the book. "See, there's this whole page of writing at the back. He wrote it really fast but it doesn't tell us much we haven't already figured out. But this stuff that smeared the inside edge of the page, that's on top of the writing. Whenever it got there, it was after. And it isn't ink."

"He did while I make thing to go in window," Barzo said seriously. "Little rope, just to grab after wall-step? Give book, help me get out. I say I help him."

Triss looked up, interested. "You did a wall-step? Don't tell me you used Herr Mauer as a boost?" Barzo glanced away, saying nothing. "Well, that means he didn't have much time whatever he did."

"Ah! I see him pick up some of the glass from broken window," Barzo added.

"I found a map! Um, but it's a little awkward here ..." Willem waved a large roll of paper. "I don't think we can unroll it fully," he said, looking around the room, which was small to begin with and now full of people.

"Someone hold it up for me." Triss had a look of grim determination. She said something in the zigane tongue to Barzo, who nodded fervently and scrunched up his eyes in fierce contemplation.

Jens-Peter grabbed the map from Willem and started unrolling it. With a bit of jostling, he and a confused Dieter managed to get it right side up for Triss to study.

"Why is she looking at the map and not asking him questions?" Dieter muttered to Jens-Peter behind the map.

"Once she's got it in her head it will be easier."

"What?"

Jens-Peter ignored him. It would take too long to explain and even longer for him to believe. The map was large and had quite a bit of detail, so he wasn't as confident as he seemed. But after ten minutes Triss turned away and started asking Barzo questions. He was a lot more communicative in his own language.

"He reached the bargemaster's office by crossing the river from the Schilling Bridge. Before that he could see the Memorial Plaza on his left— at least I think it's the Memorial Plaza. How many other places have a giant column made of cannon barrels? And he didn't cross any big streets after escaping, and he's sure it was less than three leagues. It has to be in the place that says Rogasti on the map. A big stone building, with a broken basement window, with a large tree near the entrance. Oh, and he thinks the stone was dark in color but there wasn't much light at the time."

"I'll let them know." Willem ran out again.

Triss and Barzo were talking again, quietly. Triss looked up.

"Is there anything else you want to ask him? If not he should rest."

Jens-Peter shook his head. "Let's move to the office area. I want to look at the map again."

Spread out over two desks, the map was a lot easier to examine.

"Do you think we got the location wrong?" Dieter asked, frowning.

"Just an idea I had. See, this is where Mauer lives." Jens-Peter tapped the map. "And this basement dungeon place is all the way over *here*. To get Mauer and Barzo there, they must have crossed Brunnenstrasse at some point, and that has police stationed at every crossroads for most of it because of the army base there. I wonder if they noticed anything suspicious,…"

"But when did they get captured?"

"Barzo said it was morning, the day you and Herr Mauer returned the cart." Triss thought for a bit. "And he couldn't see much, but he was awake even when he was frozen by magic. It was just getting dark when he escaped, and they were in the cellar for several hours before that. So … sometime before noon."

The door opened and Markus Asgaya entered.

"What are you discussing so energetically? I understand you think you have located where Mauer was brought." Asgaya walked up to study the map.

"Yes, Willem went out to have people search. We were thinking maybe their carriage was seen while taking him there."

"Speaking of searching, do you have the book?"

Triss, naturally, was carrying the book and handed it to Asgaya, who promptly opened it to the very back.

"We already looked for any other messages," Jens-Peter said. "Besides that note, he didn't write anything."

Asgaya studied the book carefully, flipping the back pages. "The writing isn't the important thing," he said slowly. "What he said is essentially what Barzo told us. I think it is a decoy, and the real message isn't the writing but a method by which he can be found wherever he is." Asgaya put the book down, open to the back endpapers. "If I understand the reference he quotes, the substance smeared inside is his blood. If so, we can find him with magic."

"But Mauer isn't a magician," Dieter objected.

"True. But he's seen me use blood tracking magic before. He must have believed his captors would move him after we learned his location." Asgaya stood and went to an unusual metal cabinet that had no visible handles or hinges, just a pattern like the rays of the sun streaming from a central design. He took out a slim leather folder with a metal badge inside and held it up to the design, and the pattern unfolded to reveal several shelves with various boxes and bottles.

Reaching inside, he took out a leather case the size of something used to hold spectacles. Inside was a small glass vial and a bundle of silvery tissue that when unwrapped revealed a slender, carved rod of blue-black metal. It was either poorly decorated, partially corroded, or both. "A good thing I remembered we had this. The trouble with the tracking spell is that usually only the magician casting it can actually do the tracking. Somewhat inconvenient at the moment since I cannot stay here for long. But with this device, assuming I can get it to work, that will not be an issue. However. This is the only blood we have. If it doesn't work, there isn't a second chance."

"How much blood is needed?" Triss asked.

Asgaya sighed. "What you see here is barely enough."

She picked up the book and looked down the spine. "If there was more, could it be done twice? It would damage the book, but it looks like it soaked into the backing."

After careful work with a penknife, Mauer's book was in pieces and a pile of binding, thread, and paper, all bearing bloodstains, was heaped on the desk.

"That's better. With luck, that will give us a second chance if we need it. I'll need to concentrate now, so please do not distract me."

His eyes focused intently on the bloodstained scraps, one hand hovering over but not touching them. The scraps of paper and thread started to shiver, as if they were in a breeze, and Asgaya's jaw was clenched. A fine, dark dust drifted up and collected midair. Asgaya placed his other hand over the rough metal rod and grimaced, fine beads of sweat appearing on his forehead. The floating dust swirled and flowed toward the rod, which began to glow. The rough decorations were actually very intricate inscriptions. There was a gust of warm, metallic air, and the glow vanished.

Asgaya snatched the small glass vial and quickly gathered the remaining blood dust before it fell. Then he collapsed in a chair, wiping his face with a handkerchief. "Well, that was unpleasant, but I felt it take. Now we must test it." He grinned and held up the glass vial, handing it to Jens-Peter.

Dieter peered at it. "Will that work?"

"Shall we find out?" Asgaya looked around the room. "We'll need a string or something similar."

Jens-Peter looked down at his ragged coat and pulled a fraying thread free. "Will this do?"

"Admirably." Asgaya tied the thread to the middle of the rod, which had a convenient indentation. Holding the other end of the thread, he let the rod dangle freely.

One end turned, just like a compass seeking north. Jens-Peter moved the glass vial from side to side, and the needle faithfully followed.

"I understand you can also float this in water, if needed. Well! That's one worry dealt with." Asgaya placed the little rod back in the wooden box.

"The lining shields the magical effect, by the way. To protect it from being overwhelmed by other magic. I should also mention the range is not very large. One league at most, according to the notes that came with it."

"Better than nothing at all." Jens-Peter felt some of the tension in his body relax. He heard footsteps on the stairs. "Is that Willem? Maybe we won't need the tracker if he's found them already!"

It was Willem, and his expression was grim. "We sent people to the place Barzo described. We found the cellar prison but your friend was not there. Nobody was there. They'd already fled."

Asgaya stood up. "Any indication which direction?"

"We've got searchers out, sir. And von Ries requested assistance."

"From whom?" Asgaya gave him a hard look.

"The … the Kriegsa, sir. We still don't have the manpower, and—"

Asgaya gave a short, sharp curse and ran out of the room. The clank of metal indicated he had opened the elevator door.

"Did von Ries do something wrong?" Willem murmured. "I thought we wanted to find them."

"We do, and so does the Kriegsa, but maybe for different reasons. The Kriegsa wants to find *me* because they think I'm behind the levitation ship attack!" Jens-Peter thought for a moment. "Well, they've got no reason to suspect Mauer of that, so maybe it's all right."

Triss picked up the vial of blood dust and tried out the tracker for a few minutes, then packed it away carefully in the wood case. "Where did Willem put the extra blankets? Herr Theusen will need some, and since Barzo is in the only bed, I'll have to find another place to sleep. Maybe the meeting room. That table is certainly large enough."

It didn't seem right that Triss would have to sleep on a table, but even with concentrated thought Jens-Peter couldn't come up with a better option. Barzo was injured, and at least they could leave Triss in her own room at night while Dieter and he made do in the office. Willem, or one of his colleagues, had indeed found a large pile of blankets and the three of them, taking an armful each, started to arrange their temporary sleeping accommodations.

To only be interrupted by the sound of the elevator descending, followed shortly by the immediate appearance of a very worried Asgaya with a long strip of paper in his hands. It appeared to have words printed on it.

"You all need to leave. Immediately." He glanced at the pile of blankets and winced. "And take all of that with you."

"What?"

"Why now? Can't it wait until morning?" Triss frowned at him.

"No. There isn't time to explain all the details, but von Koller is coming *now*. I just got this reply from the court. That request for assistance was strongarmed into authorization to stuff his people in any of our facilities, and he's always wanted to get in here. Suspecting, correctly, we are hiding something." Asgaya grinned. "Which means we need to get all of you, and the ship, away and out of sight before his people get here. Gutr—Fräulein von Kitren is delaying them but she can't do that for long."

Jens-Peter felt a horrible sinking sensation. "But we *can't* leave! It's still daylight! More importantly, the altitude adjuster isn't fixed; it sticks for descents. If we launch we might not be able to get down again!"

Triss sighed and matter-of-factly picked up the blankets again.

"Can't you fix it in flight?"

"If I had nothing else to do and five trained crew, maybe! But it's just me!" What added to his frustration is he knew the danger of staying. He didn't want to deal with von Koller even before the incident, and now it would be fatal.

"You aren't by yourself. I can climb, and Herr Theusen can hold on to ropes. If you don't go too high, can't you pull the ship down like that? Oh, and Barzo is really good at acrobatics. We'll have to take him anyway, you know. I'm not leaving him behind." Triss picked up her bundle and the basket of food.

"But he's injured!"

She shrugged. "No broken bones. Mostly it was hunger and fatigue bothering him, he'll be much better when he wakes up. What else do we need from here?"

Jens-Peter gave up and gathered his belongings. In the face of Triss's pragmatic attitude he felt he had no choice.

"Here's some money." Asgaya stuffed some bills and coins in his hand. "We'll try to find you … You'll want this, don't forget." He slipped the leather case with the tracker in Jens-Peter's coat pocket. "Oh, and this map of the city could be useful."

"Already seen it," Triss commented, darting out of the office. Asgaya paused, nonplussed.

"She remembers things she's seen. Perfectly," Jens-Peter said as he ran. Triss passed him on the stairs, going up.

"I'm going to get Barzo," she panted.

"Get Dieter to help you!"

"I can manage. You have to untie all the ropes holding the ship down first!"

She was right. There was too much to do and not enough people to do it. He had Willem and Dieter cutting the ropes if they couldn't untie them fast enough, while he loaded every piece of equipment in the yard, even the broken engines. With more weight the ship would fly lower, and they could always toss it in a river later.

Strangely, Asgaya was simply standing in front of the large carriage doors to the outside, eyes closed and hands spread slightly at his side. Just as Triss came staggering down the stairs with a barely-awake Barzo, Asgaya spun sharply and gestured.

"They're here. My tripwire spell was just triggered a block away. Go!"

Jens-Peter pulled on Barzo's arms while Triss pushed until the man fell onto the ship, then she swung aboard herself. Jens-Peter pulled at the altitude lever—and nothing happened. He soon found the problem.

"There's still two more ropes holding us down!" he hissed. They'd missed them before because they were tied in an odd place on the building. And if they cut it from the ship end and someone saw rope in the courtyard, they would be bound to ask questions.

"I'll get them." Triss jumped down and climbed the courtyard walls, pulling out the knife he'd forgotten she carried. Jens-Peter could hear voices outside the building now.

One rope suddenly came free, and the ship tilted hard. Triss scrambled to the second rope.

If she cuts that one, the ship will float free and leave her behind!

Before he could call out a warning, he remembered he couldn't do that now. He tried waving instead, but Triss didn't seem to notice.

Another sharp jerk, and the ship floated up, level again. Jens-Peter rushed to the side and looked down, but there was no sign of Triss.

The ship rocked slightly, and then a familiar shawl-covered arm reached over the rail. "Good thing I held on," whispered Triss.

Relief made his legs weak, but he didn't forget to keep nudging the altitude. There was a low cloud cover and a slight breeze that moved the ship as it cleared the warehouse. It was risky to go too high if they couldn't be sure of coming down again, so drifting away was better if they had time.

The sun was starting to go down, but there was still enough light to see the levitation ship if people looked up. They couldn't start the engines without detection, yet they needed to move away, fast. All he could do was increase altitude and hope for a good wind—and that he could get them down again.

Jens-Peter shifted to the viewscope, getting the view from underneath. As he watched, the large main doors opened, and a crowd of uniformed Kriegsa officers streamed inside just as the bright courtyard lights went out. Someone, probably Asgaya, had shut them off to give them a little more time to escape without being seen. None of the people in the courtyard looked up, and Jens-Peter held his breath until the drifting clouds concealed *Einzl* from the ground.

CHAPTER 18

They came for him a few hours after Barzo's escape. The only warning Mauer had was the creak of the iron hinges, and he barely had time to turn, in pain, to get a glimpse of their faces before he was frozen again and a dark cloth covered his head.

In a way the freezing was a relief. Barzo's jump had broken at least one rib, and any motion, including breathing, was agonizing. Mauer didn't recognize any of the people at the door. They had a similar odd, haggard appearance, especially in the face, and they didn't talk.

As before, he could still hear even if he couldn't see. From the sounds of the people carrying him and the motion, it appeared he was being carried up a series of stone steps and then out to an open space. Something was clinking and rattling in a familiar way, but while he was trying to figure it out, a harsh voice started yelling.

"Where's the other one? I told you to bring them both."

"Not there." The person answering spoke in a dull tone.

"What do you mean, not there? There's no way they could escape!" Rapid footsteps faded into the distance. When they returned a few minutes later, they were even more rapid and followed by shouted orders. Mauer couldn't make out what those orders were, but the voice sounded fearful. "Take him to your master, as fast as you can without being suspicious. Only let him out at night, out of sight of strangers. Go, now, quickly!"

He was moved again, up and then down. Matching the creaking noises, and at last he remembered where he had heard it before. A carriage with springs. But where was he being placed? Something made a thump above him, and all remaining noises became muffled. So, inside the carriage. But the leader had said he wasn't to be visible. Perhaps there was a hidden compartment in this carriage?

The swaying motion of the carriage increased. Mauer couldn't tell which direction they were going, but they seemed to be traveling on rough cobblestones.

"He will be angry," a cold, precise voice spoke.

"We were ordered to capture him. We did this." The other voice was deep, and slow, as if tired.

"Two people were brought. Why?"

"The other was there and saw us. We cannot be discovered. This is also the command." The deep voice seemed briefly tense and continued in a tight, pained voice. "If he asks he will be angry." At the end, he was almost gasping.

The cold voice replied immediately. "He will ask. Gehrig came to the city hideout. The one who escaped may contact the enemy. The highest order is to not be discovered."

"We will be punished."

"Yes."

It was a very odd conversation, almost detached. And now that he thought about it, why hadn't these people thought to interrogate *him* about what had happened? Mauer hoped he could withstand pain, but he didn't have any illusions about prolonged torture. His only chance of avoiding it was if Barzo had gotten well away and was bringing help.

After what seemed like an eternity Mauer woke from his doze by pain. Not only could he feel again, but when he tried to shift instinctively to a more comfortable position, he could. He tried moving his hands. It was like being covered in glue, but he *could* move. Just like the first time, the freezing effect only lasted a few hours.

He wasn't going to escape like this. For one thing, he was still in the hidden compartment under the seat and at least two people were inside the carriage. What could he do with his temporary freedom? Searching the hidden compartment by touch, he found nothing useful. The only things he had were the contents of his pockets.

A fountain pen. His watch. A coin purse containing a total of two guilder, fifteen pfennig. A linen handkerchief. The key to his lodgings. A small notebook he'd been looking for and thought he'd lost, but which was actually deep inside a vest pocket he rarely used. *I am not going to be performing any heroic deeds with this.* Mauer sighed, continuing to dig, until a sudden sharp pain lanced his fingertip. He stifled his yelp, hoping it had not been noticed by his captors, then remembered. He'd put the fragment of glass in his pocket after dripping blood in the book he'd given Barzo.

He couldn't tell how yet, but having something that could cut could be quite useful in the future. Not wanting to get stabbed again, he wrapped the shard of glass in the handkerchief and put the whole bundle in the same vest pocket the notebook had been in. It would not be noticeable under his jacket but would be easy to reach at need.

Mauer felt fortunate that he had taken advantage of the unfreezing when he did because minutes after he had finished, the carriage came to a halt and he heard the lid of the secret compartment open. He decided to pretend to be half unconscious. They would know the freezing magic had faded, and he didn't think he could fake being asleep if they decided to test it.

He was roughly pulled out of the carriage and dumped on the ground, then dragged until something pressed against his back. His feet were tied and then rope wound around his chest and arms and pulled tightly, making him groan when his broken rib shifted. Then the black hood was removed from his head.

It was dark, and the carriage had stopped near a thick stand of trees such that it was not visible from the road. One of the people from the carriage came and dumped a heel of dry bread, a wedge of cheese, and a pottery jug in his lap before silently moving away to watch him. His hands were free so he could eat, and he did so. He was starving. The pottery jug contained either stale water or weak beer—he couldn't tell for sure.

Thinking furiously, Mauer ate as slowly as he could. His captors would likely use the freeze spell on him before continuing on the journey. If he was going to do anything useful, it would have to be now. And the only thing he could think to do would require concealment. He sighed. What did he have to lose except his dignity?

"Any chance I could relieve myself?" He waved his hands. "I'd do it here, but it's awkward without standing."

The captors looked at each other, blinking in silence. The larger man, the one who acted as coachman, came forward and untied his arms but not his feet.

Mauer struggled to his feet, tears of pain leaking from the corners of his eyes as he was forced to put pressure on his injured ribs to stand. He rested for a moment to catch his breath, then hopped cautiously around the tree, glaring in feigned resentment at his captors.

For whatever reason, it worked. They remained standing motionless. It wasn't like he could escape; by the time he got the ropes off his feet, they would easily recapture him. No, it just looked like he wanted some privacy.

He did need to relieve himself, but more importantly he could shift his clothing without suspicion. He quickly brought out the handkerchief, noting the bloodstains from his cut finger. Using the shard of glass, he cut away one section of bloody cloth and tucked it out of sight in the branch of the tree.

The coachman came over soon after. Without a word he grabbed Mauer's coat collar and dragged him back to the coach. At least this time they had the courtesy to let him get settled in the hidden compartment before freezing him. He wondered if the blood on the scrap of handkerchief would be enough for tracking. He had to find a better way to leave a trail, maybe by leaving a note with any useful information he could gather.

What if Barzo couldn't get help? He tried to think of who would miss him. His professors would be irritated by his absence, but not to the point of alerting anyone. His friends—well, Jens-Peter was in hiding somewhere, Dieter either immersed in his work to the point of forgetting to sleep or helping Jens-Peter, and Stefan … They'd all been tired after the night with the mule cart. His abduction might not be noticed for days.

He really hoped someone was looking for him.

"Trisstela, why am I in a boat?"

Triss scrambled to the draped blanket tent where Barzo was sitting up, looking very confused. Fortunately he was still half asleep, and he spoke in a low mumble.

"We are escaping enemies. Hush." She peeked over the rail. The courtyard of the warehouse was still in view but no longer directly below them. The ship was drifting to the south-east, away from the river and the center of Baerlen. She dropped back down next to him. "I think we are safe, but do not make any sound. How do you feel?"

"A new man." A flash of white in the darkness from his smile. "But how are we in a boat? That place, I smelled no water nearby."

She wasn't sure what she could safely tell him. As soon as he looked around, he'd figure it out for himself, unless he was blindfolded. It would be better to convince the others to let Barzo join the group.

"Rest here for a while longer. I'll explain later."

Triss carefully made her way across the deck, greatly hampered by boxes and gear tossed and shifted when the levitation ship flailed about during the launch. She wanted to move everything back, but that would make noise, too, and they couldn't risk it. Finally she reached the control station and Jens-Peter. Dieter Theusen was hanging on to a cable with a death grip, and she could hear his teeth chattering.

"How far away are we now?" Jens-Peter spoke so quietly that she could barely hear him.

She looked over the rail again. "Two streets. If we keep going this direction, there's a bridge with lots of lamps lit on it. And after that, a tall building."

Jens-Peter muttered something. She couldn't see his face to be sure, but he sounded worried and stressed. "I told him this was a bad idea. How far away is this bridge?"

Triss grimaced. She didn't really know official distances like leagues or miles. The zigane measured in terms of travel time. "I think it would take me a little more than half an hour to walk."

"Peh. I've seen you walk. Fine, there's no help for it. I'll have to take us up higher before I can start the engines. If I do it over the river the sound will be harder to locate." He reached over and started pulling levers and adjusting knobs.

"Um. I want to tell Barzo about all this. I think he could help."

"How? He can barely stand at the moment."

Triss waved her hand. "He was mostly starving. That *cude* is a stomach on legs. A lot like Dieter, actually." She shook her head. "Anyway, food and a good night's sleep have him mostly back to normal, with a few bruises. He's worked through worse. And he's better at acrobatics than me. In addition, he *also* lost his job because of this nonsense. So. He needs work, you need someone who can dangle from a rope with one hand and use a wrench with the other. Hire him."

Jens-Peter groaned. "I am already in too much trouble as it is. You do remember this is supposed to be completely secret, right?"

"You've already got me mixed in." Triss threw her arms wide. "You aren't worried about me keeping these secrets of yours, are you? I'll be his vouchsafe. He's family. If he agrees, it will be just like me saying it. This is a zigane custom. It means, if he does something wrong we both get punished. Family is the most important thing for us. He won't betray me and if he swears through me he won't betray you either."

Jens-Peter was silent for a while. "Dieter. I need you to watch the ground for me. As soon as you can't see the lights, tell me."

"Got it," Dieter croaked. "Are we going to die?"

"Not if I can help it." Jens-Peter sighed. "All right, if Barzo agrees. I even have some money to pay him, while it lasts. But why didn't you run with him? You could have escaped before von Koller showed up. You didn't have to come with us."

"Fräulein von Kitren gave me an advance on my wages," Triss said, surprised. It hadn't even occurred to her to let Jens-Peter and the others go alone. "I have to come. Besides, Barzo can't walk very far just yet."

"I haven't forgotten my promise," Jens-Peter said quietly. "And since Barzo got caught up in this mess too, I'll help him as well."

Triss carefully went back to Barzo, who was still awake and looking about in confusion. "Heya, *nadu*," she said in the zigane language. "Can you not sleep?"

"I see no trees, no buildings. Even at night I should see something, no? What river is this?"

"A river you have not traveled before," she said and laughed. "Can you move? Come out of the tent so we can talk together."

She had to help him in places since he still was moving stiffly, but shortly Barzo and Triss were together with Jens-Peter and Dieter.

Jens-Peter nodded at him. "Triss says you are even better at climbing than she is, and we need help. This boat we escaped on has to be repaired while we're on it. And it has to be kept a secret, so you can't tell anyone about it. Of course, you'll be paid."

Barzo blinked, then looked at her. His understanding of Preusan was fairly good, but limited to the level of vocabulary found among dockworkers. Jens-Peter spoke like a university student. Triss quickly translated, and Barzo nodded his head.

"You want me climbing, fixing? Ha, that easy! Carry heavy things, maybe not so good now." He rotated his arm experimentally and winced.

"You do understand you can't talk about this to anyone, even family?"

Barzo stared at Jens-Peter. "Is no harm to family, yes? Trisstela says not bad thing, yes? I no say to anyone."

"Wait, you want him to work *now*?" Dieter said, his expression troubled. "We are hundreds of feet above ground! It's too dangerous."

"Ey? So high?"

Triss sighed. "Barzo. Hold on to that rope and stand up. Look that way." She started to point, then realized he couldn't see much in the dark and took him by the shoulders and turned him.

Barzo stood. "What I see, eh? Oh." He was quiet for a long time. "How is ..." he switched to zigane. "Trisstela, these are *bruje* you travel with? We fly like birds in this boat?"

"No, not *bruje*. This is a boat made with magic anyone can use, and it does fly. Evil people want to steal it. We are all helping to keep it from them. It was damaged in the fight and needs work in the ropes above to go as it should." She pointed up to the dark, creaking shape of the levitation balloon.

"These evil ones, they take me and that other? You go to free him, yes?"

"Um." Triss switched back to Preusan to query Jens-Peter. "We're going to look for Mauer now, right?"

"Yes. He doesn't have to help with that, just the ship. Who knows what we'll find there. If we find him."

"I go with you" Barzo stated firmly. "Ah, is not just ..." He glanced at Triss. "Not just *obeza*. You go for this friend, caught with me? He no help, I still there. I promise, bring him help. *Ayo*, this works well, eh?"

"The lights are starting to look foggy," Dieter said, looking up from the viewscope.

Jens-Peter immediately pulled a lever down. "We'll drift up a little more, but that should be enough. Let's get out two lamps and stow as much of the gear as possible. Where's that building you saw, Triss?"

The wind must have shifted, because the building, now barely visible in the cloud, was well away from the ship. Triss considered what she had seen before and decided nothing higher was anywhere near them. Dieter found the shielded lamps and set them up on the deck so that even if people looked up at the sky, they wouldn't see them.

Triss found her bundle of belongings and stowed it first. She wouldn't put it past anybody on board to accidentally toss it or stuff it somewhere never to be found again. This way she knew where it was. Then she secured the food and blankets, again so she knew where they were. Dieter and Barzo handled the larger boxes and pieces of equipment, with direction from Jens-Peter, who remained at the controls.

The ship wasn't that large, so after an hour or so it was as organized as it was ever going to be. Jens-Peter started the smaller stern engine, which coughed alarmingly at first but then settled down to a soft puttering noise.

"Now we can steer. Where was that place Barzo escaped from again? Probably should start there, while it's dark, since it was inside the city."

"He's not there and hasn't been for a while," Dieter pointed out. "How will that blood-seeking needle thing find him? Unless he bled going out ..." His voice faded unhappily.

"I know, but I can't think of anywhere else to start searching."

Dieter shifted his seat. "Well, we can narrow it down. Willem found them gone around eight in the evening, and Barzo escaped at noon, roughly. It's unlikely the escape was detected immediately since Barzo got away without them giving chase. Call it eight hours maximum. They can't be riding horses since they have to carry Mauer around like a sack of potatoes, so a carriage or cart or something. I remember somebody saying the post coaches have stages about three leagues apart, and it takes an hour in good weather between them."

"So the farthest they could have gone is twenty-four leagues then. But that's a large circle to search, especially since we can't go that fast."

Triss closed her eyes, recalling the map. "What's a place that's ... um, fifteen leagues from Rogasti?"

Dieter and Jens-Peter looked at each other.

"Maybe Zossen?" Dieter suggested.

She nodded. In her mind she searched for that name and where it was in relation to the kidnapper's hideout. She could see where a circle would go from that central location.

"Well, I doubt they'd go east. That goes through the city itself and is more likely to be discovered. South and south-east also have lots of little towns. There's always people out in those places, again hard to hide. North or west. West has a forest. We'll need someplace to hide out during the day if there aren't any clouds."

Jens-Peter nodded. "Then let's start to the north and circle to the west. If we find any trace we'll follow it. Ah, and where are we now?"

Triss looked over the railing and could see nothing. They were truly engulfed in the clouds. Dieter had seen a few details when he looked which allowed her to mentally map their last location. "Probably off Ritterstrasse, near the Boulevard."

"Right, got it." He glanced at the compass mounted near the controls and turned a wheel slightly. Triss didn't feel any change in the movement of the ship. They were still floating serenely in the sky, in silence. "I'm going to start the other engines. It will still take more than an hour to get close, so you might as well get some rest."

It was cold, but they had a lot of blankets. Triss had slept in worse conditions. She closed her eyes and felt the gentle motion of the ship as she fell asleep.

CHAPTER 19

"It found him! It's moving!" Triss peered at the blood-seeking needle, sounding excited.

Dieter scoffed. "That's just the wind. Look, if I stand in front it stops!"

Jens-Peter sighed, wishing he had the thick wool coat he usually wore when going on night excursions on the levitation ship. He'd thought briefly about wrapping himself in a blanket, but it would make movement awkward. With *Einzl* in a fragile state, he might have to move quickly.

"Eh, you do not have ... for the lamp?" Barzo gestured with his hands. "The glass. To keep wind away." He had been awoken by the argument between Dieter and Triss but still lay on the deck.

"A chimney? Well, the only ones we have are in use by actual lamps ..." Dieter cast a look around. "Oh, but it doesn't have to be shaped like that exactly since there's no smoke to deal with. Anything clear should work, right?"

Much searching ensued. A bottle of beer was found but vetoed on the grounds of lacking good visibility. Jens-Peter wondered how that had gotten aboard and also how nobody had found it previously. Then Triss discovered the mostly empty bottle of ink he'd brought to help write his paper, and the bottle was clear even if the ink wasn't.

"There. Not a lot of room, but it doesn't really need it." Dieter examined his work with a critical eye. He'd even re-used the lid, poking a hole in the center with a nail to feed the string through. It was, as he said, a working solution that didn't need to be elegant.

"It doesn't sense anything." Triss had inkstains on her fingers from cleaning the bottle. She had been chosen as the navigator and thus inherited the detector needle.

"Not surprising. We still haven't reached the outer area."

The cloud level had varied a few times, enough that they had been able to check their bearings. The engines were not producing their full power, unfortunately. They would have to cut short their planned route or be caught out in daylight. He'd tried lowering the altitude but the change was so small that he couldn't detect it.

"I'm hungry," Dieter said after a while. "I hope we brought some food in all the confusion."

Triss looked up. "I grabbed that big basket. It definitely has bread and cheese, but it's heavy, so maybe there's more."

Dieter found the wicker basket and started rummaging around. "*Ach*, tins! Do we dare hope there's an opener on board? That we can find before we starve?"

"Before *you* starve? No. The rest of us might last a few days."

Dieter gave Jens-Peter a scowl before digging into the basket again. "Ah, and a jug of something. Oh, do we have water?"

"There's a cask up front. Don't drink it all. We need some for replenishing the boilers."

"Do we have anything to drink from?" Triss asked.

They did not, except for a very sad and dented tin cup that Jens-Peter had been keeping screwdrivers in. Triss pointed out the tins could be used as drinking containers after finding the tin opener thoughtfully included in the basket. Which ended up with Jens-Peter enjoying some bean-flavored hot water, but he was past caring. It was warm and didn't have metal shavings.

Triss operated the tiny heater for this, after Dieter showed her how, while Dieter watched the detector needle.

"It hasn't moved," he said when she finally sat down near the controls with everyone else. "See, I lined it up on this crack for reference."

"Assuming we find Mauer, what do we do then? These people won't just let him go because we ask them." Triss dunked a crust of bread in her tin of hot water. "We'll need help."

"Send a telegram." Jens-Peter wished they had a better, or at least quicker, method. "Asgaya gave me a safe address."

"But if they move him, like they did this time?"

He scowled. "We'll just have to keep following. As long as we have the detector and the ship, we can do that."

He braced for more questions but Triss just nodded and finished her hot water. Getting to her feet, she grasped one of the guy wires and leaned over the railing, staring at the ground below for several minutes. She closed her eyes, apparently to check the map in her head. "We aren't in the right place anymore. Too far north."

"Hang on, I'll adjust course. Probably wind shifted us a bit." Jens-Peter checked the compass and turned the wheel. They couldn't be too far off course; they weren't moving very fast. Unfortunately.

Dieter sat up sharply. "Hey, it moved!"

Everyone stared at the detector. It definitely was no longer aligned with the crack in the board it was resting on.

"It didn't move very much," Triss said. "When it was tested with the blood dust it moved a lot."

Dieter reached out and rotated the glass jar. After drifting slightly the needle again pointed in the new direction, same as before. "It's sensing *something*, it seems. But not very strongly."

Jens-Peter felt a sudden surge of optimism. "Yeah, but we're detecting enough! If we just follow it, we'll find Mauer. I wonder if we can use this to find out how far away he is? Triss is right; when the blood was right there, the deviation was quick and strong."

Dieter thought for a moment. "How about how long it takes to adjust? If I move it like I did, it takes time because of twisting the string." Triss gave him a blank look. "Torsion."

Her expression indicated she thought he was making it up, but she dutifully noted "response time" every half-hour. She also did a regular check for any landmarks.

"We'll be hitting the post road soon," she said, moving away from the rail. "Where do you think they are going?"

Jens-Peter shrugged. "Probably not a big city, if they want to hide."

"Small towns are harder. They know who belongs and who doesn't." Triss wrapped her blanket more snugly around her. It was bitterly cold now, and Jens-Peter was miserable. "If it was me, I'd rather hide in a city."

Jens-Peter picked up the pocket watch. Four hours past midnight. In winter, dawn was more than two hours away but at their speed, they needed to start finding a place to hide. Just a bit more, so they could be sure they were in the right direction. He hoped Mauer was warmer than he was.

"Dieter. Take the controls."

Dieter blinked and got up. "What is it, are you tired?"

"I need to set up the winch." Of course, the real hook anchor was missing. Jens-Peter had to improvise something that would work out of scrap and spare parts. The really crucial thing was rope. It had to be long enough, strong enough, and able to fit through the winch opening.

"Are you planning to lower someone to the ground?" Triss looked dubious.

"Lowering the whole ship, if it works."

He'd been thinking about it all night. They couldn't continue without altitude control. Moving only at night left too much time for Mauer's kidnappers to get away, and they could run into clouds that blocked them from navigating. Even if it delayed them, they needed to fix it. Repairs at this height were just too risky to count on. Even if Triss and Barzo were amazing acrobats, it was too cold to do that *and* do precision repair work on mechanisms they had never seen before.

So, he'd figured out that if he deliberately snagged the hook anchor in a sturdy tree and used the winch, he could *pull* the ship down. Except that, as he soon discovered, they didn't have nearly enough rope to do it. Maybe tying everything together would get it close, but the knots would jam the winch.

"We're maintaining constant altitude, right?" Dieter was puzzling this out as soon as Jens-Peter explained what he wanted to do. "So if we can't go down, go somewhere the ground is … up."

"Oh!" Thinking about it like that, it made sense. Height was a relative measurement after all, so they just needed a hill. With a tall, sturdy tree at the very top.

Triss huddled against the bulwarks and watched the world spin rapidly around her. This was a mistake, as her mild queasiness ramped to full nausea. How long was Jens-Peter going to do this if he didn't succeed? She recognized the stubborn expression on his face. He had figured out something he considered particularly clever, and he was going to get it to work no matter what.

"These *gadje*, are you sure they are not crazy?" Barzo wanted to know. He was awakened by the rapid, sharp motion of the ship, and seeing Triss in distress, he was unable to stop worrying.

A whoop came from Dieter on the prow, followed by a muttered curse. "Almost had it, but it came loose. Try again."

Triss whimpered and closed her eyes.

"What does he do?"

"He wants to wrap the rope with the hook around a tree. So he … urk … spins the ship to get the hook to fly out."

"Trisstela."

"Yes?"

"How does this boat stay up in the air?"

Triss nodded, hissed, and stopped moving. "There is magic in that." She pointed at the compressed bag. "Made small, the ship goes higher. Larger, it goes lower. There are also engines that push it around. I was climbing on the roof at night and saw it get stuck and helped out. And then the god of travel and the god of luck got drunk together, and the rope I pulled loose pulled me up." She sighed. She couldn't leave someone in trouble like that, especially on a rooftop. But when could she have avoided this *zumala*? It couldn't have been because of the books, could it? She always put them back in the right place and never damaged them!

"They did not put you back?"

"Only when they were sure of me. Because this is a big secret, like they told you. Their Great Chief has said it cannot be known."

Barzo sobered at the mention of the King. "Aiy, it is not good for you to be seen by such people. It brings bad luck."

"I know, but what can I do? I am already doing what I can to avert the bad luck of losing my position. And now you lost yours as well."

The ship spun hard again, but this time, it stopped with a jerk. Tools and gear fell to the deck.

"Dieter! Is it holding?"

Dieter leaned halfway out of the ship. "Uh … yeah! It wrapped around, and one tine is hooked on top!"

"Finally!" Jens-Peter sagged for a moment, then snapped upright with determination. "Right, now let's get the winch going!"

It was much less dizzying, but the process of lowering the ship by winch was nerve-wracking. Slowly inching down, the manual winch got harder and harder to turn the closer they got to the ground. Barzo was the strongest of them, and even he had to rest after a while.

"All right, I think that's the best we can do for now." Jens-Peter looked down. The top of the tree was a little higher than the rail of the ship. It was a sturdy pine, close to the crest of the hill. "Let's tie it down fore and aft. Triss, can you climb down this tree, or will we need the rope ladder?"

Triss looked at the tree dubiously. Pine trees had lots of smaller branches that didn't always hold a lot of weight, unlike oaks. "I can do it with a rope, but you can't. Better use the ladder. Unless you want to do the winch again?"

Nobody wanted to use the winch any more, so ladder it was. Triss went ahead and marked the branches strong enough to bear weight by tying a rag to them. She was followed by Barzo, then Dieter and Jens-Peter. Looking around, she saw a stream in the valley below and a meadow next to it. The hillside had several large boulders emerging from the soil, and a breeze made the location chilly.

Dieter shivered. "Do we dare try a fire? It's not that far from the post road, so smoke might bring attention."

"If you use dry wood, it won't be noticeable." Triss walked to the edge of a small cliff and looked around. At the base were more tall boulders, in a rough circle. "We can camp down there."

It had been a long night for all of them but especially Jens-Peter who could not nap like the others. Triss got a fire going and tied some of the blankets over the rocks to make a rough shelter. It would keep out wind, diffuse any smoke, and keep the heat closer. Jens-Peter was already stretched out on the ground inside.

"We should get supplies if we can. The food we have won't last long. It's too clear to fly now, but it might cloud up later. I'm going to try and get our altitude control fixed." His eyes drifted shut, then snapped open. "Oh, and we should probably tell Asgaya where we are, just in case. Where are we?" He turned to look at Triss.

Triss reviewed the mental map. "I think the town we saw in the distance is Schopsdorf. We're on the Baerlen-Magde postal road, definitely." She closed her eyes to focus. If they kept going on the post road, then … "Um, we should see if we can find a map too. The one I saw in the warehouse ends thirty leagues ahead."

"Oh, that's a problem." Dieter rubbed his head. "So, we definitely need to pay the town a visit. Who should go?"

"Whoever can't work on fixing *Einzl*," Jens-Peter mumbled.

Barzo came up the hill with an armload of firewood. Triss gave him a serious look. He was limping, but not badly, and it would probably be better for him if he were off his feet and hanging from ropes instead. "Are you well to work?" she asked in zigane, gesturing at the floating levitation ship above them.

Barzo leaned back, one large hand over his eyes. Barzo had not really seen the levitation ship before since he had been brought in unconscious and then spent the rest of the time either asleep or in the dark. His eyes went wide, and he tilted his head back to take in the huge canopy bag with the bronze lattice mesh and rope webbing. He grinned. "Aiye, just move it over the water, and even a fall won't hurt."

Triss scowled. "Freezing will kill as well as broken bones. Do not grieve the family, eh?" Switching back to Preusan, she glanced at Jens-Peter and Dieter. "I'll go into town. How do I send a message? And I'll need money."

Jens-Peter sat up stiffly, going through his coat pockets until he pulled out a purse and a scrap of paper. "This is a telegram address. Use it just like that, and make up anything you like for the message. They put the town location in the telegram itself by default. There's an office, and you speak to a clerk to get a form, then write it and hand it to the clerk again."

It all sounded needlessly complex. Why couldn't she just tell the clerk the message and save a lot of bother? And would she seem out of place in this telegraph office, enough that people would ask questions?

Triss sighed. It wasn't like they had any choice, and taking one of the others would definitely draw attention. She'd just have to do her best.

To that end, she climbed back up the ladder and found a wicker basket. It didn't have a handle but she made one with a piece of rope. She also got out both of the long scarves from her bag of belongings. A lot of the country women wore scarves tied under their chins in winter, and she could use the other to kilt up her skirts which she had also seen them do if they had a long way to walk. It would help her blend in a little or at least be an excuse for not knowing how they did things in the town.

Back down on the ground, she took the money and the message and stowed them both safely in her inner pocket. "From what I saw of the map,

I should return in three hours, four at the most."

"You take some food, eh?" Barzo reminded her. "No good, you get cold or hungry on the way."

Nodding, she took a sausage and a roll from the supplies they had brought down. She wasn't that hungry, but Barzo was right—it was cold, and there was no point leaving food if they had it.

The countryside was more hilly than the area around Baerlen, or the southern farmland the troupe had traveled in. It was even a little pretty, though bare, and the snow and ice on the road minimal. It was true there were some definite advantages to traveling by levitation ship. Judging from the huge frozen ruts, going by cart would have been extremely uncomfortable. And much slower.

By the time she reached the outskirts of the town, Triss was warm enough to feel comfortable again, if a bit tired. She hadn't been walking enough in Baerlen to keep in practice.

People were beginning to stir and go outside to do chores, and Triss found an old gentleman who directed her to the telegraph office. If she finished quickly, she could ask around while looking for a map. If the people noticed any odd travelers or strangers—not including her—it might be useful to know.

The telegraph office had a very shiny, newly lettered sign as an attempt to make up for the fact that it was in a very old half-timbered building with a slight lean to one side. The clerk was also quite young and eager to please. Triss wondered, coming in the otherwise empty office, if he was worried that no one wanted to send telegrams.

Triss quickly filled out the form and brought it to the clerk, who fussily added up the word charges. She had to stifle a gasp at the cost—a month's wages, just to send ten words?

"I-if it's too much, we can remove a few words," the clerk said, blushing.

"No, that's what the mistress wanted sent," Triss said hastily, stopping the motion of his pen. She could tell he was very curious why a young, poor girl like her was sending a telegram. A good story would stop questions and gossip. "If it's changed, I could get in trouble." She blinked as if she were fighting back tears, and the clerk sighed.

"Ah well, it can't be helped then. Oh, the return address is empty. If you expect a reply, that should be filled in."

Triss felt a spike of irritation. This clerk was too helpful. "Mistress is traveling, so we don't have an address, not yet. I was sent ahead to do this. She didn't mention a reply."

"Oh." The clerk took the coins Triss had put on the counter. "Um, if your mistress will be sending other telegrams on her trip you can take some forms back with you. To save time."

"I can? Thank you! That is very helpful." *Free paper!* Triss exulted and took a few of the forms to place in her basket before leaving. It was nice sturdy paper, too, better than she could usually afford. The cost of the telegram seemed less extortionate now.

Noticing several cook and maid-type people on the street with full baskets, Triss went in the direction they were coming from and soon found the market street. It was late for the market so the best goods were gone. That just meant she could haggle with the sellers for the remaining goods and get a better price since they were often slightly damaged or the stall owner didn't want to carry it back.

She looked at her haul: a handful of potatoes, a hambone from a kindly butcher, three day-old bread loaves, a packet of butter, and best of all a small battered pot from a second-hand stall. It would fit on *Einzl*'s small cookstove as well as the fire at the camp, and she could make soup with the hambone.

Then she found a map for her traveling (and increasingly eccentric) mistress and with the map, asked the locals for "a quiet, isolated house" that her fictional mistress wanted to rent. She could have made up a different excuse, but in towns like this one, the bored telegraph clerk would likely be spreading her story half an hour after he left work. With a consistent tale, she would be a one-day wonder and forgotten. Caught in a lie, however, she would become a mysterious and dangerous stranger that could be discussed for a month or more.

The map was very crude compared to the map of Baerlen and environs from the warehouse office, but Triss wasn't too worried. The post road and towns were marked, and any other roads would be small dirt paths to farmhouses and unlikely to be where Markus was held. Her attempt to find likely hideouts did not yield much, but the few she did hear about might work for *their* hideout needs later.

She picked up a few more necessities such as matches and the like in the time remaining. She wanted to get lamp oil, but her purchases were already heavy, and here in the country the oil-seller only dispensed to containers people brought themselves. They could live without it for a few days.

By the time she returned to the campsite, the basket felt like it was full of rocks, and her feet were sore. She had gotten soft, working as a maid.

"Oh, right on time!" Dieter was sitting near the fire, whittling and tossing the scraps to burn. "Did you have any trouble?"

Triss pulled out the map. "I sent the message. I also asked around. There are two old houses, empty, north of the town and accessible by the post road. Nobody noticed an unusual carriage going through but if it was at night they might not have seen it." She unpacked the rest of the basket. "Here, fill this with water and I'll start some soup." She handed the pot to Dieter, who stared at it with a puzzled expression, then shrugged and headed down to the stream.

Barzo saw the hambone and smiled. Then he saw the pot, and without Triss needing to tell him anything, limped out to find some green saplings to make a tripod for the fire. They had both done enough rough cooking to know the pot could not be put directly on the flames, and damp wood would not catch fire easily.

Triss eyed the immobile lump that was the sleeping Jens-Peter and decided not to forcibly wake him up. He'd gone all night without any sleep, unlike the rest of them. A few more minutes wouldn't hurt.

The potatoes were cut and added to the hambone in the pot and placed over the fire, Triss got up and nudged Jens-Peter with her foot. Hearing a faint moan, she nudged harder.

"All right, all right! Stop kicking me." Jens-Peter sat up, blinking groggily. He stared at the fire for a moment then out at the sky. "Oh. It's already daylight? Time to work!"

Barzo and Dieter watched him stumble out of the shelter and up the hill.

"This crazy *gadje,* I can help him?"

"It is ropes in the air. You do not even have to catch anyone," Triss said in zigane. "You can do it well. Go and help."

Barzo scrubbed his head, looking embarrassed. "His words I do not always understand. He speaks different, aiye?"

It was true that Barzo's Preusan was almost a different dialect than what the students used. "Aiye, he learns from books, this one. They speak like this. Come, I will go with you for a while and help you learn his words."

The soup would take a few hours to cook. It should be safe enough to leave, and she could add extra water just in case.

Everyone climbed back up to the levitation ship. Barzo studied the rigging, tugging on the cables and ropes, and pointed to different things. Triss translated his questions, and Jens-Peter's replies. Then Jens-Peter sketched out a gear mechanism on the back of one of the telegram forms.

"This is the thing that needs fixing. When I pull this lever, it loosens the ratchet, and then this control allows it to go in or out. The ratchet bit isn't working correctly, so we can't control our altitude. Also it is made of bronze since it is right next to the levitator bag. You have to be careful and not use too much force or it can break. Not like iron. Now the tools are here ..." He picked up a pair of pliers from the box and went through all the names and how the tools were used.

"They use all these? How can I carry all this and climb too?" Barzo looked a little worried.

Jens-Peter rubbed his head. "I guess you'll have to come down and get the tool you need."

"That will take forever, and not good for his injured leg." Triss switched to zigane. "Eh, we do this too, yes? Go up, I will show him." It shouldn't just be Barzo learning new words, should it?

Barzo ran and jumped, fluidly grabbing the rope mesh and swinging his legs up and *into* the mesh above. In a few seconds he was dangling upside down on the curve of the canopy, supported by his legs, which were wound around the rope mesh, and with both hands free.

"*Hup'le!*" He called down to Triss, who took a hammer lying on the ground and hefted it in her hand.

"*Hoyt!*" Triss tossed the hammer. Barzo caught it easily and swung it at the astonished spectators.

"This easy!" Barzo grinned. Then he grabbed the net, swung his legs free, and climbed down until he could jump off the canopy to the deck.

"I told you he was better than me," Triss whispered to Jens-Peter.

CHAPTER 20

"I'm trying again!" Jens-Peter firmly tugged the release. "Did it work?"

"Na, no good!" Barzo's faint voice came from up top. After a bit, the ropes vibrated and he slid down to the deck. "This thing, I can see it move, but it no touch the other side." He handed over a bronze lever with serrations on one edge.

"There wasn't anything else there?" Barzo shook his head. "No wonder it wasn't working. The whole assembly broke off. Great. That's a custom-made part too." Then Jens-Peter started thinking. It was true that he couldn't use the console now since only one side was connected. But how many times did they actually need to change altitude? Could they make do with a manual release? Opening, if they were careful about it, would happen anyway as the other controls worked and the bag expanded. The compression grid would be forced open. It was the closing, for higher altitude, that might stick. It would take extra force.

"Here. Take this metal cable and fasten it to the holes in the …. um, the place this came from. Looks like this." Jens-Peter did a quick sketch. Barzo studied it, nodded, and gracefully leaped up into the rigging again.

He had to rummage around and eventually scavenge a metal eyebolt to run the cable through, but then he could feed the end of the cable through it and into the winch mechanism. It was horribly crude, and it meant they couldn't use the winch for anything else, but it *worked*.

They practiced while *Einzl* was still tied up to the tree. It turned out Barzo was a disaster at running the winch, nearly getting his fingers jammed, but he could climb at a moment's notice. Dieter, on the other hand, was quite good with it, and after an hour or so the altitude adjustment was nearly as smooth as when the controls weren't broken.

Feeling daring, Jens-Peter cast off and let the ship drift away from the hill and over the stream. He still didn't want to fully expand the envelope,

145

so he couldn't bring the ship all the way to ground level, but it was certainly close enough that the shorter rope ladder could be used. He drifted the ship to the meadow near the stream and then had Dieter and Barzo tie it up safely before descending. There was ice between the rocks and withered grass of the stream edge, so he walked carefully until he reached clear ground.

"Are we going to leave now?" Triss looked up from the pot she was stirring. It smelled delicious, and Jens-Peter was suddenly aware he hadn't eaten anything.

"We'll wait for dusk. The sky is too clear today." He was also surprised at how long they had been working. It was worth it, though. Now they could actually *use* the ship instead of flailing around.

The four of them quickly disposed of the potato-and-hambone soup Triss had made, along with hunks of bread. To his surprise Triss insisted on bringing the hambone along, in the pot, when they packed up.

"We may need it again," she said darkly. "You people eat like wolves in winter."

"It *is* winter!" Dieter ducked his head. "So which way are we going? Back to the post road?"

There was no point retracing where they'd already searched, but they had to be sure they could still trace Mauer. "Check with the needle. If we can still sense him, we'll use that first."

Triss quickly pulled out the wooden box and assembled the glass jar and the string with the hanging needle. "Looks much like it did before," she reported after staring at it for a few minutes. "Almost exactly."

"Then we follow it."

It would save a few leagues while the light remained and also serve to check that the kidnappers were staying with the post road. Jens-Peter checked the wind, and grimaced. It would have been truly bad luck to have headwinds, but he was hoping for an assist, and there was not a breath of wind. They had fuel but not as much as he would have liked, and even if Triss had been able to carry it he was reluctant to buy it here in a small town. It was unusual enough that it might be noticed. They would simply have to make do with what they had and go at half speed.

He wanted to go as fast as the engines would allow. Mauer was still a prisoner, and they had no idea if he'd been injured—accidentally or deliberately.

By now it was fully dark, and he was remembering exactly how cold it could get in the levitation ship. Then Triss suddenly sat up.

"It moved. A lot!" She pointed, and Jens-Peter quickly steered that direction. "Um, again?"

After a few minutes, it was clear they were circling something.

"I don't see any lights, or people," Dieter whispered. "There's a tree and bushes."

He can't be dead. They took him for a reason, so they wouldn't kill him, right? Please?

Even if nothing were down there it would be a good idea to practice an altitude change. "Ready with the cable," Jens-Peter said quietly. Dieter tugged on the cable, making sure it was attached to the winch, then glanced over at the console.

Jens-Peter took hold of the altitude control with one hand and raised the other, and as he lowered the lever, he lowered his hand. As they had practiced, Dieter ran the winch to match. It wasn't perfect, with a few shuddering jerks due to the uneven expansion, but *Einzl* slowly descended to a reasonable ten-foot height.

"Let's go and see." Jens-Peter found a wrench and tucked it into his belt before descending. Barzo was already down and looking around.

"No one here," Barzo said.

"Take the lamp." Triss lowered it down on a rope. "The needle says something is definitely there."

"Bring it down, then. I don't see anything." It was a good thing. They would have seen a body if it were there. So it had to be something smaller. He really hoped so … and tried not to think of lots of blood and a moved body.

With Triss and the needle, they finally found a tiny white bundle tucked in the fork of a tree. A piece of paper with drunken letters scrawled over it was wrapped in a torn scrap of handkerchief. The cloth had bloodstains.

"Well, now we know he was here. What does it say?" Dieter peered over Jens-Peter's shoulder.

Jens-Peter squinted. Triss held the lamp closer, but it didn't help. "'Liver'? No, 'alive.' Then I think that's 'tuoma'…"

"'Two Men.'" Triss frowned. "Then something about a seat?"

"Hid under seat. WM, his initials. They are hiding him under a seat? Or are there two men hiding under a seat?"

"Sounds crowded. If I were a kidnapper, I'd stick Mauer somewhere he couldn't be seen. He's telling us there are only two kidnappers." Jens-Peter sighed. "He's not here, anyway. Now how are we going to track him if the needle is pointing to that piece of handkerchief? Wait, Dieter, you're a magic student. What should we do?"

Dieter stared at him. "Do you have any idea how advanced this magic is? Asgaya is a *schutzmagus* and nearly mage level. Never mind that the spell's been placed in an object, which I didn't even know was *possible*."

"Oh."

Triss shifted her feet, then mumbled, "If the needle is protected by that silver tissue paper, would it work the other way? Wrap the cloth, instead of the needle."

It turned out Triss had to wrap the scrap of bloodstained handkerchief in several layers of the silvery tissue to completely block the needle from detecting it. Jens-Peter, impatient at the delay, wanted to simply burn it.

"We don't even know if that would work," Triss pointed out. "What if it's burned but the magical thing in the blood is still there?" Of course the *bruje* hadn't explained precisely how the detection worked. All Triss was sure about was the blood being the most important factor.

"Is also very bad luck for the *gadje*," Barzo muttered in zigane, looking uncomfortable. Magic with blood was already dangerously close to black magic, which the zigane would refuse to even speak of and feared greatly.

"Worse luck if we are late to find him," Triss pointed out. "He gave the blood to us willingly so we could rescue him. It does not have *mala kru*."

Barzo frowned, then nodded reluctantly. Fortunately, at that point Triss succeeded in using the silver tissue, and the question of burning or destroying the blood was no longer an issue.

With the strong source shielded, they could look for the next trace. Of course when Triss found it, the new signal was quite faint, and they spent nearly an hour getting back on track.

"I think we're getting close to one of the empty houses," Triss said after hanging over the railing for a minute. She pointed. "It's over there."

"With the white walls?" Jens-Peter turned the wheel slightly, and the ship drifted on a new course. "Looks like it has three stories and a steep roof."

"Sounds right." Triss leaned over the railing. The building showed no sign of life and also caused no twitch in the detector needle.

"Looks empty."

Triss sighed and nodded glumly. "That's what the people in town said."

From the memorized map she was very much aware of how close they were to the troupe's wintering location in Eisenach. As tempted as she was to go and find them, she and Barzo would just be more mouths to feed if they did. Besides, Mata Sheri would give both of them a blistering lecture if not a beating. It was better to stay and hope she would eventually get a decent job. Besides, Fräulein von Kitren had paid her for three months, so she couldn't abandon Jens-Peter now.

They passed by the second house she'd heard about, but the needle never moved, and Jens-Peter decided to keep going. If they still couldn't find Mauer they could go back and check more carefully.

A few hours from dawn, the needle got another strong signal, and again they circled around. This time there was a pond and a rutted area where vehicles had stopped, presumably to water horses. This time the note and scrap of bloodstained cloth were under a rock.

"His handwriting is horrible," Dieter said while squinting at the note.

Triss stared at him, eyes wide with incredulity. "He's a prisoner! It's amazing he's able to write anything, and he's remembering to leave a blood trail for us too."

"Yes, yes, but if it's so important he should make it so it can be read, right?"

"Oh, let me look." Triss got up and peered over Dieter's shoulder. She'd gotten accustomed to Mauer's handwriting after seeing so much of it recently. Even allowing for haste, it still seemed bad. Was it dark when he was writing? His captors would definitely be suspicious if they saw him writing, but he still was managing to hide the notes without being detected. So he must be writing the notes beforehand, then quickly leaving them with a scrap of handkerchief when he was allowed out of captivity. For, she presumed, an urgent necessity even captors could not prevent. "How far apart were these two notes?"

"You're the one with a map in her head," Jens-Peter grinned, then frowned, thinking. "Ah, it was eight hours, at half speed. You think they might be making regular stops?"

"If there aren't people watching, probably." Triss focused on the scrawled writing again. "I think it says … 'Tall thin one is magician. Both act strange. Not sane. Freeze me but it …'" She stared harder. "Maybe 'warzone?' No, that doesn't make sense. Oh, 'wears off early. Going master place.'"

Barzo sat up on the railing. "Yes, the freezing they did to us. It becomes weaker with time. I am thinking four hours, maybe little longer?"

"So they think he's immobile," Dieter said, "but instead he can move and writes in the dark. But he can't get free. What is the master place?"

"No idea. Their master's headquarters maybe?" Jens-Peter looked at the sky then at the rest of them. "Good news for a change; we've got cloud cover, so we can keep flying during the day. If Triss is right and they are making regular stops, it won't be complicated. Follow the indicator and stay aloft. We might be able to catch up to them! I'm going to get some sleep. Barzo, do you think you can steer?"

Barzo grinned. "This? Go you, and rest well. My *nadua* will tell me if we go adrift."

"Good. Then, Dieter, you should sleep too. I'll need you later for any descent."

Triss made sure the detector needle in its glass bottle was securely in place next to the compass and aligned with their current course before going to the tiny stove and making some thin, hambone-flavored soup. She handed a tin mug of soup to Barzo before wrapping herself in blankets and sitting nearby. Jens-Peter was already gently snoring in the bow next to the unconscious Dieter.

"We go on like this, we get even closer to our people," Barzo said softly in zigane. "Last I hear, the wintering place, they go by Einbeck to get there. What would we say to them?"

So Barzo had also noticed their location. "We don't." Triss sipped the hot soup and shivered. "There is nothing you or I could say to soothe Mata Sheri. Even if all the money I sent reached her, she will still be angry at both of us. And we can't explain without speaking of what must be kept silent." She gestured at the looming bulk of the levitator bag.

Barzo went pale. "Truth. Sheri will be angry. Even more so if she learns why we are here. Rescuing a *gadje?* Is that not for the men of the law to do? Are they so weary they must make us do their work?" His tone had gone high and forceful, imitating a certain voice.

Triss choked, stifling a laugh, then nervously looked around. She *knew* Sheri could not possibly be on the ship, but a lifetime of habit was hard to break. "Aiye, sometimes being sent away is not so bad."

"Not so bad? *Nadua*, what do we do when we find this person? The people that take him will not give him back for asking. He is *gadje* of status, him. To do what they did earns them prison or worse. He says there are only two, but where they are going, I think there will be more."

"So we find him before they reach this place." Barzo gave her a strained smile. She knew what he was worried about. Even if they did catch up to Mauer, it would not be easy. One of the men was a magician. They would figure something out because they had to. Mauer had helped her, after all. She looked at the needle and saw that they had gone slightly off course. "He's that way," Triss said, pointing.

She hoped it was true.

CHAPTER 21

The next drop was almost exactly where they had expected, and at a similar distance as the previous location. This time, however, they found no useful information other than that they were still on the right track.

"I hope this was not conveying anything crucial," Jens-Peter said, holding up the sodden scrap of paper. If there was any writing, it had long vanished.

Dieter shrugged. "He's still alive and able to leave messages. That's good to know anyway. I guess we keep going then?"

"We don't have much food," Triss said from the ship, above. " And I've run out of map again. There's a town ahead. We should get some supplies."

Jens-Peter frowned. He knew she was right, but he really didn't want to delay even for a minute. The sky was not looking good either—patchy clouds that could clear up any time. On the other hand, if he could get fuel they could go farther and faster. He eyed Barzo.

"Have your injuries healed enough to carry something heavy?"

Barzo grinned and flexed an arm. "All good. Maybe not big rock, eh?"

"Just some canisters of benzine if you can find it. And if it won't cause comment."

"What do people use benzine for if not for engines?" Dieter wanted to know.

"They must use it for *something*, or it wouldn't be sold in shops, dunderhead!"

"Yes, but what?" Dieter pointed at Barzo. "He'll need a plausible story if they ask. And don't say he can just pretend not to understand. That will also draw attention! Oh, maybe he can say he's going to go around peddling benzine …" His voice drifted off into convoluted thought.

Jens-Peter gave him a doubtful look. "I've never heard of anyone going door to door selling benzine. Maybe he has his own engine?"

"I'm telling you, we don't want the word 'engine' to come up at all! All right, what about horseshoe polish?"

"In this weather, who would be polishing horseshoes?"

Triss heaved a sigh. "It's used in cleaning, you know. For removing grease stains. I'll just say I'm taking in washing and he's helping me carry it so I'm getting a lot at once."

Now this actually made sense. Jens-Peter had not realized laundry was so technical, but it was a good thing. Nobody would look at Triss and think of mechanical-magical airships.

"I also want to send another telegram. And this time, wait for a while and see if they will send a response. So we'll rendezvous on the post road. Dieter and I will keep searching, but we'll come back and find you."

"Is it a good idea to delay?" Dieter asked, doubtful.

Jens-Peter rubbed his head. "I get the feeling we are getting close to their destination. And even if they don't reach it, we might catch up to them. I don't want to meet up without some help or the prospect of help on the way."

"So how do we know which town has a telegraph office?"

Now that he did know, courtesy of many, many night flights. "The telegraph wires. They follow the post road here, and if there's an office, a branch line connects up. You can't see the wires in the dark, but the posts show up fairly well, and the white insulators."

Dieter nodded. "So if we see a branch line ahead, we'll drop off the two of them and keep going. Sounds good."

Jens-Peter thought of something else. "Triss, do you have any of those forms left?" He turned his head and discovered she was tying a rope between two of the support cables, one on either side of the ship, and Barzo was draping a blanket over the rope.

"It's to keep the wind out," she said in response to his stare. "I have a few forms left." Triss took them out of her pocket and glanced at them, then looked more carefully under the light of the lamp. "Oh. They have the name of the previous town on them. Will they refuse to take it?"

"Doesn't matter. You can copy it again on a new form, right?" He could see her expression brighten with this thought and knew she had realized she could take *more* extra forms for writing on. He stifled a grin. "You and Barzo should rest now. I'm going to check the telegraph lines and then find a place to set you down."

He liked doing high-altitude scouting. It was quiet, and he could see everything laid out like a real map. He slowed the engine speed going over the town, just in case it could be heard, which also allowed him to check things out carefully.

There was, in fact, a branch line—not surprising given the size of the town. The more difficult part was finding a location for lowering the ship without being seen. All the forests in the immediate area had been cut down and the town was surrounded by fields, mostly with livestock that were probably cows. Cows weren't bad, in his limited experience. Geese, now. Geese were a danger to all humanity and should probably be exterminated if they weren't so delicious.

"I think this is the best we can do. Wake them up, Dieter." It was a smaller field, but there was a good-sized tree offering concealment from the road and the nearest house, if they were quick. And there was only one cow in this field.

Strangely, Triss was not happy with his choice.

"No! Anywhere but that one!"

"Why? It's just one cow!"

Barzo was doubled over with laughter. "Aiye, that is a bull, *gadje!* He have bad temper anyway, and now you insult his manhood! *Zumala!*"

"I cannot believe that idiot didn't know about bulls," Triss grumped as they walked back down the road to the town.

Barzo shrugged. "How much has that city-born *gadje* seen of farms? We go everywhere and stay on their fields. Of course we know more."

"I suppose ... but still! How is he even still alive?"

"The god of fools loves his children?" Barzo grinned at her, then sighed. "Ah, Trisstela. We go together, your hair ..."

Yes, her hair. And her face. She was not worthy of comment on her own, but put next to the bronze skin and heavy black hair of Barzo, it could cause trouble. Barzo was clearly zigane blood, and she was clearly not. *He's still my kin, no matter what I look like.*

This was not the first time, and Triss knew what to do. She tied the kerchief around her head tightly, concealing her blonde hair. Meanwhile Barzo had burned a willow switch, and she used the soot to darken her eyebrows. A mixture of mud and soot smeared on the part of her face exposed by the scarf wound loosely about her neck served to make the contrast in skin tone less obvious.

"We should go to the telegraph office first if we have to stay in this town to wait for a reply," Triss said once they were within the streets of stone buildings. It could be her imagination, but the people they encountered seemed to stare at them with curiosity mixed with worry. An attitude she had not seen before, but she hadn't gone with Barzo.

"I go by myself?" Barzo whispered.

"No. And speak Preusan, not zigane." It was safer to stay together. They both knew how to spot true hostility as opposed to general unfriendliness, and she didn't sense that the people here were going to cause trouble.

It was early, and they had to wait a while for the telegraph office to open. This gave them plenty of time to overhear gossip on the street, and even a curious "... *More* zigane? Are they visiting the town for some reason?" But then the telegraph office opened, and by the time Triss looked back, the speaker was no longer in sight.

Triss felt quite at home in the telegraph office now. She sent the message, paid, and even remembered to ask when the office would close for the day before taking a handful of forms and stuffing them in her pocket. She reminded herself that she owed *obeza* for them. Even if she had paid money, it was for the message she had sent. The paper was a gift, and she should give a gift in turn.

"We get food now?"

Triss shook her head. "I don't know how much benzine costs here. It was not cheap in Baerlen. The housekeeper would only let us use it for really bad stains. Whatever money we have left will determine what kind of food we can buy."

Asgaya had given them a goodly amount of money, but between expensive telegrams and feeding three large male appetites in cold weather, it was disappearing at a rapid rate. She hoped that their message would get a reply along the lines of "Coming soon, bringing supplies and funds."

They found benzine, after asking at several shops, at a warehouse specializing in lamp oil and other combustible substances. The owner was an old, bent man with disordered tufts of white hair and a mischievous look in his eyes.

"I don't usually sell to individual customers in the shop," he commented with a raised eyebrow. "Wouldn't it be easier to get a small bottle of the stuff for this laundry of yours?"

"It's a long walk, especially in cold weather, and I ran out last week. Since my cousin is here to help me, I wanted to always have enough on hand." Triss tried to appear like a shy and timid girl, the kind who wouldn't want to go into town on her own.

"I just thought, since you folk live in those little carts, that space would be precious." The old man took the filled canister, carefully screwed the cap on tightly, and started filling the second canister. Triss and Barzo exchanged worried glances. "But if that other fella didn't find the missing cart, maybe you are staying in a house at present?"

"Other fellow?" Triss asked and noticed that Barzo was looking away and shoving his hands in his pockets.

"Zigane, like you. Had a grey hat with a yellow feather and a long drooping mustache. He was asking around if anyone had seen this cart, see. You're not with him?"

Barzo still wasn't saying anything. Triss smiled. "Ah, we travel all around you know. That sounds like a distant relative of ours. I hope he is well." And what was Toa Babik doing here? She was sure it was him; no one else had that yellow feather.

"Seemed to be in health, aside from worry about that cart." The old man closed off the second canister and wiped both carefully with an old rag. "There you go, two guilders if you please."

"How long ago he pass through?" Barzo asked.

"Ah, was it two days ago? No, three, it was market day." The old man smiled gently, his teasing manner gone. "Don't fret. A green cart with gold and red trim? Who wouldn't notice such a thing going by? I'm sure he'll find it eventually."

If she hadn't been suspicious, she would have missed Barzo's sharp intake of breath and briefly frozen expression. Before, he had been trying to conceal something. Now, he was surprised.

Triss thanked the old man and left the warehouse. While still in the yard but out of sight of the street, she took out the crude cloth purse and opened it.

"Is it beans again?" Barzo smiled, referring to an old family joke.

"If we are lucky. If I can't find cheap beans it's stone soup for a while." Triss pretended not to notice his awkwardness. Something was going on that he didn't want her to know, but it looked like he wasn't being told everything either. A missing vardo, one that looked exactly like Tia Drina's, and someone who looked like Barzo searching for it? The troupe didn't have much and losing a cart would be a heavy blow to them. But what could she do if she knew everything? They wouldn't let her go back to help, and the only thing she could do was earn money to help replace it, which was what she was doing right now.

By searching the entire market area and bargaining hard, Triss managed to obtain some sausages (slightly overdried) and a hunk of cheese. With her last pfennigs she bought a loaf of stale bread. Toasting the bread with cheese would remove the stale flavor, and wrapping the sausages in a cloth soaked in hot water would make them more edible too.

"Let's go back to the telegraph office. I want to hear they are coming to help us." With more money or food or both.

"Yes. Then we leave this town." Barzo was looking around, jumpy. "Wait for them to find us outside."

He was probably worried about running into Toa Babik, and she should be too. Nobody knew the whole story of her new sort-of job or that Barzo had lost his.

Somewhat to her surprise, there was a message waiting for them at the telegraph office. While they were waiting for the clerk Triss assuaged her guilt by dusting odd corners with the edge of her coat for *obeza*.

The message was very short. "Coming soon."

"That says nothing of use!" Triss waved her arms as they walked. Now that they were outside the town, she felt it safe to revert to zigane. "When is 'soon?' Who is coming? How will they find us?"

"I am thinking, Trisstela. From when I was injured, they have my blood. They can find me and then from me find the others."

It was true. She had forgotten; Mauer was not the only one they could track. Once the magicians got to the town, they could track the ship or even Mauer himself if they were close enough. Asgaya still had a little of that blood too.

"Well enough. Now tell me. There are no *gadje* that can hear. What has been happening to our people, and why is Toa Babik looking for Tia Drina's *vardo* here?"

Barzo took a deep breath, removed his knit cap and scrubbed his head. "I do not know everything. Before, I was working on the river near Kassel, close to the wintering place. Then Nicu came to me there and said, Tia Drina's *vardo* was stolen. We need more money, can you hire on to the barge work up north to earn more?"

"But why steal a *vardo*? They are for living in. Everyone knows they are zigane too. They point and gossip. Why not steal the larger carts that carry the equipment? They don't look special at all."

Barzo shrugged. "Maybe they want to be noticed?"

"In a stolen cart?"

"Stolen from zigane." He gave a wry smile. "Who will care?"

CHAPTER 22

Mauer found being a prisoner extremely boring. It was too uncomfortable to sleep for long. Even when he was frozen by magic, he was awake, and most of that time he was stuffed in the hidden compartment under the carriage seat. It was cold too.

In his great boredom, Mauer had taken to scraping at the inside of the seat-box he was confined in using a loose nail he'd pulled free. He didn't have much paper or handkerchief left, and the darkness and lack of space to move in was driving him mad. A task, even a stupid one, helped.

Then he discovered it wasn't such a stupid idea as he had thought. His fingers found a crack where cold air came in. Several hours of scraping later, he could see light, and then when the hole was large enough to put his eye to it, the passing landscape. Just being able to see outside was a relief.

The two men did not change their established patterns. They traveled through the night, changing horses as often as they could and only allowing Mauer to move around when they stopped to eat. He wasn't sure, but he suspected that the taller of the two, who wore a pearl tiepin, was the magician. He was always the one facing him when the freezing magic was applied.

After a while he noticed they had made a turn onto a road in much worse repair than the post road. It slowed their progress, and he saw no further signs of civilization, not even a milestone or a fencepost. This went on for several bone-shaking hours, and then the road changed again, to dressed stone. The stone road wound up a hill with switchbacks, and the horses were clearly struggling. Mauer stared, trying to figure out where this place could be. There was grass between the stones, and some were missing or tilted at the edge of the roadway. Well built, but not currently in use.

It was awkward only being able to look at where the carriage had come from and not their destination. Where were they going, and what would happen to him when they got there?

The carriage leveled off, and the sound of the horses' hooves changed, thudding on wood. It proved to be a drawbridge, and from what he could see and smell, the drawbridge was of recent construction. A castle? Then they passed through some kind of stone gateway into a large open courtyard. Along one side was a rough shed, also new, where a few shaggy horses were standing. Nearby was an unusual cart with a rounded roof, painted yellow with green trailing vines and white flowers. It had a tiny window on the side, just like a cottage on wheels.

The carriage stopped, and he was hauled out and his hands bound before being pulled along through a ruined stone courtyard. He had seen enough earlier to realize his first guess, a castle, was incorrect. A wall, yes, but no fortifications of any kind and instead many instances of the trefoil spiral symbol of the Albionate monks. It seemed rather remote to be a church, so this must have been a monastery or something similar. A third man with a lantern joined them silently. The other two did not speak or even seem to notice the new arrival.

A heavy door blocked the way. Unlocked, it revealed a flight of stone steps leading to an unusually clean passageway. The passageway was decorated with more of the trefoil spirals carved in the walls and a few dim oil lamps, and it had a dry, musty smell in the air. At the end of the passage, past some dark arched openings, was a metal grate. One of the original kidnappers took out a large iron key and opened it. Like the drawbridge, the grate was clearly new and showed no signs of rust. Mauer was pushed through and the man with the lamp lit it. It revealed another arched opening and a room with several stone columns, niches with skeletal remains, and two other bays with iron grills, also new.

None of the three men spoke. They pulled Mauer to the far wall where one of the columns had an iron ring embedded in the stone, and a long chain going through it. The shackle at the end was placed on his leg. He watched them turn back to the iron grate door, darkness following them.

"Hey, can't you at least leave the lamp?" He heard a slight waver in his own voice. Skeletons were bad enough, but skeletons in the dark were definitely excessive. He'd also recently made the mistake of reading his friend Hoffman's latest story about a skeletal hand that moved on its own. If he survived this, he was going to make Hoffman very much regret that particular flight of fancy.

He tugged on the chain out of habit. It was very solid and completely unbreakable by his strength alone. Then he sank down on some very dusty straw and tried to distract himself from the various small scratching noise that could only be caused by rats and absolutely *not* by self-propelled bony hands.

There had been something odd about the shackle and chain, but he couldn't figure out what it was. The whole arrangement was odd. The shackle looked new, now that he thought about it. No sign of other prisoners before him unless that was where the bones came from. Mauer shuddered.

Before he could get himself worked into a complete state of terror, a faint light flickered through the grate, and gradually grew stronger. One of the men had come back with a lantern in one hand and a jug in the other. The jug had a dark round loaf on top. The man placed the jug just inside Mauer's reach before backing away.

"Wait. Can you at least tell me why I'm here?"

The man glanced at him, grimaced, and left almost at a run. Mauer dragged the jug and loaf back to the pillar and attempted to eat. The jug was full of water. The bread was dry and extremely dense. The only way he could make a dent was to soak it with some of the water first and then gnaw on it. It was, he realized, something to do. He almost wished he were back in the carriage box.

He hadn't wasted his time when the food delivery came. While the lantern was there, he'd stared at the chain, especially the part that wasn't directly attached to him but had fallen on the other side of the ring. It was concealed by the straw, but he'd seen the edge of another shackle. It must be attached to something or he'd be able to pull the chain free. He felt around with his fingers. There was a rusted grating in the stone floor, clearly not part of the new furnishings. The other shackle was attached to one of the grating bars—and it wasn't fastened. It just looked like it was, and the very strange jailers had never bothered to check it.

Mauer shifted the shackle free, at the cost of a few pinched fingers, and hurriedly pulled it through the iron ring. Now he could move about the room, and he immediately went in the direction of the iron grate door.

He could barely see some reflected lamplight on the far corridor wall, but it helped tamp down his bubbling panic. Something other than pitch-black darkness. Enough so that Mauer started thinking about how he could escape.

Not being chained to the wall was an improvement, but there was still the (locked) iron grating door and beyond that the wood door between him and the courtyard. He couldn't remember if it had been locked or not. There were no windows, and the floor drain was not large enough to escape from. What about the rooms with the gratings?

He fumbled his way along the wall, not sure what he could learn when he couldn't see anything. Until he realized he could. It was very faint light, just enough for him to see that beyond the iron gratings were piles of crates. The light was coming from carved inscriptions on the walls. Most were inscriptions in a language he had never seen before, but he could, with the benefits of a classics education, read one of them. *O Powers, defend us from evil and watch over our souls.* A sentiment he was in full agreement with, although he did wonder how the ancient monks had managed to get their inscriptions to emit light. And why he'd never heard about such a thing before.

The light was strong enough that he could even read the label on one crate. *Salis Mineralis—Roma.*

"Why must we keep walking?"

"To keep warm." Triss sighed. She couldn't blame Barzo. He was the one carrying the two heavy canisters of benzine. "We can't stop on the road. If anyone sees, it will look suspicious. And if we go off the road, the others won't be able to find us." Feeling guilty, she broke off the softer end of the heel of bread in her hand and offered it to him. Barzo opened his mouth and she fed him.

"Who will be on this road so late?" he mumbled while chewing.

"Someone like us, with business in town and returning home before dark." She knew her answer was vague, but she didn't have any proof to back up the itchy feeling in her bones that someone was watching them. Something she should be aware of but could not pin down. She'd thought she had seen Cousin Nicu in a crowd, but before she could get close enough to be sure, the man had moved away.

It was not a comfortable time to be out and away from the safety of the town. The deepening twilight was full of shadows, and if it were not for the snow on the ground, it would have been too dark to walk. Even the air seemed to be mysterious, with a soft hum that came from nowhere and everywhere at once, causing the hairs on her scalp to rise.

Triss looked up. A large cloud of darkness loomed over them, blocking the wind and the emerging stars. She gaped. She hadn't realized how quiet and menacing the floating ship could be from the ground. She really hadn't heard anything, and it wasn't until the rope ladder descended that she was able to relax.

"Did you get the fuel?"

Triss nodded at Jens-Peter, resigned to his fixation. "Two cans, just like you said. It took most of the money, though, so I couldn't get much food."

Dieter threw over a line and shortly pulled up the first can of fuel. "Oof. It's a lot harder without the winch. It feels like lead."

"What about the telegram?"

Triss handed over the terse response. Jens-Peter scanned it urgently and then sagged in relief. "I was afraid they would pretend they didn't know us anymore, the way our luck has been going lately. Anything else?"

Triss rolled her eyes and made her way to the tiny stove. "Yes, Barzo and I are nearly frozen solid, so I'm heating water first. I'm not sure that message was worth waiting for. When are they coming, how many of them, and will they bring food?"

Jens-Peter laughed. "We'll find out when we see them, right? And how could they send anything secret when the telegraph office could read it? We still don't know who is behind all this, so they are being careful."

"Maybe." Triss did not place a great deal of reliance on what she had seen so far. "Did you find any further trace of Mauer?"

"Yes!" Both Jens-Peter and Dieter chorused.

"A really strong indication from the needle. But we didn't dare get too close. There's a big hill with ruins or something on the top, and if there are people in there they might see us. So we circled around to make sure. Needle kept pointing to the hill, and it didn't even vibrate. I'm sure he's in there somewhere."

Triss sipped her hot water and observed how his expression changed from detached analysis to hopeful enthusiasm. "What do we do now? Wait for that Asgaya person?" *Please wait for that Asgaya person. Please notice that we don't have a single weapon and that Barzo is the strongest person here, and I don't want him hurt again.*

"No. I want to scout it out when it's dark." Jens-Peter's eyes blazed with excitement. "If we cut the engines, we'll be completely soundless."

"If it's dark, what can we see?"

"If it's *not* dark, like a light or a fire, we can see that!" he pointed out. "And there will be a bit of a moon later. It's worth a try. Asgaya will need that information for the rescue anyway."

Triss gave up. When Jens-Peter had that crazy look in his eyes, he was not really listening to reasonable objections. He was just completely determined to satisfy his curiosity. So she wrapped herself in a blanket and slept for a while in the little jury-rigged tent.

When she emerged again, the sky was completely dark, and the ship was as well. Even the small, shuttered emergency lamp had been extinguished. A sliver of moon was the only light in the sky.

Moving carefully so as not to make any sound, Triss went to the railing and leaned over. She could see roads and paths with the edges of snow against the darker background of the trees. After a while her eyes adjusted, and she could see more. The levitation ship was headed for a deeper darkness with occasional pale glimpses as they got closer. This must be the hill Jens-Peter had mentioned. But where were the ruins? There were craggy rocks at the top, and ...

And some of the rocks had arches in them. *There really are ruins.* She hadn't quite believed it before. There was no road, no nearby town. Why would there be ruins here?

It didn't matter. Mauer was in there somewhere, taken by the same evil people who had taken Barzo. Vengeance was also something zigane believed in. Triss stared at the approaching hill, looking for anything that might be useful.

Jens-Peter stopped the engines, and the ship drifted silently closer. Now she could see a light, just at the corner of her eye. The pale rock, now revealed as the road up the hill, lead to it. There was a dark mass, then an area of light. A gateway to a courtyard? And there was something in the courtyard …

She blinked, shook her head, then looked again. It was hard to be sure in the dim light and awkward viewing angle, but was that … Mata Sheri's *vardo*? Barzo had only mentioned that Tia Drina had her *vardo* stolen. And more to the point, why would it be *there*?

The ship passed over the hill. Triss moved to see as much as she could, but the other side was uniformly dark. She shifted over to where Jens-Peter was guiding the craft, close enough to whisper.

"Can we go back again? I think I saw something."

The ship shifted slightly, and Barzo came up. "Did you also see?"

Triss grimaced. "That's what I want to check."

"What did you see?"

"One of the troupe's carts," Triss mumbled. "One was stolen. Can we go back on a different path? More like this." She gestured. "It was along the north wall of the courtyard. I think."

"Sure. But also take the detection needle, and watch it close. I saw it spin around once. That should be where Mauer is."

The wait to turn the levitation ship was agonizing to Triss, and she couldn't even discuss it with Barzo to distract herself. At least two *vardos* stolen! The troupe would be devastated. Some of those carts were over a hundred years old and lovingly maintained. They belonged to the women, as zigane tradition dictated. And some idiot *gadje* had stolen Mata Sheri's *vardo*, meaning his life would be short and very painful. Mata Sheri was the person no one, not even Faad Tobar, wanted to be on the rough side of. Now there was even more vengeance to pay.

Again, Jens-Peter cut the engines as they approached the hill. Triss was glad of this when it became apparent that now there were people in the courtyard, moving things from a dark, ordinary carriage. She couldn't tell from this distance if any of them was Mauer, just that there were at least five. The carriage hadn't been there on the first trip, so it must have arrived recently, meaning it had made most of the trip up in the dark.

Triss kept an eye on the needle while she glanced at the courtyard. Barzo was beside her, watching closely. Just before they crossed over the eastern wall of the courtyard, the detection needle quivered and swung sharply. *He's there.* And there was the *vardo*. The distinctive roof and even the tilted stovepipe, legacy of the vanished and unlamented Toa Ferka's poor repair skills.

As soon as the levitation ship was safely away from the hill Triss relit the lamp and quickly pulled out a pencil and one of the blank telegraph forms. She sketched the outline of the courtyard and every feature she could see, marking the location where the needle changed direction.

"That's where it happened," she said, holding it up for Jens-Peter to inspect. "And that is Mata Sheri's *vardo* down there, undoubtedly."

"Right." Jens-Peter took the paper and held out a hand for the pencil. He sketched an oval then lines from the mark Triss had made to the edges and shaded the area between them. "Mauer is somewhere in that area, underneath the courtyard. That was a good idea, getting two lines of measurement." He grinned at her. "I wonder what they are up to, moving goods in the dead of night."

"If it was river, easy to say. Smuggling." Barzo joined them, sitting crosslegged on the deck. "Here, no easy road. No place to send cargo, eh? Is just, valuable thing to hide, maybe."

Triss suddenly thought of something. "Or people." They'd tried for Mauer and Barzo. "What if Mauer isn't the only they've captured?"

CHAPTER 23

Gutrune rubbed her eyes and turned up the lamp. There had been too many late nights recently. The pressure to get results was increasing, and even the King was not immune to it. Naturally, she had to help shoulder the burden.

She heard the rough floorboards of the warehouse corridor creak, recognizing the tread. Asgaya opened the door and waved a strip of telegraph paper.

"They are in Bielefeld. They even requested a response, so I believe they are close."

"Bielefeld." She got up, feeling stiff, and went to the large table where the maps were laid out. "Interesting. If they are correct …"

"Yes. Too close to the coast to be a coincidence. The cases are clearly linked." He came up beside her. "As we suspected, Korda wanted the levitation ships to move the salts and is desperate to the point of kidnapping anyone with a connection to them to get them."

Gutrune turned, raising an eyebrow. "And are you desperate to the point of sending two college students, a bargeman, and a housemaid to confirm it?"

A small muscle at the corner of his mouth twitched, but otherwise he maintained his calm, detached expression. "They were quite determined to rescue their friend. It would be cruel to stop them."

"You were quite capable of being cruel to von Koller. He was so certain he could find the ship here … or something to our discredit."

Asgaya threw his detached persona to the winds and scowled. "Von Koller needs to suffer even more. Why can't he point all this boundless energy into something that would be actually useful?"

"He may be the victim of circumstance," Gutrune said mildly. "Given what has happened, we know Korda must have his people—or people he

164

controls—in the Kriegsa. If he is given faulty information, he will make faulty decisions."

"Aided by his strong and biased opinions." Asgaya sighed, then smiled. "You are, as always, correct. I allowed my frustrations to get the better of me. It's bad enough with that madman running around Aerope with a magical compound capable of destroying entire countries, and now we have to dodge von Koller as well." He paused for a moment. "I suppose that means we should plan for a convincing distraction for him in addition to moving on this hideout. But what if Korda is not present when we do move in?"

It was a risk. They knew so little, and Korda was paranoid to the point of insanity. He had not been in his right mind when they encountered him in Bhuta, and from his subsequent actions, it had only gotten worse. Gutrune tapped the map.

"Even if he isn't there, the fact that Mauer is being held there shows it is an important location. If he isn't there now, he will go there at some point. I also suspect he may be storing the salts there. We know he's been moving them around and wants to move more. If we are careful, we can take it over and just wait for him to appear. But we will need to be cautious and avoid alerting von Koller and, through him, Korda's spies."

Asgaya rubbed his chin thoughtfully. "Even more, if we capture the salts, Korda becomes less of a threat. I finally got word from our colleagues in Ostri after threatening to visit them in person. Korda was never much in the way of powerful magic originally. He was at best a research assistant for their late Mage Guardian Baron Kreuzen. Nothing outstanding, but a decent sort of person, if unimaginative. Now, of course, with the magic salts he can easily wield mage-level magics but he doesn't have the knowledge or the training to use them effectively. Remove his access to the salts and he is not a danger."

"True, but he *does* know the *geas* spell and has controlled other, more capable magicians." That was what frightened everyone. The horrifying spell of control, long thought forgotten but revived by the monster Denais.

Asgaya leaned back against the table, gesturing in argument. "Ah, but again, he's not very good at it. Remember what Frau Kermarec told us? His *geasi* are uneven, patchy, and fragile. She mentioned he never removed Denais's *geasi* before placing his own. To me that shows he knows he isn't that good, so he doesn't dare rely solely on his own work. He's a magical parasite. Mage Guardian Kreuwel thinks that may be why we've had such poor luck removing the *geasi*. The sudden shock of releasing magic, that was never done right from the beginning, causes devastating damage."

The bleak look in his eyes made her reach out and clasp his hand without realizing it. "You must also remember, these people often had their original *geasi* placed years ago by Denais. It is not surprising such a terrible thing would cause mental harm, increasingly so the longer it was present." They were both silent, thinking of the horrible cost in lives and in sanity. "Do we have any estimate of what quantity of magical salts is out there?"

Gutrune rubbed her forehead, wincing. "Some of the survivors claimed there were written records. But they were kept in Denais's house, and—"

"—and Herr Kermarec blew it up. Rather thoroughly, as I recall. Not that we had much choice in the matter at the time, but now I have regrets."

"We can make a rough estimate, however. From the amount we captured before it was shipped out of Bhuta and how long the extraction facility was in operation. We also know Korda could not steal all of it without alerting Denais."

Asgaya frowned. "If Korda knew where Denais was hiding it, he could reach it too."

"Not necessarily. Denais was very careful to guard the salts, so even his own people could not reach it. And Korda only took over *some* of Denais's people, not all. If Korda ordered them to open the vaults they would not obey him."

"Well, that is one saving grace. So how much can Korda access?"

"After subtracting what we found in Anatoli and Bhuta? Something like two hundred crates. We *think*."

"And each crate had ten of those jars, and each jar as much power as Ardhuin Kermarec, the most powerful mage I've ever encountered." Asgaya's face was pale, and she was sure hers did not look much better.

Gutrune had no magical ability. But once, while secretly investigating some suspicious crates in Anatoli, she had accidentally breathed in dust from a jar labeled "Salis Mineralis"—and then blue magefire covered her hands. She had, briefly, felt what it was like to be a magician.

That was why the salts were so dangerous. *Anyone* could use that power. Not just trained magicians. The previous Mage War had devastated Aerope, with Denais as a junior mage. If the salts got out, the destruction would make the Mage War look like a minor brawl.

Asgaya lifted her hand and kissed it. "Don't look like that. We will win in the end, love," he said softly. "Recall that you went against Denais with only a knife in your hand, and where is he now? Scattered at multiple ends of a valley and buried under a mountain of rock."

She couldn't help smiling, even as she remembered. "Yes, and this is what you want to send those overeager students into?"

Asgaya waved an airy hand. "Precisely, they are university students— well, not the bargeman or the maid—and they are quite intelligent enough to realize they can't launch an attack on their own. See?" He waved the strip of telegram. "They are asking for help, and we will give it to them. It may take a little longer to prevent von Koller from learning about it, but I've already started moving people there. I'm sure Oberacker and his friends will be perfectly safe staying in the levitation ship. What could possibly reach them? "

It was too much to expect to be left alone in the crypt, Mauer realized. After all, these mysterious people had gone to a great deal of effort to capture and bring him here. He'd even felt a small spurt of interest when he heard the creak of the large wooden door at the end of the passageway. It gave him enough time to stealthily replace the shackle chain through the iron loop and hide the open end with straw. He'd even practiced earlier, to make sure he could do it fast and quiet.

If he was lucky, it was food. He was not lucky. Two men entered, one he recognized from his time in the carriage, holding a lantern. Older, wearing clothes that were once quite high quality but were now slightly shabby. They hung loosely on him, as if they had been made for a different person or he had lost a great deal of weight. The pearl tiepin glowed in the lantern light.

Without a word, the older man gestured. Mauer felt a bolt of agony strike him, so strong and sudden he couldn't even draw breath to scream and could only groad. As he recovered, gasping and blinking tears from his eyes, the man spoke.

"Where is the flying ship?"

"W-what?" The old magician hadn't even asked him anything before attacking. Mauer was deeply afraid now. They were going to torture him for information, probably kill him. He'd been in danger previously but this was the worst so far.

Another magical bolt darkened his vision for a moment. After he recovered from the agony his throat was raw from screaming. The man with the lamp never moved, but his eyes were wide and full of mute horror.

"Where is it? Tell me now. I must know."

As soon as Mauer saw the man's hand twitch, he yelled, "I don't know! I don't know what you are talking about! Hurting me won't make me know!" Maybe if he kept talking, he could distract the man from hurting him or open another line of inquiry. Even as he recovered from the smothering wave of pain, he couldn't help thinking how odd this interrogation was. The man's face was a frozen mask, and his eyes, like the man with the lantern, full of pain.

Why?

What could possibly compel the magician to torture him if he didn't wish to do it? And wouldn't an educated magician know better ways to ask for the information he wanted?

After what seemed like hours the question did change. "Who knows where the flying ship is?"

Mauer regained consciousness and could barely open his eyes. He lay on the floor unable to move, even when the power hit him. He had given up speaking, since the result was the same no matter what he said. Pleas, jokes, denials—nothing worked.

The expected pain did not come, and he cracked one eye open, just enough to see the two men standing together. They were talking quietly, but he was able to make out what they were saying with an effort.

"You have stopped. The master wants the information."

"The master said he must not be killed until the ship is found. He is too badly injured to continue."

Silence, then "The master is coming. The master will make him talk."

"Yes."

Was it his imagination, or was the voice full of grief?

Even taking into account his lack of experience with torture and interrogation, this still seemed very odd. The two men's conversation was stilted and abrupt, the questioning perfunctory. They seemed to only want to know where the ship was, and they never asked other questions that might yield the same information if put together.

Footsteps left the crypt, and the iron grating crashed shut. Mauer took deep, sobbing breaths trying to get his body to move again, stopping when he heard the footsteps return. He kept his eyes closed, hoping he would still be considered "too injured" and would be left alone. But all that happened was a muffled clink on the stone floor near his head, and when the man left again and it was safe for him to open his eyes, he found a wooden plate and a ceramic stein nearby.

Groaning with effort, he managed to prop himself on his elbows and drag the stein close enough to drink from. It was beer this time, not stale water, a strong, hearty brew. The plate held a chunk of bread, still soft, and a piece of stewed beef. He barely had the energy to chew it, but it was the best meal he'd had since being captured.

He'd learned something during the interrogation. Someone was in charge of all this, a mysterious and apparently powerful "Master." This person desperately wanted to obtain the levitation ship, and knew that Mauer was somehow connected to it. But who would know such a secret? The Kriegsa carefully controlled that information. And why had that zigane fellow, Barzo, been captured too? Simply because Mauer had spoken to him?

Mauer hoped Barzo had escaped successfully and had gotten word to someone, but he'd seen no sign of rescue. He was glad he had no idea where Oberacker and the ship were. Even if he wanted to, he could not betray him.

I wonder where he is now.

CHAPTER 24

The trouble with hiding a levitation ship, Jens-Peter knew, was the balloon. Because it was full of levitator dust and the intact, solid levitators had the greatest effect, compressing it produced maximum lift. This required very secure tiedowns and strong cables. Leaving the balloon in the fullest expansion made it easier to fasten, but harder to find a place large enough to conceal it. And just because they had had the argument multiple times did not mean they had found a consensus on the topic, but Jens-Peter kept trying.

"We have to conceal it even better than before. That place is on a hill and they could look down and see it, like we do from the air."

Dieter gave Jens-Peter a scornful look. "And how do you intend to do this? Look, even in the dock building, it took four cables to tie *Einzl* down in full compression, and we don't even have *one*. Not to mention we also don't have strong tiedowns anywhere to fasten them to if we did. And if it gets loose, it launches to maximum altitude, and how could we even get it back from there?"

"Well, nobody could steal it, that's for sure," Jens-Peter muttered. "All right, so we can't compress it. But we do need to hide it well since we'll have to be reachable from a road or path whenever Asgaya's people get here."

"We don't have to stay right next to the ship," Triss pointed out. "It can go anywhere when we need it to. It might be better to camp away from it. If anyone sees us, they won't see the ship."

"I'd like to get the balloon below the treetops anyway." The color of the balloon was a grey-brown that did not stand out very much in the leafless trees. It was just the shape and size that were too obvious.

Dieter nodded. "A valley then, like before. Maybe that lake we passed over would do? It wasn't far from the road or the path to the ruins."

169

"Water brings people," Triss said, shaking her head. "Especially close to a road."

"There aren't any houses! Where are these mythical people coming from?"

"Travelers like us. Anyone with horses needs to water them, right?" Triss stared at Dieter.

Jens-Peter sighed. "Let's look around the lake then. We don't have much time before sunrise."

Taking the lack of vociferous argument as agreement, he steered the ship at full speed for the lake.

The sun had just peeked over the horizon by the time they had found, approved, and started to descend into a small valley. It had a stream that fed into the lake, making it easy to find. The descent, however, was not easy. Because the valley was so small, too many branches scraped the balloon and Jens-Peter was afraid their repairs would get damaged.

"Barzo. Can you climb up and cut those branches?" Jens-Peter waved. "Anything that would touch the ship."

Barzo shimmied down a rope and started up the most problematic tree, an axe stuck in his belt.

"I can help too," Triss commented.

"I know you are good at climbing, but we only have one axe."

Dieter looked up, an expression of enlightenment on his face. "Oh! The branches Barzo cuts off … We could stick them on the balloon! You know, to break up the outline."

Triss gave Jens-Peter a glance and went off to toss Barzo a line to tie to the branches before cutting them.

"Be careful, and don't let the branches hit anything on the ship!" It was the only thing he could say. Triss was going to help one way or another, so he should look like it was his idea.

Triss stayed aloft all the way down. Jens-Peter really didn't like this, so he was even more careful descending. Once they found some sturdy trees, they tied up *Einzl* securely.

Triss landed on the deck with a thump. Her hair was full of dead leaves and twigs, even with her head kerchief, but she was smiling.

"It looks mangy, but not like a flying ship so I suppose it will do."

"What do we do if we need to leave fast?" Dieter asked. "Won't the branches block the mechanism?"

"I used the fly-away knot," Triss said, shrugging. "It stays put unless you tug on the end the right way. The branches should just fall off."

"What we do now?" Barzo took off his cap and rubbed his head before replacing it.

"Sleep. Who knows when anyone will show up, but it's bound to be a night attack, and we'll need to be rested."

Triss had become accustomed to organizing their camp setup, and she directed them to move gear to a spot halfway between the ship's hiding spot and the lake. Barzo said something to her in zigane while shaking a tall sapling, and she nodded before grabbing their only bucket and heading out.

"Going for water? Why not set up near the lake?" Jens-Peter took the bucket from her and walked alongside.

"If there are any ordinary people showing up, I'd rather not be seen."

"Then why not the stream itself? It's closer."

Triss shrugged. "Zigane custom. Take drinking water from where it comes in to a lake, do all washing or unclean things where water leaves."

"What was Barzo talking about when we left?"

She brightened. "He will make us a bender tent. We can all fit inside and even have a fire. You use saplings that are flexible and stick both ends in the ground, so it makes a half-circle, and then drape fabric over that. You'll see, it is very comfortable."

"Did you camp like this often?" He had noticed how many handy skills Triss and Barzo had.

Triss shook her head. "Not me. The main camp is where I usually lived. Bender tents and the like were for side trips away from the troupe, so I only did that a few times when I was young."

They had reached the point where the stream met the lake, and Jens-Peter dunked the bucket in the water but with all his efforts could not get it more than half-full.

"Let me. You're stirring up the mud that way." Triss took the bucket and moved closer to the stream. She rested the bottom of the bucket on the rocks of the lake and tilted the edge down. With the stream flow, the bucket filled almost to the top.

Jens-Peter took it back and hefted it up, mentally wincing at the thought of how far he'd have to carry it. Why was courtesy always so much work?

Then he noticed that someone else was crouched at the waterline on the opposite side, a woman in full dark skirts and a red scarf wound around her head. Triss had been right—people would come to the water. He edged back, reaching to tug on Triss's sleeve to alert her. "Quick, I don't think she's seen us."

And that was when the abused bucket handle decided to break.

The woman snapped her head up. "Eh? Who is there? *Trisstela?*"

Triss gaped, sputtering and trying to speak, but was quickly drowned out by a stream of zigane delivered in a forceful tone and ending with the woman glaring at them, hands on her hips. He thought he heard the word "*gadje*" several times, which he remembered meant non-zigane. She finished up with a a sharp gesture and a single word of command, then turned and walked away.

"I have to go talk to her," Triss said, her voice shaky. Jens-Peter stared at her. He'd never seen Triss afraid of anything. "If she comes to our camp, she'll yell at Barzo too, and ask all sorts of questions."

"I'll go with you." Triss started to protest, and he held up a hand. "She wants to find out what I'm doing with you, right? It will look worse if I run off. Who is she?" He set the broken bucket down. Assuming they lived, he could pick it up again later.

"She's the *mata* of our troupe. That is ... um, there really isn't a Preusan word for it. She is the female chief and has final say on what happens inside the camp. There's a male chief, too, the *faad*. Usually the *mata* is the wife of the *faad* but she's dead, so Sheri does it now. But why is she here? She should be with the troupe."

"She doesn't seem, ah, very friendly." Spitting tacks, more like.

Triss's shoulders slumped. "I'm not supposed to be wandering around on my own, remember? They were the ones who sent me off to be a housemaid. And I really, really am not supposed to be with strangers." Then she frowned. "Even so, she seems angry. Be very careful what you say. She may not speak much Preusan but she understands a lot."

Jens-Peter helped Triss jump over the stream to get to the other side of the lake rather than take the long way around. Sheri's camp was behind some bushes and looked very similar to what Barzo was currently constructing. The difference was the large amount of gear and a very colorful red cart with large wheels nearby. The cart was tilted, as if something wasn't right with the frame.

Logs were arranged around the fire, and Sheri was seated on one of them. She ladled out water from a pot hanging over the fire into two pottery cups, sprinkling something in it before handing them silently to Triss, who in turn handed one to Jens-Peter.

"It's salt water. Hospitality, and also supposed to drive out evil spirits," Triss whispered.

It was unlikely to be poison if she'd given the same thing to Triss. Jens-Peter swallowed the hot salt water. It wasn't bad, after being cold for hours. He sat on his log, glancing out of the corner of his eyes at Sheri and Triss. Nobody was talking. Triss was sitting bolt upright and completely still.

Sheri looked at Triss for a long moment, then turned her gaze to Jens-Peter. He suddenly recalled a legend Mauer once told him, about a Graeco-Roman legend of an eagle that was eating somebody's liver for having done something one of the gods didn't like. Sheri was giving him the same kind of look, as if she were wondering which end of the liver she should start from.

Should he say something? Apologize? He didn't know what he should apologize *for*, but that was often the case.

Fortunately before he could make the attempt Sheri began to speak. She was apparently asking Triss what she had been up to because Triss was responding with increasing heat. Barzo's name was mentioned after a while, and Triss was waving her hands in agitation and pointing to him. Jens-Peter sat up and tried to look honest and trustworthy.

"I was telling her about how Barzo and I met up with you after Barzo was kidnapped and escaped," Triss said but with a meaningful quick grimace. From which Jens-Peter deduced it was crucial that Sheri not know about, say, midnight rambles on rooftops and the like.

He nodded quickly. "Yes ma'am. My friend is still a captive. He helped Barzo escape, so Barzo is helping me find and rescue him." Every word was true, just not the *complete* truth.

"Why you here this place, *gadje* boy?" Her Preusan was heavily accented, but the scorn came through clearly.

"Er, the people who took him are close by. We think."

Triss asked her own sharp question in zigane. Sheri smoldered for a moment, then exploded. Jens-Peter didn't mind her ranting because it wasn't directed at him. He glanced at Triss, questioningly.

"She's very angry. Someone stole her *vardo*—the cart like that one, that we live in. Three were stolen from us. They are like our houses, you understand? The troupe can't afford to lose even one. She and the others have come to look for them. They asked everywhere near the wintering place, and followed the reports to the road. People saw the *vardos* near here, and the troupe even found this one, damaged, nearby." Triss pointed at the red cart.

"You mean like the yellow one at the ruins—"

Triss glared at him and made a hissing noise. "Don't say anything!"

"But why is she here, if … um, is there a specific reason they stopped here? At this lake?"

Triss translated, and Sheri pointed at the dark red cart. "*Zerbriste,*" she said gloomily.

"That means 'broken,'" Triss said. "Something in the axle that our people can't fix. The men went off to see if they can find something to repair it with in town."

Jens-Peter perked up. "Maybe I can take a look?" He held out his hands, still marked with engine grease around the nails. "I know how to fix things."

Sheri gave him a distant nod, slightly less glacial than before. She pointed to the front axle, the one with the pivot for steering, and Jens-Peter crawled underneath to take a look. Triss crouched nearby, glancing over her shoulder as Sheri went back to the fire.

"The real problem is they can't afford to get it fixed. These *vardos* are quite old, and they get used a lot. I think the rough road was too much for it."

Someone had taken the cart on a hard road or hadn't steered it properly.

The underside had deep gouges and dents in the frame. Jens-Peter poked and found a handful of rusted fasteners that had given way, making the gearing come apart. "Yeah, I can fix this. At least for a while, but as soon as they can they should get this redone by a blacksmith. I'll go back and get some tools."

Triss shook her head. "She wants you to stay here, where she can watch you. Tell me what you need." Then she whispered, "I also need to warn Barzo."

Put like that, Jens-Peter had to agree. He told Triss the tools and supplies to get from Dieter, and she left quickly. He decided it was safer to stay under the cart until she returned, so he started banging at the rusted fasteners with a rock to get them out.

Then he noticed the dark skirts standing by the cart, and soon Sheri's intense dark gaze was piercing him, like a hungry eagle.

"Where you see my *vardo, gadje* boy?"

CHAPTER 25

As soon as she was out of Mata Sheri's sight, Triss ran as fast as she could through the forest, her thoughts frantic. The flying ship had to be kept secret. The troupe couldn't know about her and Barzo being out of work … No, that was impossible, not the way Mata Sheri asked questions. She always could tell when someone was hiding something. In a way it was good that Dieter and Jens-Peter were there. With outsiders present Mata Sheri would not be quite so fierce. Or get out the wooden spoon.

Barzo was lying inside the completed bender tent. Triss dropped to her knees beside him and shook him awake.

"Bad luck, bad luck! Mata Sheri is here!"

Barzo sat up sharply, drawing a breath so suddenly he started coughing. "What? How? She's in Eisenach with the others!"

"She is *not*. She is here and very angry about her missing *vardo*. There are others with her, and they have camped on the other side of the lake," Triss said grimly. "Also they found one of the *vardos* on the road near the ruins. It was damaged too badly to use. Jens-Peter is there trying to fix it and to distract her. I must find Dieter and get tools for him. You go and keep her there, yes?"

"No?" Barzo looked at her with pleading eyes.

"You must go!" Triss pulled him up ruthlessly. "She already knows you are here. I had to say! She saw Jens-Peter too!"

He knew what she was hinting at, and he groaned. "Aiye, bad luck. What did you say to her? I must know so our words do not cross in her ears."

Triss quickly repeated what she had said, then added, "As long as she thinks I have always been with you, it is well."

"Oh? And the reason you are not safely within doors, sweeping and dusting?"

175

They needed a story that included all the important and true points but skipped over the troublesome ones. "Let me think. Does Mata know you went to Baerlen?"

Barzo nodded. "They tell me to look for you, even."

Good. They didn't need to explain that part. "All right, I think I have an idea. You *did* find me, at the house of Baron Heufritz. Everything was fine." Next they needed a reason for Barzo and Mauer to meet up. Well, she had met him to get the books back, hadn't she? "When we talked, you found out I was being sent on an errand to the university to get back some books from a student named Mauer. You didn't like me meeting this strange man, so you offered to go in my place, and I gave you a letter so he knows you can take the books. That's when the kidnappers grabbed you both. Everything that happened after that is what really happened."

Barzo thought for a while, rubbing his chin. "Eh, so why is Jens-Peter here?"

"Mauer told you to find him to get help. He's looking for his friend Mauer to rescue him."

"Ah, but why are *you* here?" Barzo held up a finger.

Triss grinned. "Because I got in trouble when the books weren't returned and lost my position. You didn't want me wandering the city alone, after all."

"But Father Rito could have let you stay at the church."

She knew what he was trying to do, come up with all the possible objections Mata Sheri could raise. "Not without bringing him trouble, *zumala*. Because of the school, the church fathers check often. To have a young girl in his house? Forbidden."

He gave a short laugh. "And we are here because of hearing word of Mauer?"

Triss frowned. "Better to say he left messages and you saw the road they left on. Who has seen him for us to talk to? Also, we heard the people in that city mention seeing one of our *vardos*, and we were curious."

That should cover all the main points, explain their presence, and distract Mata Sheri. Barzo left the tent, and Triss went to find Dieter, warn him about staying with the ship and not coming out, and to get the tools and other things Jens-Peter had asked for.

When she returned to Sheri's camp, she was shocked to see Jens-Peter backed up against the damaged *vardo*, hands up in a futile attempt to placate an irate Sheri, and a very worried Barzo trying to calm her down.

"Mata, he is *gadje* and doesn't understand you! Why are you angry with him?"

This just changed Mata Sheri's target. "Why didn't you mention you saw my *vardo*? Where is it?"

Jens-Peter took advantage of Mata Sheri's distraction and quickly slid under the *vardo* for safety, and Triss could not blame him.

"It is a very dangerous place. With *bruje*," Barzo blurted.

To Triss's shock, Sheri stopped yelling and folded her arms, frowning fiercely. "So. This dangerous place, why do you go there? To rescue this *gadje*? Just because he was imprisoned with you?"

Barzo squared his shoulders and lifted his head. "Because he made it so I could escape. I have *jaina*, Mata Sheri. He saved my life. This is outside the camp. Only *Faad* can tell me not to do this." He stared at her, brows furrowed.

Triss stifled a twinge of happiness. If Sheri saw her smile, the temper would erupt again. It was true, the *mata*'s authority only extended to the camp and people of the clan. Anything outside, such as dealings with other clans or an obligation to a *gadje*, was for the *faad* to say what was permissible.

"Aiye. Obligation should be repaid, *jaina* repaid fully," Sheri said grudgingly. "Speak with *Faad* when he returns. This is a bad business. We cannot invite more bad luck."

Triss blinked. "Is *Faad here*?"

Sheri nodded. "All except the children and elders, who stayed in Eisenach, have come to search for our missing *vardos*." She stared at Triss. "You will stay in this camp, you hear? Barzo did right to watch over you, but now he has men's work to do."

Triss knew better than to argue with her. There were ways around Mata Sheri, and her being sent out to work was one where *Faad* had won an argument over her. She crouched down at the side of the tilted *vardo*.

"I brought the tools. Everything is secure," she said quietly, then held up a finger to her mouth to indicate no questions.

Jens-Peter, looking a little frantic, nodded and whispered, "Thanks."

Triss edged to the back of the *vardo* while Sheri was lecturing Barzo about getting captured with a *gadje* stranger. She needed to find a way to stay busy and out of sight until the others returned, or Sheri would start interrogating her. Since Jens-Peter was working on the outside, she should see if the inside needed work.

She didn't mind staying in the camp. Sheri was bound to have more and better food, and this way they could intercept any of Asgaya's people more quickly. And if she and Barzo stayed here, Sheri would have no reason to go to where Jens-Peter and Dieter would sleep. In fact, the same rules would prevent her from going to a "stranger" camp.

The exterior of the *vardo* was scratched and dusty but not obviously damaged. Then she opened the door with the tiny glass window and gasped in horror. The wood floor was covered with mud, straw, scraps of broken wood, and garbage. Triss recognized the interior. This *vardo* belonged to Araunya, and she had always kept it spotless and gleaming. A wave of fury blinded her. What had the thieves done, and why?

Looking more closely, the fine finishings were smashed indiscriminately—but they were all there. She found one of the copper pans under a pile of dirty straw, unharmed. It was a valuable thing, but it had not been stolen. If anything, it looked like something heavy and bulky had been crammed in the *vardo*, and that was how the damage came about rather than deliberate vandalism.

She definitely had to get this cleaned up before Araunya saw it, or she would fall down dead in anger. Triss started gathering up the debris and shoving it out the door. The broom that should be hanging from the underside of the *vardo* was long gone, so she made a rough version from twigs. Eventually more of the original interior became clear, and she wanted to cry all over again.

The built-in bed was a complete loss. The blankets were missing and the mattress stained. Had the thieves slept there? Then there were countless pieces of broken crockery, nearly everything in the cupboards. Triss sighed. *Obeza* wasn't just returning favors. It was also not creating animosity or danger, and simply tossing out sharp pieces of pottery, when many people went barefoot in the troupe, was bad. They would have to be gathered and buried.

She started piling the shards in one corner. During all of this she could hear muffled clanking and banging underneath the *vardo*, indicating Jens-Peter was still hard at work, and she smiled. It was good he could help. Mata Sheri was temperamental but honest, and this would give Jens-Peter some points in his favor.

Some of the shards were strange, a kind she had not seen before. Red clay, rough and coarse, with the exterior unglazed. The interior, however, *was* glazed. Triss frowned, remembering Araunya's belongings. She could not recall anything like that or Araunya keeping anything like that in her *vardo* or wanting to. So, had it come from the thieves? The inside surface felt slightly greasy. Maybe it had held some kind of food or salve. Hopefully, it hadn't spilled anywhere. Grease took too much work to clean, especially from wood surfaces.

Triss knelt down where she had found the red clay fragments, at the edge of the built-in bed. There was a gap between the bottom edge of the storage cabinets the bed was built on and the floor to allow the doors to open. Feeling with her fingers, she discovered a layer of oily sand in the gap. *Well, at least it wasn't salve or something sticky like treacle.* She might be able to get most of it just by scraping.

Using a piece of stiff paper and one of the pottery fragments, Triss gathered up the oily grit and then took a rag to get the last few fragments. She placed it on top of the pile of shards so it would not fall on the floor and get it greasy. Feeling the area where it had spilled, it didn't seem like the oil had been absorbed by the wood, but she wiped it again just to be sure.

Before she could do anything else, Mata Sheri called her out to help with the cooking. "That *gadje* boy needs to tilt the *vardo* to set the wheels. No reason for you to be inside to make it harder," she grumbled. But for all her unfriendly words, Triss noticed that Jens-Peter also got a share of bread and cheese, like Barzo, for lunch. "The others should be back before dark. We'll have hot food to greet them."

"Who came with you?" Triss asked. From the bender tents she could see, it was at least ten people, possibly more.

"Lasho, Khulai, Oti, the Uraje men, Toa Vann and his son. Faad Tobar and the rest will be coming in a day or so."

Triss blinked. That really was most of the men in the troupe. "Where is Toa Mihai?"

"He stayed with the elders and children. Which is a good thing, so he does not see the treasure of his heart wandering outside when he thinks her safe," Mata Sheri said with a meaningful look.

"Others can come out but I cannot?" That was as close as Triss dared come to criticizing Mata Sheri, but if she was to blame for disobeying her elders, why was Mata Sheri away from the main camp, her responsibility? "I have already said I had no other choice."

"We come out to save our tribe. No, wait for the others to come. They will have questions for you as well," Mata Sheri said, overriding Triss's attempt to ask more. "You make flatbread now. Use half of the flour."

Of all the chores Sheri could assign her, making flatbread was acceptable. It gave her an excuse to stay near the fire, and a cold wind was gusting through now and then. It wasn't like Triss could escape chores, not with Sheri.

The camp didn't have much in the way of utensils, not surprisingly. Triss had to make the dough in the stewpot and then use a clean cloth and a relatively flat rock to roll out the flatbreads. Once the dough was made Sheri took the stewpot and started making *terrangi*, a lentil stew. It was usually served with a main dish but Triss saw no other ingredients. If they were living on only *terrangi* money was very tight indeed.

Jens-Peter left for the other camp, saying he needed to get other tools but more likely because he wanted to check on Dieter. Triss surreptitiously handed him one of the flatbreads to share. Dieter was always hungry. When he came back in the afternoon he went back under the *vardo* and made more banging noises for a while, then came out again.

"Hey, Barzo! I need to lift up the body to get the axle back in the right place."

Barzo scratched his head. "How? I not strong enough, lift whole *vardo*. Wait for others, maybe."

"No, we'll use a lever. I just need to tilt it a little. Cut down one of those trees, the tall slender ones."

Triss looked up from her frypan, rubbing flour off her nose. "Wait! I want to clear out the sweepings first." If they tilted and jostled the *vardo* the pile of pottery shards would fall and the oily sand would spill again.

"Stop jumping around and finish your work," Sheri snapped. "Don't burn the flatbread!"

"It will only take a minute. If I don't, it will make a mess and undo all the work I did." Triss flipped the finished flatbread into the pile and got up. Sheri continued to grumble while stirring the *terrangi*, but it was more out of habit than conviction.

Triss used the old cleaning rag to gather up the pieces so she wouldn't cut her fingers, balancing the paper with the oily sand on top. She stepped carefully down the *vardo* steps, which were uneven because of the axle problem, sighing with relief when she reached the ground again. Now where could she bury it? The latrine pit would work, and it would be quick too.

Just as she turned to go into the woods, a gust of wind went through the camp, and the paper with the dust launched into the air, landing on her face.

Triss dropped the pottery pieces, eyes watering as she scrubbed the dust from her face. She sneezed twice, staggering. Why did she feel so ... tingly? Her skin was shuddering, a feeling like drips of warm honey running over the surface. The feeling intensified, then faded. Triss hurried to pick up the fallen pieces and toss them, making a quick detour to the lake to wash her face clean. Now she was feeling dizzy and had to take careful steps.

"Triss? Is something wrong?" Jens-Peter was staring at her with a frown, a hammer in his hand.

"I'm ... not sure." She looked at him and immediately regretted it. She could see *everything* about him in minute detail, even the frayed threads on his shirt cuff and the thin line of dried blood on his hand from a scraped knuckle, and he was at the other end of the camp. She glanced at Barzo, and that was even worse. Every pore on his skin, even a small, pale scar on one ear she had never seen before. She stumbled and fell to the ground. Looking at the trees didn't help either. She could see every twig of every branch, even insects on the trunk. "I can see everything."

She heard the thump of the hammer falling to the ground and running footsteps. "What do you see?" Jens-Peter asked, sounding worried. "Does it hurt?"

Triss shook her head. She closed her eyes and tried to focus on how to explain, thinking of what she had just seen.

"Aaah!"

"Spirits, *mala kru, mala kru!*"

Quickly opening her eyes, Triss saw the flash of an image before it vanished, the very thing she had just been trying to visualize in her mind. Now all she could see was Sheri, Barzo, and Jens-Peter staring at her with varying degrees of horror and astonishment.

"You … that … that was magic!"

Sheri and Barzo glanced at Jens-Peter. Sheri frowned.

"Eh, a curse? Was the *vardo* cursed by the *chor* who stole it from us? Aiye, Trisstela! I will make a charm for you, drive the curse away!"

Barzo narrowed his eyes, facing Sheri. "Why do you say the *vardo* is cursed? Those are heavy words from you, Mata."

Mata Sheri's eyes closed, face etched in grief. She seemed suddenly older and more weary. "You will hear from the others when they come. The *vardos* … Magic was used to steal them. The thieves must have used magic to make sure we cannot take them back."

CHAPTER 26

Jens-Peter didn't know what to do. Triss, even wrapped in blankets next to the fire, was shivering and staring at the flames in silence. Something had happened, but nobody knew exactly what, or what to do about it. Barzo and Sheri were convinced it was a curse. Jens-Peter didn't believe in curses but had seen a lot of strange magic in his activities with the Dragonhunters, and he suspected this was more of it.

Triss was quite vehement about not having any magic, and Sheri agreed. If it was magic or related to it, they needed a magician's help. He'd asked Dieter, but it was outside his experience and skill. There should be better magicians on the way, but he hadn't seen a trace of them. Were they delayed? Or reluctant to show themselves in the presence of outsiders like the zigane? Dieter hadn't seen anybody either. Should he go to the town and send another message?

While he worried, he worked on the *vardo*. With Barzo's assistance he got the turning axle correctly aligned under the cart body, and the fasteners tightened one more time.

"Should be able to take that on the road," Jens-Peter said to Barzo. "If you can, have a real blacksmith look it over. I did the best I could, but I don't have all the tools to really fix it."

"Aiye, better than it was!" Barzo lowered his voice, glancing over his shoulder. "A good thing, Mata will not be so angry with you."

Jens-Peter raised a skeptical eyebrow. But before he could say anything the sound of hoofbeats and voices came through the woods along the track to the road. Shortly an open cart, brightly painted in blue, green, and yellow drove into the camp pulled by two shaggy, sturdy ponies.

There were seven men of varying ages in the cart, all with bronze skin and black hair. Their arrival caused Sheri to heave to her feet, waving a wooden spoon while saying something in loud, forceful tones. The men were shocked, glancing at the *vardo*, then looking again at *him*. Jens-Peter tried to smile, waving a greeting.

Now Barzo joined in, waving at Jens-Peter and pointing at the *vardo*. Hopefully, he was explaining who fixed it. But since Jens-Peter did not understand a word of the increasingly loud discussion in zigane, he could not be sure.

Then one of the new arrivals recognized Triss, wrapped in her cocoon of blankets, and that started another round of exclamations and greetings, gradually transforming from happy to worried as they understood her plight.

Sheri shouted, hands on her hips. Then she pointed at the stewpot. Jens-Peter was familiar with this behavior. It was the "I don't care if the house is on fire, you will eat your dinner properly first" that Frau Zinkler firmly believed in. Sure enough, food was parceled out. A portion was served in a bowl, covered with two of the flat pancakes, and placed next to Triss, and another was ladled on a pancake and served to him on the cookpot lid. The rest was plonked down in front of the men, who took turns spooning the stew on the pancakes. Sheri and Triss shared the bowl.

Jens-Peter wasn't sure what was in it, but it was delicious, hot, and surprisingly filling. It did not escape him that although Sheri still viewed him with suspicion, he had been fed. Separately from the zigane men, sure, but fed. If this were Frau Zinkler, he would say he was on probation.

"Barzo say you fix," one of the older men said, pointing at the *vardo*. He was wearing a patchwork leather vest and a red neckerchief, and he had a long mustache salted with grey.

Jens-Peter hastily finished chewing the last bite of food and swallowed. "Fixed enough to take on the road, but I wouldn't plan any long mountain trips."

The man grunted. The expression in his eyes was hard to read, a mixture of caution and wariness. "You tell, why you here." Barzo attempted to speak but was smacked into silence again.

Jens-Peter took a breath, mentally reviewing the agreed-on version of events, and started talking. The old man heard him with an impassive expression, eyes squinting at the fire.

"We go everywhere in that town. Nobody will come help us. Too cold, we cannot pay enough to change this. It is good fortune you are also here, with knowledge and tools." A narrow stare. Yes, definitely suspicious about something.

"I'm here because I want to rescue my friend from university. I study mechanics there, so of course I know how to fix things!" Jens-Peter grinned with all the innocence he possessed. "And, er, I'm not rich either, so my, ah, cart always needs work. Keeping tools in it just makes sense, especially for a long trip like this."

The man's hard gaze shifted down, looking at the fire. "Still, you have saved one of the Vetsayo *vardos*, our only treasure. We have obligation to you, Yans. For this, and for Barzo's rescue."

His voice dropped to the point of being barely audible. Triss was looking at him, worried, and Jens-Peter suddenly realized this was a very proud man forced by his desperation to be humble.

"Um, well, I don't think it's quite to the level of a serious obligation. Sir. More like *obeza*, maybe? Triss has helped us an awful lot and we're gratef—" He stopped, suddenly worried. All of the zigane, except Triss, were staring at him in utter shock. "Er, did I say it wrong?"

"How you know *obeza*?" That was one of the younger men, standing up and looking belligerent.

Was he not supposed to know? He couldn't help glancing at Triss, hoping for a clue on how to proceed.

"I told him." Triss stirred in her blankets, glaring back. "Why, is this a bad thing, to teach a *gadje*? If more knew, would that not be better?"

The young man mumbled something and sat back down, looking sullen. The old man on the other hand, had cheered up. "This *obeza*, I accept it for the Vetsayo. Come, Yens. Sit and talk with us."

Room was made around the fire, and Jens-Peter took a seat. He noticed that nobody had moved near Triss, forcing him to sit next to Barzo instead. At least he wasn't next to Sheri.

"Yes, we must talk. Tobar, the *vardo* may move now, but there is evil on it. The evil struck Trisstela. How can we bring it back like this? The other *vardos*, too … They could be the same. Think how they were taken!" Sheri's face was tired and sorrowful.

"Er, how were they taken? Ma'am." Jens-Peter hoped his new acceptance extended to permission to ask questions. They were speaking Preusan instead of zigane for his benefit, so it seemed reasonable.

"Witch-work," The old man snapped. "We were in the camp, yes? Many people around. No one saw any stranger. Then, like that!" He clapped once. "Three *vardos* vanished. All in different places, not together."

"And nobody noticed anything?"

A quiet, middle-aged man looked up. "One child, he say he try get inside, steal candy. Say it was like ice, not cold. No touch door. He cry, think he make bad thing."

Yes, that sounded like magic.

The old man rubbed his forehead, looking tired. "So. If the *vardos* are now cursed, why take them back? We have enough bad luck."

"No!" Sheri cried, then her face crumpled. "It is all I have …"

"Er. I, ah, I'm not a magician, but I know a few," Jens-Peter said hesitantly. "I don't think the *vardo* is cursed." *Because curses aren't real, but even I know better than to argue that now.* "There may be a spell, but not a curse.

And if it's just a spell, a magician can remove it. What the child found, the not-cold ice? That sounds like a ward, from what I've heard."

The zigane sat up, interested and listening. The old man, though, frowned. "Magician, they want gold, yes? If we have gold, would we go so far to find our stolen *vardos*?"

Jens-Peter pondered for a moment. It all seemed connected somehow, and if that was so … Then it clicked. "If you want the other *vardos* back you will need magicians anyway. The yellow *vardo* I saw was in a building up there." He pointed to the hill. "I know because that's where my friend is imprisoned, so I was looking around to find a way to rescue him." Looking from the air, but never mind that detail. "There are definitely magicians there. They used magic to capture Barzo and my friend. And"—he gulped—"I sent a message to the magicians I know, asking them to come and help. And they will. But they can't do everything. What if … what if you could trade with them? Offer your help in exchange for theirs. I can at least ask."

The zigane began to discuss the idea in their own language, their limited Preusan not up to the strain. Some were doubtful and depressed, others excited. With attention diverted for the moment Jens-Peter took the risk, and whispered to Triss.

"Are you feeling better?"

She glanced at him, and he noticed her eyes were red. This was very bad. Triss never cried. She nodded, hesitated, then shook her head. "I still feel like tiny ants, all over. And I still see *everything*." She shuddered and wrapped the blankets more tightly about her.

"I'm sure Asgaya will know what to do. Or whoever he sends."

"When will they get here?"

He really wanted to know too. He could only shrug. "Soon."

Barzo nudged him. "Better you go, now. They will talk easier without an outsider, and it is night soon."

Jens-Peter waved a hand in acknowledgment. He returned the stewpot lid to Sheri, remembering to thank her for the meal, and headed back to his own camp. It would be cold, since Dieter let the fire go out, and depressing. Of course Triss had to stay with her own people, but he'd gotten used to her being around.

And with nothing to do, he'd spend entirely too much time fretting about how to figure out what had happened to her. And to the reinforcements they had been promised.

No, Asgaya was definitely—strangely—interested. He would send people to protect the levitation ship.

"But when the hell is Asgaya going to get here?" he mumbled.

One of the shadows on the trail thickened, then shimmered. A dark-clad figure stepped out with a lurking grin on his face. "I've been here for over an hour. Do tell me, who are all these intriguing people you've collected?"

Triss put up with it for as long as she could, but eventually the loud voices and multiple, simultaneous arguments made her head throb. "I'm going to go to sleep," she told Mata Sheri.

Mata Sheri gave a sharp nod, then rummaged in her pockets until she brought out a blue glass *ojo* threaded on a green-and-yellow ribbon. "Take this, keep evil from invading your dreams."

Triss smiled and took the amulet. Mata Sheri was always fierce and often bad-tempered, but she truly cared about her people. It was just hard to remember that sometimes with all the yelling.

Mata Sheri had a medium-sized bender tent set up, originally to share with her sons, but now that Triss was here, the sons had been shifted out and it was just the two of them. That meant there was just enough room and she might get some sleep. Would she sleep? Would the … whatever it was get worse in the night?

But before she got to the tent, she heard a familiar voice going "Pssst!"

Jens-Peter? Why had he come back? "You shouldn't be here!" she whispered urgently. "Mata Sheri will get angry!"

"She won't see anything." A different yet also familiar voice, and her hopes rose. It was that strange magician, Asgaya! "I've got an avoidance field around us. I'll know if anyone comes near. Try to keep your voice low, though."

"We know where Mauer is," Jens-Peter said quickly. "But we've got other problems. These zigane are Triss's people. They didn't know she was here; they were trying to find their stolen wagons. They were stolen using magic. And when Triss was in the one they found, near the mountain where Mauer is held, something strange happened to her. I think it's magic too. Maybe they left a spell as a trap or something. Can you help her?"

Markus Asgaya held up a hand. "First things first. Is the, ah, special equipment safe?"

"Yes. Dieter is with it now. It's hidden nearby."

"Good." Asgaya sighed in relief. "Next, where exactly is Mauer?"

"At the top of that hill. There's some old stone ruins at the top. We've located where he is, pretty much, even if we don't know exactly how to get there. Somewhere underground."

Triss recalled the overflight, trying to describe it more exactly for Asgaya. Forgetting what had happened before, she closed her eyes to concentrate. The sharp, indrawn breath reminded her.

"Is this the 'something strange' you were referring to?" Asgaya's voice sounded strained.

"Um, yes. But you can see it here." Triss squinted one eye open. The exact mental image was once again floating in midair, like a picture on an invisible wall. She pointed. "Right there. We went over twice, different ways. The detector needle switched direction right there." The image flickered and vanished, but Asgaya didn't even seem to notice. He was staring at her.

"Well. I believe I can state with confidence that this is not a curse or a spell. However, it is *highly* unusual and will take further investigation. Tell me more about why you think the stolen wagon was connected to this new behavior."

"It happened after I cleaned it out. Well, no, I was cleaning it most of the morning." Triss thought back, trying to calm her panicked mind. When had it actually started acting strange? When she had thrown out the broken crockery. "Jens-Peter and Barzo were going to tilt the *vardo* to get the axle set again. I had swept up some broken pieces of plates and other ceramic things, and I wanted to collect them up to bury them safely. As I was carrying them down the steps, the wind picked up and some of the dust went in my face and … I felt very strange. And I could see everything. Every leaf on every tree."

"Where are those broken pieces now? I want to see them."

Puzzled, Triss glanced at Asgaya. His voice sounded strained. What did broken crockery have to do with saving Mauer or protecting the flying ship? "I can show you, but can you fix what's wrong with me first? It's hard to move when my head hurts."

"I regret, but to fix what is wrong I need to be sure that … and if I am right, I need to see those pieces first."

Jens-Peter came closer. "Is all the extra stuff you see making your head hurt?" Triss nodded. "You keep your eyes closed then. I'll guide you."

And he did, better than Triss had expected. He had her put one hand on his shoulder, following him from behind, and he held her other hand in his. Once she told him the general location of the latrine, she closed her eyes and stumbled along with them.

"All right, we're here."

Triss opened her eyes and looked around. "In that pit," she said, pointing. Then she noticed that in her haste, several of the pieces hadn't made it in to the pit and were scattered around the edge. "Those too."

A tiny ball of bright light floated from Asgaya's fingertip, drifting over the broken pieces and down into the pit itself. Then the light came back and hovered over one piece. "This … Do you recognize it?" It was one of the rough pieces.

"Um, it was in the *vardo* but Araunya didn't own anything that looked like that. I guessed it was from the thieves."

"Did you notice anything strange nearby when you found it?"

Triss shook her head, then frowned. "Well, there was this greasy sand,

and I was worried about clean—"

Maybe it was the little magical light that was making Asgaya's face look so horrified as he backed away. "Shh. Don't say anything more. I know what happened now."

"So it *is* cursed!"

"No. But it does involve magic. Let's not talk here." He gestured off into the dark forest before leaving. Triss let Jens-Peter guide her again, away from the zigane camp. "I can't tell you anything more about it except the effects will fade over time." Asgaya looked suddenly weary and grim. "I apologize. I can assure you ... Well, you recall the lady you met, Fräulein von Kitren? The same thing happened to her, and she was back to normal within a day. That said, it is very, very dangerous. Please. For the safety of your people and mine, don't mention anything further about the sand or the pottery you found." Asgaya sighed. "To anyone. Your people found that cart after it was stolen? Near the hilltop road?"

"That is what I was told. Can you please tell them the *vardo* isn't cursed? My family is poor, and they are afraid they might have to leave the *vardo* even though they need it desperately. You can ask them more about how they found it."

"Very well. I must let my colleagues know first so we can plan. I shall 'discover' your camp in an hour or so." He grinned and vanished into the shadows.

Triss stared at the darkness for a moment, then sighed. "Are you sure he can be trusted? I have the feeling he is not being completely honest with us."

Jens-Peter nodded without hesitation. "He's a bit odd at times, but he was once a defensive magician of the King himself. Now he's with ... a different group but still defending Preusa. He's got a lot of secrets. You know one of them." He pointed into the woods toward the flying ship. "Looks like you've found another. I don't know what it is, but I *do* know it has him scared. And I didn't see him scared the time I was pulling him off the side of a mountain half-frozen and half-burned and nearly dead. So I don't think I *want* to know what this new secret is, but you're involved, so I guess I'll have to find out."

He was reluctant, grumbling, but a tiny bit of the terror gripping Triss faded. Someone knew what had happened to her and what to do, and someone else was going to stay with her until she was normal again. Someone she knew and trusted. Someone who cared about her.

CHAPTER 27

After seeing Triss back to her tent safely, Jens-Peter ran for the other camp. As he expected, Asgaya and the others were there, talking with Dieter. Several horses were tied up nearby. Besides Asgaya, he saw five unfamiliar faces. They were dressed similarly, in dark clothing, but not in the uniform of the *schutzmagi*. Asgaya was briefing them on the situation.

"... So we know this is a hideout for his people, and I have now confirmed he is shipping the contraband here. I don't know for sure he's also storing it here, but considering the location, it's highly probable. Ah, and here's Jens-Peter. I saw the layout"—he coughed lightly—"but the others haven't."

"I'll draw it for you, if you've got any paper." Yes, it was important but he didn't want Triss bothered, especially when she was shaken by whatever had happened to her.

One of the other magicians produced a map with a blank reverse side, and Jens-Peter got to work, talking as he went. "This side is almost all sheer rock, except for some boulders at the bottom. The road is steep and fairly narrow." He sketched the switchbacks he'd seen, wishing he had Triss's memory for visual detail. "That cart they found showed signs of damage on the undercarriage, and I think it was from going up that path. It's stone and much better than the rough and muddy road here. Old fortifications along the ridgeline, mostly ruined. Didn't see any intact roofs." He made an X and circled it. "That's where the detection needle indicated Mauer was. Nobody saw anything when we passed over, so he must be underground."

"How big is this place?" One of the magicians, a stocky man with short, dark hair asked.

Jens-Peter quickly added some estimated dimensions on the diagram. "And judging from the altimeter, I'd guess the height is eight or nine hundred feet."

Asgaya frowned at the map. "Is there any way up there other than the stone road?"

Jens-Peter shook his head. "I didn't see anything else. With that steep hill, the road is pretty much the best the builders could do. I can't think of another way up myself."

"Right." Asgaya gave a sharp nod, then tapped the map near where the stone road met the country road. "Gunther, Albecht, I want you to set up detection magic here and here. If anything comes or goes on this road, I want to know about it. Uwe and Rudi, scout the approach for any defenses, especially magical ones. Be aware there are likely to be one or more magicians inside, and be extremely cautious. I want to get inside before dawn."

"What do I do?" a tall, thin magician asked.

"You'll be coming with me to the zigane camp. We need allies and they are already involved."

As the four left on their errands Jens-Peter shifted. "Um, if this is so important, why can't we call in more Dragonhunters? I want to rescue Mauer as soon as possible but not if it puts him in danger."

"As much as I value Mauer, securing that contraband is even more important. And dangerous." Asgaya's face was hard. "We also need to be very discreet about this. The fewer people involved, the better. I also can't risk assuming that the contraband is only being stored here temporarily. If we lose track of it ..." He shook his head. "*Many* people could die, not just Mauer."

"I thought you said it wasn't—" Jens-Peter stopped, reminded by Asgaya's frosty glare and glanced at the remaining magician and Dieter.

"Evil people want it, badly. That's enough to put everyone involved at risk. And what they want it for ..." He gave a bleak smile. "I can't think of any good purpose." Asgaya sighed. "Never fear, I do intend to summon help. *After* I am ready to take action here. We must seize the moment, and even a slight delay risks failure."

"That's all very well, but what can we do to help?" Dieter shrugged. "I'm not much of a magician, and Jens-Peter isn't one at all. Or the zigane, if I understand correctly."

"You can run that highly useful levitation ship, for one thing." Asgaya paused. "Ironic in a way—we think the attack on the facility that started this mess was provoked by the same people, who were desperate for a way to transport the contraband in a secure and secret way. You effectively removed levitation ships as an option"—he inclined his head politely to Jens-Peter—"so they stole the zigane wagons instead."

"But aren't they rather colorful? How is that secret transportation?"

"Colorful and *already known*. What would you think if you encountered one? Unlikely to be considered as transporting dangerous materials. Zigane go everywhere, as well."

Jens-Peter was feeling more and more uncomfortable. Matters could very well be as desperate as Asgaya said, but he didn't like Mauer's rescue becoming a side issue and the whole operation a desperate roll of the dice due to time. "So what are you planning to use the levitation ship to do?"

"Transport us up to the ruins, for a start. We can scry and even attack from the air."

And that was what he was afraid of. "You said there will be people there, guarding the … the whatever it is. If they are attacked from the air, even in the dark that's where they will attack *back* and *Einzl* has no defenses. Worse, cut enough of the cables and there is nothing I can do to prevent a crash. The levitator balloon is a huge target." Unlike any of the other levitation ship operators, Jens-Peter had been shot at and did not want to repeat the experience. "And what if the magicians there can detect the levitators?"

That made Asgaya sit up. "Were you found when you flew over the ruins?"

"No, I don't think so."

After thinking for a moment, Asgaya's expression lightened. "Then it is likely they do not have very many magicians, or are not doing active scans. And since their leader is more than a little paranoid, if he knew it was a threat, he would order them to do so. But you are right, we should not reveal our trump card until they are no longer in a position to do anything about it." He thought some more. "That does remove some of the use of the ship, however."

"Maybe not." Jens-Peter took a deep breath. It would help Mauer and in a way help the zigane. "Is this contraband so important that you would be willing to let a few more people know about *Einzl*? Because if we don't launch magical attacks from it, and it's all done without detection, we could get more people inside before they realize it."

"I know you want more people, but it will take two days at minimum to get a message out and the people here."

Jens-Peter shook his head. "I mean the zigane. These zigane. They are an acrobatic show. Barzo and Triss took to the rigging like they had done it all their lives. They already know about *Einzl*, so why not the rest of them? If we take the zigane in the levitation ship, we can get our attack from the inside first, before they even know we're there."

Mauer could only guess if it were day or night without any windows. His watch had stopped during the trip, and while he had rewound it, he couldn't tell what the actual hour was—only that time had passed. It was enough, however, to figure out that his captors now only came once a day, to feed him. They had also taken to giving him a hot sort-of stew instead of a hunk of bread. The contents were often scorched and alternated between bland and too salty, but it was worth it for the brief warmth while he ate.

Then he had far too much time alone in the dark. His injuries were still painful, and the cold only made them worse. He continued to search every inch of his prison to keep his mind away from the pain and fear even though it hurt to move, and he made a few interesting discoveries.

One, there were old torches still in their holders in his cell. Two, if he took one of the old torches and held it outside the metal grating from the tips of his fingers, he could just reach one of the burning lamps outside and light it. Just having light again helped his mood tremendously, and it let him see even more. And at night, it was a tiny source of heat.

He had the feeling he was running out of time. While he had not been beaten and questioned since the last time, he was sure that this mysterious "master" the men were fearful of was coming soon, and that there were worse things than broken bones and bruises awaiting him. So as soon as his captors left after bringing his food, he hastily ate then unfastened the chain to light a torch and go exploring.

What he hoped to find was something that could be used as a weapon. If there was only one man, he had a chance of taking him down and escaping, but aside from the long iron chain, he hadn't found anything yet—and he would have to remove it from the ring on the pillar to use it.

The niches with bones, once he worked up enough courage to search, yielded nothing but scraps of cloth that could be used to extend the burning time of the torches. The bones themselves were brittle. Everything else was bare stone, even the floor when he kicked away the straw to search every inch. The grate cover might work if he could pull it free fast enough.

Then Mauer turned his attention to the bays blocked by metal grill doors. The wooden crates looked identical … No, some were clearly damaged. What if he could pull one of the pieces free? *Even better if it has some nails in it.* The grill doors were chained and padlocked, but he could reach through the spaces in the grill and touch the crates. He could also see that the crates, strangely, had ropes tying down the lids instead of the expected nails.

After several hours, even after the torch completely burned out, Mauer had barely managed to shift two crates to the grill. They were surprisingly heavy, so if they were stacked, he could not move them. Going by touch he wedged the edge of the shackle under one of the ropes and started sawing.

As he worked, Mauer wondered if this was a good idea. What if the cut rope or the damaged crate lid was noticed? Considering how only the lamp was brought in and how quickly they came and went, they might not see anything since the bays would be in complete shadow. It was worth the risk.

He checked his watch. There were still a few hours before he expected

192

any interruption, but he had to be back in place before then. He sawed harder. If nothing else, it was keeping him warm, and it wasn't like he could sleep.

One rope broke, and Mauer started on the next. Every now and then he would try to lift up on the lid to see how loose it was and after one attempt, he could feel the rope start to give. Using all his strength, he gripped the edge and heaved, and the lid came free with a scrape and clatter that startled him with its loudness.

Heart pounding, he froze and listened for several minutes, ready to dash for the pillar he was supposed to be chained to. After a while it became clear that no one had noticed, and he went back to work trying to extract a piece large enough to be used as a weapon.

It didn't work. For some reason the lid was not coming apart, and in the darkness he couldn't tell why. Sighing, he got up and found one of the remaining forgotten torches. He should gather all of them up, if there were any more. He couldn't remember how many he'd seen and how many he'd already used.

With light he made an interesting discovery. The crate top was not, as he had expected, put together with nails. Instead, wood pegs kept the pieces together and still stuck out from the inside surface. It seemed like a lot more work, but perhaps they had been short of nails at the time. He could also see the inside of the crate, full of straw and rough, fist-sized pottery jars. They did not look anything like they were valuable enough to be locked up.

There was a bracket for a torch nearby so Mauer stuck it back in place so he could use both hands on the crate. It was awkward enough having to work through the grill. He braced one end of the lid against the far inside surface of the crate itself and shoved with all his strength.

Something gave way with a sharp crack, but it wasn't the lid. One of the side panels cracked and sagged, and the contents of the crate slid to the side as the whole end came loose. Several of the pottery containers fell, smashing against the stone floor. A grimy, gritty sand fell out of the broken containers, which continued rolling until one came to rest against the metal grating.

A small, blue-white thread of light darted along the base of the grating where the grains of sand made contact, writhing with a sharp, crackling noise. The tiny lightning bolt lasted for nearly a minute and left a thin trace of acrid smoke when it finally died out. Mauer knelt to examine the grating more closely. The metal at the edge was pocked and corroded. When he poked at it with the manacle, the metal crumbled like rust.

Mauer sat back, trying to think through his fatigue. The jars were labeled as mineral salts, but this was acting more like the acid he'd seen Dieter work with once. It ate metal. And, remembering Dieter's protective gear and caution, probably anything it came in contact with. Still, despite the danger, this was much more useful for his escape plans than a piece of wood.

For one thing, he could use it to break open the main door right now instead of waiting for his jailers to appear first. He immediately reached for the remaining containers in the crate only to discover the jars were not small enough to pass through the bars. He would have to create a large enough opening first, but how to do that when he couldn't open the closed jars and didn't dare touch the stuff that had spilled?

Then he remembered the stew, or more precisely the wooden spoon he'd been given to eat with. That worked quite well indeed, and after etching away at the corner of the grill, he was able to extract several of the sealed jars.

He'd been thinking again, though. He didn't know where his captors were located or how many were here. He was also weak and injured and not the best fighter when he was healthy. How far could he get once he got out of this catacomb? It might be better to make it *look* like he'd gotten out. They would start searching for him outside the cell, so the safest place for him to hide was *inside*. Specifically, in the padlocked bays with the crates. They wouldn't search a place he clearly hadn't gotten into and would have no reason to get into, right? But he'd have to make it look like he'd gone somewhere else or they would search anyway.

The main metal door was the last resort. It was too easy for someone to notice that it was damaged and to know he couldn't have escaped that way if the hall was guarded. There were no windows … but there was the drain. A fairly good-sized drain and more than likely close to an exterior wall. Maybe he could use the acid salts to make it look like he had somehow broken it up to get out that way?

In a desperate emergency, he could throw the acid jars at anyone who attacked him. So first he had to break into the bays. Then he could decide what else to do from there.

CHAPTER 28

The sound of voices raised in argument woke her up. Triss wondered drowsily why—arguments were a constant background of her childhood, and she'd slept through them without a problem—until she heard Jens-Peter's voice, and she woke up completely. She was not back with the troupe, except by accident, and she also wasn't going to be able to go back to sleep in this situation. She might as well join them.

She noticed that her hands weren't shaking as much as before and that the overwhelming detail in her vision had faded too. Maybe Asgaya was right and it would all get better with time.

When she reached the large campfire, Asgaya was already there along with another dark-clad *gadje* she did not recognize. Jens-Peter was trying to persuade everyone about some clever idea he'd come up with, and around the fire were most of the men of the troupe, over twenty in total, regarding him with doubtful expressions. The rest of the searchers must have come while she was sleeping.

"—But if we work together it will be even better!" Jens-Peter said. "Herr Asgaya is a powerful magician, and he also wants to retrieve things stolen by those people."

Triss sighed and came closer to the fire, near Jens-Peter. "They don't understand you. Even if they understand Preusan, they don't understand your city dialect." She looked at the men of the troupe, and gave a quick translation in zigane. "They are going to attack, too, and want to work together with us."

Toa Babik snorted. "Two *gadje*? How much help are they going to be? They can follow us if they like, but not to make noise and give us away!"

"They are *bruje*, uncle. They can use their magic to help us."

"Still only two ..." the uncle muttered.

Triss knew it was less a matter of numbers than their strangeness. This was a clan matter, and bringing outsiders in just didn't feel right to them.

A pale ball of light drifted through the woods, ahead of three men coming from the road. Some of the troupe stood up, fingering the hilts of their knives.

"Ah, they are with me," Asgaya hastily interrupted, holding up his hands. "I did say I brought several men with me, if you recall." He glanced at the newcomers.

"Do we, ah," the man said and gestured uncomfortably at the zigane. "We've got some bad news."

"Go ahead. They will need to know as well."

The man grimaced. "I don't know if it will help them to know, though. That place has a barrier up. I went about half way around, scrying, and it's even around the part with the cliff."

"Enclosed or simple?" Asgaya asked quickly.

"Er, simple. I think. I didn't detect any curvature."

Asgaya took a deep breath, looking worried. "I see. What that means is, the magicians inside have put up a wall of magic around the ruins," he explained to the troupe. "Even if you climb up, you won't be able to get in."

Triss translated this as well, and winced internally at the frowning faces. They were so close, and now to hear this …

"*Gadje*. You can break this wall?" That was Sheri, ignoring the customs to speak. Well, it wasn't customary to have outsiders at vengeance meetings either, so maybe it wasn't such a bad thing.

"Yes, madam." Asgaya answered with a slight bow. "Unfortunately, the magicians inside would know the instant we did so—and we would still have to break down the door of the entrance to get in. With angry and alert magicians to greet us once we do."

More argument. The troupe was doubtful of the true presence of a wall of magic but too polite to say so directly. "They don't believe you," Triss whispered to Asgaya when the others were distracted. "Can you take one of them to prove it is there?"

"There's so little time … We should already be moving," Asgaya muttered, a crease between his brows. "But I also need to make sure we will succeed. I suppose it is a good sign the barrier is not enclosed. That means their magical capability is limited."

"I didn't scry any detection spells," the other magician said. "Not even the easy ones."

Asgaya didn't say anything. He just rubbed his head and grimaced.

"Why not go with my idea? If the top is open …" Jens-Peter stood up. "You can't keep everything secret, not and get in tonight. Which secret is more important?"

Asgaya looked up at him for a long moment, then sighed. "You are right. If it wasn't an order ... Frankly, we've been fortunate *Einzl* hasn't been seen before now." Triss gave him a skeptical look, and Asgaya's customary faint, mocking smile returned. "Excepting housemaids on rooftops, I should say."

Triss angrily hushed him. "They don't know about that!" she whispered, glancing around to make sure.

Asgaya got up from the log he was sitting on, giving her a wink. "There is another option if you are willing to take a risk," he told the assembled zigane. "By means of a—well, call it a magical raft—I can lift several people over the top of the ruins, allowing them to drop down from ropes. I understand that most of you are quite comfortable going up and down ropes, given your profession?"

"Aiye?" The reactions amused Triss. The older men were more skeptical, but the younger ones were eager to try just for a chance to see this marvelous contraption.

"Yes. How do you think I was able to obtain this?" Asgaya held up a paper with an eagle-eye view of the ruins. It was ragged and not completely precise, and she recognized the handwriting. Triss glanced at Jens-Peter, who was trying hard to look innocent. "We saw one of your painted carts inside, by the way."

"This *gadje* magic, strong enough to lift people?" Toa Babik asked. "How many?"

Asgaya gestured, and Jens-Peter suddenly floated up with a shout, flailing, until he was dropped back down again. "A good question. It is more a matter of the size of the raft, which means ..." He looked away as if calculating, and Jens-Peter whispered something with his head turned. "Oh, ten or twelve at the most. One of which will need to be Oberacker here as he has seen me use this before."

"I'll go too," Triss said before she could stop herself.

"You will not fight, Trisstela!" snapped Toa Babik. "Vengeance is for the men to do."

"Vengeance only for men?" Sheri erupted. "Those dog-sired *gadje* have my *vardo*! Tell me again I no get my vengeance!" She pulled out the long knife from her skirts, startling Asgaya and the other outsiders.

"I wasn't planning on fighting," Triss hurried to explain. "But, um, I can translate. And help with the ropes. You know I can do that much." She grimaced at Jens-Peter. It was all very well to say it was going to move by magic, but if left to themselves, the men would soon figure out that it wasn't just magic moving the levitation ship. "I think Barzo should go, too, since he was working on a barge. It might help."

The expression on Barzo's face was troubled. It was true that he had to keep secrets, but he also had to protect his family. She hoped he understood that she was trying to make it possible for him to do both. It was absolutely crucial that Sheri not find out exactly how long the both of them had been on this "floating raft" and why.

"Certainly. If I may suggest it, perhaps the lighter members of your company? That way more can fit on the raft. As for the rest of us …"

"You do not go on this flying thing?" Sheri asked, eyes narrowed.

"Once it is empowered, a magician is no longer needed," Asgaya said smoothly. "Oberacker knows what to do. More importantly, I must be with my team to break down the barrier for the second attack."

"Then I go with you. To help. Make sure you remember, keep our people safe with this magic you do." Sheri smiled while tapping her chin with her long dagger.

"Why do so many women want to threaten me with knives?" Asgaya muttered as Sheri went off to continue organizing the two teams.

"Going by what I've seen, it must be something you said," Jens-Peter observed matter-of-factly.

"No doubt, but it is polite to pretend otherwise. Now, it would be best if *Einzl* is not connected with your earlier appearance, so rather than have them go to it, let's have it come here. Will you and Dieter be enough?"

"I'll help too," Triss grumped. "I wouldn't put it past Toa Babik to forbid me to go. He's still mad that I showed up in the first place. So I just won't give him the opportunity to stop me."

"Very well, but let's start moving. I have a bad feeling that we do not have much time." Asgaya frowned in the direction of the hill. "Bring the ship to their camp but keep it in shadow as much as possible. If von Koller ever gets wind of this …"

The lingering effects of the strange magic had one positive effect. It was much easier to run in the dark forest without tripping. Triss got to the levitation ship before any of the others and started climbing the ladder as soon as she reached it.

"We're going to the ruins with my family," she gasped to Dieter when she swung over the railing. "But they shouldn't see anything secret. That magician Asgaya told them it was a raft he used magic on."

"We're going to rescue Mauer *now?*" Dieter gasped. "Er, right! Um, what do we need?"

"All the ropes. And a way to put the men in that tent. That way they won't see much."

Now Jens-Peter was panting and gasping his way over the side. "We'll have to coast in like we did the first time, silent. But first we have to get this thing to the lake."

The first thing he did was drop off anything that wouldn't be used in the attack, to lighten the weight. Jens-Peter had kept some things like the old, damaged engines as ballast to help with the broken altitude controls, but now it was more important to carry as many people as possible into the ruins. And it all had to be done by hand since the winch was still in use as the altitude control substitute.

"I think that's the last of it," Jens-Peter wheezed, feeling limp. "Let's go pick up the raiding party." It was a good thing the plan called for him staying with the ship during the attack. He could rest.

Triss calmly coiled rope, piling it on both sides of the ship after fastening one end to a cleat. Dieter was pouring more benzine in the engine tanks and wiping them down.

"Er, what exactly are we doing? I know we're taking a whole bunch of zigane up to the ruins, but after that it gets a trifle confusing."

Jens-Peter started the main engine and slowly turned *Einzl* around. "No doubt Asgaya and the rest are still arguing about it. I figure once we've dropped off our passengers, maybe we can help search for Mauer. If he's hidden underground, it won't be easy to find him."

He glanced at the sky. It wasn't the worst weather possible, but it wasn't that good. A strong wind scattered clouds, sometimes exposing and sometimes hiding a half-moon. If it stayed covered, the shadows were deep. If not, there was enough light to expose the ship to whoever might be watching in the ruins.

Fortunately, the wind was not strong down in the valley, or coming in to the camp would be tricky. "Get ready with the ropes. We're over the lake now." It was surprising that nobody was shouting in alarm yet even though they were on alert. They weren't even looking in the right direction.

When the ropes dropped down, *then* there were startled cries, quickly stifled.

"As I said, the magic also makes it hard to see." Asgaya's urbane voice could be heard in the midst of the group. "Come down for a discussion of strategy, Oberacker."

Jens-Peter, out of habit, looked around for Triss, but she had ducked out of sight and he remembered her mentioning that one of her uncles was very much against her taking part. He sighed and climbed down the rope ladder.

He was quickly surrounded by a crowd of ferocious and armed zigane, ready and eager to fight. Besides the broad knives all of them seemed to carry, many had cudgels and one even had a woodcutter's axe. None of them were as tall as Asgaya but all of them were taller than Jens-Peter, and he hoped they would remember he was on the same side. More, he had discovered where the yellow cart was, so didn't that count as rescuing it, at least partly?

"All right. We have two groups. One, with the magicians, will be up the hill on the road but out of sight of the gate they have there. The second group will go with Oberacker to enter the ruins by air. The first group will wait for your signal to bring down the barrier." Asgaya handed Jens-Peter three long objects he recognized as signal flares, which he accepted with some reluctance. He really hoped he didn't set anything on fire this time.

"When the barrier is down, two magicians will guard the gate and the lower road so we don't get surprised, and the rest will attack and draw the attention of the defenders. You in the airship party, stay unseen as long as possible so they won't attack you, and keep the element of surprise. Oberacker and Theusen, once everyone is down and deployed in concealment, fire the signal. You stay on the ship to provide retreat if needed. Once we're in control, we can find Mauer." He glanced over to where one of the magicians had brought an open carriage. "Ah yes, and if you would like to arm yourselves with something more than a knife, we do have some firearms to spare for our allies. If you can shoot, please make yourselves welcome."

"Why you have guns, *gadje*? Magic not so good?" one of the younger men asked with a hard tone.

Asgaya didn't even blink. "I have learned, from hard experience, not to rely on a single method of attack. Does everyone understand what they need to do? Right, then let's get the ship loaded."

The older zigane man with the hat, the one Triss had referred to as Faad Tobar, issued orders in a quiet voice. One or two of the men started to protest, but a single glance from the leader was enough to silence them.

Not surprisingly, the ones sent to the levitation ship were primarily the younger men. They scorned the rope ladder and swarmed up the ropes like flowing water. Jens-Peter had felt clumsy compared to Triss, but they were at an entirely different, higher level. He clambered up, only to see that their smooth competence had collapsed into childish glee, running about and peering over the edge of the deck. A few adventurous sorts were starting to climb the cables up to the barely visible balloon.

"Get down! That's dangerous!"

They stared at him without comprehension until Barzo said a few words, and they reluctantly complied.

"Thank you. Can you ask them to stay put until we get there? It's bad to let the deck get tilted. It affects the steering." Not to mention the railings were not that high and they could fall off, but he didn't want to give them a challenge.

"Ya, like water boat. *Oi!*" Barzo gave the attentive zigane a short lecture, and surprisingly it worked. Everyone sat down, evenly arranged in the available space on the deck.

"Oberacker. How long do you think it will take to get in position?" Asgaya peered up from the ground.

"Half an hour. It could be faster but I want to coast in without power so it's silent."

Asgaya nodded. "We'll be waiting for your signal then. Good luck. And remember, don't leave the ship!"

Of course I won't leave the ship. Someone has to look after it. And he had to admit he'd be even more useless in a fight than doing acrobatics, but it didn't help his gloomy mood. Then he brightened. What he *was* good at was handling a levitation ship, and nobody else here could say the same. And would they be able to rescue Mauer without the ship? No, they would not. Yes, he was short and not much of a fighter, but he could do this!

After flying nearby recently, Jens-Peter had a sense of the local wind patterns and how they varied by elevation. So he took the ship higher than usual to get in position before dropping and making the approach run. As soon as they moved away from the camp, Triss came out of hiding to startled exclamations and then what sounded like teasing. She ignored them all and went to the viewscope.

"Watch for drift. The wind isn't direct this time, and I don't want to turn on the motors to correct it."

She nodded. "Maybe shut them off early, and I can check it then?"

The zigane, apparently understanding the purpose of the viewscope and forgetting the need for staying still, started to get up to take a look until Triss scolded them back in place. Jens-Peter felt a twinge of sympathy. He remembered his own excitement the first time he went up and how he spent all his spare time just looking.

"Tell them that when we go back I'll let them all take a look," he murmured. "But now they have to be silent. We're going to be shutting off the engines soon."

The wind was tricky, and Jens-Peter had to adjust altitude more than once before he got the ship lined up and confirmed by Triss. Dieter, who had been working the winch, made his way cautiously to the controls.

"Um, something's off with the cable, I think. It acted like it was stuck on something."

Jens-Peter grimaced. "Not surprising; the cable part is all improvised. I will be glad when this is over and I can fix it properly. At least we have the right height now."

Dieter nodded and watched the approaching black shadow of the hill with the ruins. The direction Jens-Peter had chosen had them coming in over the rocky cliff section of the hill, from the north. Seeing the landmarks, Jens-Peter waved Dieter back to the winch, then leaned to whisper to Triss.

"Have one of them secure the line when they drop. There's too much wind, and the ship may drift out of reach if we don't tie up."

She nodded and crouched down near the zigane to pass on the request, then went back to the viewscope. Jens-Peter watched her intently until she held up one hand. They were over the ruins, and it was time to attack!

He gestured to Dieter. The manual action of the winch seemed loud in the silence, but he knew it was his imagination. He'd heard it himself from the ground and it was barely a ticking noise at this height.

Then there was a larger clunk. Dieter's face wasn't fully visible in the moonlight, but his eyes looked disturbingly wide. Yet the ship was descending, so Jens-Peter decided to pretend everything was under control. He could check it later, while waiting for the attack to end.

The ship jerked and tilted slightly. He felt his confident grin stiffen, and he gestured to Triss, pointing to the zigane and then down. As smoothly and swiftly as they had ascended the ropes, they now descended in silence. As soon as the last of them was down, Jens-Peter turned immediately to the winch and Dieter.

"What happened?" he whispered as softly as he could. He noticed that the ship was still descending even though Dieter wasn't moving the winch handle—and that the cable was slack.

"I don't know! It sort of twanged and then it looked like this."

Triss glanced at them, then swung up into the rigging before Jens-Peter could stop her. After a minute the cable drooped even more, falling free, and then Triss descended by sliding down the rope.

"It was supposed to be connected to something, right? There's nothing left up there. The cable was snagged on part of the canopy webbing, which tore. The mechanism is completely gone."

Jens-Peter looked at the altimeter. It was slowly but steadily dropping. The ship, on the other hand, was definitely tilting to one side. He felt a distinct sinking sensation in his stomach. One side of the balloon was expanding, letting the ship descend, but the other side wasn't. And he had no way to fix it.

He took a quick look through the viewscope. They were still over the ruins, thankfully, and one of the zigane had indeed tied off the ship as requested. That might not be a good thing now. If the attack failed, *Einzl* could be captured. There was only one thing he could do now. But first he had to light the signal flare, or there wouldn't be an attack at all. He lit the fuse and watched the red flare shoot into the sky, then sighed.

"Prepare to abandon ship," he said as quietly as he could for rising panic. "We're sinking."

I'm in so much trouble …

CHAPTER 29

Inside the carriage, no one spoke. The nursemaid because she was under a *geas* and had been ordered to stay silent, Sita because she was asleep. Korda himself was deep in thought. Using the painted carts to transport the magical salts worked, after a fashion, but they could still be seen and potentially stopped and searched. Which is why he still wanted the flying ships that his contact in the Kriegsa had told him of. The salts were his one weakness that he could not expose, and he hadn't found all the salts Denais had extracted. Without the salts, he was a powerless low-ranked magician being hunted by mages all over Aeropa—because of Denais. Who had captured and enslaved him. Of course he'd had to fight back!

With the salts, he could control magicians far more powerful than himself if they had already been put under the *geas*. Even now, he was protected by two magicians acting as coachman and guard on his coach and followed by another two coaches, each carrying three magicians. It enabled him to travel safely and securely, without detection.

He could do so even more quickly and discreetly without Sita or her nursemaid, but something wouldn't let him leave the girl behind. Ever since she had found him in the mountains of Ynde, after escaping the death of Denais and the vengeful Aeropans hunting him, he had not been able to make her leave. He was even more incapable of placing a *geas* on her. That had been what Denais would do and what he had saved her from the first time he'd seen her.

And it was Sita who had given him the idea of using the painted carriages to transport the salts. They had been traveling to another of his hiding places when they encountered a string of them and carts with gaudy signs advertising some tawdry acrobatic show on the road. Sita had been completely fascinated, especially by one in yellow with white flowers.

He'd ordered his subordinates to save that one for Sita. It was waiting for her in the old monastery now as a surprise. He wasn't sure why he'd done that either.

They were getting close to the monastery by now. Korda glanced out the carriage window, searching for the dark hill in the moonlight. He couldn't see it, but what he did see was a bright red light launching into the sky and then falling in an arc.

His eyes widened, and he felt his breath catch. His people would never do that. Which meant they'd found him. The cache was under attack. His magical salts …

Korda hammered the roof of the carriage. "Go faster! Faster! Get me there immediately!"

The crates in the formerly locked bays yielded a surprising number of the rough clay jars. Wolfgang Mauer took two of them out of the straw packing with care, placing one near the outer door as an emergency precaution and taking the other to the old rusty grate in the floor. It was more difficult than he had thought to use the oily sand to damage the grate; it kept falling through before doing anything to the metal, and it wasn't as corrosive on the rusty surface.

Mauer looked around for ideas. He still had the beer pitcher with the dregs remaining and a wooden bowl and a crust of bread. Maybe if he made a paste of the stuff and applied it with the bread?

He didn't have a lot of options if he wanted them to think he'd escaped through the drain. Mauer sighed and dumped a generous amount of the sand into the wood bowl. Adding the beer, even a small amount, did not result in a paste. Instead it made a fizzing, foaming liquid that smelled strongly of ammonia.

Gagging, Mauer poured the mixture over the drain as best he could for his watering eyes, hoping it would do something.

It did. A dull boom shook the floor, and a cloud of choking white smoke billowed from the drain. He couldn't tell if the metal grating had been damaged and he couldn't take the time to check. He had to hide *now*.

Stifling the urge to cough, he lunged for the open door of the nearest bay and scrambled behind the crates, wondering if he had the time and the energy to stack another crate for better concealment before deciding it was too dangerous. He'd know soon if his plan succeeded.

Sure enough, he heard shouts and running feet in the passageway soon after, but to his astonishment, the men ran past his prison without even looking inside.

Don't they care that I just blew something up? Is something out there more troubling than an explosion?

He could hear more shouting outside now, faint but definite. There was also a loud crashing noise. Mauer rubbed his forehead, trying to think of what to do now that his clever plan was being completely ignored. Someone was attacking. They probably thought the drain thing was caused by the other people. Did he really want to be trapped in here facing a different group of violent strangers who might think he was connected to the kidnappers?

No. Getting out was better. He could always run back if it was too dangerous. He went to the outer door, made sure no one was in the hall, and started etching the lock. The grains of sand kept falling even after the lock came loose, due to his shaking hands, and he made sure not to step on them when he pushed the door open.

Still empty. All the noise was up the stairs. That was a way out, but that was also where all the people were. What if there was another, less crowded route?

He hadn't been in any condition to notice such things when he was brought in, but now he noticed the passageway extending some distance into the gloom past the crypt he'd been imprisoned in. The lamps, however, did not go that far.

Just as he was about to liberate a lamp to investigate, he heard rapid footsteps descending the stone stairs. Before he could reach the crypt grating, the other came in view. It was one of his original captors, the one who wore fine clothes and a pearl stickpin.

As soon as he saw the man's face, Mauer instinctively flung the jar of acid sand at him. He missed his target, but the jar hit the stone wall and shattered, scattering sand everywhere—including on the man's face.

He screamed, a horrible, high-pitched sound, convulsing in short snapping motions until he collapsed against the wall and slid down, motionless. Rivulets of pale blue light ran down his face and hands, which were otherwise completely undamaged.

Mauer was sure someone would come now after that kind of noise. He reached up to grab the lantern, frowning as he thought about what had just happened. What kind of acid would destroy iron yet leave human flesh intact? Yet it had clearly had a strong effect of another sort.

"It's gone ... Thank almighty God, it's gone."

The voice was so faint that Mauer would not have heard it if he wasn't standing right in front of the man. He clutched the lantern and backed away. He'd thought the man was dead, but now there was a glimmer from barely open eyes. He still hadn't moved, slumped like a broken doll on the floor.

"Run. He's coming. Run, but kill me first! He'll put the *geas* on me again ... Don't let him ... get you ..."

The man was clearly in pain, but he spoke in a natural manner completely different than before.

"Who is coming? Is that what is happening up there?"

The man gave a gasping laugh. "No, strangers. Go down the tunnels. There's a passage in ... the stone. He doesn't know. Get out now!"

"And why should I trust you? You did kidnap me, you know."

The man closed his eyes, and a tear trickled down his thin, sunken face. "The *geas* ... forced me. You are right to mistrust me. But to be free ... I never knew you were a magician. How did you remove it? I am ... in your debt."

"I'm not a magician." Mauer stared at him. "Why would you think I was?"

"Only magic removes *geas*. The compulsion."

Mauer shook his head. The man was not in his right mind, and he had to focus on escaping. He turned and ran for the stairs, ignoring the frantic, whispered pleas behind him.

He reached the landing at the top of the stairs and carefully eased the door open just enough to look out and saw utter chaos.

The floating ship was no longer floating very well. Triss held on to part of the railing to peer over the edge, and saw that the bottom of the deck was resting on the edge of a cliff. That support plus the taut cable tied to a stone pillar were the only things keeping the whole thing from falling down the mountain.

A wrench slid off the engine housing it had been resting on and rattled all the way down to the stern of the ship, and it was followed by an empty wooden box that Triss had to dodge. And she could see more loose gear about to follow it. "We can't stay any longer. If that rope breaks ..."

Jens-Peter muttered a curse. "I know, I know. It's just ... Well, it will do better if we lighten the weight. You get down first. I'll follow in a minute."

The railing the rope was resting on creaked, then snapped off under the pressure. "Look, it's about to collapse! It's not going to get any better if you wait!"

"There's something I need to get first. We'll decide what to do next once we're on the ground. Go!"

That was harder to do than she thought. The ship was tilted, so she had to climb to even reach the bow. Then she had to climb down to reach the cliff top while avoiding the sharp pieces of the broken railing. It was cold and windy, and she could hear the sound of fighting in the distance. Dieter stumbled off the ship next to her and then, after what seemed far longer than a minute, Jens-Peter.

She shivered, and not just from cold. Being on the ship, she'd been safe from the danger. Now she was stuck in the middle of it, and the only way out was through the fight.

"I hear gunshots. I think we shouldn't get any closer."

Dieter crouched down near her, behind a broken wall that kept out some of the wind. "Jens-Peter or I should see what's happening, though."

"No, we stick together." Jens-Peter was firm. "It's too dangerous—and too dark—to go wandering around separately. This is a ruin, for heaven's sake. You could fall down a hole and never be seen again."

We could all fall down the same hole, and that way we'd have company. Triss was beginning to regret insisting on joining the attack—but then if she were back at the camp, she'd just be frantic from worry, not knowing what was happening at all.

They ended up following the broken wall, which led roughly in the right direction. Triss went last, so Jens-Peter had her hold on to the edge of his coat so she would not get lost. She also had the sense that he wanted to know she was still there, so she stifled her protests and went along with it. If she argued, he'd start making too much noise and get them noticed.

Closer up, she noticed that the fighting seemed to have died down in intensity. A few blasts of flame, a few shots. Were they actually winning?

"If you see Barzo," Triss whispered, "tell me. I will call him over."

"Won't that be noticed?"

"We use a special whistle."

Dieter sighed. "Sure, like there would be any birds around this late at night, after all this."

"It doesn't sound like a bird!" Triss bristled. "As if we would be so stupid—"

"Shh!"

Jens-Peter suddenly crouched down, so Triss did too. Now she could see the open space, the one behind the entrance gate. At first it was hard to tell what was going on, in the darkness, but then she started to figure it out. One group was fighting a pinned-down magician. The zigane had guns, the magician was throwing fire, neither was getting much accomplished, but the magician couldn't get away.

Another group Triss didn't recognize, so were probably the magicians Asgaya had brought, were doing something odd that created darker shadows with nothing to cast them, and two strangers were struggling in those shadows.

And farther back, along the far stone wall of the courtyard, Mata Sheri was harnessing a horse to her stolen yellow *vardo*, ignoring the fight in progress. Triss grinned. No matter what, Mata Sheri was taking back what was hers.

Some of the zigane were lying on the ground behind a pile of stones. They were still moving, though, so they should be alive. The air was full of strange smells, metallic and sharp. Some of that was probably gunpowder, but not all of it.

"I can't find Barzo," she murmured. "I hope he is not injured."

"He was clever enough to escape these people, so I doubt he'll let them take advantage again," Jens-Peter said, sliding down the wall to sit at the base. He dug into his coat pocket. "Meanwhile, why not try and find Mauer?" He held out their hand-crafted detector needle bottle.

Triss stared at him. "Is that what you went back to get?"

"We have no way to fight," Dieter pointed out. "What if he's being guarded?"

"If he is, we can still find him and tell the others. But I doubt any guards would stay put while everybody else is getting thrashed, don't you think? They probably ran out to help a long time ago." Jens-Peter had regained his cheerful optimism.

Triss gave him a highly skeptical look. "And if you are wrong?"

"Oooh, look how fast it reacts! I think he's really close!" Jens-Peter said, oblivious. He was already moving, hunched over behind the ruined wall. Triss grimaced, realizing he was too focused to hear anything. At least he was making some effort to stay out of sight. She was going to have to stay with him to keep him out of danger. She reached back to touch the handle of the knife hidden behind her neck.

She could see the needle gleam in flashes of light. At first she thought Jens-Peter was not seeing it correctly, then she realized he was going around the outside edge of the courtyard. At the far end was a large wooden door bound with metal. It was slightly ajar.

"That's the only way down I've seen," Jens-Peter said quietly after stopping. "Dieter, did you notice anything?"

Dieter hesitated. "No, but just now the door moved."

Jens-Peter glanced down at the needle bottle. "That's exactly where Mauer is so we have to go there."

"But someone could be there waiting to kill us!"

"Or it's the wind ..."

Triss rolled her eyes. "*That* door? That very thick and heavy door?"

The door opened wider. A grimy hand appeared on the edge then a pale, worried face. "Jens-Peter? Is that you?"

Before Triss could stop him, Jens-Peter vaulted over the ruined stone wall and dashed for the doorway. "Mauer! You're alive!"

The door was open wide now and there was enough moonlight for Triss to see it really was Wolfgang Mauer, very much the worse for wear and in bad need of a shave, but definitely alive. Jens-Peter was darting about in excitement, talking so fast his words were barely comprehensible. Triss decided it was probably safe and scrambled over the wall after Dieter.

"I wasn't sure anyone could find me ... I mean, I don't even know where I am right now. Did you find my notes?" Mauer's voice was slightly rough, as if he were fighting a cold.

"Some of them, but mostly we used the blood from the book you gave Barzo. Asgaya created a tracker from it!" Jens-Peter held up the ink bottle proudly. "And it worked!"

"Why did they grab you anyway?" Dieter asked, after thumping Mauer on the back.

Mauer staggered, gasping. "I am not clear on that myself, but I still have a fractured rib, so could you postpone your violent gestures of affection?"

Triss smiled to herself and looked around. It seemed that all the fighting had stopped. The black-clad magicians were walking about without concern, and they even helped Mata Sheri steer her *vardo* out the narrow entrance. One of her sons was sitting beside her on the bench of the *vardo*, and Mata Sheri had an expression of wild glee on her face as she drove away to the cheers of the zigane.

Now they'd found two of the three stolen *vardos*. It would be good if that happy mood continued long enough for Triss to find new work and conceal the fact that she'd lost her other position.

Mauer frowned. "How did you deal with the magicians, though?"

"We brought some!" Dieter gestured broadly around the courtyard. "Well, we tracked you in the levitation ship and then Triss sent telegrams back to—"

"What are you doing here? I told you to stay on the ship!" Markus Asgaya glared at them from his position on top of a broken section of pillar. He turned back, shouted some orders, then jumped down and made his way over to where they were standing.

Jens-Peter hadn't moved his position since discovery, but he did appear to have shrunk in an attempt to evade notice. It didn't work.

"Er, about that. Um, it wasn't possible to stay on the ship. Not at present." Jens-Peter took a deep breath and looked up. "And it wasn't my fault! The altitude control armature broke completely off while we were dropping off the zigane. I couldn't tell you."

"Where is the ship?" Asgaya said through gritted teeth. "Can it be seen?"

Jens-Peter pointed. "It should be out of sight for now. At least it is if the rope hasn't broken yet."

Triss nudged him to stop talking. As bad as it was, he didn't need to tell Asgaya everything at once.

Then Asgaya saw Mauer, and he gave a sigh of relief. "Well, that's some good news. It seems there are no other defenders inside if you are here. Do you require any medical attention? I assume they rescued you from your imprisonment?"

Mauer blinked. "No, I rescued myself. There's one of them down there still, but he can't move, and when he can speak, it doesn't make much sense."

"Wait, there's one of them still down there? How did you escape?"

"I … am not quite sure, actually. That is, I found this acid sand in the place they locked me up. I used it to break open the metal door. Then when that guy surprised me, I threw the jar at him, and then suddenly he collapsed." Mauer shrugged.

Asgaya shifted closer, frowning hard. "He's still alive? What is he saying?"

"Oh, things like 'I'm free' and 'He's coming, don't let him put a *geas* on you.' What's a *geas*?"

"A very evil spell that compels obedience," Asgaya said grimly. "What do you mean by acid sand?"

Mauer held up a fist-sized ceramic jar. "It works quite well on iron."

Asgaya had gone completely still, his eyes wide with horror. Triss glanced at the jar and frowned. It looked very familiar, the rough ceramic surface … and sand …

"Is there more of this … acid sand there?" His voice was a hoarse whisper.

"Yes, about ten large crates." Mauer looked puzzled. "Why?"

"It's a kind of contraband I've been tracing. It's good to find it at last." Asgaya was putting in a good effort to seem relaxed, but Triss noticed the small tremor in his hand. "But don't mention it to anyone else. It's dangerous stuff."

Mauer nodded. "I understand, I have seen it in action."

Asgaya gave a quick, twitchy grin that didn't reach his eyes.

And then a huge explosion rocked the courtyard. A beam of blinding white fire hit one of the black-clad magicians, slamming him against the stone wall with a crack. Blue halos appeared around the body and the white beam.

Asgaya cursed. "Oh, of course. He's here, damn him. And we're tired from the fight already. Quick. All of you, back down that stairway, and bar the door behind you! We'll do our best to keep him out, but if we don't, he *cannot* get those salts! Do you understand? This is for the safety of all Aerope! Hide it, dump it out a window, anything! Go, go!" He shoved Mauer back through the doorway. Then he pulled off a bag he had slung over one shoulder and tossed it at Dieter before he ran off, yelling to his magicians and pointing to the new threat.

Jens-Peter gaped, motionless, but Triss snagged the collar of his coat and dragged him inside the doorway.

If Asgaya was frightened, she wanted them to get as far away as possible.

CHAPTER 30

The stairs were dark and even darker when Triss slammed the door shut. "I can't find a bar or anything," she gasped. "We have to keep it closed somehow."

Jens-Peter shifted over. "Do we have any light at all? How did you see to escape, Mauer?"

"Sorry. I forgot I had this." Mauer held up a flickering lamp. It wasn't very bright, but in the total darkness it was a welcome sight.

Triss was right: the door had no bar. There was an iron bracket for one, but the wood bar itself was nowhere to be found.

Jens-Peter studied the iron hinges thoughtfully. "I need something wedge-shaped. We can block it with that for a while. You said there were iron grills in the place they kept you, right?" Mauer nodded. "Were the iron bars as long as the door is wide? Excellent. You and your jar of acid sand have some work to do. Bring me one of those bars. And what about light, are there other lamps?"

"Torches. I think there's one or two left."

Triss came up with a collection of rock fragments in her hands. Jens-Peter picked out the most likely ones and quickly hammered them in place under the bottom of the door. It wouldn't hold for long, but it was better than nothing.

"Let's get those iron bars."

At the base of the stairs a gaunt man lay sprawled, eyes half-open and twitching. "Is he here?" he whispered.

"I don't know if it's that master person you mentioned was coming, but somebody with powerful magic just showed up." Mauer started dribbling sand on the iron door a few feet away. "And is attacking."

"No don't do it like that, take out the grill hinges and then take it apart on the ground," Jens-Peter protested.

The man wheezed. "What … are you doing?"

"Trying to block the door that leads to the courtyard." Jens-Peter noticed it was a little brighter, and then Triss came out with a very short torch.

"Are the crates where that came from?" She pointed to the jar in Mauer's hands. He nodded.

"There's no windows in that place, and there are a lot of crates. How can we get rid of them?" Triss glanced at the man on the floor. "Does he know? Even if he did, it will take a long time to toss everything. And I don't think we have a long time." Her voice trailed off as she looked down.

"I can … buy you time …" the man said, his face twisting. "My body … is weak, but my magic is not. Take me … to the door. I can seal it more than iron."

They looked at each other. Jens-Peter remembered Asgaya's frantic instructions, the fear in his eyes. He didn't know what exactly was going on, but it was something he could not afford to make mistakes with. He also knew that with the power of the attack he saw, the door itself would disintegrate no matter what was holding it shut—but magic might work.

"Aren't you one of the people doing the attacking?" Triss stared at the man, hands on her hips.

"He was, but under compulsion," Mauer said, looking up from his work on the grill. "He's not like he was anyway. And he warned me the attack was coming."

"I'll be able to tell if he's doing what he said he would," Dieter added. "And provide magefire, but, um, not for very long."

I only have bad choices and no information. It's worth the risk.

"Mauer. Keep working on the grill. Dieter, help me get him up the stairs."

Jens-Peter took the depressingly small torch in one hand and tried to find a way to help carry the man, who was a dead weight, but failed as the torch went out with his fumbling. They'd just have to go up in the semi-dark until Dieter used his magelight. He stuck the stub of the torch in a pocket so he wouldn't lose it.

"You have a name?" Jens-Peter managed to gasp out. Even with Dieter's help it was hard work.

"Hans Sollveg."

Dieter stumbled and grunted. "Is all this really a danger to Aerope? Enough for Asgaya to fight to the death to keep whoever it is away?"

"Yes." Sollveg's voice was still weak, but the intensity was fierce. "Korda is insane, or close to it. And he is the most powerful magician I've ever seen."

Jens-Peter sighed. "Doesn't that mean he'll be able to break through anything you do to stop him?"

"He is powerful but not clever. It will delay him. He also does not wish to damage the crates. He values the contents more than anything." Sollveg gasped. "What he did to me ... the *geas* ... he would do to everyone. Forced to obey his every command ..."

They were finally at the top of the stairs again, and Jens-Peter fought to catch his breath. He could hear distant shouts and feel shaking underfoot, so the fight was still ongoing. He wondered how long Asgaya could hold Korda off since he was already tired from the previous fight.

Dieter grimaced, holding out one hand, which suddenly was enveloped in pale blue light. It was just enough to see the door and the landing.

Sollveg stared intently at the heavy wooden door before taking a deep breath, gritting his teeth, and raising one arm in a complex gesture.

Suddenly the sounds from outside disappeared. Dieter reached out to the door handle, but before his fingers could reach it a ripple of pale blue light spread across the door and vanished.

"It's a barrier, and it's working," he said, nodding. "Quite strong."

"One more ... thing." Sollveg could not even keep his head upright now. "Don't let him take me alive. Please."

Jens-Peter compressed his lips. It wasn't a matter of wanting to save Sollveg; he wasn't sure he could save anybody. "I'll take you with us, whatever happens. I can't promise more."

"It is enough." Sollveg had a ghost of a smile on his face. He gestured with one finger. "I heard there is a passage down to the base of the hill, somewhere in this catacomb. Find it ..." His body sagged.

Then Jens-Peter noticed light. "Where is it coming from?" Dieter's magelight had blinked out already.

"Your pocket."

"Ah, the torch relit!"

When he pulled it out, he saw that while the torch was the source of the light, it had not relit itself. Instead, a bright bluish light came from the tip of the stub.

Dieter gaped. "He cast magelight on the torch! I didn't know you could do that. I guess he's still trying to help." He dragged Sollveg's arm over his shoulder, preparing to head back down.

"Hold on, what's this?" Jens-Peter could now see a dark bag on the ground. It looked familiar, and then he remembered Asgaya tossing it to him before running off. Inside was a tied-off leather sack, some stiff cord, a few nails, and a wooden box. The sack contained roughly a pound of gunpowder and inside the box, which was padded, was a glass bottle of pyretic acid.

Despite the danger they were in, he couldn't help grinning. He'd wondered why Asgaya wanted him to have the bag, and now he knew. He also had a pretty good idea what to do.

"Come on." He picked up Sollveg's other arm. It would be easier going down, he hoped. "I need to do some structural analysis with ill intent."

While Mauer worked on the iron grill, Triss searched the passage and the crypt as much as she could for the lack of light. She found another dry, fragile torch stump in a wall bracket but decided against lighting it. They might need it later.

She wanted to stay as far away as possible from the oily sand Mauer was using. The sharp, sour smell was exactly the same as the sand she'd found in the broken *vardo*, and the thought that it could etch metal made her even more reluctant to come into contact with it. Yet Mauer, strangely, did not seem to fear it but considered it a useful tool. She could only conclude he was not subject to visual hallucinations or had avoided contamination so far.

"There!" Mauer pulled one of the long vertical iron bars free. "Now, where's Jens-Peter?"

"Make sure to shake any loose grains of sand off before you touch it," Triss said as his hand went out. "That ... It's probably dangerous."

He nodded. "You have a point."

A dull boom echoed, and a trickle of dirt and pebbles fell from above. *Still fighting. I hope the troupe got away already.* What could they do against a powerful magician like that? And what would she be able to do to help even if she were up there with them? It still worried her, and being trapped down here wasn't reassuring either.

"I don't know what Jens-Peter wanted this for if not to bar the door." Mauer carefully picked the iron bar up using his jacket, tapping it on the ground. "Let's see if there are any other rooms or passages."

Triss nodded. "Hopefully with windows." She wanted that sand destroyed and away from her.

The passage was very dusty, and a few places had roots growing through the stones of the arched ceiling. Triss kept a careful eye out for spiders. They found a few doorways, one to a similar crypt but clearly not recently used and another where the structure had caved in and was full of masonry and dirt. Triss found a few more old torch stubs.

Then she noticed a light, brighter than the lamp, coming from the direction of the stairs, and footsteps. Triss immediately grabbed Mauer and pulled him into the disused crypt.

She hadn't heard anything, no yelling or ... But there had been that loud noise previously. Had the magician gotten past Asgaya? Was Jens-Peter still alive?

And then she heard his voice, cheerful as ever. "—and with the light now it's really clear! I've only seen Early Romasque barrel vaults from

214

illustrations in books! There's hardly any of them left since they were only used for about a hundred years or so."

Dieter only grunted in response. They were still carrying the gaunt man, now completely unconscious.

"Why did you bring him back with you?" Triss was still not convinced he could be trusted.

Jens-Peter took a few deep breaths and wiped the sweat from his forehead. "Sollveg did seal the door with magic for us. And gave us this." He waved the blue light. "Even if he is working with Korda—the bad guy attacking right now—it's better to keep an eye on him than to leave him behind to cause trouble."

Mauer handed him the iron bar. "What are you planning to do with this?"

"I was thinking about breaking a wall or something to get access to the outside, but Asgaya gave me some explosives. But here's the problem." Jens-Peter gestured at the crypt. "I don't know how thick the walls are. We could blow it up and not get an opening to toss the sand stuff out from. However, I *do* know something about the vaulting. The reason there aren't many surviving examples of Early Romasque is it has some crucial structural flaws. If it isn't done right—or is damaged— the whole thing can collapse on you."

Dieter glanced up, his expression relaxing. "Oh, you want to bury the crates. What's the problem with that?"

"If I take out the critical support in the crypt, this hallway might collapse too."

No one spoke for a moment. "Well, that would certainly keep the crates away from Korda," Mauer said finally. "But it would also trap us. I suppose we could wait for Asgaya to find us, if …" Triss knew he was tactfully not completing the rest of his thought.

"Sollveg said there could be a passage here out to the bottom of the hill," Dieter mumbled.

"Which he's never seen himself, only heard about."

Another long silence, which only irritated Triss. They didn't have time to waste!

"What choice do we have?" she said, her voice sharp. "We can't go back up and leave this undefended. Asgaya is so worried about the oil sand getting into the wrong hands that he was willing to reveal the levitation ship to stop it. He's fighting right now. Even if … if he can't rescue us, I am certain Fräulein von Kitren knows he came here, and if he doesn't return, she'll come looking for him." If she could, and if she could bring help able to dig out a mountain in time. They had no food or water. "Maybe he'll win and we won't have to blow it up, but we have to be ready to do it. Whatever we do, we need to do it now."

Mauer then Dieter nodded. Jens-Peter prodded the stone wall with the iron bar and grinned. "Right! Fortunately, it won't take much to bring down the vaulting. The gunpowder here will be enough, and save the pyritic acid for emergencies. And there's always the chance, you know, that this is Transitional Romasque."

"What does that mean?" Triss couldn't help asking, although she had a strong feeling she would regret it.

"It looks the same, but it doesn't have all the flaws. If it is, only the crypt vault will collapse and the hall will just be weakened, probably staying intact. We might be able to get out if so." Jens-Peter took the iron bar and went into the crypt where the crates were. "Right, perfect. They removed the sub-piers to make the bays larger, so it's even weaker. The gunpowder needs to go right where the vaulting support meets the vertical wall. I'll mark the place. Everybody grab something to smash with!"

They weren't going to make a dent in the stones with what they had, so Jens-Peter had them dig out the mortar between the stones, as deep as they could. Triss was using the old iron shackles that had held Mauer, which were quite awkward to use to excavate, but she managed.

Then Jens-Peter packed the holes with gunpowder. "There really isn't enough fuse," he muttered. "We have to set it off all at once for it to work for sure."

The problem was the distance. The fuses hung from the wall, one in each bay. Rubble from the damaged bays made it awkward to run from one bay to the other.

"Dieter, is there anything you can do?"

Dieter shook his head. "Not that precise. I could set it all off at once though."

Triss looked at the others and gritted her teeth. "I'll do it." When Jens-Peter started to protest, she held up a hand. "I can move faster than any of you, especially over broken ground like that. Give me the lantern, then get far away from the door."

Mauer was holding the lantern. His face twisted as she reached for it, but he let her take it away.

"I'll set the furthest fuse to be longest," Jens-Peter said, taking some of the nails and holding them in his mouth. "The rest of you take Sollveg far down the passage," he mumbled, cutting some fuse and fixing it in place.

Dieter had already left. Mauer, still injured, was slower. When he reached the doorway, he looked up at the stairs. "Um, I think we have a problem," he called back, his voice shaking. "The door is glowing."

There was an indistinct murmur, and then Dieter yelled, "Sollveg says the seal is breaking! We can't wait!"

Jens-Peter looked up, eyes wide. He started to protest but Triss grabbed his arm and pulled hard. "Get out! I'll start the others without a fuse!"

She lit the long length of fuse, glancing up to make sure he was nearly out, then sprinted for the next bay, vaulting over the pile of rubble while keeping the lantern aloft. She couldn't drop it now.

At the base of the second bay pillar she fumbled with the lantern, unscrewing the cap to the base where the oil was. Using a tossing motion, she got oil on the gunpowder and dripping down the pier before running to the last column and repeating the process but leaving a trail of oil on the straw underfoot.

"The seal is gone!"

Triss hurled the lantern at the pier and launched herself out the doorway, dropping into a tuck to roll away from the opening, but she hit something that grunted and fell, and then wrapped arms around her tightly.

Jens-Peter! He didn't run, the idiot!

A blast gushed fire, smoke, and rubble out of the doorway. Jens-Peter scrambled to his feet and half carried, half dragged Triss.

"What? Why? The explosion is over!" Triss could see the passageway and, at the top of the stairs, a man staring down at them with a cold, murderous expression.

"Just the start!" Jens-Peter gasped. "Hold on!"

And then the walls collapsed with a thunderous roar. It seemed to go on forever, sounding like a mountain falling, but eventually it did stop. The air was full of dust, smelling faintly sour.

Jens-Peter was huddled on the ground, hunched over her. Triss got up carefully. Some of the rubble had hit her leg, and she was not sure how badly she was hurt.

"Is everyone all right?" Mauer's voice came out of the gloom.

"Alive, anyway." Jens-Peter sounded almost cheerful. The blue magelight torch got closer, and they were able to see that the passageway was completely blocked by fallen masonry. "Ha! It *was* Early Romasque!"

Triss took a deep breath and then coughed hard. She couldn't kill him after he'd saved them. Not right now. But if anyone deserved a beating …

CHAPTER 31

There was, Jens-Peter admitted, a slight problem with minimal light, lack of water, and lack of a guaranteed escape route. Other than that, though, things had turned out rather well. It would take a long time for anyone, even a magician, to get through all that rock. The contents of the crates were now safe.

Dieter and Mauer had sustained no additional injuries, the same for Sollveg who was still unconscious. Triss had a sluggishly bleeding scratch on her forehead and was limping slightly. She was also covered with dust, making her sneeze.

"I just want to know if I will ever be clean again," she muttered, patting off the worst patches from her skirt.

They had gathered together in a rounded area at the far end of the passageway. The only real light was the magelight carried by Dieter. As far as supplies went, they had only what they were originally carrying and the satchel Asgaya had given him, now much lighter since the gunpowder was used up.

"I suppose we should look for this alleged escape route," Mauer said with a doubtful expression. "I am not seeing much to search, frankly."

It was true. The rounded space had no obvious openings that weren't full of rubble or broken beams. Jens-Peter was reasonably sure the rubble *here* was not their fault as it was all covered with cobwebs and none of it extended to the passage itself.

And he was starting to feel jittery. He'd never had a problem with closed spaces before, but then he'd never caused a roof collapse either. He just wanted to run as far as he could.

"I brought all the torch stubs I found," Triss said, dropping them to the stone floor. "Good thing the ceiling didn't collapse that far. But they won't burn very long."

"Do you … need light?" Sollveg groaned and sat up, gesturing to the pile of torch stubs. He no longer looked like a fresh corpse even if he did still sound like he was about to become one. "I can make more like the first I did. It would not be wise to use up what air we have with flame."

As soon as Sollveg mentioned it Jens-Peter realized they had another thing to worry about, and it could kill them faster than Asgaya could reach them.

He crouched down next to Sollveg. "I don't suppose these stories you heard mentioned *where* the passage came out?"

Sollveg shook his head. Triss handed him a torch stump, rubbing her eyes. The magician gestured and another of the bright lights shimmered. "It is strange … I feel stronger than I did before." He frowned at his fingers. "That should not be. And I recovered much more quickly from the magical exhaustion than I expected. Could it be the result of removing the *geas*?" He gestured for Triss to hand him another torch stump.

She took a step, then staggered and rubbed her eyes again. Jens-Peter got up and went to her.

"Are you all right?" he asked in a quiet voice. Even with a limp, Triss had good balance and had never stumbled before. Had she been injured more than he'd realized?

"It's starting again. It went away just like he said but now it's back. I can see everything …" Her voice was taut and choked, like she was holding back tears.

Well. It appeared that dropping a ton of rock on crates had loosened some of the sand and spread it. "I think you said it felt like ants all over your skin?" Triss nodded sharply. "So that's what's happening to me. I agree, it is unpleasant. But I'm not seeing anything special."

"I can even see the individual specks of dust move …" she whispered.

Jens-Peter put his hand on her arm. "You got through this once, you can do it again. Remember? Just close your eyes for a bit, I'll guide you." Then he thought back on what she had said. "Um, where is the dust moving?" The passage was surprisingly clean, and nobody had moved for a while now.

Triss pointed at the opening in the wall with the fallen beams. Jens-Peter went up to it, even sticking his head inside. It might be his imagination but the air seemed to smell fresher. He guided Triss over to take a look.

"Oh, it's moving even more over there."

It wasn't like they had much choice. They might be able to move the beams or get past them. The stones were too heavy to lift.

"I think we should try exploring," Jens-Peter said to the rest. "If nothing else, it seems to be getting fresh air from somewhere. Maybe there's a way we can signal for help. But it is going to be awkward going." He looked at Sollveg. "And it might not go anywhere. I don't even know how close we are to the outside of the ruins."

A glow of light blinked in front of Triss, who gasped. "Ah, no …"

Jens-Peter stared at the image. It took a moment for him to realize he was looking at a simple outline of the hill in cross section. There were the ruins, the courtyard, the stairs, and the passageway, which had a distinct slope he hadn't realized previously.

"This is good," he said, walking around it. "See? We're about halfway down. Triss, this is useful. Can you do it the other way? As if we were above?"

It wasn't as detailed, but Triss did manage to come up with another image, still floating in the air and glowing. He hadn't realized how close they were to the edge of the cliff. He felt a very slight twinge of hope.

"Young lady, how did you train such a gift?" Sollveg was staring at Triss in awe. "I have never seen such clear imaging art."

Triss shook her head. "I wasn't trained. I usually can't—"

Jens-Peter gripped her hand, warning her. If Sollveg didn't know, they couldn't tell him about the oily sand and what it could do.

"I think we should try it," Mauer said. "All of us. We'll probably have to move some of that to get out, and it's just as awkward going back and forth. Besides, we should stay together."

"I believe I can walk, with assistance," Sollveg said. "And I too think we should try this way."

Progress was awkward and agonizingly slow. The fallen beams were most visible, but there were also sections of masonry that had fallen. They crawled through any available opening, and if necessary created one. Dieter and Jens-Peter levered up some blocking beams while Triss and Mauer shoved rocks underneath, then crawled through. Even when there seemed to be no way forward, Triss could see the air movements in the dust or fractures that meant part of a beam could be removed.

Sollveg tried to walk, but mostly crawled and he and Mauer had to be helped through the tight sections.

"Are we making any progress at all?" Dieter wondered. With all the dust and exertion everyone's voice had gone rough. Jens-Peter felt like his mouth was full of grit.

"We're … we are getting closer to the ground," Triss said. She clenched her eyes shut, and a flickering image showed their path.

Jens-Peter shook her shoulder. "That's enough. Don't visualize unless we really need it." He held up the magelight for a better look at her, but the blue-white light made everybody look like ghosts. He still thought she looked exhausted.

Triss would get sharp headaches if she held the image for more than a minute, so he wanted to reserve that skill only for when they got lost. And he didn't think they would get lost now. The walls were hand-cut living rock with frequent steps, all heading down. The beams that had troubled them for so long had vanished, and there were only occasional rockfalls to climb over now. No side paths had appeared either. If this wasn't the escape route, they were truly stuck.

They were surprisingly close to the level of the base of the hill now, according to the image Triss had produced. Jens-Peter trudged down more uneven rough-cut steps, almost wishing there were no way out so he could give up and stop moving.

Then the steps ended. They walked slowly into a wide space that seemed different than the passage, with worn rock walls that had no sign of being chiseled.

"This looks like a natural cave," Mauer said, panting and clutching his side. "Did the builders find it first and then cut the passage up from here?"

Jens-Peter looked around, seeing no passageways or other openings. "I hope so, because that means there's an exit somewhere that I'm just not seeing."

He glanced at Triss, who shook her head. No helpful swirling dust here. They would have to search the hard way.

He went over every inch of the large cave and found nothing of use, with the exception of three old coins, a cracked wooden bowl, and a pile of lumber and rust that might have been anything from a large cart to a small siege engine.

Sollveg had long ago stopped searching from fatigue and was sitting on one of the fallen rocks. "What have you found?" he called out to Dieter. Dieter was staring fixedly at a wall of large boulders mixed with smaller rocks.

"I'm hungry." Jens-Peter was only surprised it had taken Dieter that long to mention it. He needed a constant source of food, especially when exerting himself.

"We all are. That's why we're trying to get out." Jens-Peter sighed and started looking again, only to notice that Triss was now staring at Dieter. What was she seeing?

Dieter frowned, looking puzzled. "I was just generally hungry before, but when I walk past this place I get *really* hungry."

"Your nose twitches too," Triss said. "What do you smell?"

Mauer limped over and started sniffing the air. "It's very faint, but there is something."

"Oh, I guess that's it. Now that you say that, I can smell it too." Dieter pondered some more. "It reminds me of something. That scary zigane woman."

Jens-Peter froze. The supreme unwisdom of even *thinking* about Mata Sheri in the context of bad odors had him terrified. If she found out …

Suddenly Triss smiled, a shaky smile but a real one. "It's *terrangi!*

Someone outside is cooking *terrangi*! It's that lentil stew you had. There must be air from outside coming through here!"

Mauer slumped to the ground. "That's great. In case you hadn't noticed, there's still half a mountain's worth of rock in the way. That one in particular isn't moving even if all of us were in perfect health." He pointed to a large boulder, squarely in the way and touching the solid rock walls on either side.

Jens-Peter opened the satchel and pulled out the small wooden box. "That means it's a job for engineering! You've never seen pyritic acid in action, have you?"

"Possibly because it's extremely dangerous," Dieter muttered, but Jens-Peter had seen the gleam in his eye.

"Yes, yes, it's very unstable and explodes at the slightest impact, but only when it is dry! Oh, phooey. I should have brought some straw from your prison cell." Jens-Peter nodded at Mauer. "That was nice and dry, but I forgot in all the excitement."

Triss folded her arms. "You like exploding things, don't you?"

"It's an occupational hazard," Dieter said with a grin. "They don't like it when we do it at the university, so we have to take our opportunities when we find them. What can we use if we don't have straw? I suppose we could make wood shavings, somehow." He glanced at the pile of wood.

"It's damp." Triss shook her head. "What kind of material do you need? Something that burns?"

"Something that can absorb the acid and then dry out, the faster the better. I've seen it done with paper and straw."

"What about cloth?" Triss ripped off a scrap from her tattered skirt and held it out.

They had a wide variety of cloth, from thin muslin to the knit scarf he was wearing, if they didn't care about being cold. Jens-Peter stuck with the thinner fabric that would dry faster and wouldn't keep too much of the unstable pyritic acid. Then they had to figure out where to put it.

"Bunch it up, but loosely. Then tuck it underneath. No, on the other side." Jens-Peter pointed. "Then the rest here."

Dieter glanced up. "Are you sure? That's not going to crack the boulder much."

"We have to have some where we can throw a rock from the stairs." Dieter nodded and arranged the scraps of fabric, then stood and dusted his knees.

Jens-Peter turned to look at the others. "You should take a piece of wood to cover your heads from that pile, then go up the stairs as far as you can." The stairway was cut from the rock, so it should be more stable than masonry. He hoped that would be enough, but they didn't have any better options.

He carefully took out the bottle of pyritic acid, turning it upside down for a minute before taking a deep breath and unsealing the lead stopper. Sometimes crystals would form inside if the acid was left without being moved for a long time, and opening the bottle would cause an explosion. Letting the acid dissolve again was the best fix, if so.

The bottle did not explode. The itchy, sharp smell of the pyritic acid drifted past his nose, and he fought the urge to sneeze. Sneezing now would be very, very bad.

He sprinkled the pyritic acid on the fabric, being careful to never let it pool anywhere and to save enough for the last scrap to act as the detonator. He wasn't sure what to do with the bottle but ended up re-sealing it and tucking it in a gap in the rocks.

Then Jens-Peter went as far as he thought he could throw accurately, almost to the base of the stairs, and waited. It was cold and lonely. If it failed or he tripped, he would probably die. The others would die too if they couldn't get out.

He checked his pocket watch. It had been an hour, and even in the damp air of the cave, pyritic acid would be dry by now. He stood, rolled his shoulders to warm up the stiffness, and flung the rock in his hand at the rag detonator.

Even though he spun and sprinted as soon as the rock left his hand, the sudden blast lifted him off his feet and flung him painfully against the stone stairs with a thundering roar. Lying there, he was too dazed to move and just gasped, coughing in the dust and acrid smoke until he felt hands pulling on his arm and turning him over.

Why can't I hear anything? Triss's face was hovering over him, and her lips were moving. Her face was twisted with worry as she stared at his face. *Oh. The detonation.*

"The explosion hurt my ears," he said, or tried to say. It was strange not hearing his own voice.

Are you hurt? Triss mouthed slowly. Was he? He patted his sides and then tried to stand up. A wave of dizziness nearly made him fall, but nothing hurt. Well, besides the general, all-over ache, but he was nearly accustomed to that.

He pointed back at the cave. He couldn't see if they had succeeded because of all the dust in the air, but perhaps Triss and her enhanced eyesight could see more. Triss shrugged. Bracing himself against the stairway wall, Jens-Peter started to edge through the murk. He could feel if it worked, maybe.

Triss yanked his arm over her shoulder. From her expression she was yelling at him, but she still helped him across the cave, and he couldn't help grinning at her.

In the magelight, close up, he could see that the boulder had been shattered into several pieces. One of the larger pieces was still in the way, so he had Triss help him to the pile of old wood to see if there were any beams large and strong enough to serve as a lever.

"… idiot! And … old, so …"

Jens-Peter turned sharply, setting off another wave of dizziness. Dieter was right next to him, frowning. The dust was settling enough he could see Mauer helping Sollveg back down the stairs.

"Hey, I can almost hear you! Anybody hurt?"

Triss's mouth moved again, probably explaining his sudden deafness. Dieter shook his head.

Jens-Peter tugged on a long pole that looked sturdy, lost his grip, and fell. Triss and Dieter picked it up instead. With pointing and gesturing, he got them to put the end where it needed to go, and then Dieter moved another rock to act as a fulcrum.

They didn't have to move it very far, just enough to let them squeeze past. Triss went first, as the smallest of them. Now Jens-Peter heard a constant ringing noise, like being in a church belfry, but with faint voices.

"… light!"

That was very good news. He started shoveling dirt and rock with his hands while staying on his knees so he wouldn't fall. Soon he could see not just light but a pair of hands making the hole the light came from larger and larger until he could see Barzo's face.

"You there! I find you! That *bruje*, he say you moving, so alive, come out at bottom somewhere!" For some reason he could hear Barzo's deep voice better, even through the ringing in his ears. "I wait for you, Trisstela!"

"Um, I don't suppose you have any food?" Dieter asked. "We've had a long day."

CHAPTER 32

Triss drifted awake, feeling confused. She was lying on something soft, she was warm, and the confusing double and triple vision caused by the strange sand had gone away. She sat up with a groan. All her bruises and sore muscles had stiffened since ...

She blinked. The ruins. They had found the secret path and escaped the ruins, and Jens-Peter had blown things up ... at least twice. Then Barzo had found them outside and sent up a flare to bring help. She vaguely remembered hot *terrangi*, even more delicious after starving an entire day, and then a carriage ride that somehow ended with a glorious hot bath, the first since she had left Baron Heufritz's house. Even if the tin hip-bath was tiny, she was *clean*.

But where was she? The room was small but tidy, clean even in the places careless maids often missed, and Triss nodded approvingly. Then she saw her cloth bundle on the rush-seat chair next to the bed.

So. Someone must have gone back to the flying ship then and retrieved it from the cabinet she'd stuffed it in. Which meant the ship was still there and the fight had been won by the zigane and Asgaya's magicians.

On the foot of the bed she found a plain blouse and a dark-blue skirt. Judging from the size, it was a loan from the same source as the nightgown she was swimming in. She got dressed as fast as she could and left the room.

She was in a little hotel in Bielefeld, and it appeared that Asgaya had taken over the entire building with his people and others who had arrived that day. Triss had to squeeze by several groups of men in the hallway while looking for anyone she recognized. At last she caught a glimpse of Asgaya in the hotel parlor issuing orders to a group of people in uniform and edged into the room.

Asgaya looked tired but happy. He had a bandage on one hand but otherwise appeared to be uninjured. When the uniformed men left, in a rush, Triss approached.

"Ah, Miss Trisstela! You time your arrival well. I have almost completed what needs to be done here." Asgaya quickly wrote a few lines, blotted the paper, then folded it and handed it to someone standing nearby.

"I don't want to disturb you. I just wanted to know where I can find Jens-Peter. And the others," she added quickly.

"At last report Herr Oberacker was still snoring in bed, as was Herr Mauer, who has more of an excuse for such behavior. We brought in a doctor to look at their injuries as well as the magician you rescued. What was his name? Ah, Sollveg. Mauer is in the worst shape, but a few weeks of rest and he should be good as new." Asgaya stood up. "I believe your family is busy having your carts repaired at the moment, but some of them may be about outside."

From the position of the sun, it was past noon. She had slept longer than she ever had before and still felt slightly tired. Outside she found Barzo and some of the other young men from the troupe, who saw her looking carefully for Mata Sheri and laughed at her.

"Mata Sheri, she is still cosseting her *vardo* like a rescued chick," one said.

"Is the same yellow as one, no?"

Barzo grinned. "Trisstela, you are a fine lady now? Sleep like a cat in the sun, then wear skirts like a tent!"

Triss stuck out her tongue at him. It was true that the skirt was very full and so long that it covered her toesl, but it was clean. "Ha, and do you poke at gifts? Tell me, how are our people after the fight?"

Barzo rubbed his head, and the grin faded. "All still breathe, for the luck. But Oti, his leg hurt bad. And others, but he is the worst. I do not know if we do our usual show even by spring."

They had recovered the *vardos*, but now the troupe had lost its means of making a living. Oti was strong and reliable, an important anchor for the more skilled acrobatic tricks. Without him, it would be nearly impossible.

"I wait for word from Faad Tobar, what to do now. The *bruje*, he send the doctor to our people. He pays *jaina* in full, that one." It was high praise from a zigane speaking of a *gadje*. Then Barzo frowned at her. "But what were you about, to be on that hill? You said you would stay with the flying ship, no?"

"The flying ship stopped flying," Triss said with exasperation. "What, I should fall to my death instead?"

"Do not say such ill-omened words. We have enough bad luck. Ah, your *gadje* boy comes."

"He's not my *gadje*," Triss protested but turned to see Jens-Peter limping out of the hotel. He had visible bruises and scrapes on his face. "Can you hear now?"

Jens-Peter nodded carefully. "It feels like I have cotton in my ears, but it's a lot better than yesterday. Now that everybody is up except Mauer, Asgaya wants to ask us about what happened in the underground passage." He wasn't looking at her or Barzo, so she suspected there was something he was concealing.

"Eh, you go. I tell you when word comes." Barzo waved and walked off down the street.

Asgaya did indeed want to talk to them, and in such privacy that he even set up a magical barrier against eavesdropping. "I regret not giving you more time to rest, but I must know with certainty. Did you block access to the crates?"

"I brought down the vaulted ceiling on them, so anybody who wants to get to them will have to move a lot of stone to do it," Jens-Peter said.

"Good, but for that material they might." Asgaya looked grim. "I put some of my own protections in place, but I do not like having two routes to that area of collapse. It does look like there's enough rubble to hold matters for now. I will call in more powerful mages to seal it permanently."

"Speaking of more powerful mages, what happened to that Korda person that showed up?" Dieter asked.

Asgaya sighed and ran a hand through his white-streaked hair. "A draw. He escaped, but we captured several of his enslaved magicians. A pity we couldn't get him, too, but he'll be much weaker now. And he doesn't have the crates, which is a definite victory for us. Thank you." His eyes were solemn. "On behalf of Preusa, and of Aeropa, thank you. You do not know the danger you have saved us from. Once the passage to the crates was blocked Korda panicked and ran. He's not actually very skilled. He just has access to tremendous power. And that makes him dangerous."

"That reminds me—what will happen to that Sollveg fellow? He was with Korda, at least at first, but he did help us."

Asgaya nodded. "He's imprisoned until we can confirm everything he did was under compulsion, but he is free from the *geas* now and has been telling us everything he knows about Korda. He is profoundly grateful to you and claims you were the ones who removed the *geas*. Since none of you are mages, I find that claim incredible, but he is obstinate about it. And lucky. It doesn't always work well when the removal is attempted." He rubbed his forehead with one hand, shading his eyes, and was silent for a moment.

"I want to know what happened to *Einzl*," Jens-Peter said. "The ship," he explained to Asgaya's inquiring glance.

"Ah, yes. We had to lower it down, but it is still intact and under guard. They know about it, so I expect they will be sending people to repair it soon."

Triss looked at Jens-Peter and then at Asgaya. "Does that mean he's not being chased and shot at anymore? Because I really need to find work, especially now that the troupe can't perform and—"

The door to the parlor opened, and the familiar, bedraggled figure of Mauer stumbled in.

"What are you doing out of bed? You are lucky to be alive, you know." Asgaya got up and reached out to help support him. "There's nothing for you to do here."

"No, I think you need to know what I saw." Mauer's voice was strained but determined. "Did you bring any people from the Kriegsa with you?"

Asgaya stared at him for a moment, then shook his head.

"That's what I thought. After all, you can't stand them or they you ... but I saw one of them during the fight. After I broke out and found Jens-Peter and the others, I saw a man at the top of the stairs after the magic barrier failed. I recognized him from when I went to the Kriegsa to tell them about Jens-Peter."

Triss blinked. "That wasn't the evil mage?"

"No, he never got to the stair entrance." Asgaya looked startled, then grim. "What did he look like?"

"Rather thin in the face, with light brown hair. Blue eyes, oh, and he speaks with a slight Pladt accent."

"Thank you. I know who that is." Strangely, although Asgaya spoke softly, Triss felt a chill of fear. "Are you willing to identify him to a military court?"

"He was behind my kidnapping and imprisonment, of course I will," Mauer snapped.

"Then I must leave for Baerlen immediately. Holtzer! Guard them well and bring them to Baerlen as fast as their injuries permit. All of them." Asgaya gathered up a caped coat and a handful of papers and strode out as one of the black-uniformed men came in. He stopped in front of Triss. "I have not forgotten my obligation to your family. We will talk again in Baerlen when you return."

"Return? Why do I have to go to Baerlen?" The troupe would not understand, and eventually Mata Sheri would remember her and start asking questions.

"You saw that man too and that puts you in danger. He has powerful connections, and I am going to try and stop him before he can take action."

Triss gaped in shock. She was in danger? *Barzo is not going to be happy about this.*

CHAPTER 33

Jens-Peter was bored. He knew he had to stay inside and out of sight, but there was nothing to *do* in the warehouse. Last time he was here, at least he could work on the levitation ship. He was pretty sure Triss was bored too.

Why was he even here? He should be back at the ruins, fixing *Einzl*. They were probably doing it wrong. They didn't even *ask* him.

At least Triss had something to do even if it was just daily cleaning. Barzo tended to smoke his pipe in the sun, occasionally helping when Dragonhunter carriages came in. "So why is your cousin here? He didn't see that Kriegsa spy."

Triss kept polishing metalwork with a rag. "That was the agreement with Faad Tobar. I can only stay here if Barzo is with me. So Herr Asgaya agreed. And Fräulein von Kitren hired me to clean this place, so I need to be here anyway."

Jens-Peter sat cross-legged on the desk. "I suppose. And why is the troupe leader in Baerlen too? It's all odd." He sighed. "The only thing I do that's useful is run the levitation ships, and even then I realized I can't do much without crew." It had been fun with Triss and Barzo helping. They didn't complain about heights or climbing the rigging to do things. He'd made do with help from his friends, but they didn't always have time.

The faint sound of creaking hinges came from the courtyard below. Desperate for anything interesting, Jens-Peter jumped down and went to a window to take a look.

"Ah? It's Stefan! Oh, you haven't met him. Stefan Arendt, he's a magic student, and more importantly, his brother works at the Kriegsa. I wonder why he's here."

Shortly Barzo opened the door to the office area, followed by an agitated Stefan. Jens-Peter had never seen him anything less than calm before, so he started to worry.

"What on earth did you do this time, you magnet of disaster? The Kriegsa is like a beehive that's been kicked. According to my brother, half the senior staff has been booted, and one of the head's aides is supposedly in *prison*."

Jens-Peter stared at him. Stefan didn't seem drunk, and to be fair it was a bit early in the day for that. "Why are you blaming me? I haven't done anything!"

"Ran off with a levitation ship, participated in a midnight raid with that levitation ship, nearly wrecked that levitation ship on multiple occasions … and that's just what I saw personally," Triss said calmly, still polishing.

"Yes, but none of that would create such a stir. I think."

Stefan rubbed his forehead. "Von Koller is in a vile mood and snapping at anyone who even looks at him, my brother says. He was speaking to Herr Asgaya in his office and yelling so loud everyone could hear him. Your name"—he pointed rudely at Jens-Peter—"was mentioned. Repeatedly. Then one of the sub-commanders came by and gave my brother's office the day off, with a strong hint that clearing out would be healthier for everybody. He came and told me about it." He snapped his fingers, his brow clearing. "Oh, and Asgaya passed on a message as he left. That whole mess with the ship fire and so on has been cleared up, and nobody is accusing you. And he'll be by soon to explain."

"See? It isn't my fault. Von Koller was just mad he couldn't blame me."

Stefan grinned. "Oh, it's more than that. Rumor is they are going to build more levitation ships, and they *aren't* going to be under Kriegsa control. There was something else I was supposed to tell you—was it that? No, this was Dieter. He came this morning before I'd even had any coffee and blathering about somebody mad at you. Somebody *else*. Shacht? Slenck?"

Jens-Peter froze, horror shuddering through him like being immersed in a bucket of icewater. "Schenk. Professor Schenk. I completely forgot about that cursed paper! I barely started … I was working on it when all this happened! I'm doomed." He looked around frantically. Calendar, didn't this sorry excuse for an office have a calendar?

Finding one only made it worse. If the deadline had already passed, there was nothing he could do, but it hadn't. Not yet. "Three days? That's impossible. The books I need are still on *Einzl*, assuming they haven't gotten tossed off at some point." Not to mention he still needed a real case of structural failure to analyze.

Barzo was looking about, ready to fight the threat but confused about what it was. Triss put down her polishing rag.

"His teacher at the university has threatened to expel him if he doesn't write a satisfactory paper. And he promised his father to graduate. It is *jaina* for his departed mother." Barzo blinked and looked even more serious.

"Those books, the ones on the ship? I remember *Treatise on Structural Elements, Masonry Construction,* and *Elementary Architectural Design Principles for Industry.* Were there any others?"

"Did you ... by any chance ... read them?" Jens-Peter saw a faint thread of hope before him.

She nodded. "I was bored. What do you need from them?"

"Citations. Equations." Jens-Peter rummaged through desk drawers and shelves while he talked until he found a stack of foolscap, a pen, and a bottle of ink. "It won't be perfect, but if I can produce *something,* I will have a chance to argue my case to the provost."

"Wait, are you going to write the whole thing now? Without your references?" Stefan glanced at Triss and then back to Jens-Peter.

"She *is* the references. Triss can remember anything she's read. *Anything.*"

Jens-Peter started writing, ignoring Stefan's expressions of doubt. He had mostly organized his thoughts previously, and had even written most of the introduction, his least favorite part. It should be enough to just put the main points for now and then go back and make it pretty later.

"Triss. In *Structural Elements* there's a page with a heading 'Span-weight transfer' and a paragraph about width of span limitations."

Triss closed her eyes. "'Consideration for the weight of the construction materials limits the extent to which ...'" As she continued to recite the text, Stefan stared at her in sudden silence.

Triss also found some equations he needed, but in these cases she had to draw out what she remembered, not knowing the symbols or what they meant.

"That is completely uncanny. Will it be enough?" Stefan rubbed his head. "Didn't you also need a case study or something?"

"It occurred to me that I can just use the vaulting we blew up to —" Triss coughed, and he remembered that Stefan wasn't in on the secret of the crates. "Blew up in our escape. Er. Will anyone believe it if I use that? It's completely buried now."

"Not much you can do about it." Triss went back to polishing. "What choice do you have? It's not like they can prove it *isn't* there."

He wanted to point out that Professor Schenk wanted nothing more than for him to fail, but she was right that he had no choice. And he was right that Schenk would toss it out as pure fiction and he'd get expelled, but damn if he wouldn't fight it all the way!

Having delivered all his messages, Stefan left. Jens-Peter waved goodbye and focused only on the page before him and the calculations for arch strength, dimly aware of Barzo saying something about going back out. There wasn't much to interest Barzo inside.

After asking Triss for yet another paragraph of text, he noticed that the light outside had dimmed. The door opened and instead of the expected Barzo bringing food, the tall and elegant figures of Fräulein von Kitren and Herr Asgaya walked in. Fräulein von Kitren observed Triss reciting with her eyes closed, only one raised eyebrow showing her surprise.

"Oh yes, her memory is phenomenal," Asgaya said, nodding at Triss. "So, did Arendt give you my message?"

Jens-Peter blinked, dragging his attention away from weight-bearing walls. "Oh, the new ships? That's great, but I have to deal with this thing first." He thumped the pile of scribbled-on paper. "Whoever's getting them won't want a failed engineering student."

Asgaya gave him an exasperated look. "Did he not give you the full message, or were you not listening? The Dragonhunters are getting the new ships, I will be making the decisions on the engineers, and I believe your practical experience far outweighs any university credential. It's not as if they are able to instruct on the topic, after all."

That got Jens-Peter's full and enthusiastic attention. "Truly? That's fantastic! The Kriegsa were always afraid to try any of my suggestions." Then his happiness dimmed. "Ah, but the real problem is finding crew. Any of the people I've tried are terrified of heights or have hands made of thumbs." Then he remembered the exceptions. "I suppose we could hire Barzo. He did a good job."

He glanced toward Triss, to get her opinion, only to see her being quizzed by Fräulein von Kitren, holding one of the books from the office shelves. Triss was standing rigidly straight in front of her, hands clasped in front like a schoolgirl.

"Page 117, an illustration with a castle with fighting going on and a pencil drawing of a man smoking a pipe in the margins. The words underneath are 'Battle of Zondernberg'. Something sticky made pages 118 to 220 unable to open. Page 221—"

Fraulein von Kitren held up a hand. "That will do. Most impressive. I am afraid you are not suited for a maid position here, however."

Triss appeared to droop but maintained her posture. "I'm not afraid of hard work, ma'am. Did I not meet your requirements?"

Fräulein von Kitren actually smiled. Jens-Peter was shocked. "You misunderstand me. Your talents are desperately needed elsewhere. I have long thought the Dragonhunters have great need of a librarian."

Triss seemed to mouth the word to herself, thinking hard, then suddenly looked up with a glowing expression. "Ma'am, do they, do librarians work in *libraries*?"

Von Kitren gently inclined her head. "Indeed. They must know the contents of the books and be able to locate requested information. As you have been doing already."

"That's all very well, but I need her first. I have to finishe my paper,"

Jens-Peter objected.

Asgaya grinned. "Yes, yes, finish your paper. Now that we've got the young lady settled, let's call up Barzo for the rest. You young idiot, did you really think we hadn't noticed such a prime opportunity? Not just Barzo, but the entire troupe. They were having difficulties before their carts were stolen, so I believe when I suggest they send any extra people not needed for performing to crew our new levitation ships they will be inclined to listen."

"And those who travel about will be equally useful as eyes and ears for the Dragonhunters, and will excite no comment wherever they appear," Fraulein von Kitren added.

Asgaya nodded. "I really should thank Korda for giving us the idea."

"Do you think you can have this discussion *somewhere else*?" Jens-Peter grumbled. "I really wish I had *Structural Elements*, there's a graph of material compression as a function of load but it would take forever for you to draw it out …"

Triss had not lost the blissful smile on her face ever since she had heard the word "library" and Jens-Peter was sure she had not heard him … until an image of the page came into view before him. It was only there for a few seconds, but it was enough.

"Oh! It still works?" Triss rubbed her forehead.

"I think you will find it becomes easier with practice," Asgaya said, after a warning glance to Jens-Peter. "It is a natural ability. You simply discovered it under stress."

Triss glanced at him. "Did you see it long enough to be useful?"

"Thanks," Jens-Peter managed to croak. "I got what I needed."

"Even more useful than I had imagined," said Fräulein von Kitren. "Even as you are, you will be the most valuable resource in the library."

Jens-Peter surreptitiously wiped his hands on his trousers, wondering how much longer he would have to wait. He was having trouble keeping his eyes open after finally finishing his paper at the end of a marathon twenty-four hours of writing and drinking coffee. Fortunately, most of the research was done at the beginning, and he could send Triss off to sleep while he did calculations and sketches of the vaulting for the case study.

Now he just wanted to get the humiliation and failure over with so he could sleep. It wouldn't be too bad. He'd still have a place with the new levitation ships, but in his heart he would be failing his mother and making his father grieve.

The door creaked open. Jens-Peter stood as Professor Schenk entered the small conference room, bare except for a worn table and a few chairs.

"I see you made use of every possible second of the time allotted you,"

Professor Schenk snapped. He narrowed his eyes at the bundle of paper, tied with a narrow black ribbon. "And this is the result of your labors, is it?" His expression was that of having discovered a dead rodent in his soup.

He could just take it to read somewhere else, but not when he can make me suffer too, Jens-Peter grumbled to himself.

Schenk's scowl only deepened as he read, and when he got to the case study, he flung the paper down in disgust.

"What nonsense is this? You—"

A firm knock sounded on the door. Shenk got up, still in a temper but curious too. "I distinctly remember reserving this room …"

He opened the door and stood there, mouth agape. Jens-Peter was equally astonished. The last time he had seen Sollveg the man had looked like a living corpse, one welcoming death, at that. Now, while still thin and worn, there was a trace of color in his face and a definite strong presence in his expression—and no sign he was still in official custody either.

"Good heavens, is it Stinky Schenk? How many years has it been? But what a delightful surprise to meet you after such a long time. I have not been in good health recently or I would have tried to keep in touch."

Jens-Peter heard the gentle voice rise and fall, wondering if he would ever be able to see his professor again without thinking of the appellation "Stinky Schenk"— or refraining from grinning.

"But … that is … you say a surprise? Were you not looking for me?" Schenk stammered.

"Oh no! I was looking for young Oberacker there. I do apologize, young man, but your professor and I were at school together. So many memories, it is amazing we were never caught up by the watch, haha."

Jens-Peter's shock had worn off to a degree, so he noticed a certain dangerous edge to Sollveg's voice. He also noticed how pale and nervous Professor Schenk had become.

"Well! It is fortuitous to find you both together. I am in Baerlen to consult with certain official parties, and we have need of Oberacker's expertise, it seems. Will your remaining business take long to conclude?"

"It should not take long at all. This alleged research paper is a collection of utter nonsense, with a completely fictional Romasque structure I've never heard of as proof!"

"*Early* Romasque," Jens-Peter murmured.

"Oh, would this be the old monastery ruins near Bielefeld?" Sollveg's expression contained nothing but polite interest.

Schenk drew a deep breath. "You *know* of this place?" He picked up the paper and waved it at Sollveg. "Is this accurate?"

Sollveg calmly paged through the paper, pausing at the sketches. "Yes, this matches my memory exactly."

I'm not surprised, you were there when I blew it up.

Professor Schenk's face turned red, then pale. "I see." He clenched his jaw. "Still, this is a paper to show that this student has mastered the material and applied it in the correct academic fashion. Oberacker is still a long way from displaying the conduct of a proper student, and to see him continue in this fashion will—"

"Truly? I had understood he is all but done with the required course of study. Why not take this research paper as proof? No doubt he is impatient to leave the university and make practical use of his knowledge. The University of Baerlen still does degrees by examination, does it not? As I recall, you are a good friend of the provost. Perhaps you could request a review and allow young Oberacker to obtain his degree that way?"

Now Professor Schenk looked like he had been saved at the moment of execution. "What a splendid idea. I shall put it in motion immediately!"

As he left, Sollveg turned to Jens-Peter and gave him a wink and a gentle smile. Jens-Peter realized he was actually going to get his degree. He would never have to sit in one of Schenk's classes again, and he could start with the Dragonhunter ships immediately instead of waiting.

Really, it was a solution that satisfied everyone.

EPILOGUE

"You are sure of this *gadje*? The money is good, but do we trust him? He is *bruje* as well."

Toa Mihai sat back and tapped his pipe on a stump, then spat into the fire. "The money is good. The work is honest. Barzo has seen this. We have not done well with the acrobatic shows the last few years. This will keep us alive and even more."

Faad Tobar sat back and tossed another log on the fire, staring out at the starry sky. "I think of your Trisstela too. To have a family connection to these Dragonhunters is good, but not at the price of her happiness. We can find another way."

"To know this, does it not take time? Barzo will be close by and watch them both. The boy has a good heart and already has taken up some of our ways he learned from Trisstela. He may be *gadje*, but so was your *Anki* and her daughter is our family now." Toa Mihai smiled. "They do not even know their own hearts now, but Mata Sheri sees the beginnings of it. It is not wrong for us to watch over them before they know. And if they do, and it is well …" He shrugged. "Then it is family!"

The matter of Trisstela's marriage had troubled him for some time now. Not zigane by blood, too old, in truth, to marry a zigane boy. But what *gadje* would be worthy of her, would accept her and her family?

This way, it might work. And be good for all.

He would watch and see.

236

ABOUT THE AUTHOR

Sabrina Chase was originally trained as a Mad Scientist, but due to a tragic lack of available lairs at the time of graduation fell into low company and started working in the software industry. She lives in the Pacific Northwest and is owned by two cats.

Further sordid details may or may not be available at her website, chaseadventures.com

Made in the USA
Middletown, DE
30 July 2021

44773160R00149